Duty and Honor

A Novel of the Civil War

Book Two of the Drieborg Chronicles

Michael J. Deeb

Duty and Honor

Addison & Highsmith

Addison & Highsmith Publishers

Las Vegas ◊ Chicago ◊ Palm Beach

Published in the United States of America by
Histria Books
7181 N. Hualapai Way, Ste. 130-86
Las Vegas, NV 89166 USA
HistriaBooks.com

Addison & Highsmith is an imprint of Histria Books dedicated to outstanding works of fiction. Titles published under the imprints of Histria Books are distributed worldwide.

Library of Congress Control Number: 2023948279

ISBN 978-1-59211-388-0 (hardcover)

ISBN 978-1-59211-414-6 (eBook)

My thanks to all those who encouraged me
in the pursuit of this adventure.

Prologue

In June of 1863, General Robert E. Lee led the Army of Northern Virginia into Pennsylvania. They were fresh from a major victory in May over the Union's Army of the Potomac at Chancellorsville, Virginia. There, Lee's army of 60,000 men defeated General Hooker's Union force of 140,000 men who were better fed, clothed, and equipped.

Now, Lee would take his army north and thus lure this same Union Army into another major battle. This time, the armies would fight on Northern soil. And this time, Lee planned to destroy the Union forces.

Such a confrontation took place on the hills surrounding a small Pennsylvania town called Gettysburg. There, the Union Army commanded the heights. If General Lee were to gain his victory here, his men would have to fight both the very steep hills and a numerically superior foe. Despite this, he chose to attack.

For three days, the armies struggled for control of the hills. But no ground changed hands. The Union still dominated the heights around the town.

Late in the afternoon of the third day, July 3, Lee gambled on one final attack. Preceded by the most intense artillery bombardment of the war, he sent a division under General George Pickett to assault the very center of the Union line.

At the same time, he wanted the Confederate cavalry of General Jeb Stuart to attack this Union line from the rear.

Barring Stuart's way was the outnumbered Union cavalry of the Michigan Brigade.

First Blood

And so, in a cornfield three miles east of Gettysburg, elements of the Michigan Cavalry Brigade and Stuart's Virginia Cavalry would fight for control of the approaches to the rear of the Union lines at Gettysburg.

Earlier this day, a thousand of Stuart's Rebels had badly bloodied an equal force of Union cavalry, the 5th Michigan Regiment. The Michigan men had used their newly issued repeating rifles well. The Rebel advance toward Gettysburg had been stopped; at least for the moment.

Now, the rest of the Michigan Brigade blocked Stuart's way. Lieutenant Michael J. Drieborg, a platoon leader in I Troop of Michigan's 6th Cavalry Regiment, knelt in a grove of trees waiting for the Rebs' next attempt to break through. Tall for a cavalryman, Michael stood over six feet and carried fifty pounds or so more than anyone else in his unit. Under a three o'clock afternoon sun, sweat rolled down his torso under his blue wool shirt.

He looked across a one-hundred-yard-wide field of knee-high corn. In a grove on the other side of the field, he could see Troopers of the Michigan 4th Cavalry Regiment and what was left of the 5th Michigan. They, too, were waiting.

His attention was drawn to his right by the glare of the sun shimmering off hundreds of drawn sabers carried by gray-clad horsemen. As he watched, more of them moved into the open field; their unit banners and flags showed clearly in the stiff breeze. Almost a mile away, they formed ranks clear across the end of the same cornfield.

"Must be thousands of them," he thought. He wished he had more men. The Rebs slowly moved forward as though on review. Born to the saddle, they had fought together since the war's beginning. These Rebs had earned a reputation as the best. As they moved down the slope toward the waiting Michiganders, Michael could tell they believed it. The Michigan men had only been together a few months. For most of them, this would be their first battle; Michael's, too.

Until last week, he had been assigned as an Aide in Washington, City, to Congressman Kellogg, who represented Michael's hometown area in Michigan. But, with Lee's invasion of Pennsylvania, many able-bodied soldiers stationed in the capital had been sent to bolster the Army of the Potomac and oppose Lee's army. Lt. Michael Drieborg was one of those soldiers.

He was assigned to I Troop of Michigan's 6ᵗʰ Cavalry Regiment. He had originally joined this same unit when it formed in the summer of '62 back in Grand Rapids, Michigan. Despite the dangers of warfare, he was glad to be back with his old comrades.

The lead rows of Confederate cavalry were still beyond the range of his men's Spencer repeating rifles. They could fire this rifle seven times a minute before reloading. At up to three hundred yards, the weapon was quite accurate. Such a rate of fire was new to the war and would be devastating to Rebel cavalry tactics.

Along with their saber, Rebel cavalrymen usually carried a musket, a shotgun, or a pistol. None of these would prove to be any match for the Spencer repeating rifle.

Captain Hyser, commander of Drieborg's Troop, was a typical cavalryman. He was a stocky five foot seven, and he wore a mustache with long sideburns, common among officers. Unlike the commander of their brigade, General George Custer, Hyser was plainly dressed and soft-spoken. He had previous battle experience in the infantry before taking over I Troop of the 6ᵗʰ Michigan Cavalry the previous summer.

He walked over to Drieborg's position.

"Mike, I want you to mass your rifle fire on the Reb flank. And remind your men to hold their fire until I give the order. Clear?"

"Yes, sir," Drieborg responded. "I'll pass the word." Michael moved among his Troopers, giving the order.

"Will they ever stop coming out of those woods up there?" asked George Neal.

"The captain told us that there should be several thousand of them, George," Mike informed him.

"This time last year I was back in Grand Rapids at the bakery sweating by the ovens waiting to pull out fresh bread," George said. "Now, I'm sweating under this wool shirt, waiting to kill some people. Being a baker's assistant was sure a whole lot easier than being a soldier. I'm just a city-bred boy, Mike. Never had to fire a rifle, and certainly never tried to kill somebody. Look at me now."

"Yep, George," Mike shot back. "Look at you now. You've become a pretty good horseman and not a bad shot. Of course, those guys attacking us are pretty good, too."

"That newspaper article you read us called 'em the Invincibles. They're supposed to be the best cavalry in the world. Think we can beat 'em, Mike?"

"We are all that stands between them and our boys on the hills at Gettysburg. If nothing else, we had better slow 'em down some. I think we can do that."

"But why is it so quiet? Even our horses aren't making much noise." "Don't know, George. I'm new to this, too. Now, just shut up and stop worrying. You'll do just fine."

Sgt. Riley, Drieborg's platoon sergeant, was a battle-tested veteran from the early days of the war. He had told the men to expect strange things to happen when waiting for a battle to begin.

Mike moved to Riley's position. "Sarge, move along the firing line, will you?" he directed. "The cannons will begin their fire pretty soon. Don't want the guys spooked. Keep them calm. They'll listen to you better'n me. Remember, no firing until the Captain gives the signal."

The attacking horsemen were still almost a mile away. Despite the distance, fire from twenty Union cannons suddenly broke the silence, startling the green cavalry Troopers. The four batteries of five cannons each fired without pause. The solid shells were meant to explode in the air over an attacker and shower them with sharp pieces of metal.

The rows of Confederate cavalrymen rode only a yard or two apart from one another. The hot metal from the exploding artillery shells tore great gaps in their ranks, often causing both horse and rider to be sent to the ground. Nonetheless, the other Rebs kept coming.

At three hundred yards from the artillery positions, the Rebs began to charge at a gallop.

Within range of their Spencer repeating rifles now, Mike's dismounted Union cavalry opened fire. The Union Troopers on the other side of the field joined the firing on the advancing Rebel horsemen.

Closer now, the screams of the wounded horses could be heard even over the roar of the artillery pieces. At two hundred yards, Union artillery began to fire shells filled with small metal balls. Once fired, the casing of the shell exploded, releasing seventy-five of these balls into the oncoming cavalry at a very high velocity. The effect was devastating. Mike felt sorry for the horses riding into such a curtain of steel.

He could see blood spraying into the blue sky. Wounded horses screamed, some catapulting into other rows of attackers. Some mounts stumbled over the fallen, carrying their riders to the ground, too. Wounded riders fell and disappeared under the hooves of the following horses.

Still, the Reb horsemen charged ahead.

One hundred yards in front of the attacking Rebels, the 1st Michigan Regiment waited. As the brigade's only battle-tested unit, they would take the brunt of the Rebel attack.

Suddenly, a bugler sounded the charge. The Union artillery stopped firing, and the 1st Regiment burst from their positions with sabers drawn and flags flying.

In the sudden quiet, the new commander of the Michigan Brigade, General George Custer, shouted, "Come on, you Wolverines."

Drieborg's platoon and the other Yankee cavalrymen on the flanks continued to fire into both sides of the advancing Rebs. Custer continued to lead the 1st Regiment toward the oncoming Rebel cavalry.

When the two forces met, the sound of their collision was as loud as a cannon blast. Horses somersaulted, and men were thrown into the air. With sabers and pistols drawn, the charging 1st Michigan Regiment cut through the Rebel center.

Mounted now, Michael directed his Troop toward the Rebel force. "I Troop," he shouted, "charge!" His men joined the other nine hundred men of Michigan's 6th Cavalry Regiment and attacked from one flank, while the Troopers of the 4th and 5th Regiments attacked the other flank. Hit from three sides, the charge of the Rebel cavalry began to slow.

All military formations now forgotten, thousands of mounted men, some in blue and others in gray, found themselves in their own battle for survival. One-on-one fighting shut out all other sounds or concerns.

Maneuvering his horse with leg pressure, Mike led his platoon into the Rebel flank. He raised his saber in his right hand while holding a pistol in his left.

Private George Neal was on his left, protecting his blind side. As Neal turned away to engage an attacking Reb, Mike was left exposed and vulnerable for a moment.

In that moment, he felt a sharp blow on his back. His left shoulder stung with a burning that numbed his whole left arm. He lost his grip on the pistol.

Dizzy now, his grip on the horse weakened. He fell to the ground and lay dazed as the battle raged on above.

Lying on the ground still dazed, Mike heard the faint sound of a bugle.

"Is it the call to reform? Maybe it's a call to retreat? Which side is signaling?"

Around him, a thick haze of blue-gray cordite smoke from the gunfire hung low over the battlefield like an early morning fog. George Neal suddenly appeared, moving slowly on horseback as he looked for missing comrades.

He spotted Drieborg on the ground. "Mike," he shouted as he jumped off his horse. Kneeling by Drieborg's side, George nudged him with his left hand but continued to hold the reins of his horse with his right. "Are you alive?" he asked, panic-stricken.

Mike moaned. "Yeah, but my shoulder hurts like mad."

Just then, George heard his Troop's bugler sound recall.

"Damn! I gotta go, Mike. But I'll tell Sergeant Riley that you're alive and back here. He'll send one of the orderlies to check on you. Hang on, Mike." George left his water canteen by Mike's side, mounted his horse, and rode to the sound of the bugle.

Mike slumped back onto the ground. Evening was approaching and it would soon be dark.

"Did George say he heard a bugle sounding retreat? That could only mean we failed."

"Did we stop 'em, George?" No one answered.

"Don't forget me," Mike murmured. Then he fell asleep.

Lowell, Michigan: 1862

In 1862, Lowell, Michigan, was a small farming village located on the western side of the state a few miles east of Grand Rapids. Typical of most Michigan farming communities, Lowell had fewer than fifty permanent residents. These townspeople provided goods and services for the farm families who lived in the area.

Buildings were located on either side of Main Street, a dirt road running north and south. The Grand River ran east and west through the center of town. Lowell had a general store/post office, a doctor's office, a lawyer who was also the justice of the peace, a grain-processing elevator, a bank, a smithy, a restaurant, and a bar. The town also had a new library and was home to several churches.

Farmers were seldom seen in town during the week, but most Saturday mornings found the little village crowded with them.

It was not yet seven in the morning, but the Drieborgs had finished their morning chores. Jacob was driving the farm wagon the five miles to Lowell. With him were his seventeen-year-old son Michael and his sixteen-year-old daughter Susan. Pulled by the plow horse, they carried grain to be ground and a list from his wife Rose of things to buy at Mr. Zania's general store.

Jacob was taller than most of his neighbors. He had blue eyes, blond hair, and stood a good bit over six feet. He was a serious sort, keeping his thoughts to himself. He had the reputation of being an honest, hardworking, and successful farmer who always paid his debts on time.

He and his wife Rose had come to the United States when they were about Michael and Susan's ages. They had left the Netherlands, a country in Western Europe, to escape the constant warfare between the major countries there. Their respective families sent them to live with relatives in the Lowell area. They worked for their host farm families until the cost of their passage was repaid and they saved money to marry and have a farm of their own.

It was said that his two sons, Michael, seventeen and Little Jake, now twelve, were virtual clones of Jacob Drieborg. Some wondered, though, why Michael was not fighting for the Union like most of Lowell's young men his age.

When the Civil War began, Michael's parents insisted he remain at home instead of volunteering as he had wanted to. They had not forgotten the European wars they fled years ago. Now that war had come to the United States, they feared its spread, and they feared Michael's involvement. He obeyed and stayed home. Besides, no one thought the war would last more than a few months at most.

There was never a shortage of work on the farm, but there was a shortage of farm workers. The first war fever in the spring of 1861 had taken most of the single young men and landless workers around Lowell. The next wave of volunteers, with cash bounties being offered, took the rest of the single men and many family men, too.

The Drieborgs' field hand, Willi Becker, was a cousin from back home in the Netherlands. Jacob paid for Willi's passage to the United States in early 1860 before the war began. He was a hard worker and especially good with animals. He also became very adept at butchering and sausage-making. So good, in fact, that in his spare time, other farmers hired him to do their butchering and meat preparation. Even Mr. Zania, the owner of Lowell's general store, sold some of Willi's sausage.

Willi was one of the bounty volunteers of 1862. All the Drieborgs were sorry to see him go. He wasn't just a farmhand. He was treated as part of the family. The children thought of him as an older brother. He had a room of his own in the barn but he ate with the family and spent his free evenings in the house, as well. Rose Drieborg taught him to understand and speak English. Even the kids helped him with the language.

"Speak English, Willi. Speak only English," everyone would say when he struggled and fled back to the comfort of his native Dutch language.

When Willi left, the children had to do his chores as best they could. Even Susan, who was sixteen, and Ann, fourteen, had to take on outside chores. Little Jake had to help with the cattle and pigs in addition to keeping the barn clean. When he didn't have school, he had to get up at five in the morning to help with the milking. He really missed Willi. Ann took over the sheep flock, and Susan the chickens and ducks.

Jacob wrote his brother, who still lived in Holland. Hopefully, another good male worker who wanted to come to the United States could be found.

Even without Willi, the Drieborgs were more fortunate than most farm families. Jacob had over eighty tillable acres for corn, hay, and wheat. Few others could handle that many acres alone, but he had two strong sons old enough to work a full day in the field and help him with the cattle and pigs along with the early morning milking. His two daughters helped with the afternoon milking, worked a good-size garden and managed the chickens, sheep, and goats. They also helped their mother in the kitchen.

Consequently, the Drieborgs had more security than most small farmers. They were more diversified with their crops and their cattle and sheep for market, cows and goats for milk, and pigs for their table.

Smaller farms often had difficulty, especially if the papa had no sons to help, was injured, became sick, or had gone to fight in the war.

Rose often told her children that the Lord had been good to the Drieborgs. So, the family thanked God at every meal, before bedtime, and of course on Sunday at St. Roberts, the Catholic Church in Lowell. Jacob agreed with his wife, but he insisted that the Lord helped those who worked hard.

Saturday was a work day as far as he was concerned. "Da cows and goats need milking," he would tell the children. "Dey don't care that it's a Saturday or a Sunday."

This Saturday, the three Drieborgs arrived in Lowell before eight in the morning. Despite the hour, the village was crowded with people and wagons, so all of the stores and the grain elevator were open. Even Harvey Bacon's Lowell Bank welcomed customers at that early hour.

In fact, dozens of people were in evidence on the wooden sidewalks in front of the stores. The main street was full of wagons and horses, and there were already six farm wagons in line waiting to have grain processed at King's Grain Elevator.

Farmers wanted to get their town business done and use the better part of the day more productively on their farms. Jacob Drieborg was no exception.

It was often a social time, too. Michael's mother Rose usually accompanied his father. But this time, his sister Susan had come in her place. She would help Michael with the order at the general store and eagerly join him at the new library to pick out some books for herself and her younger sister Ann. A very pretty and shapely blond girl, Susan hoped to see some of the boys who flirted with her at school.

"Come on, Susan," Mike said over his shoulder as he briskly began to walk into the main part of Lowell. "You know how Papa gets. We haven't got all day if we are going to spend time at the new library."

"Oh, just hold your horses," she responded. "You can walk as fast as you please. Just don't expect me to run around all day trying to keep up.

"Besides, I don't need to stay right by your side. I'm old enough to take care of myself, you know."

"Look here, Susan," he told her. "I'd just as soon I didn't have you to watch after. But Papa told me that you're my responsibility. He also told you to stay with me, so stop whining and come along."

At Zania's general store, Susan browsed while Michael gave his mother's list to Mr. Zania.

"Pretty busy this Saturday, Mike," he told him. "There are several orders ahead of you. So, it will take me a good hour till I can fill yours." Mr. Zania was quite a bit shorter than Mike, no more than five foot three inches tall. He was stout, with a barrel chest and strong-looking hands that he frequently used to stroke his full black beard. *Not much fat on that frame, either,* Michael observed.

Mr. Zania owned what was called the Lowell General Store. Through a large glass window on either side of double doors, passersby could easily see a store filled with goods from floor to ceiling. He seemed to stock everything, from shovels and Shaker garden seeds to clothing, shoes, canned goods, candy, building supplies, and weapons.

"That's all right, sir," Mike responded. "Susan wants to browse, and Papa will be tied up at King's for at least that long. My sister and I want to visit the new library, as well. So that will suit us just fine."

"Mr. Zania," asked Susan, "can I take a new order catalogue home with us? We would really love to go through it."

"I'll include one with your order, Susan."

As Susan and Michael walked out of the store, she noticed a smallish man in a Union soldier's uniform standing on the sidewalk in front of the store to their right. His back was turned to them as he was strutting in front of a group of young boys.

"My goodness!" Susan exclaimed. She gripped her brother's arm and pointed. "Do you see that man in a military uniform? I can't believe it. I think its Carl Bacon."

"Yep, I think you're right, Susan. That's our old classmate Carl, all right."

He was also the Lowell banker's son. Carl was quite a sight in his blue wool uniform, with highly polished knee-high boots and a wide-brimmed blue hat with a bright yellow feather. No more than five foot five inches tall, he could not have carried more than one hundred pounds on his slender frame. He had been a grammar-school classmate of the Drieborg children.

They stood on the sidewalk with some other bystanders and watched the performance Carl was putting on for the benefit of several boys who had nothing better to do.

"I thought he was at the university in Ann Arbor," Susan remarked.

"He was," said Michael. "Word is that he was expelled for cheating, drunken behavior, and poor attendance. Then I heard that his father purchased him an Army commission in that cavalry Regiment being formed this fall in Grand Rapids."

Mike and Carl Bacon had never gotten along when they were in school together. Carl bullied small kids and thought his father's position as owner of the only bank in Lowell entitled him to special treatment. He did not hand in his homework and was disruptive in their one-room schoolhouse. He liked to tell the teacher that he didn't have to behave or do his work because his father was the banker and schoolboard president.

Carl didn't like Mike much, either. At six foot two and one hundred seventy-five pounds, Mike was not to be bullied. In fact, the smaller kids looked to Mike for protection. Carl felt Mike's anger often, especially on one occasion when Carl had pushed Susan into a puddle when she refused to kiss him.

Even when it seemed justified to Mike, Mr, Clingman, the teacher, and his parents got after him for beating on Carl.

Part of the reason for his father's anger was that Jacob was trying to borrow funds from the Bacons' bank to purchase one of the new threshing machines, as well as a metal plow. He needed Carl's father, Harvey to approve the loan.

As Mike and Susan watched, one of the kids in his audience laughed at Carl's strutting. Angry at the ridicule, Carl grabbed the kid by the shirt and began shaking him. Then, right in front of his audience, Carl raised his riding crop to hit the little boy.

Still holding her brother's arm, Susan could feel him tense up and begin to move away from her side toward Carl. "Don't, Michael." Susan tried to hold him back. "You'll only cause trouble."

"That arrogant little shit's going to hit that kid with his riding crop," Michael said.

"And this is none of our business, Michael," she insisted, holding him tighter.

Michael pulled away and moved toward Bacon. From behind, Mike walked up and grabbed the riding crop from Carl's upraised arm. "That's enough of that, Carl."

Surprised, Carl released the youngster. He turned to face the intruder. "Not this time, Drieborg. I'm an officer in the Union cavalry now," he spat with hate in his eyes.

"That may be," Mike replied. "It still doesn't give you the right to push others around."

Facing Mike with hands on his hips, his composure restored, Carl retorted, "Not much you can do about it, farm boy. This uniform gives me all kind of rights. Come to think about it, most of us in this town are doing our duty to defend our country from the slavers. Maybe you're one of those Copperhead traitors who would like to see this country destroyed."

"Watch what you say, little man." Michael flushed with anger. His hands tightened into fists at his sides.

"Lookee here, everyone," Bacon said, turning to the kids and the gathering adults on the sidewalk. He pointed toward Mike. "Look at Lowell's Rebel lover and real-live coward."

Susan came up to Michael's side, holding his right arm. He pulled away from her.

"Please, Michael!" she said, but it was too late.

Mike jumped forward, enraged. He grabbed Carl by his wool jacket and lifted him off the sidewalk as though he didn't weigh a pound. Michael walked him backward toward the street.

Carl gripped Mike's wrist and tried to kick him with his polished boots. Stumbling backward, Carl turned his head toward the water-filled horse trough by the side of the road where Drieborg was heading.

"Cool off, Lieutenant," Mike ordered. With that, he dunked Carl to the cheers of the kids and the laughter of the adults who had witnessed the entire episode. Each time Carl pulled himself above the cold water, Mike pushed him under again.

"That will be enough, Mike," said Mr. Zania. He had heard the cheering of the small boys in the crowd by the water trough and left his store to investigate. "Let him up and go about your business. Go on, you kids. Entertainment's over."

Carl was left sitting on the edge of the water trough, soaking wet, catching his breath and sputtering.

Susan was once again at Michael's side, pulling him away from Bacon and across the street toward the library.

From behind them, they heard Bacon shout. "I'll get you yet, Drieborg. Just you wait."

"Michael," Susan said, chuckling, "it was funny watching Carl flaying his arms around and sputtering each time you dunked him. All the adults on the sidewalk couldn't help but laugh, too."

"Can you imagine that arrogant runt beating on a little kid with a riding crop?" Michael fumed aloud. "Why didn't anyone stop him?" "I wish someone else had. You still seem so angry; I think you could use a dunk in that water trough yourself." Her laugh did not calm him down a bit.

"Very funny," Mike shot back. "I don't need your humor right now."

"Maybe not, Brother," she replied. "But you're going to need to be much calmer when Papa hears of this. You know you're in trouble with him."

"I probably am," he admitted. "I shouldn't have lost my temper, either. But he really got to me with that coward business. Others around here probably think the same. I can handle that. But coming from that little bully, I lost my temper."

A bit later, Michael sat at the reading table in the center of the single room which served as the Lowell Library. He was reading the latest war news in the *Grand Rapids Eagle* newspaper. Susan was checking out several books for herself and her sister.

The Lowell Justice of the Peace, Joseph F. Deeb, entered the building. He looked around and headed directly for the table at which Michael sat. He stopped there, and Michael stood up. Without hesitation, he asked Mike, "Did you push Carl Bacon into the horse trough a few minutes ago?"

"Yes, sir, I did. He was beating a little kid with a riding crop, and I stopped him."

"Witnesses have attested to that. But others have said that you attacked him only after he called you a Rebel sympathizer and a coward. Is that true, too?"

"Yes, sir it is."

"Well, son, Carl's father has filed assault charges against you. You'll have to come with me. Where would your father be about now? He'll need to know of this situation."

"I expect he will be at the elevator or at the Zania general store right about now, sir."

The Justice of the Peace was the closest thing Michigan's small towns had to law enforcement. Any serious breach of the law would be referred to the sheriff at the county seat. In this case, that would be in the nearby city of Grand Rapids. This situation did not call for a referral to the sheriff's office.

Susan collected her books, Mike put away the newspaper he was reading, and all three left the library. Mr. Deeb walked a few feet ahead and heard Mike talking to no one in particular.

"For beating on a little kid, you'd think Carl would be the one arrested. Not me for stopping him."

Mr. Deeb stopped, turned and walked back to Mike.

"I would arrest Carl, but the parents of the boy he was hitting with his riding crop refused to file charges. I asked them. They are probably afraid of what Carl's father would do to them. He could call in their farm loan. Ruin them, probably. And if they don't have a loan from the bank right now, they might need one in the future. No one I can think of would cross that banker. That's something you might have thought of, too, Mike."

He left Mike standing in the street and headed for his law office. Mike, stunned by the comment, just stood there hanging his head. It now dawned on him that he had made a major mistake this morning. Furthermore, he realized that his family might very well have to pay for his foolishness.

Jake Drieborg had just pulled up to the general store. He had begun to load the supplies on the farm wagon.

Michael approached his father and told him that the Justice of the Peace wanted to see him in his law office.

"Why would Mr. Deeb want to see me, Michael?" Jacob asked his son.

"I got into a fight with Carl Bacon, Papa."

Mike expected his father to react with anger. Instead, Jacob looked at his son with such surprise, as if he had been slapped in the face. He turned toward the wagon, put his hands on the sideboard and hung his head. In a few moments, he turned around. Michael could see that the look on his face still wasn't one of anger, just disappointment. He looked directly at Michael, put his hands on his hips, and shook his head.

"Come, you two," he said. "We go see Mr. Deeb about dis now."

In the office of the Justice of the Peace, the three Drieborgs sat in straight-back wooden chairs in front of Mr. Deeb's desk.

"Thank you for coming here so quickly, Mr. Drieborg," Mr. Deeb said, looking directly at Jacob, ignoring Michael and Susan. "Charges of assault have been filed against your son here. This is what happened." With that, he related the events of the morning. When he finished, Jacob turned to Michael.

"Is what Mr. Deeb says true?"

"Yes, sir, it is. But I just stopped Carl from beating on this little kid."

"Mr. Drieborg, I can understand Mike's reaction to Bacon's bullying children. But he and Carl are not kids having a schoolyard disagreement any longer. Mike can't just take things into his own hands however justified he believed it to be. He should have called me. Besides, formal charges have been filed. Herb Bacon intends to see to it that the law is enforced. There are plenty of witnesses. Mike himself admits to attacking Carl. We have a nasty situation here, Mr. Drieborg."

"They're talking about me like I'm not even here, as if I have no part in the matter. I feel bad enough about what Mr. Deeb told me out in the street. But now I could be going to jail for assault. What was I thinking? I wasn't. Instead, I allowed my temper and my own arrogance to rule my head."

"Mr. Deeb," Jacob began, "you have known me and my wife since we moved here twenty years ago. We work hard and pay our debts. You have had no trouble with da Drieborgs. Dat Bacon kid has been a pain to da people of dis town since he was old enough to walk and talk."

"All true, Jake. But charges have been filed."

"Mr. Deeb, how about I take care of Mike in my own way, at home. You can have my word on dat. Will dat take care of dis business?"

"Not this time, Jake. I have little choice. Mike is guilty of assault by his own admission. He attacked Carl Bacon in front of nearly the whole town on a Saturday morning. Herb Bacon already told me he would not drop these charges for any reason.

"But I'll tell you what I can do. First, Mike has to plead guilty. Then I will release him to you until Monday. You have him back here by eight in the morning when my court opens. At that time, I will accept his plea of guilty and give him the choice of spending thirty days in the Kent County Jail or paying a one hundred dollar fine."

"Go to jail!" Mike exclaimed, rising from his wooden chair.

"Michael, sit down, und be quiet," his father directed. "Right now!" Mike had never known his father to speak to him with such force. His father was shaking as he stared Mike into silence.

Mike sat with a thud and slumped forward, looking at the straw hat in his hands.

"But, because of the war, I can offer one other alternative," Deeb continued. "Mike can volunteer for service in the Union Army. If he joins the cavalry Regiment now being formed in Grand Rapids, there will be no jail time or fine."

"But Mr. Deeb," Jake asked, "isn't dat da Army unit where da Bacon boy is an officer?"

"Yes, it is, Mr. Drieborg. But that's the best I can do for you. Think it over. I'll see you Monday morning at eight when I open my courtroom. You can give me your decision then."

Michael's Decision

As the Drieborgs left the office of Lowell's justice of the peace, Jacob turned to his son. "Michael," he directed, "you sit in da back of da wagon. Susan, you ride on da bench wit me."

Michael looked at his father and, for the first time, saw anger on his face.

Jacob snapped the reigns, and the horse began to walk home. "Michael, tell me everything dat happened."

Michael told him everything in detail.

"Susan, you watched dis entire thing, ya?" Jake asked.

"Yes, Papa, I did."

"So! You tell me everything you saw and heard. Leave nothing out." When she finished, Jake said to Michael, "So! You did not dump Bacon in da horse trough because he had hit da little boy. You attacked him because you lost your temper when he called you a coward. Is dat right, Michael?"

"Yes, Papa. It is."

"I thought so," he concluded. "Neider of you talk now."

The remainder of the trip home seemed to take forever to Michael. Jacob directed the wagon off Fulton Street and into their farmyard. He told Susan,

"Do not say anything to Mamma just yet, Susan. I will decide when."

"Yes, Papa."

Michael watched Susan go into the house and his father move around the back of the wagon.

"We are late, Michael. Mamma will have dinner ready. Help me now." "Yes, Papa."

They both took a sack of flour into the root cellar under the house. The ground corn went into the storage box in the barn. Michael carried the box of cooking supplies into the house. He avoided his mother's gaze and swiftly left for the barn to help his father unhitch the horse and get it settled with a rubdown, water, and grain.

When they finished, they both washed before going into the house for dinner.

The house was built some thirty yards north of Fulton Street. The Drieborgs owned 180 acres, ninety of them south of the road, stretching all the way to the Grand River, a good source of water.

The Drieborg home was constructed of wood, typical for that time. The main room had a front door in the center opening on Fulton Street, a stone chimney to the left, and a window to the right. This fireplace was called a Dutch Oven. Rose and her daughters used it to do all their cooking and baking. Jake and Rose Drieborg had a bedroom on one end of the house, and the two girls had one on the other. The two boys slept in a loft above the girls' room.

Jake had designed his home carefully. Most farmers used rainwater for cooking and washing. Rain was channeled from the house roof to a barrel in the cellar. Others used well water brought to the surface by a pump located outside the house. Instead, Jacob installed a hand water pump on the kitchen sink that connected to the well in the yard. He also enclosed the back porch where they hung their coats and cleaned their boots before entering the house. This rear entrance also had a stairway to the cellar on one side and a water closet on the other side. Much to the boys' disgust, the job of cleaning out the chamber pots in this closet fell to them.

The barn sat about twenty yards north of the house. There were stalls for the two milking cows and another for the plow horse. A fourth stall was currently empty. The double doors at the east end of the barn opened into a series of pens for the pigs, sheep, goats, and cattle. One part of the loft was full of hay for the animals the other had a good size room for their farm hand.

The rest of the buildings and the animal pens were sufficiently distant, to keep farm-yard smells away from the house.

Now, all the Drieborgs were at the dinner table with heads bowed as Jake thanked God for His blessings. Then, Rose began passing the plates of food for the midday meal they called dinner. Supper would come later in the day.

Dressed like most farm women of her day, Rose's homemade long-sleeved dress was plain and covered her from neck to toe. She was of a cheerful disposition. In her early forties, she was five-foot-ten inches tall and weighed not much over one hundred fifty pounds.

Michael considered his mother very pretty, especially when she pulled her long blond hair into a bun behind her head. Her bright blue eyes sparkled, except when she was upset with him or one of the other children. He believed she could be tougher than Papa at times. He feared this would be one of those times.

She passed a dish of freshly baked biscuits, hot from the oven, and another of beef stew. Everyone loved her stew over biscuits. Applesauce, milk, and apple pie were on the table, too.

Once the food was passed and everyone's plate was full, Mamma spoke. "So, tell me the news from town."

Without hesitation, Jake responded, "Michael got arrested by da Justice of da Peace today."

"What do you mean arrested, Papa? Arrested for what?"

Michael and Susan sat silent. Michael's sister Ann and his young brother Little Jake excitedly asked questions too.

"Quiet everyone!" Jake interrupted. "Let Michael tell you."

Mike told them what had happened and the decision of the Justice of the Peace.

"What do we do now, Papa?" Mamma asked.

"We have no choice, Mamma. We must pay da fine," Jake responded without hesitation.

If Michael had any objection to his father's decision, now was the time for him to say so.

"No, Papa," he said firmly. "I intend to volunteer. It's time I got into this war, anyway."

The other members of the family sat in stunned silence.

Michael knew that none of the children had ever dared to disagree with either of their parents, especially not their father. Now he was telling them he would leave the farm and go off to war against their wishes.

"Michael," urged his mother, "listen to your papa. You cannot join this war. Your duty is here. This war is none of our business. Besides, with the new land to clear and all the work with Willi gone, we need you here on the farm. Tell him, Papa."

Michael put down his fork and faced his mother. "First, Mamma, I want to apologize for my actions in town today. I had no right to do what I did. I acted without thinking of the embarrassment I would cause my family. Susan tried her best to stop me, but I allowed anger to cloud my judgment. I apologize to you all for my actions.

"But Mamma, when this war began over a year ago, I stayed on the farm as you asked. Besides, everyone thought it would end after a battle or two. But it didn't end. And now our President has asked for more volunteers for the Army. He is trying to keep our country together. I can't stay home any longer while others, my schoolmates and neighbors, go off to fight and die for our country. Even that worthless son of the banker has joined. How can I live here and not be considered a coward? No Mamma, I know I have a duty to my family. But I have a duty to our country, too.

"I hope you understand Papa," Michael said quietly, but without hesitation. "It is time for me to join in this fight. So, I want to tell the Justice of the Peace that I accept my guilt for assaulting Bacon. I hope you will not try to pay the fine. Instead, allow me to take the option he gave me of joining that cavalry Regiment being formed in Grand Rapids."

Everyone sat silently, waiting for Jacob's reply.

"So, Mamma," he said. "It is decided! Now, finish your dinner everyone. We all have things to do yet today."

***

It was Sunday morning. As usual, the Drieborg family was at St. Robert's Catholic Church for ten o'clock Mass. The two girls and Rose wore their best summer dresses. The two boys and their father wore a white shirt and tie under their black wool suit jackets.

A head covering was mandatory for ladies attending a Catholic Church service. The Drieborg girls and their mother chose to wear a white lace cap pinned to their hair. The custom for men was quite the opposite. They were to uncover their heads when entering a Catholic Church.

The pastor, Father Bernard Dumphy, delivered a sermon in which he stressed controlling one's temper. Michael thought his pastor looked right down from the pulpit at him. The priest probably knew of the scrape Michael had gotten into the day before with Carl Bacon. Every-one else seemed to know.

Attending Sunday services was important to Lowell area families. Few missed what they regarded as their Sunday obligation, and few wanted to miss the opportunity to socialize. With homes widely scattered throughout the area, there was infrequent contact during the week. So, after the Sunday service, most churchgoers gathered for awhile around a potluck meal.

After Mass concluded, the families in attendance went directly to the tree-shaded area next to the church. There, they sat at wooden tables while the women passed the plates and bowls full of food they brought from home.

Once everyone had their fill, the dinnerware was washed and the tables cleared. The adult men stood around, some smoking pipes, and talked about farming and the war. The women spoke of family matters, and some even shared a little gossip, too. The young boys played a new game called baseball, while the girls talked about the boys.

There were only a couple of single males Michael's age left in the church congregation. Most of the others had already volunteered for service in the Union Army.

"Hey Mike!" one of Michael's friends called out. "I hear you got into another scrape with Carl. Didn't know he was back in town. I thought he was still at the University."

"He was there Billy," Mike responded. "But they threw him out. After that, his father bought him a commission in the Union Army. And yes, we did have a fight. Not much of one, though. I just dunked him in the horse trough for beating on a little kid with his riding crop."

"Were you arrested or what, Mike?" Tom asked.

"You might as well hear it from me. You heard right. Carl's dad filed charges and the Justice of the Peace arrested me. No other way to say it."

"Why aren't you in jail, then?" asked Billy. "I thought when a person's arrested, they're in jail."

"I don't know that much about such things, either," Mike responded. "I guess I thought the same thing. The Justice of the Peace gave me a choice. Serve thirty days in the Grand Rapids Jail, pay a fine of one hundred dollars, or join the cavalry Regiment being formed over in Grand Rapids."

Tom's eyes grew wide. "What are you gonna do, Mike?"

"We talked about it at home yesterday. My folks want to pay the fine, but I decided that I would volunteer for the Army. Like you, when the war broke out last year, I obeyed my parents and stayed home. But this war is lasting longer than anyone thought. Besides, it's time I helped keep our country together. So, that's my choice."

Leaving the Farm

Even though it was still dark outside, Michael was awake. He just lay there in bed, looking up at the roof beams. For a number of years, his internal clock had awakened him a few minutes before he heard his father in the kitchen just below his sleeping loft, starting the morning fire in his mother's Dutch Oven. Once he got it going, she would begin her breakfast preparations. By the time chores were done, she would have fresh bread and a big breakfast ready. That would be his favorite meal of the day.

This day was different though. He couldn't remember a night when he had slept less. After all, this was the day he intended to plead guilty to a serious crime. He had assaulted someone. He wondered if the Army people would know what he had done. He hoped that they would not know he had been given a choice of jail or joining up. The thought kept coming back to him — how could they trust a criminal? How would they treat him?

At one point during the long night, Michael thought, "*Maybe my decision to volunteer was a mistake. Let Papa pay the fine. Stay home until after harvest, and then volunteer. The Army people would never know, would they? Mamma would like that too.*"

He rolled over and punched his pillow again. Little Jake was snoring, safely asleep beside him. "*No*," he thought. "*That's not right. In the first place, where would my parents get one hundred dollars? And then have me skip out to volunteer in three months or so. How could I use them that way?*

"*What's the matter with me all of a sudden? I assault someone in town, on a Saturday no less, just because he made me angry. That was bad enough. But it was not just someone. No, it had to be the son of the only banker in Lowell.*"

This was the banker whose approval his father needed for financing the farm operation from time to time. This was the banker who held a note on their farm. He was known to have denied people loans if he didn't like them or ruined people if they angered him." *And my reckless behavior put my parents in danger of both.*"

His Papa's head showed atop the ladder to the loft.

"Michael, come now, da chores."

Mike swung his legs out of bed, stretched, and rubbed his eyes. In a few minutes, he was by the back door pulling on his boots. There was a morning chill, so he put on his wool jacket, too.

"Here, Michael," his mamma whispered. "Eat this biscuit."

He took a good-sized bite. It was left over from last night's supper. But his mother had warmed some of them this morning. She had butter and strawberry preserves in the middle.

"Umm," he mumbled. "Thanks, Mamma."

He stuffed the rest into his mouth and joined his father in the barn to begin milking their two cows. All told, the two men had about an hour of early chores. Once he had swallowed the last of his mamma's treat, he wanted to talk with his father.

"If the word I have is correct, Papa," Mike began, "the cavalry Regiment I'm joining in Grand Rapids will not be forming until late August or early September. That should give us time to clear a few more acres of the river land and get the new sheep flock settled. Don't you think?"

There was a separate wooden stall for each of the two cows in the Drieborg barn. Each of the men sat in one of these stalls on a low three-legged stool alongside the cow in order to milk it. Mike heard the barn animal sounds, the chickens in the yard, and the sound of the squirted warm milk hitting the bucket. He did not hear his father's reply to the farm questions he had asked. Just silence.

Michael remained silent as well.

When his father walked by his stall, he carried a full bucket of milk to empty into the separator. Then he commented absently,

"Ya Michael, der is plenty of time for dose tings. We see, eh? Now we finish da chores. Mamma has got breakfast for us early so we are not late for your trial. This morning, at least one of the Drieborg men will be a man of good character. He will be on time. Come now, Michael, we have chores to do."

"Ouch! That hurt." Michael thought.

The two of them finished quickly and washed up for breakfast. As usual, it was a hearty meal. Mamma and his sisters had fixed freshly baked bread and biscuits, meat with fried potatoes and gravy.

"Michael," said Rose, "put on your Sunday suit and tie. I won't have you in that courtroom today looking like a farm hand."

Michael just shook his head and headed for the loft to change his clothes.

She turned and said, "You too, Jacob." But he was already behind the closed door of their bedroom.

Papa drove the wagon into Lowell. According to his watch, it wasn't yet eight o'clock. In fact, they still had fifteen minutes before the court would be open.

Michael turned to his father. "Papa, I am so sorry that I let my temper cloud my judgment Saturday. I would give anything if I could take it back. I wish that it had never happened. I know I embarrassed the family, let you down and exposed you to Mr. Bacon's anger. I hope you and Mamma can forgive me."

Jacob just sat on the wagon's bench seat. While Michael spoke, his father had leaned forward, arms on his legs, still holding the reigns in his hands.

"Please say something, Papa," Michael silently wished.

He finally did.

"Michael," he said, still not looking at his son. "Neider Mamma or I could ever believe you would do such a thing. We never thought you would act like a bully. Yes, you let us down. But you are my son, und you are going away soon. Maybe I never see you again, mit dis war you are going to fight. So, you und I, we have no time for anger, I tink. So, I forgive this mistake you have made."

Jacob looked directly at Michael.

"Thank you, Papa," Michael asked, looking back at his father.

"Parents, especially da mamma, love der children, no matter what.

"But children must earn da parent's trust, especially from da papa. Now listen to dis, Michael. You have my forgiveness and you will always have my love. But you have lost my trust."

Michael slumped against the back of the wagon bench. The air seemed to have been punched out of him. His hands clutched the seat. He broke eye contact with his father.

"I want you to promise me that you will do everything you can to earn back my trust. Will you do dat, Michael?"

Michael looked again at his father. "Yes Papa," he promised.

"So," his father continued, "you promise me dat every time you feel your face flush with anger or you are tempted to do something you know is wrong, you will remember us sitting here dis day and da promise you just made. Ya?"

"Yes, Papa. I'll not forget."

"Und," Jacob went on, "will you promise me dat whatever you do in dis army you are joining will make me and Mamma proud. Ya?"

"Yes, Papa," Michael replied, still shaken by his father's words. "I promise."

Jacob had never hugged either of his sons, but he put his hand on Michael's shoulder and gave it a light squeeze.

"Good. Now, it is time for da court."

Michael and Jacob entered the building and took the same seats they had used Saturday, in front of Mr. Deeb's desk.

Mr. Deeb wore a long black robe this time, Michael observed. Seated across from the Drieborgs, he called his court to order and read aloud the complaint brought against Michael Drieborg for assaulting Carl Bacon.

"Good morning," he greeted them. "What have you decided, Mr. Drieborg?"

Michael's father straightened up in his chair. "Dis was a big decision for da family. Since Michael is da person who will have to live with dis, I'll let him tell you."

Mr. Deeb looked directly at Michael. "Well, Michael?"

"It was decided, sir…" he responded. "It was decided that I would join the cavalry unit being formed in Grand Rapids, sir."

"Fine. That then will be the ruling of this court," Mr. Deeb pronounced.

After filling out some paperwork, he turned to Michael again. "You are to sign here. By so signing, you are pleading guilty to the charge of assault. Further, you choose to enlist in the Union Army instead of spending thirty days in the county jail at Grand Rapids, or paying a fine of one hundred dollars."

"Yes, sir," responded Michael. "Will that stay on my record forever?"

"No, son. In fact, one year from today, as long as you are still serving in the Union Army, or upon your death or an honorable discharge, it will be stricken from your record. I also prepared this other document, whereby you agree to volunteer in the Sixth Cavalry Regiment. By signing it, you are agreeing to report to their training area in Grand Rapids the first Sunday of September before five in the afternoon. Do you both understand?"

"Yes, sir, we do," Jacob answered "Michael?"

"Yes, sir, I understand too." Michael signed both documents.

"This court stands adjourned."

They rose, shook Mr. Deeb's hand, and left the building thirty minutes after arriving in Lowell.

***

Several weeks later, Jake and his sons were just finishing the morning chores early one Sunday morning.

"Come boys," he told them. "Mamma will be angry if her breakfast gets cold waiting for us."

As they entered the house, the three male Drieborgs could smell the freshly baked bread and the bacon waiting for them on the dining room table.

"Well, Jacob," Rose announced. "Another few minutes and the food would be cold. Were the animals cranky this morning, or were you just slow today?"

Jacob reacted to Rose's frosty greeting lightly. "See why I told you that we must hurry mit da chores, boys? Good thing da food is not cold."

Without further comment, Rose took her accustomed seat at the table. Jacob said the prayer, and Rose began to pass the plates of food. After finishing, they would all go to church in Lowell as was usual on a Sunday morning.

But this was not the usual Sunday. Today, Rose's eldest child, Michael, was leaving home. He had agreed to report for training this day as a soldier in the Union Army, eventually to fight and possibly die in the War of Rebellion now raging.

At the breakfast table this morning, it was unusually quiet, Michael thought. He didn't know how to act or talk. He knew that his parents, his mother, in particular, did not want him to leave. So, he remained silent. His brother and sisters were silent, too, not knowing what to say. His father remained impassive. His mother picked at her food. He could see that she was near to tears.

Toward the end of the meal, she broke the silence. "Papa," she said, "I want to go with you when you take Michael to the training camp."

"No, Mamma," Jacob announced. "You and I have talked of dis already. After church and we eat da dinner der, I will drop you and da girls off here at home. Little Jake and I will take Michael to da camp in Grand Rapids. You will stay here with da girls."

"But Papa!" Rose pleaded.

"No more Mamma," Jacob insisted, softening the tone of his voice. "Michael will say his goodbye to you and da girls here at home, not in front of hundreds of men. Besides, the roads might not be safe. Der will be hundreds of men going to dat camp in Grand Rapids today. And there will be many others returning to der homes after taking men to da same camp. It might not be good dat you, a woman, be traveling on da road today. Come now, we must clean up and leave for church. Da Drieborgs are not late for Sunday Mass eh, Mamma?"

***

Despite the sunny September day, the women of the Drieborg family hardly sang at the Sunday church service. With Michael leaving for training camp that afternoon, the other women of the church understood their feelings, since most of them had already gone through the same thing themselves.

Later, Jacob dropped off the women at home despite their tears and pleading and headed toward Grand Rapids to drop Michael off at the training camp. However, he did take Little Jake.

The three men traveled west on Fulton Street. Heavy woods lined both sides of the road. Every now and then, a clearing would appear and show a farm house, a barn, and other small buildings much like theirs.

"Not much different from our layout eh, Papa?" suggested Little Jake.

"Dey haven't cleared enough land for crops, son," his father replied. "Dey will have a tough time paying da mortgage on dat place."

Michael had seldom traveled this far from home, so he found the changing landscape fascinating. He knew that the big city of Grand Rapids wasn't much more than two hours from his home. As the time passed, the road seemed wider and more worn than it was near Lowell.

He knew that Fulton Street would not take them directly to the camp. As they neared the city limits, they looked for a road running north called Prospect Street.

"I think that's the street, Papa," Michael pointed out.

His father pulled up. They sat in the wagon, allowing the horse to rest before turning.

"My goodness Papa," Little Jake exclaimed. "We can see the whole city from here."

And they could. The city was located on both sides of a wide river. The hills on each side made it look as though the city was in a bowl.

"Look at the boats on that river," Mike observed. "And see all the tall buildings. It sure is a lot bigger than Lowell."

"Maybe," his father said. "But I would not want to live in such a crowded place. Lowell is better for us, I think."

Jacob alerted the horse and pulled on the reigns to turn the wagon onto Prospect Street. The old plow horse struggled up the street's steep incline. But it didn't take long to reach the next cross street, Fountain Street. They had been told that the training camp would be one hundred yards or so east.

The street looked like downtown Lowell on a Saturday morning. Dozens of horse-drawn wagons were coming and going near the entrance of the camp. Families were milling about or picnicking nearby.

Jacob spoke to his youngest son. "Little Jake, I don't want you telling da girls about all da families we see here today. They are upset enough. Do you understand me, son?"

"Yes, Papa."

Michael pointed to an opening, and his father pulled the wagon off the road.

"Give me those two packages, little brother," Mike said.

Little Jake handed him the small bundle of clothing. His mother had insisted he take several changes of underwear. Then he passed up the other small package. This one contained cookies, fresh bread, and slices of ham and cheese.

"You never know how long it will be until they feed you, Michael," she had warned him.

"Stay with the wagon, son," Michael's father told Little Jake.

"Hey Mike," Little Jake told his brother with a wide grin. "Do you realize that's the last time you'll give me orders?"

Mike gave him a big hug. "You take care, Jake," he urged him. He was several years younger, but Little Jake was as tall as his brother.

"I'm sure you'll do fine. Remember, you have to look after our sisters now."

"You know I will."

"Come, Michael," his father urged him. "We walk a bit."

As they walked side by side, Mike felt his father's hand on his shoulder. When he stopped, they both looked into the camp area. They could see men hurrying everywhere.

Jacob turned to his son. He still had his right hand on Michael's shoulder. "It will be almost dark when we reach home, son. And you must report in. I wish you were not going to fight in dis war. But you have given your word. Remember Michael, our talk about controlling your temper. Stay away from dat no-good Bacon boy. He will cause trouble for you if he can."

"Yes, Papa," Mike responded.

Jacob's grip tightened on his son's shoulder. "You must do your duty, son. And always behave with honor."

"I promise, Papa," Mike responded. "I will do my duty and bring honor to the Drieborg name."

Jacob embraced his son; turned and walked away.

As Michael watched the wagon pull away toward home, he repeated his promise.

"Don't worry Papa. I'll do my duty and bring honor to the Drieborg family."

Boot Camp: September 1862

Grand Rapids, Michigan, was a city of some 15,000 residents located in a valley. The town had been built on both sides of the navigable Grand River. East of the river at the top of the very steep Fountain Street hill, a military training camp was set up in late August of 1862.

Wooden barracks to accommodate a thousand men, and tents for officers and some noncommissioned officers had been erected. Fields had been cleared for training men and horses, too. Now that housing issues had been addressed and training areas prepared, the men who would direct the training were hard at work on personnel matters.

"What about this Drieborg fellow who has been assigned to I Troop?" asked Captain Hyser commander of a one-hundred-man cavalry unit called a Troop. He was meeting in his tent with his Troop's first sergeant, Williams. They were looking over the names of the men assigned to his Troop. "Do you know why he was forced to volunteer?"

Hyser was a veteran who had fought in the first battle at Manassas. A cavalryman not much over five-foot-seven, he was a stern leader of men who would immediately punish breaches of military rules. Nor would he tolerate immoral or crude behavior. In fact, as his men would soon discover, he insisted they attend church services and write home regularly, as well as keep away from card playing and drinking.

"No, sir," Williams responded. "But there's a lieutenant over in G Troop who's been saying Drieborg's a troublemaking bully. They come from the same town, it seems. I can talk with him if you wish, sir. If Drieborg was a problem there, the local Justice of the Peace would know about it. Want me to find out from him, too?"

Williams was the first sergeant of I Troop. He had served with Hyser earlier in the war. He demanded respect with his six-foot-two husky frame. Seldom smiling, he was not someone his men would cross a second time.

Hyser nodded. "Yes, Sergeant, That's a good idea. For now, put Drieborg on the list of men who could be a problem. Assign him to Riley's platoon. You and Riley have a serious conversation with him when he reports next week. He must understand what will happen should he break the rules here. Now, let's finish going over the roster."

Later that day, First Sgt. Williams was going over the completed platoon assignments with his platoon sergeants.

"What?" exclaimed First Platoon's Sgt. Riley. "You give me three men who are on the trouble list? Thanks a lot."

Several inches shorter than Williams, Riley had a fiery look about him, with a head and beard of red hair. He was a perfect fit for the type of disciplined unit Captain Hyser wanted.

"I don't suppose any of these boys have ridden a horse a' fore, either."

"I don't know about that, Riley. But you got 'em in your platoon, riders or no. Don't worry so much. You and I will meet with these three men the first day they are in camp next week. I think we'll be able to get 'em in line. But we gotta jump on 'em early and hard, and you're just the man to do it.

"You've had a year of this stuff," Williams continued. "You're the best one to take this bunch as soon as they walk in the gate. So, are you with us on this, or not?"

"You know I am," Riley responded.

"But let me know as much about each of these boys as you can. Now, let's finish lining up the rest of my platoon."

Over one thousand men reported for duty on the first Sunday of September 1862. They would become the new 6th Cavalry Regiment. Few of the volunteers had any military service experience. Some of the officers and noncommissioned officers had been fighting in the war in other units. They had been given promotions to transfer here and help form the new Regiment.

Most of the volunteers came from farms. They were accustomed to rising early and working long hours outside in all types of weather. They were also experienced with animals and were handy with a musket. Those volunteers who had lived and worked in towns were new to living and working out of doors. Few of them had much experience working with animals or using firearms, either.

The Majority of officers and noncommissioned officers had no military experience. They had been given their rank for one of several reasons. Because some had recruited a pre-agreed upon number of recruits, they were promised officer's rank. A commission could be offered to someone who helped outfit a Regiment of men, or the governor might simply give a person of influence a commission.

Once given a commission, an officer might give a friend a position of authority like that of a sergeant. Some units elected their leaders.

***

"No pushing over there," commanded a soldier clothed in the blue uniform of the Union Army. "And don't you worry boys, the Rebs will wait for you. There are plenty of uniforms to go around, too."

A new cavalry unit, the 6th Michigan Regiment, was being formed this day. An area for training the green volunteers had been established between Fountain and Lyon Streets at the eastern outskirts of the city of Grand Rapids the second largest city in Michigan.

"Will you look at all these men?" Mike said to no one in particular. "With everyone standing so quiet and serious-like around here, you'd think they were giving away free money in this building."

A thousand men reported for duty that sunny day in September 1862. Just inside the main gate along Lyon Street, a large sign directed the arriving men to a one-story building called a commissary. "This line is pretty long," the man in front of Mike said. "And it's moving mighty slow. I'd sure be mad if it turned out to be the wrong line."

"If that soldier over at the gate is telling everyone the same thing," Mike said, "we're supposed to get all our clothing and such in this building. So, I think we are in the right line."

"This fellow is right, though, about how slowly this line is moving, Mike thought. *Papa dropped me off at one-thirty, according to my pocket watch. Looking at the sun, I would guess it's now almost three o'clock, and I haven't moved more than ten feet closer to this commissary building. Hope we don't miss supper."*

It took another hour, but Mike walked out of the commissary by four o'clock with his arms piled high with clothing and other gear.

"What Troop are you assigned?" Mike asked the recruit right behind him.

"After I got my stuff, they told me to find the I Troop barracks," the man responded.

"That's what they just told me, too. That man sitting by the doorway over there looks important to me. Let's check with him." The two recruits walked up to the man.

"Sir," said Mike, "we've been assigned to I Troop. Do we go into this building?"

"I'm not a sir, Private," he snapped. "I'm First Sergeant Williams of I Troop. Who might you be?"

"Michael Drieborg, First Sergeant."

"So, you're Drieborg," observed Williams. As he said this, he stood to his six-foot-two height, hands on the table in front of him. He leaned forward and looked Mike in the eye.

"I'll be having a serious talk with you real soon, Private. For now, go inside the barracks here," he ordered.

"Report to Sergeant Riley. He's looking forward to seeing you too, Drieborg."

Michael and the other recruit stepped through the door of the barracks.

"You know that guy?" asked his companion.

"Never met him," Mike answered.

"The way he looked at you, I'm glad he's not meeting me later today. Good luck trooper."

"Why did he single me out?" Mike wondered. Once inside the one-story building, he noticed a red-haired man with sergeant's stripes on his sleeve. He looked angry.

"Sergeant Riley?" Mike asked. "Sergeant Williams told me to report to you. I am Michael Drieborg."

"Ah, yes, Drieborg, 'tis it now," he responded. At six feet two, Mike was a good six inches taller than this sergeant. A stocky man, Riley had pink cheeks on each side of a bulbous nose. To top it off, his head was covered with brilliant red hair.

"Take that bunk over there, Private." Riley pointed.

"All a'you men," he directed, "change into your uniform, and then make up your bed. I'll be talking with all of yas in a bit. Don't just stand there gawking! Get on with yas, now!"

The bed above Mike's was already covered with bedding and civilian clothing. A young guy was standing barefooted in his underwear along one side of the bunk.

Mike dropped everything he was carrying on the lower bunk and turned toward the barefooted fellow who, Mike assumed, would occupy the bunk above his. Holding out his right hand, he said, "Hi, I'm Mike Drieborg."

"I'm George Neal," George responded. "Nice ta meet ya, Mike. I'm from Grand Rapids."

"Mind if I change, too, while we're talking?"

"Be my guest. It's probably a good idea not to waste any time. I'd hate to be caught without my pants on or my shoes unlaced with that red-headed sergeant yelling at me."

"That's exactly what I was thinking." Mike chuckled. His first impression of Riley gave him the feeling that he would not want the sergeant mad at him.

Mike unlaced his shoes and stripped off his civilian clothing. Looking around, he realized how much taller he was than everyone else, except for Sergeant Major Williams.

Over his long underwear, he put on the blue woolen blouse and trousers he had been issued. Once he buckled his belt and put on the shoes he had been given, he had to admit, that things fit rather well.

"What do you think, George?" Mike asked pleasantly. "Do I look like a soldier?"

"Probably do, as much as anyone in this corner of the barracks," Neal answered.

While Mike laced up his new shoes, the two men talked more.

"What's it like living in a big town like this, George?"

"Well," Neal responded, "I was born here in Grand Rapids, actually. So, I don't know any other place. But I can lead you around this town blindfolded. The last few years, after my father was killed in an accident, I worked as a baker's apprentice. I lived in the back of the bakery, too."

George was about five-foot-six, a brown-haired, chubby kid. Mike thought he looked too young to be in the Army, with his smooth, pale face.

"I was born and raised on a farm located between the villages of Lowell and Ada, just east of here," Mike explained.

"These are small farm villages. I never had much chance to go to Grand Rapids until now. I read the *Eagle*, your newspaper, all the time, though."

"I didn't care for school much," George added. "Don't remember my mom. She died when I was little. I guess I just grew up not reading much."

"We read every day in my house. My mother insisted. In fact, my father read the Bible out loud to everyone each night after supper."

"I never saw my father read. But we attended church every Sunday when he didn't have to work."

Suddenly, they heard a loud command from the other end of the building.

"First Platoon! Attention!"

Some men jumped off their upper bunks, others rose and stood up by their beds and looked about quizzically. Mike and George looked at one another. Neither knew what was expected of them.

In fact, Mike didn't see anyone move. Then he heard another command.

"Line up at attention in front of the barracks," Sergeant Riley shouted from the barrack doorway.

"Move it, now," he continued yelling loudly as he followed the running men out of the barracks.

Outside now, Mike still didn't know what to do or where to do it. It didn't appear to him that any of the other men did, either. Except for Riley, that is.

Riley was standing in front of twenty-five recruits, none of whom knew what he wanted of them. Mike was tempted to smile, thinking that the sergeant was enjoying every moment of his men's confusion. So, Mike just stood still, looked his sergeant in the eye, and waited. Riley did not disappoint.

"When you fall in," Riley instructed, "ya look straight ahead, hands at your sides, feet together, and back straight. When I call ya to attention, don't move again 'til I tell ya to. Understand what I just told ya?"

Mike heard no response.

"When I ask a question, shout, 'Yes, Sergeant!'" he ordered. "Now, once again, did ya understand what I jus' said?"

This time Mike shouted, "Yes, Sergeant." Some of the others joined him.

And so it went for almost an hour. Riley would dismiss Mike and the other men. Then he would call all of them to the position of attention again. Time and again, he asked them questions that required only a shouted yes or no response. Riley taught them the moves in response to commands of right-face, left-face, and about-face.

Mike could not help but laugh during the execution of that about-face command. It seemed the hardest for these newcomers to execute. He saw some men lose their balance in the attempt. Sometimes, men ended up facing one another. It truly was amusing to witness. Some others joined in with Mike's laughter. Riley's patience was sorely tested. However, Mike and the other men were finally able to execute the command.

"That's much better. We will continue these drills later," Riley promised.

"Chow will be in about one hour. Right now, I want ya ta store the clothing an gear ya was just issued in yer foot locker. I'll be back to inspect just before chow.

"An' each of ya will also write a letter home today. I'll be checking on that, too. Those who can write, help those who can't. Stay in this barrack until after inspection. I don't want ta see any'a ya outside getting lost or in trouble. Besides, all'a ya have plenty to do. Now get to it! Platoon dismissed!"

Back in the barracks, Mike and the other five men of his squad stored their gear or just sat on their beds, stunned by the events of the afternoon.

Unwanted Attention

"Private Drieborg, front and center," shouted Sgt. Riley.

Mike was storing his gear in the wooden box at the foot of his bed. He was startled by a command from the doorway of the barracks.

"Private Drieborg," repeated Sgt. Riley, "front and center."

He quickly moved toward the sound of Sgt. Riley's voice. At attention, he said, "Private Drieborg reporting as ordered, Sergeant."

"Get your cover, Private," he ordered. "That'll be yer hat. Button yer blouse and tuck it in, man. Then, meet me outside the barracks door here."

"Yes, Sergeant." *Well, here I go*, Mike thought. "*This must be that conversation Williams promised.* He wondered if Bacon was behind this."

Mike found Riley just outside the door.

"Follow me, Drieborg." Riley led him along a row of tents. He stopped at the last one. "Wait here." Then the sergeant entered the doorway of the tent.

Michael stood nervously rocking back and forth. He stood with his feet a foot apart and his hands behind his back. Being singled out like this was a new experience. It was not a good one for him thus far. He could feel that his hands were sweaty. So was his forehead.

It wasn't but a minute before Riley returned.

"First Sergeant Williams is ready for you. Put yer cover under the left arm an' follow me in. Stand at attention in front of his desk."

At the far end of the small wall tent, Mike could see the first sergeant facing him from behind a field desk. He stood at attention in front of that desk.

"Well, young fella," observed First Sergeant Williams. "It seems that you bring a reputation to our happy family here."

As he had done earlier in the day, Williams stood to his six-foot-two height and leaned forward on the table. He stared intently into Michael's eyes.

"I'm told that you are a bully. I'm told that you were given a choice of jail for assault, or joining up with us. You might wish that you had chosen jail, Drieborg. Without lying," Williams shouted, "tell me exactly how you earned that reputation."

Still standing at attention, a startled and terrified Michael Drieborg remained silent, as though he didn't hear Williams' order.

"You was asked a question, Private," snapped Sgt. Riley. "Answer the first sergeant!"

"I don't know what to say about your question, First Sergeant," Mike stammered. "I'm puzzled, mainly because I am not considered a bully, not in Lowell, anyway. It is true — I was given the choice you mentioned. That was the result of my stopping another fellow from beating a little boy with a riding crop. The father of the fellow I stopped is the town banker. He is the one who filed assault charges. I was guilty of dumping his son in a water trough. Several times, actually. So, our Justice of the Peace told me I was guilty of assault."

"That's not the way Lieutenant Bacon of G Troop tells it, Private," challenged Williams. "He's an officer. Are you saying he is a liar?"

"It was Bacon, after all," Mike thought.

He felt the anger begin. He took a deep breath and unclenched his hands. *"Relax, relax. Remember your promise."*

After regaining control of his anger, Mike responded, "I don't know exactly what Lieutenant Bacon told you, First Sergeant. But I went to school with him since first grade. He was always picking on little classmates, and I was always stopping him. Sometimes I punished him, too. His father, the banker, always blamed me for starting it. But in all those years, I never did. Not once."

"Answer my question, Private," demanded Williams. "Is he lying?"

"Knowing Bacon as I do, First Sergeant," Mike responded, "yes, he is."

The questions continued.

The Lowell Justice of the Peace had already told the I Troop commander and First Sergeant Williams the details and the history of Drieborg's relationship with Lt. Carl Bacon. Mike's answers to their questions were supported by the Lowell official. Bacon had not been truthful. But he was an officer in this army, and his rank gave him power, or at least authority over enlisted men.

"Wait outside, Drieborg," ordered Williams. "Sergeant Riley and I will decide what to do with you."

Once again, Michael stood nervously outside the tent and waited.

"Calm yourself, calm yourself," he repeated.

It wasn't more than a minute or two before Drieborg was called back in the tent.

"Here's how it will be, Drieborg," explained Williams. "We will give you a chance to prove yourself. But hear me clearly, trooper. You do any bullying in this unit, and we will come down on you like you never have experienced. Remember, if we kick you out, it will mean jail time back home. Do you understand what we are telling you, Private?"

"Yes, First Sergeant. I do."

"And stay away from Lieutenant Bacon," warned Williams. "Should you experience any problems with him, remember, he is an officer. Assaulting an officer in this army will get you jail time for sure.

"Sergeant Riley, I expect you will have some private words with Private Drieborg. We want him to clearly understand his position here in I Troop. Don't we, Sergeant?"

"Yes, First Sergeant," responded Riley. "I'll be sure he understands." "Very well," Williams concluded. "Drieborg, you are dismissed."

***

Mike returned directly to his squad area in the I Troop barracks. He had barely entered the door when he heard a bugle call.

"First Platoon," Sgt. Riley ordered. "Get yer mess gear and fall in." Mike was amazed to see that this entire group of men knew what to do, and did it to Riley's satisfaction.

"Right-face," he ordered next. "Forward, march."

The First Platoon marched to another building and lined up for supper. Mike's squad of six men sat together at a long table to eat their first meal as soldiers.

"Mike," George said, "we sort of got acquainted after Riley took you wherever you went." With that, each of the other four men introduced himself and shook hands with Mike.

"So," Neal asked, "can you tell us what happened? What made you so special to be called out by Riley?"

"There is an officer over in G Troop who told First Sergeant Williams a bunch of lies about me," Mike told the others in his squad.

"He was the guy I dunked in the horse trough back in Lowell, my hometown, when I caught him beating on a little kid with his riding crop." Mike continued to relate his history with Harvey Bacon. He also told them that he had to either join this unit or go to jail as punishment for assaulting Bacon.

"Don't worry about it, Drieborg," urged Stan Killeen, the farm worker from Cadillac, Michigan, a city north of Grand Rapids.

"Instead of having to look after yourself with guys like this Bacon, now you have the five of us to help. Right, you guys?"

There was a murmur of assent by the others.

The oldest man, Bill Anderson, a generalstore owner from the nearby farm town of Wyoming, appeared as old as Mike's father.

"I hope you will stay away from that guy, Michael," he urged. "He is an officer, after all. An enlisted man is no match for one of them, you know."

"Bill's right, Mike," agreed David Steward, who owned a small farm near Newaygo, a small village northwest of Grand Rapids. "He gave you good advice."

"That's exactly what Williams and Riley told me, too. With Riley running us ragged, I can't imagine I'll have any time to wander to the G Troop area, anyway," Mike joked.

The fourth member of the squad was Gustov Bjourn, who wanted to be called Swede. He just sat quietly eating his food.

"Any of you guys need help writing that letter Riley wants to see?" Mike asked. "I'll be glad to help." They had until Wednesday to turn their letters in.

George Neal piped up. "I don't have anyone to write to, is my problem. Can you help with that?" Neal had no family. His mother had died bringing him into this world, and his father had vanished shortly after, leaving George with the baker's family.

"Sure can," Mike responded. "I have two sisters who would love to get letters, especially from someone as handsome as you, George."

"How about you, Swede?" asked Bill Anderson. "You have anyone to write to?"

"No, I don't." He had been in the United States for just a year, working in the copper mines of Michigan's Upper Peninsula as an animal handler. "You got anoder sister, Mike?"

"I sure do. She'll love it. Do you want me to write it for you?" Swede nodded. "Ya, cause I can't rite da English eider, Mike."

Everyone was soon busy writing. Mike helped Swede first. Then he tackled his own letter home.

Dear Family,

I hope this letter finds you all well. I am fine, except I miss you already. It is hard to believe that I have only been here less than one day. Seems like I have always lived in a building called a barracks with five other men, worn this hot uniform, and been yelled at by a red-headed sergeant who makes us run everywhere.

Not much to tell you tonight. The first meal was all right. Not anything like you cook, Mamma. The other five men in my squad seem like very nice fellows. One of them, George, is going to write you, Ann. The other fellow, Swede, is going to write you, Susan. Sergeant Riley told us today that each of us has to write home this week. They have no relatives. I volunteered you two. I hope you do not mind.

George is about my age, was born right here in Grand Rapids. Before he enlisted, he was a baker's apprentice. The other fellow, who wants to be called Swede, has been in the United States for only a year. He worked in the copper mines up north. I'll tell you about the other four men as we become better acquainted.

Please write and tell me everything that is going on at home. That's all I have for now. God bless you all.

Love,

Michael

Training

It was day two of Michael's new life as a soldier in the United States Army. He was one of twenty-four men who made up the First Platoon in I Troop of the 6th Michigan Cavalry Regiment. He stood at attention with them in front of their barracks. There were four rows of six men each, called squads. Sgt. Riley was in front of Michael's platoon, facing the platoon leader, Lt. Thomas.

"Good morning, men," Thomas began. "I am your platoon leader. During your training here, Sergeant Riley will be in direct charge. I will only deal with you directly if Army regulations require it, or he has a problem he can't solve. That means you go to him, not me, with your questions and problems. Take over, Sergeant."

Sgt. Riley saluted the lieutenant. Once his salute was returned, Riley did a smart about-face, and Thomas left.

"Platoon," he ordered, "at ease."

This was another type of military position. Michael and the other new Troopers learned this one yesterday after noon chow. It went like this: from the position of attention, the at-ease command allowed each man to place his hands together behind his back, relax and even talk to one another. But each man had to keep his right foot fixed in place. Thus far, Mike and his fellow Troopers had been very quiet, and Riley had done all of the talking.

"I want ya all ta look around." He directed their gaze by waving his hand around. "We are standing in what we call a Company Street. The four barracks along this street are all I Troop. The tents in that row behind the buildings are housing for the officers. First Sergeant Williams and me, share a room at the far end of this barracks here.

"The door to our room will be open. But ya don't jus' walk in as ya please. Knock on the wall and stand at attention outside the door if'n ya need something. If the door is closed, keep away. 'Tis closed for a reason.

"An' look how clean this street is. Our platoon is responsible for keeping it that a'way. So, every morning after this formation, we'll go over every inch of it. That's called policing the area. Ya miss anything in our platoon area an' the whole lot a'ya will be on hands and knees going over every inch, every morning for a week.

"An' notice men, there are no servants around here to pick up after ya. No moms or wives, neither. So, each of ya is responsible for making yer own bed each morning, picking up the area around it, and keeping yer gear an' uniform neat an' clean. Jus' to make sure ya don' forget, we'll have an inspection each morning after chow.

"Speaking of chow," he went on, "we don't have anybody cooking or waiting on ya, either. So, in the cavalry, each squad must do their own cooking and cleaning up when the eating is done. Also, after we police our Company Street this morning, each squad will prepare a duty roster. Our platoon will have one, too.

"And what might that be for, ya might ask? We have to have a latrine for the platoon. No indoor chamber pots for ya here, lads. We don't even have an outhouse for yer tender backsides. But 'bout a hundred yards or so back a' the barracks is an area set aside for latrines. We must dig one for this platoon every now an' again.

"Yer turn to fill in the old one an' dig the new will be shown on the duty roster. It will be posted on the wall outside my door. It will not go well for ya if ya miss yer turn.

"Oh, yes. By the middle a' next week, our mounts will arrive. Each of ya will be assigned one of these horses. The real work starts then. The farm boys here think they know something about taking care of a horse? We'll see 'bout that. But I'll wager none of ya have any idea 'bout training a horse for riding; specially, not a hardly broke horse which don't want ya on top a' him in the first place. We'll see how ya do when these animals get here.

"Now lads," he warned, "jus' like we practiced yesterday. I will call ya to attention. Then I will tell ya to fall out. The new part is for ya all to stay in place, 'cause we have to pick up our street here. Do it right the first time, lads. Platoon attention! Fall out."

It only took Mike and the others a few minutes to pick up the street around their barracks. Sticks and leaves, mostly.

"First Platoon, fall in! Not bad, lads. The street looks clean. Trash ya jus' picked up goes into that wooden tub by the door. Remember where those bits of trash go, men. Ya don't want ta get me riled if I see ya dropping something on the ground instead of putting it into that tub. After I dismiss the platoon, each squad will go to the cooking area. Finish cleaning up. I'll be around to inspect shortly. Ya can show me the duty roster for the week.

"One more thing," Riley continued. "Each squad will select a leader a'fore chow this noon. Each man selected will report to me a'fore anyone in that squad eats chow again. I don't care how yas do it. Draw straws, take a vote; arm wrestle, with the loser taking the job. Aside from an increase in pay, squad leaders will be responsible for making up a duty roster for his squad, an' t'other duties I'll tell 'em about."

"First Platoon," Riley commanded. "Attention! First Platoon, dismissed!"

***

Mike was the last of his squad to reach his bunk. The others were already sitting or lying down. No one said anything.

Bill Anderson broke the silence. "If any of you think I should take this responsibility just because I am the oldest, you have another think coming. I had to make decisions for years in my General store. I kind of like not having to do that here. Count me out, fellas."

Mike thought that Bill was probably as old as his father. At least, he looked older to Mike than anyone else in the squad. He was clean-shaven like Jacob Drieborg, but slenderer and a whole lot shorter.

Bill had told everyone that Wyoming was just a small village near Grand Rapids. Mike guessed that Bill's store was probably a lot like Mr. Zania's general store in Lowell.

"Count me out, too," added Dave Steward. "I'm just a small farm owner from the sticks."

Dave had told Mike the previous night that he had a fruit farm outside of the village of Newaygo. Not far from Lake Michigan, Mike concluded that the soil up there was not good for crops like the Drieborgs planted in their Lowell fields. But it was evidently perfect for peach, pear and cherry trees. Dave had two milking cows, some cattle, pigs, and goats. Of course, he had chickens, too. He called it a small operation, but it evidently supported his family. He told Mike that his wife was in charge now.

Stan Killeen spoke up next. "I don't care how much more they pay; it's not enough for me to be in charge of anything but me and my horse."

Stan was a talkative fellow who had described his background the previous night at chow. It seemed that he was from a hundred miles or so north of Grand Rapids. He was raised on a farm just like Mike's, but he had also worked for wages the last two years, cutting big trees in the Upper Peninsula of Michigan. His face looked wind-burned, and he had a bushy mustache.

"That pretty much leaves it between you and Swede, Mike," George concluded.

"Not me, by golly," protested Swede. "I can't even read or write da English."

"I say Mike gets the honor," announced Dave. "Anyone opposed, speak up."

No one spoke.

"Wait a minute," Mike protested. "I have enough problems with Riley and Williams, not to speak of Lieutenant Bacon over in G Troop. Besides, I'm probably the least experienced of everyone in this squad. Every one of you worked for someone other than your parents, and you were paid for your work. So, I'm the real rookie of this bunch. Besides, don't I get any say in this?"

"Nope!" Stan announced. "You are now our leader, Drieborg. Go tell Riley so we can eat."

***

Later that day, the weather had cooled some. There was also a nice breeze that evening. Many of the men were outside walking, smoking their pipes, and talking. Bill Anderson and Stan Killeen were taking a stroll and puffing on their pipes.

"So far, life around here seems pretty easy to me," commented Stan. "We'll see how easy you think it is when those green nags arrive in a couple of days, Stan," Bill responded. "I know I'm not looking forward to it."

"Why didn't you stay on the farm, Stan?"

"Actually, I left my folks' place a couple of years ago. My dad is a hard case. He never smiled that I ever saw, or gave an atta-boy, either. His place was just outside of a village called Lake City, but the land around there wasn't very good. We had more rocks than crops, so there wasn't much money around that I ever saw. And my four sisters were on my back all the time. They drove me near crazy. So, I left for the Upper Peninsula to cut timber. Hard work, let me tell ya, but at least I got paid for it. I got my keep, too."

"Why did you join the cavalry?" Bill asked.

"Well, I'm pretty good with animals, actually," Stan went on. "A' course, we had animals on the farm. But in the northern woods, we used horses to move the big logs on what we called skidders. Those horses were big brutes. So, I have some experience with that kind of animal. I think I can handle most any horse."

"Besides, I'd rather ride than walk any day," Stan finished. "What about you?"

"My wife and I owned the general store in Wyoming. We raised our kids there, lived upstairs of the store, actually. The children are all gone now. Our daughter is married to a farmer and lives just outside that city. And, our son is serving in the Army down in Tennessee someplace. He and I thought it was important to keep our country together, so last year

I wanted to join up like he did. But my wife said one of her men fighting for the country was enough. That ended the discussion, let me tell you. When she made up her mind on something, discussion was finished.

"But last March, she died from some sort of infection. The doc called it a tetanus infection. She was hanging our laundry on the outside line last September. She was barefoot and stepped on a rusty nail sticking out of a board in the tall grass. She dismissed it like women do as just a trivial thing. But this red spot spread up her ankle and leg. She finally agreed to see the town doctor. He drained it and tried a poultice. It didn't do any good, though. Over the winter, the infection spread.

"She was a tough lady, but you could see that it was a painful death." Bill stood still for a minute then he resumed walking.

"Everywhere I looked, I was reminded of her, and our customers made it even worse talking about her. I had to get out of there. So, I sold the store. And then I looked to join up in the Union Army."

"But why did you join the cavalry?" Stan asked. "You don't even seem to like horses."

"That is interesting, isn't it?" Bill replied. "The short of it is that I simply took the nearest and fastest opportunity. Besides, I figured, how difficult can it be to ride a horse, anyway?"

Stan chuckled. "Well, I've been around horses all my life, first on my dad's farm, then up north hauling logs. I don't mean to frighten you, but horses are hundreds of pounds of the dumbest, most ornery and stubborn animals on God's earth." Stan paused to spit.

"I swear, if you're afraid of 'em, they can smell your fear a mile away. Until you make them believe that you're the boss, these damn animals will try to knock you down, stomp on your foot, and take every opportunity to keep you frightened of them."

Bill smiled. "That's real good news. Thanks, Stan. Thanks a lot."

"Course, Bill, I could be wrong," Stan added.

Bacon Reenters Michael's Life

Mike headed to Sergeant Riley's quarters to report the results of the leader selection for his squad. He was still frightened some of Riley. He didn't know how this particular piece of news would be greeted by the platoon sergeant, so he approached the open door with some caution.

Mike knocked on the wall beside Sgt. Riley's office doorway. Riley looked up from his desk.

"Yes, what is it now, Drieborg?"

"You ordered each squad to select a squad leader, Sergeant," Mike told him. "My squad picked me. I'm just reporting it to you, as ordered."

"Squad leader, 'tis it now, Drieborg?" commented Sgt. Riley. "Maybe what the Lowell Justice of the Peace told us is true. That you are a leader."

"I never heard that before, Sergeant," Mike responded, somewhat embarrassed. "But I'll do my best."

"*This is the last thing I wanted,*" he thought. "*But what is done is done. I'll be darned if I'll give Riley or Williams an excuse to harass me or kick me out*".

"Well laddie, you'd better, believe me," he warned. "I'll be watching ya close, now, won't I?"

"You can watch all you want, Sergeant," Mike replied, a little angry. "I'll not give you any reason to complain."

"We'll see about that," said Riley with a wry smile on his ruddy face. "But, right off, I want ya ta look at that list on the wall there. It's the platoon duty roster. As you can see, the name Drieborg is at the top of the list. So, you get the honor of digging the first latrine for our platoon.

"A latrine is a hole one foot wide, three feet long, and two feet deep. Be sure ya don't make it too wide, or some of yer fellow troopers might fall in. When you're finished with the digging, put a stick in the ground alongside the latrine. Put these sheets a' paper on it for the men to use.

"I want it done after noon chow. Ya also have to get me a duty roster for yer squad. And by the way, Drieborg being a squad leader makes ya a corporal. So, sew these stripes on ya's blouse a'fore today's inspection, too." Riley handed Michael a set of the corporal stripes.

"If ya don't know exactly where, just look at my sergeant's stripes. Give yerself enough time to clean up after you dig that latrine. Be ready for the four o'clock inspection. Got all that?"

"Yes, Sergeant."

"Off with ya, then," Riley ordered.

***

Riley sat back in his chair for a time, thinking of this young man from Lowell. He seemed likable enough. But, Lt. Bacon over in G Troop sure didn't like him. That was obvious. However, the men of Dreiborg's squad certainly did. Even after so short a time together, they trusted him, too. That counted a lot with Riley.

Lt. Thomas had selected Drieborg for latrine duty today. This type of decision was normally made by the platoon sergeant or the squad leader. In Riley's experience, the platoon leader never became involved. Did Thomas have it in for Drieborg?

Riley wondered if Thomas was doing this as a favor for Lt. Bacon of G Troop. He suspected that something wasn't right here. "*Is Bacon using Thomas to settle a grudge he has with Drieborg? What does latrine digging have to do with it?*"

For Thomas to support vengeance by another officer against one of his own men was a betrayal of all the men of his First Platoon. They would quickly recognize it as such and probably never forgive him for it.

A veteran of several battles in this war, Riley was of the opinion that any officer who mistreated his men like this would not survive his first battle.

***

"*Digging a two-foot-deep hole can't be much of a problem,*" Mike thought. "*It shouldn't take me more than a few minutes. That'll leave plenty of time to get back and get cleaned up before the platoon's four o'clock inspection.*"

He then sat down on his bunk and sewed on his new corporal's stripes, first.

Riley told Mike that the latrine area was about a hundred yards or so behind the barracks." *Yep, there it is.*" A well-marked area, it was easy to find. There were several other troopers already digging latrines in the area. Mike could see that there was a sign clearly marking the I Troop latrine area, and he also found the First Platoon stake. He set to work by stripping the top soil away.

***

"Well, well, well!" Mike heard from behind him. "We meet again, farm boy."

Mike turned, looking up from his digging. He had pretty much finished digging the small latrine.

There was Lt. Carl Bacon, standing a few yards away. He was tapping his right leg with that riding crop he always carried. Mike remembered it from their encounter in Lowell last month.

"Good afternoon, sir," Michael responded formally. He didn't know exactly how he should respond to an officer from another unit. So, he snapped to attention. Normally, in such a circumstance, the officer would say,

"At ease, Private," or, in a work situation like this, "As you were, Private."

Of course, Lt. Bacon knew nothing of military custom. In this case, he didn't care what was proper. He was here for another reason. So, he left Drieborg standing at attention while conducting an inspection of the latrine Mike had been digging.

"Who told you to dig a latrine like this, Private?" he asked.

"Sergeant Riley, my platoon sergeant, sir."

"You can tell Sergeant Riley for me that he does not know his head from a hole in the ground. Understand, Private?" Bacon thundered.

"Yes, sir." How else could Mike respond to an officer's order?

"For now, Private, fill in the hole you just dug. Replace the sod on top, too."

"Yes, sir." Michael filled in the hole he had just finished digging.

"Now, you'll dig a proper latrine over there." He pointed to an area about ten yards away.

"But, sir," Mike asked, still standing at attention. "Are you pointing to the area marked G Troop?"

"You are still at attention, Private," Bacon snapped. "It's not for you to question an officer of the United States Army, is it Drieborg?"

"No, sir," Mike responded.

"I would love to write you up for insubordination, farm boy. Just give me an excuse," he threatened. "Do as I ordered, now!"

"Barely three days in camp," Mike thought, *"and Bacon found a way to hassle me. How did Bacon know I would be out here? Did Sgt. Riley tell him? Maybe it was Lt. Thomas? No matter."*

Mike wished he and Bacon were back on at the schoolhouse. He'd throw his skinny ass in the nearest puddle. But he knew he could not do that here. He had to obey an officer here. *"Remember, striking an officer would mean prison."*

They moved to the G Troop latrine area and Mike began digging.

"This is all right with you, isn't it, Private Drieborg?" he taunted. "You don't mind helping out my platoon over in G Troop, do you?"

"No, sir." This was the response required of an enlisted man to an officer.

"Louder farm boy," Bacon ordered. "I didn't hear you. Say it louder!" "Yes sir!" Mike shouted.

It was already after three-thirty in the afternoon. Bacon, never satisfied, had Mike dig several latrines, fill each in, and dig another.

"I understand you have a four o'clock inspection, Private," Bacon reminded Mike.

"Yes, sir."

"Be a pity if you were late or not properly prepared for it now, wouldn't it?" he taunted.

"Heck! He knows about that, too," Michael thought. *"This is a set-up. This shit-head officer is going to make me late or worse. Probably wants me to shove his head into one of these latrines. He would love for me to disobey his direct order, or worse, attack him."*

"I think you finally have the knack for digging a proper latrine, farm boy. You can report back to your barracks for inspection now," Bacon directed. "Just remember, Drieborg, I can get to you anytime, and you can't stop me! Isn't that right, Private?"

"Yes, sir."

"So, until next time, Drieborg, you are dismissed."

Mike grabbed his shovel, turned and began to run back to his barracks.

Still, fifty yards away, he could see his platoon already forming. He hoped he had enough time to straighten his uniform and wash his hands and face. He didn't. Instead, he heard Riley's command to his platoon, fifty yards away.

***

"Platoon, attention!" shouted Sergeant Riley. He waited while the men quickly formed in front of him. Then he turned completely about and faced Lt. Thomas.

"First Platoon reporting as ordered, sir," he said, saluting his superior officer. "All men accounted for, sir."

"I assume that means someone's not present?" asked Lt. Thomas. Of course, he knew his friend Lt. Bacon had prevented Drieborg from making this formation.

"Yes, sir. Corporal Drieborg has not returned from latrine duty, sir." Just then Michael came running up, shovel in hand, sweaty and disheveled.

"Here he is now, Sergeant. Have him fall in as he is," Lt. Thomas ordered.

"Yes, sir," responded Sgt. Riley. He turned smartly and moved off to intercept Drieborg.

"Over here Corporal," he ordered. "Fall in with your squad as ya are."

So, with his tunic unbuttoned and not properly tucked in, Corporal Drieborg took his place in the formation with the other five Troopers of his squad.

Lt. Thomas, followed by Sgt. Riley worked their way through the formation. They stopped in front of each Trooper, checking his uniform and equipment. Sgt. Riley noted anything out of place for follow-up with the offender later. Finally, they reached the Third Squad and Corporal Drieborg. He was still disheveled and poorly prepared for the inspection.

"Well Drieborg. You were late for formation and you're out of uniform as well. What do you have to say for yourself?" demanded Lt. Thomas.

"Sir, I finished digging the latrine trench Sergeant Riley ordered, but Lieutenant Bacon made me fill it in and dig another. So, I was late getting back."

"There must have been some good reason for Lieutenant Bacon to do that, Trooper. You aren't trying to blame him for your being late, are you?"

"Sir," interrupted Sgt. Riley, "Isn't this something I should look into and report back on? Then you can decide what actions to take."

"Very well, Sergeant. Let's finish the inspection."

When the inspection was completed and the platoon returned to

Riley's control, he shouted, "Platoon dismissed."

***

Very quickly, word spread to the men of Mike's platoon about what Lt. Bacon had done to him, probably with help from their own platoon leader, Lt. Thomas.

Back in the barracks, the men of Mike's squad talked of his experience.

"What's that shrimp of an officer from G Troop doing meddling with our men?" George Neal asked.

"Isn't he the guy that Riley and Williams braced Mike about the first day we was here?" asked Stan.

"Our platoon leader should stand up to that peacock officer and protect Mike," added Dave Stewart. "It's his job to look after all of us, seems to me."

"Sarge told me he's seen this type of problem before," Mike said. "He said I shouldn't let it get to me. He figured it wouldn't last long, anyway."

"It sure is a puzzle to me, though, why our platoon leader would allow this treatment toward one of his own men," observed Bill Anderson.

"It seems we can't trust him to stand up for any of us. At least that's the message I'm getting." A bugle sounded.

"There's supper call," George reminded them. "You guys can jaw all you want. But we gotta get to fixing our food. We ran out of time to do a proper job last night. Riley reamed us out proper this morning for lollygagging around." George moved to the fire-pit area and began a fire.

The men of I Troop usually ate together in a tented kitchen area. But in preparation for living under field conditions, each squad had been issued rations for three days and required to cook their own meals.

"Leave it to George," Mike thought, *"a baker's apprentice in civilian life, to look after the cooking."*

His squad of six men trained and bunked together. Now, they also cooked meals together in what was often called a mess. They were all new to cooking, so they were lucky to have George in their mess. Mike thought that he baked the best bread and muffins outside of his mother.

***

Eventually, the Troop had its first mail call. Before he dismissed his platoon for noon chow, Sgt. Riley distributed whatever mail had arrived that morning. He simply shouted out the name he saw on each envelope or package. The lucky trooper would trot from his place in rank to get his mail from Riley and then return to his place. Michael was one of those who received a letter.

Dear Michael,

It was wonderful to receive your letter and hear that you are all right. We all miss you very much.

Little Jake is trying so hard to replace you on the farm. The family talked at dinnertime today about all the work that has to be done each day without you to help.

After we talked, Popa decided that Ann would take over the care of your four sheep. Two lambs are expected soon. I will help Papa with the afternoon milking. Little Jake will work with Papa in the field and with the firewood. Both Ann and I will help Mamma in the house, of course, too. I will tell you later how this all works out.

Papa says most of the farm families around Lowell are having this same problem getting all the daily chores done. Worse even when the papa is away fighting. He and some other men are going to help with the harvest and the woodcutting on those farms. Get this war over, Michael. We don't want Little Jake to have to go fight, too.

Michael, you must tell me about those other five men in your group. Is it really called a Mess or a Squad? We are confused. It sounds funny, anyway. Is George Neal single? Is he cute? How old is he? How about Gustov? Tell us everything about them. Papa says it is probably a good thing you do not have weapons yet. Someone might get really hurt. Farming may be hard work, he said, but nothing is better than owning your own ground.

Mamma is worried that you are not eating right. So, in your next letter, tell us more about that, too. Ann and I will take turns writing every week. We all miss you and pray for you each evening at suppertime.

Love,

Susan

Horsemanship

The six members of Drieborg's squad had just returned to their barracks from church services. Whatever their faith Captain Hyser expected all his men to attend a church service every Sunday. They were relaxing and talking in their squad area when they heard Sgt. Riley shout, "First Platoon, fall in!"

"I thought Sunday was a day of rest," complained Stan Killeen. "Obviously not," Mike retorted.

Once in formation, Riley marched his men to a supply building. There, each man was issued a saddle and other gear needed for his horse. Carrying all this equipment, the return march to the barracks was not very orderly.

"How do you like all this stuff George?" asked Mike.

"I never thought a saddle could be so heavy," George complained. "My arms almost fell off carrying it all the way back here."

Being a city boy, George had never been around horses and their gear. It was all new to him. Besides, he was only about five-feet-five and weighed only one hundred pounds soaking wet.

"You best get used to it George," teased Killeen, who wasn't much bigger. However, Stan was a whole lot stronger, and he was used to handling such gear.

"Actually," Mike said, "it's easy now. Wait until you have a horse to put all this stuff on."

After they stored the newly issued gear beside their bunks, the squad prepared their noon meal. After cleaning up, most men lounged around. Some even seemed to be taking a nap. Without warning, Sgt. Riley's loud voice got everyone's attention again.

***

"First Platoon," Riley ordered, "Fall in!"

Once outside the barracks and in formation, Stan Killeen whispered, "We are the only platoon I can see out here."

"Quiet in the ranks," warned Sgt. Riley. "I heard that barroom whisper a' yers, Killeen. Knock it off. I don't care if ya miss a bit a' yer beauty sleep. I do care about tomorrow when each a yas will have to deal with about a thousand pounds a' nasty horse flesh. If ya pay attention this afternoon, ya'll be the best-prepared Troopers in the Regiment.

"Killeen, if'n ya want ta go an' take a nap instead, ya go right ahead. But I warn ya; no one will help ya with yer horse tomorrow. What about it, Killeen? Are ya staying or napping?"

"Staying," Stan responded.

"What was that, lad?" Riley asked. "I heard ya complain clear enough. Speak up now."

"I'm staying, Sergeant!" Stan shouted.

"So, now," Riley continued, "sit down, all a' ya, right where ya stand. Watch careful. Eyes straight ahead, an' no talking, any a' yas. I'm not jus' flapping my jaw here." He looked right at Stan Killeen. "Swede, give me a hand here."

"Thank goodness we have him in our squad," Mike commented. "With his knowledge of horses, he will be a lot of help when we get ours next week."

Gustov, the Swede, had worked in the copper mines of Michigan's Upper Peninsula. He had been in charge of the horses and the mules for the mining company because he knew a lot about the care and handling of these animals.

Riley brought out two horses: his and the one Lieutenant Thomas rode. Then, he and Swede went through the complete process of preparing the two horses for riding. After mounting and riding a bit, they dismounted and took the saddle, halter, and other gear off and repeated the process for the men of the platoon to see again.

Over the next three hours, every man in the platoon came forward and repeated that same process, too.

There were some humorous sights that afternoon. Sometimes, the horse moved just as the trooper was about to lay the saddle on its back. Then it would wait quietly for the next attempt.

George Neal seemed frightened to death of even getting close to either horse. As tame as the animal seemed with other Troopers, it picked up on George's fear and got real skittish, moving away from him each time he got the courage to get close. It did look funny, this little guy chasing a huge horse around in circles.

"Come on George," someone shouted. "He won't bite."

"This is a tame horse. What are you going to do tomorrow with a near wild one?" another trooper taunted.

"Knock it off!" Riley ordered. "We'll see how well ya do when it comes to yer turn. Handling a horse the cavalry way is tough to learn; especially if'n ya never done much ridin' a'fore. So, keep yer yap shut. This is a fellow trooper in the First Platoon. Each of ya is supposed to look after each other. Help those who need it, or I'll see that ya regret it."

There was no more taunting from anyone the rest of the afternoon.

***

Michael continued to write a letter for Swede to his sister Ann. Of course, he wrote to his family at the same time.

Dear Family,

I am fine and hope you are, too. From the looks of the line at the morning sick call, it would seem that a lot of men are ill. Some are just pretending, but the trots are common, and something called camp itch is, too. Sgt. Riley gets after us to really scrub our cooking pots and pans. We also change our mattress hay and wash our bodies often. He is almost as tough as you Mamma.

We are eating pretty well. Not as good as at home, but we have enough. You'd be surprised that even I am learning to cook. The men in my squad have to take turns cooking. Some of it tastes pretty bad. But, we are learning. We all go to Sunday church, too.

Each of us was assigned a horse a few days ago. Most of them were hardly broken to a saddle. So, they were pretty frisky. I call my horse Blue after your plow horse, papa. Blue and I are getting along just fine. We still have our disagreements, but I have maintained the upper hand; so far anyway. Teaching my horse to respond properly to all my commands has been a real challenge. We spend several hours each day riding and learning. Now I know why the pants they issue cavalrymen have padding on each buttock.

I will write again soon.

Love to you all,

Michael

***

No one was surprised when very early the next morning Sgt. Riley's voice could be heard throughout the barracks. "First Platoon, fall in!"

Riding his own horse, he marched his men to the railroad station just outside of Grand Rapids. He led them to a pen holding the horses assigned to his platoon. Horse handlers, who had brought the green broke horses by rail to Grand Rapids, led each reluctant and nervous horse by the bridle to an equally nervous Trooper.

Each trooper stood at the left foreleg of his horse. He held the bridle in his right hand. Most horses jerked up their head and tried to pull away or just bumped against the Trooper. Some animals turned in a circle, dragging the surprised Troopers with them. Others reared up and flayed their hooves in the air, breaking the Trooper's grip on the bridle. Troopers cursed and shouted, adding to the confusion.

Sgt. Riley and Lt. Thomas quickly rode alongside the most difficult horses to bring them under control. It took a good hour to calm the horses and begin the walk back to camp.

"What do you think, Sergeant?" asked Lt. Thomas. "Did we get a good allotment of horses?"

"We'll soon see, sir," responded Riley. "Right now, I'm just worried about getting these nags back to camp without anybody getting killed. Swede," he shouted, "give Neal a hand there. His horse is dragging him all over the place."

Mike saw the problem, but he couldn't help George with his horse. In all the commotion, Mike knew he had his hands full with his own excited and feisty horse.

The march took almost another hour to travel barely a mile. Bucking horses had gotten away a few times, and Riley had to chase them down. But they had made it without serious injury to man or beast. Before the noon meal, all the horses were safely in camp, fed, watered, and tethered.

Mike's squad was too tired to even bother cooking.

"Let's just have some of yesterday's biscuits," Mike suggested. "I'm too tired to fix a whole meal." So, that was what the men of his squad did. They ate hard biscuits left over from the day before, drank some coffee, and then collapsed on their bunks.

The hour allotted for the noon meal passed before they realized it. "First Platoon," they heard Sgt. Riley shout, "Fall in! If yas think ya can jus' lay around, ya was wrong. Remember lads, this is the cavalry ya volunteered fer.

"An' that horse each of ya was given this morning must be cared for. Ya volunteered fer that too. Now that ya had a bit of a rest, Swede an' I will show ya just what caring for yer mount means."

After demonstrating on Riley's horse, each trooper began to brush down his own. What a sight. Horses used their hindquarters to knock troopers down. Several times, a trooper howled in pain as his horse stomped on his foot. In a pushing contest, the large horse had the advantage.

"Damn!" exclaimed Dave Steward, the fruit farmer from Newaygo. "I think this animal broke my foot."

"Don't let him see yer pain Steward," shouted Riley. "Get right back alongside him."

"Push back there," shouted Riley to another trooper. "Don't let the horse knock ya around like that."

Feeding and providing water for each horse was another responsibility. Each trooper hauled water several times daily. They had to feed their horse daily as well.

"I never knew a horse could drink so much water," complained George. "Every day, we have to haul buckets full!"

At the end of the day, the men of the First Platoon were standing at attention in front of their barracks once again.

"Good job, lads," Riley told them. "Ya did well today. Remember; only after ya take care of yer horse can ya have yer own chow. Ya always take care a' the horse first, then yerself. If ya expect yer horse to stay healthy, ya gotta take proper care of it. Groom it gently too, an' talk to it softly, he continued. "Ya will be surprised how much better yer horse will respond to ya."

***

After chow and cleanup that night, the men of Drieborg's squad returned to their barracks. They were all exhausted. Once they kicked off their boots, most of them lay on their bunks, too tired to even wash up.

Stan was the first to speak. "I've worked with animals since I was a kid. The last two winters I spent logging, I used horses to pull felled trees to the railhead. Let me tell you, this is the first time a horse has almost done me in."

"My God," moaned George. "What have I gotten myself into?"

"Riley was right," Bill Anderson said.

"About what?" Dave Stewart asked.

"This day has been the worst since we got here."

"You got that right, Bill," Stan agreed.

***

It was only eight in the morning, but Mike could see the men of the First Platoon already acting like they were tired.

"*It's no wonder*," he thought. The men of his squad had gotten up at six a.m., as usual. But instead of caring for themselves as they had previously done, they now had to spend nearly an hour caring for their horses, first.

Grooming, feeding, watering, and walking the horse was the new part of their day. For some, it was difficult if the horse was unruly. In Mike's squad, only George Neal seemed to still have problems with his horse. Mike thought that George was actually afraid of his horse. What made matters worse for George, Stan had said, was that the horse knew it.

This afternoon, the entire Troop of one hundred men would stand inspection with their horses for their Troop commander, Captain Hyser.

"Don't forget what Riley stressed this morning," Mike reminded everyone. "Polish those saddles until they gleam. We've already groomed our horses. We only have another hour before we fall in for inspection."

That hour passed quickly.

"First Platoon," shouted Sgt. Riley. "Attention!"

During the inspection, all the Troopers remained at attention alongside their horse. The I Troop commander, Captain Hyser, occasionally conducted inspections which were normally the platoon leader's responsibility.

This morning was one of those times. Captain Hyser conducted the inspection.

Once completed, the Captain stood in front of Lt. Thomas. The twenty-five men of his platoon were standing at attention behind him. Sgt. Riley stood behind the last rank.

"I Troop," Hyser commanded. "Stand to horse!"

With this command, each trooper stood at attention by the left side of his horse. His right hand gripped the bridle strapped on the horse's head, six inches from the bit in its mouth. This usually gave the Trooper good control of his horse. Not all horses cooperated. This morning, however, even George Neal's horse stood quietly.

"As you might know, men, it is my responsibility to check on your training," he reminded them. "So far, Lieutenant Thomas, your men are looking good."

He was looking directly at the Platoon Leader, but speaking loudly enough for all to hear him. "But I am concerned about the lack of horsemanship," Hyser confessed.

"I watched the men of your platoon groom their horses this morning, Lieutenant. Some of them seem scared to death of their horse. The Regiment has maneuvers scheduled in a few weeks. But from what I saw this morning, some of your men are hardly able to walk their horses, let alone ride them. You've got to step up the training, Lieutenant."

"Yes, sir," Thomas responded. "We'll be ready."

"See to it," Hyser concluded. "Carry on, Lieutenant."

"Sergeant Riley," Lt. Thomas ordered, "take charge of the platoon."

"At ease, men," shouted Riley. "Again today, we'll work in teams of three. Corporal Drieborg an'Swede will work with Private Neal this morning. Right now, Neal can't even saddle his horse without help."

"Even though I've seen the rest a' yas saddle an' mount yer horse, ya all still need more work. So, I'll be checking on all a' yas, jus' the same. Get to it now. Platoon, carry on!"

As directed, the platoon broke up into groups of three to work with each of the newly assigned horses. They would lead one of their three horses at a time, away from the tether line where the platoon's thirty or so mounts were tied at two-yard intervals.

A man took a position on each side of the horse's head and tightly gripped the rein on his side. By this method, two men led the horse to a clearing. Once there, the third man saddled and mounted the animal. They worked with their horses throughout the morning and again in the afternoon.

***

After a few days, most of the mounts were accustomed to both saddle and rider. By the end of the week, almost every trooper could saddle and mount his horse without much difficulty or any assistance.

George Neal was not one of those who could do that.

"Private Neal," shouted Sgt. Riley one morning, "how are ya coming with that horse'a yours?"

He knew that Neal was having trouble, but he wanted to put some pressure on the private.

"He still needs some help, Sergeant," responded Cpl. Drieborg

"What's this?" asked Riley. "Can't speak for yerself Neal?"

"Corporal Drieborg is right, Sergeant," Neal responded. "Another day or two, and the three of us should have my horse under control."

"See to it now," he directed. "Swede and Drieborg, both'a ya ride Neal's horse until it's so tired even a little child could handle it. As for the rest a' ya this morning, I'll watch each a' ya saddle and mount yer horse by yerelf. So, rest easy till I get to ya."

It was a long morning, but under Riley's watchful eye, each trooper walked his horse from the tether line, saddled it, mounted it, and rode it toward an exercise area. It was a long day of repetition and instructions in the basics of horse handling.

Before that evening's meal, Sgt. Riley conducted his platoon's four o'clock inspection. Each trooper stood by the left front leg of his horse, holding onto the bridle with his right hand. Each pair of man and horse stood three feet from the next row and the man and horse to his left.

Riley moved down the rows, carefully examining each horse for proper grooming and each man for proper posture and uniform neatness. Once satisfied, he moved to the next pair, until he had looked at the last man and horse. He then returned to the front of the platoon.

"First Platoon! At ease. I liked what I saw today. This Saturday coming up is a special day. Depending on the morning inspection, a' course, each of ya will be given yer first pay and a pass for town. Corporal Drieborg."

"Yes, Sergeant."

"No one in yer squad will receive a pass Saturday or any other day until Private Neal shows me he can saddle, mount, and ride his horse, without help mind ya.

"For the rest a' ya, to get a pass, write a letter home. Squad leaders will collect 'em. Platoon dismissed."

***

Back in their barracks, Mike watched while Neal got some unwanted attention.

Stan Killeen was the first. "Look here, you little twerp. I don't give a damn how good your biscuits are. You'll get on that horse of yours, pronto."

"I'm trying, Stan," he whined. "He wasn't broke in good like yours. He's a wild one."

"That's a pile a crap," Stan snapped. "Swede and Mike both rode your horse. You're the problem. You're afraid of your horse, and the animal can tell."

Usually, when Stan got riled about something, the others would step in to calm the situation. Not this time.

"We have an hour before chow," observed Mike. "Stan, why don't you and Dave work with George and his horse while the rest of us get our food fixed."

"But who is going to fix the biscuits?" asked George.

To everyone's surprise, the normally quiet Swede snapped, "No von cares about da biscuits, George. Until you do dis, we all suffer. You heard da sergeant. He punishes da whole squad. Stan is right. Me and Mike rode dat horse all dis veek. You have seen us. I vill tell Riley it is you, not da horse. You ride it now, or dey make you a cook in da infantry, maybe."

Stan jumped up. "Come on, George," he directed. "Get your bottom off that bunk. You've got a horse to ride."

An hour later, the three men returned to the barracks.

"I wish we had some wine or beer to celebrate with," Stan announced.

"Are you telling us George rode his horse?" Mike asked.

Dave put his arm around George's shoulder. "Actually, he rode two horses. Stan's first, then his own."

Stan interrupted, "Remember George said he had been given a wild horse and that I had been issued a horse that was already well broken in? So, Dave told George to saddle and ride my horse, if it was so tame." Stan chuckled. "And he did, right, Dave?"

"That's right," Dave agreed. "On the way to the tether line, I remembered watching an old horse trainer up Newaygo way, helping people learn to ride. He started them on the tamest animal he could find. When the rider was comfortable and not so nervous, he switched them to a more spirited horse. Tonight, that approach worked with George, too. So, we started George on Stan's horse. He had no problem saddling or riding that one."

"Yep, it was a breeze with Stan's horse," George gushed. "So, while I was feeling pretty good about it, I got my horse from the tether line, saddled and rode it, too."

Everyone was up and excitedly slapping George on the back and arms.

"Better be some chow left for us," Stan said irritably. "Or Neal will have another problem. This time, he'll be alone with me in back of the barracks."

First Pass to Grand Rapids

"Mike, it seems like we've been here forever," commented George. Mike nodded.

"Seems like it. And this is only our first payday. You know, I think I'm the only one of us in this squad who's never been paid for any work. Dave got money for his crops and the wool from his herd. Bill was paid every week from his store. The Swede earned money working the copper mines. You got a little pay every now and then as a baker's helper. Stan was paid to cut trees. Yup, I'm the only one of the six of us who has never been paid wages."

"But just think of it," said Stan. "You'll be getting so much more than the rest of us, being you're a squad leader and a corporal. You'll get the princely sum of fourteen dollars, while the rest of us common folk have to make due on only thirteen dollars a month."

"Thanks, Stan," responded Mike. "I'll remember your kind words the next time I have to make out the duty roster for guard or latrine duty."

Stan laughed. "There you go. Give a guy a little power, and right away, it goes to his head."

"I expect you married guys will send most of your pay on home," predicted George.

"I suppose so," said David. "My wife, Becky, has a really good garden. She has a cow for milk and a sizable flock of hens, and she can trade or sell the wool from our sheep and the fruit from our orchard. But she still needs other stuff at the general store in Newaygo. Do you have the same situation at home, Bill? Oh, I'm sorry, Bill. I forgot that your wife died not long ago."

"That's all right, Dave," Bill Anderson replied. "I plan to open a savings account at a bank in town. But I intend to buy some tobacco. I don't need to buy much else, maybe some socks and writing materials, though."

As the men talked with one another, Mike sat back listening and appraising each one. Bill was the oldest man in the squad. David was the only other man with a family. He also was the only man in the squad who owned a farm. Mike knew of men with families and farms around Lowell who had volunteered for the war. He hadn't quite figured out how they could just leave their families like that. His father spent time helping those families.

The two of these men were easygoing and seemed to enjoy looking after the other men in his squad. Mike didn't think Stan Killeen was much over twenty, and not married or anything like that. But Stan had a superior, experienced air about him that kept everyone from getting too close. He had a pretty sharp tongue, as well.

Swede kept to himself, but everyone liked him. And, for sure, all of the men respected his knowledge of horses. George Neal was likable, too, just not very dependable.

"You boys will be sending most of your pay home, won't you?" asked Bill.

"Good idea, Bill," piped in David. "You guys send even half home, and you'll have a nice nest egg when this is all over. Well, what about it

George?" David asked. "You gonna blow it, or save it?"

George bristled. "Now, wait a minute, you two. I have stuff I need. An' I don't have anyone sending me stuff, or anyone to send money to, anyway. Isn't that right, Mike?"

"Don't drag me into this George," Mike responded. "Like Bill suggested, most of mine is going home. I already asked my father to buy the eighty-acre parcel next to his for me. He's going to borrow the money now, and then use the ten dollars I send home each month to repay the note. Should have it all paid up in a year or so. Besides, I don't smoke or drink, so I should be able to manage on four dollars a month. Don't you think, Bill?"

"That's a good plan Mike. If you don't have it, you don't spend it, I say. What about you Swede?"

"I don't know vhat to do, Bill," Swede wondered. "I got no one to send money to, an' I don't need all if it to spend eider. Tobacca an' a little drink now an' den. Vhat can I do mit da rest?"

"Tell you what," Bill offered. "On our pass Saturday, we can stop at a bank in town an' open an account for you, and another one for George. My wife and I put money in our bank in Wyoming as often as we could. It came in handy during bad times or just to pay for merchandise we wanted for the store. Now that she is gone, I'm going to do that again. You could do the same. How does that sound to you guys?"

"Fine," George replied. "Will you help me with it, Bill?"

"Fine mit me too, Bill," Swede said.

"Okay you two," Bill said. "When we head for downtown Grand Rapids this Saturday morning after we get paid, we'll find a bank and get all of us set up."

***

It was a good hour before chow, so the men turned to their own concerns.

"I'm going to write home," Mike told the others. "I know it's not Saturday, but I want to tell my folks about the dirty deed you did making me the squad leader. My family should know who is responsible just in case I have a heart attack or something."

Dear Family,

Since I wrote you last, a lot has happened. The activities from dawn to dusk have not changed since then. They stay the same. But the other day the men in each squad had to select a leader. He is called a squad leader. He has the rank of corporal and could even become a sergeant.

We had a discussion about it, and everyone had his say. I expected Bill Anderson from Wyoming to be selected. He's your age, Papa, and seems pretty smart. He owned a general store in the village of Wyoming. But he's sort of quiet and refused to accept the job.

David Stewart, another squad member, is a farmer and family man from Newaygo. That's a village close to Lake Michigan, northwest of Grand Rapids. He said he did not want to be giving any orders, either.

Stan Killeen, an Irishman, worked as a logger in northern Michigan. He was raised on a small farm up around Cadillac. He said that they could not pay him enough to be giving orders that might get some guy killed.

Swede can hardly speak English and cannot write in the language at all, so he refused. George Neal, who was a baker's assistant in Grand Rapids before he joined up, refused, too. I don't think anyone would have voted for him, anyway. He is pretty immature.

Dave suggested me, and everyone agreed. I didn't want it, but the five of them selected me anyway. That makes me Corporal Drieborg. I'm not at all sure just what will be expected of me. But I am sure of one thing. Sgt. Riley will tell me very soon.

Nothing much has happened about Bacon. He has not caused any trouble for me lately. Sgt. Riley tells me to keep my temper. I will, Papa. Don't worry.

My Troop of one hundred men will be given our first pass for town this Saturday. Before we leave camp, we will be paid. As a corporal, I will receive $14 a month. I will mail Papa $10 of that each month. He can use that to pay for the 80 acres he just bought for me next to his. I hope to have it paid for by this time next year.

Girls, I don't know if George is cute. I'm not much of a judge of that. He is a very nice guy. He is trying hard to adjust to life in the Army. Just this week, he finally was able to saddle and ride his horse without help. When I watched his efforts before, I didn't know whether to laugh or cry. Swede is a real stocky five foot seven or so. Sort of quiet, he is a wizard with horses. Am I glad he is in our squad! Sergeant Riley asks Swede all the time to help others in the platoon with their horses. Unless you object, Mamma, I will invite these two to come home with me for Thanksgiving leave.

That is all I have time for now. Write me soon. My health is good. I hope and pray that yours is, too.

Love,

Michael

***

That Friday evening, the men of Michael's squad were hanging around their area after evening chow. As usual, the reveille bugle had awakened them at six that morning. The squad's normally busy day followed without letup. By the end of the day, they were all bushed and ready to hit the sack. In fact, no one was still awake when taps sounded that night.

Before they knew it, Saturday morning's six o'clock reveille bugle awakened them. They were all excited about getting their first pay and going into Grand Rapids for the day. By seven a.m., they had finished taking care of their horses. Feeding and watering was followed by an exercise period, when each man walked and rode his horse. It was only after this that the men were allowed to prepare their own morning meal.

After inspection, they were in front of their barracks, standing at attention.

"As you know, men," Sgt. Riley told them, "today is yas first payday. The pay master will be at our barracks here at nine, just about an hour from now. We will be in formation standing at parade rest.

"Now, listen really careful. When ya hear yer name called, come to attention and answer loud an' clear with a, 'Yes, sir.' Then, ya march up to the paymaster's table, right over there, come to attention an' give yer first name and middle initial, followed by 'sir.' Then, ya will sign for the pay and take the money off the table. Then, ya come to attention, turn, and take yer place in the ranks.

"Any questions, ask 'em now. I don't want ya to be embarrassing me by any'a yas stumbling around getting yer pay. There will be no passes for troopers who don't get to the paymaster's table and back into ranks proper, don't ya know."

There were no questions. No one dared reveal they had not been listening.

By ten o'clock, everyone had been paid. No trooper in Michael's platoon had lost his pass.

However, before Sgt. Riley gave the passes out to the squad leaders to distribute, he addressed his platoon.

"I expect ya all to be back here a'fore six this very day. An' while yer in town, I expect ya all to behave. Ya know by now how the Captain feels about drinking. So, stay out'a the bars. Keep yer temper under control, an' no fighting. I'll be in town, too, but I expect the squad leaders to look after yer men. The squad leaders will give out yer passes. Platoon dismissed!"

The center of downtown Grand Rapids was only a mile away from the training camp. Located in a large valley it was built on both sides of a wide river called the Grand River. The commercial district was at the base of the steep hill on the training camp's side of the river.

Almost a thousand Union soldiers walked down the Prospect Street hill into town that morning. Men in blue uniforms crowded the sidewalks and all the stores.

Saturday was the busiest shopping day of the week. The farmers and their families had come to Grand Rapids early in the morning, as was their custom. Most of them were gone before noon. But hundreds of other civilians had come downtown after their noon meal. Seeing so many men in blue uniforms crowding the wooden sidewalks caught the townspeople and visiting farmers by surprise. And they were a little afraid, too.

Youngsters dashed in and out of the groups of soldiers. Mothers shouted warnings to them, fearing the soldiers would hurt them somehow. Coquettish young girls flirted with soldiers. The enthusiastic response of some of the soldiers to this female attention made the girl's fathers very nervous. So, on this Saturday, the civilians got their weekly shopping done quickly; and their families off the streets and home.

Officers and platoon sergeants from the Regiment joined local law enforcement personnel and patrolled the downtown streets on horseback to prevent trouble. Sergeants were posted in each bar, as well. The few Troopers who got into scuffles or who were thought to be drunk were quickly arrested and taken to the local jail.

Once in town, Drieborg's squad went first to a large retail store on Monroe Street called Richmond Brothers, which sold all sorts of men's clothing. Each man looked for socks, underwear, a spare shirt, soap, and an extra towel. The store's clerks wrapped each of their purchases in newspaper and tied them with string. The men decided to leave their packages at the store while they ate lunch. On their way to find a restaurant, they happened upon a general store.

"This is a pretty good store, too," George told them as they stood outside looking in the window. "I used to shop in here for things now and again. It's packed to the ceiling with stuff."

"What do you think, Bill?" Dave asked. "Want to see how a competitor stocks his store?"

"Sure. The store my wife and I owned was just like this one; smaller though. But neither of us ever had the time to visit another one. I must admit that I'm curious. Let's go in. I need a few things, anyway."

Mike and the others entered the store. Sure enough, George was right, Mike realized. *This place is packed with stuff, even more things than in Mr. Zania's general store in Lowell.*

Mike saw Bill take a small basket from a stack by the doorway. Eventually, he and the other men got one, too. As they saw things they wanted, they followed Bill's lead and began to put them into their basket. Just about everyone bought writing materials, a hair brush, a shoe brush, shaving and sewing gear, buttons, and shoe polish. A few of them bought tobacco. Bill bought a pair of scissors, too.

"What's that for, Bill?" George asked.

"You'll be surprised how handy a pair of scissors can be. You'll see. Each of you guys should have one."

The clerk agreed to hold their packages until they returned from lunch. Then the men left to find a restaurant.

Down the street, Mike saw one called Van's. Through the glass of the front window, he could see pies on a counter. Outside, near the doorway, a menu and prices were displayed.

"Know anything about this place, George?" asked Bill.

"This has always been known as a good place to eat. I could never afford to eat in this restaurant when I lived here. Those pies sure look good, guys. Prices on this menu look all right, too."

"Not crowded in there," said Stan as he looked through the glass window. "I don't see any officers in there, either. Let's go in."

"Must be a good place," observed Dave. "They have tablecloths."

Once they were seated at a round table for six, a waiter brought a menu for each of the men. He told them that the special was beef stew, and it included pie and something to drink for twenty-five cents.

"I don't care if your stew is the best in town and the cheapest," Mike told the waiter. "I've had enough stew to last me a lifetime."

No one ordered beef stew. They'd had their fill of that in camp. Some had ham, others meatloaf. Everyone had potatoes with gravy and pie for dessert. They each consumed a big slice with plenty of fresh milk. Filled to bursting, they didn't leave for an hour.

There was no need to rush off in answer to a bugle call or to respond to a shouted command from Sgt. Riley. So, they just talked quietly, enjoying the time together and relaxing over cups of fresh coffee. Once they left, they walked up Monroe Avenue.

The soldiers retrieved their packages from Richmond's and the general store. They window-shopped as they walked. Further up the street, they found a nice park and decided to stay out of the crowded streets and rest a while.

Bill Anderson remembered that Swede and George had asked for his help in opening a savings account at the Old Kent Bank when they got into town.

"Come on, you two," Bill urged. "Let's go to that bank, open an account, and make a deposit. You do remember that, don't you?"

"I'm too stuffed to move," moaned George.

"Come on George," Swede said. "I'm full too. But let us get it over mit."

"Are the rest of you going to stay here until we get back?" Bill asked.

"Don't worry," Mike responded. "I don't think any of us could move if we wanted to."

Incident During Training Camp

Training was beginning its third week. Michael had not had another run-in with Lt. Carl Bacon since the latrine incident during the first week of camp.

The men of the Third Squad were gathered for their evening meal. As usual, it was beef stew and vegetables over some of George's biscuits. Mike was always surprised that no one complained about the frequency of this meal. But since they each had to take turns cooking, such complaints were rare. Besides, George's biscuits were delicious.

"Mike, I haven't heard a word lately about that Bacon fella," said Stan. "Did he fall off the face of the earth or something?"

"I can only hope," Mike responded. "He's probably as busy with his Troop as we are here. Fact is, I haven't given him any thought."

With the dawn-to-dusk training schedule, he had little time to think of Bacon. The respite turned out to be too good to last.

At two in the morning, it was quiet, and the men of I Troop were fast asleep in their barracks. A fall moon was high this balmy September night, and the bugler would sound the men awake in another three hours.

"Awake, you louts," shouted Lt. Thomas. "Awake!"

Mike sat up in bed and looked for the source of the shouting. He saw his platoon leader, Lt. Thomas, standing in the barracks facing the six beds of Mike's Third Squad. A half-empty whiskey bottle was in his hand, and he wavered unsteadily on his feet.

"Drieborg! Get your squad up and dressed immediately. Have them fall out in front of the barracks. Get cracking." He turned and left the barracks.

More than Drieborg's Third Squad was awake by then. The entire platoon, asleep in that barracks, heard the shouting. Everyone was awake. Thomas had been very loud.

"What the hell?" Stan Killeen muttered. "What does he think he's doing?"

"I don't know," Mike responded. "But we're going to find out real soon, I expect."

The others looked toward Mike for direction.

"Get your trousers, blouse, and boots on, fellas," Mike directed. "Fall in outside like he ordered."

Still half-asleep, the men stumbled out the door of the barracks. Michael watched as, one by one, all six men of his squad were formed in a single rank at attention.

"Third Squad reporting as ordered, sir," Michael told Lt. Thomas.

"It took your squad long enough, Drieborg, and they're all out of uniform, too," Thomas observed. "Blouses not tucked in properly, boots not laced up, and only two of your men have hats on. You don't hear very well, Drieborg. I ordered you to have the men of your squad dressed properly. A fine leader you are. Now they will have to pay for your clear disobedience to my order. What do you think of your great squad leader now, boys?"

Another figure came through the door.

"Well, look who's here, men," said Thomas. "If it isn't Sergeant Riley. What do you want, Riley?"

"Sir, 'tis two in the morning, an'tis only four more hours till reveille. Can't it wait till then, sir? Whatever it is?"

"Riley, you're too soft on your men," responded Thomas. "You baby them. We'll take care of this matter right now. Return to your quarters. That's an order, Sergeant."

"Yes, sir."

"Drieborg," he ordered, "have your men squat down, hands around their knees, and do the waddle to the end of the street here and back. Give the order now, Corporal."

Mike knew this was a very uncomfortable form of exercise. It was used occasionally for punishment. If required for long, it could be very painful, especially on the knees.

"Assume the position," Mike ordered.

All his men squatted and joined their hands around their knees.

"Forward, march." Thomas ordered.

The men began the painful waddle, one behind the other, toward the end of the street in front of their barracks. It was about thirty yards. Mike was the first in line to reach it.

"Turn and follow me, men," he directed. As each man reached the end of the street, he managed to slowly turn, following the man in front.

"Phew! This is beginning to hurt," Mike thought. *"I'm young and in pretty good shape. These other guys are much older. How are they doing?"*

Thomas followed them down the street, commenting on their discomfort. All the while he was taking drinks from his bottle. Another man came out of the darkness to join him.

"I'm sorry I missed the start of this, David, but nature called," commented Lt. Bacon. "I see you're almost finished with that bottle. Here's a fresh one."

Bacon appeared sober. Thomas was definitely not.

As the two officers stood by the road watching, the squad of men passed several wall tents assigned to officers. The front door flap on one of them was suddenly thrown back, and a man dressed in only his pants and boots stepped out.

"What in tarnation is going on here, Lieutenant Thomas?" asked Captain Hyser, I Troop's commander. "You men in the street, return immediately to your barracks."

By the light of the moon, Mike could see the fury in his Troop commander's clenched fists as he approached the two officers.

"*Am I ever glad he is not mad at me,*" Mike thought. "He then followed the men of his squad into the barracks."

Sgt. Riley was waiting inside the doorway. "Get yer men ta yer area, Drieborg. The Captain will take care a' this business, it appears."

"All right, you guys," Mike directed. "Just drop your clothes on the floor and hit the sack. The reveille bugle call will come soon enough."

***

Outside, the Troop commander was, in fact, taking care of this business.

"Come to attention, you two!" Hyser ordered. "Explain yourself, sir. I asked you a question." His words were spoken loudly and with anger. No one in the area could avoid hearing.

Thomas was too drunk to even stand with his feet spread well apart, much less at attention with his feet together.

Hyser first turned his attention to Bacon. "And just who are you, Lieutenant?" asked Hyser.

"Lieutenant Harvey Bacon III. G Troop, sir. I'm here at the request of Lieutenant Thomas, sir."

Hyser stared intently at Bacon, who was standing at attention. Then he turned toward Thomas and brought his face bare inches from the drunken lieutenant's face.

"You are drunk, and you are acting disgracefully, Lieutenant. Consider yourself restricted to quarters. I will send for you immediately after reveille. At that time, I will tell you what will become of you, sir. Clean yourself up. If you stink as badly in the morning as you do now, I will have you thrown into the manure pile. Is that clear, sir?"

Thomas recovered enough to answer feebly, "Yes, sir."

"You are dismissed," Hyser ordered.

The Captain then turned his attention again to Bacon. "As for you, Lieutenant Harvey Bacon III, I seem to remember a report that you and Drieborg had some difficulty back home. Whatever that problem was, sir, you had better let it go. I will not tolerate any officer using the power of his rank to settle personal disputes with enlisted men of my Troop. Is that clear, Lieutenant?"

"Yes, sir."

"And furthermore, if I find you anywhere near my Troop area or my men again, you will wish your father had not purchased that commission for you. I intend to speak with your Troop commander of this matter in the morning. You are dismissed, Lieutenant."

Bacon saluted, executed an about-face, and walked toward G Troop. Hyser returned to his tent.

***

It was finally quiet. Inside the barracks, the men attempted to sleep once again. It wasn't long before snoring could be heard from some.

"As much as I dislike officers in general, I gotta say that our Captain Hyser is one stand-up guy," muttered Stan.

"I agree," responded Mike. "From what I've seen so far, I would trust him. I almost feel sorry for Thomas. Maybe he'll wise up and stop doing Bacon's dirty work."

"We'll see," David cut in. "For our sake, I hope so."

Lake Michigan Maneuvers

It had been weeks since the men had been given a pass to Grand Rapids. Under the unrelenting eye of Sgt. Riley, it had been weeks of intensive work with their horses. He drove his men with drill after drill, hour after hour.

"Ya gotta become one with yer horse," he would shout again and again. "Yer life will depend on it lads. No second chances. Make a mistake in battle, an' yer dead."

During one of their infrequent breaks, George was gulping water.

"He's going to kill us, I swear," he complained. "The only reason he gives us a few minutes break is to rest and water our horse."

Bill Anderson, who almost never complains agreed. "This old body of mine is about ready to give out."

"You can always transfer to the infantry, you two," Stan kidded.

They also practiced away from the cleared and smooth training ground of their Grand Rapids encampment. Toward the end of that week, I Troop spent two days away from the camp. They had bivouacked several miles east of Grand Rapids. It was very different from the comfortable ground and the soft beds in their barracks at camp. On these maneuvers in the field, they learned to handle their mounts in all sorts of terrain and woods, and they slept and cooked in the open.

Mike had found the experience sort of fun. However, he was still glad to get back to the main camp.

"All right, you guys," Mike reminded his men. "Don't forget what Riley told us. Everything has got to be spick and span when he inspects. That means that our cooking pots and pans had better shine. Who has that duty today? Oh yeah, I remember. Dave, you've got the mess gear duty.

"Swede, you looked over our mounts after we groomed them today. What did you think? Will they pass inspection?"

"Ya, I tink so," Swede told him. "Not to worry."

"He's supposed to worry, Swede," Stan said mockingly. "That's why they pay him extra. Or maybe this squad leader stuff has gone to his head. Maybe he just wants Riley to promote him to sergeant."

"Let him alone, Stan," Bill urged. "He's just trying to keep us out of trouble with Riley. With our platoon leader, Thomas, in the hip pocket of that nasty runt Bacon, there's no chance in hell that Mike's going to get promoted. You hassle Mike too much, and he might just resign. If that happens, we would probably vote for you as our squad leader. How would you like that, my friend?"

"Point taken, Bill," Stan responded. "I got the message. With that threat hanging over my head, I'll even put up with Drieborg acting like an officer."

"All right Stan," Mike broke in, "maybe I got a bit anxious. I promise that I'll calm down. Keep in mind, though, we leave again tomorrow for maneuvers at Lake Michigan. This time we'll be with the whole Regiment."

***

The platoon inspection began that afternoon. Each trooper had his gear on the ground in front of him. Riley walked up and down the rows of men and gear.

Back in front of the platoon, Mike could see that Riley was not pleased. He was pacing back and forth as though he might begin to froth at the mouth.

"I'm not going to tell ya again," he told the men of his platoon. "Leave all that stuff here. Din any of ya learn nothing from our two-day march last week? Each a' yas only need a tin cup.

"One pot an' a skillet will do for each squad. As for the food, divvy it up among yas. An' each of ya carry grain for yer own horse. Roll up yer blanket in the poncho and tie it to the back of the saddle. Wear yer greatcoat over yer uniform, too. It'll be welcome with the chill early in the morning.

"Yer saddle will be yer pillow. Each squad will build a good fire at night, and each man will sleep with their feet up to it, just like we did on our two-day field training exercise.

"Ya probably forgot already, but yer poncho and blanket will keep you warm and dry. Does ya have any questions now?"

To no one's surprise, there were no questions.

"Now, since we leave a'fore dawn tomorrow, cook yer beef an' bake yer bread tonight. Spend extra time with yer mounts tonight, too lads. Rub 'em down extra good. Clean their hooves. Put ointment on any cuts ya find.

"Swede, go over all the mounts, if ya please. Some a' these Troopers would be walking if we left it up to them. Never forget; if yer mount gets saddle sores, ya end up walking 'till the sores heal. I'm not jus' flapping me jaw here. Remember what I tell ya. My anger is nothing to the pain yer gonna feel carrying yer saddle and gear on yer own back because yer mount has saddle sores an' the like.

"Get on with yas, now," he shouted. "An' don't forget to write home tonight. There'll be no mail call while we're gone, an' no mail going out, either."

Dear Family,

Thanks for the letter, Susan. It was great to hear all the news. George really liked the letter you sent him, Ann. I think he is in love with you already. The Swede enjoyed getting your letter too Susan. I had to read it to him, but he saved it anyhow. Please keep it up, girls.

We are nearing the end of the fourth week working with our horses. I thought I knew a lot about these animals from working with our horses on the farm, but the animals they issued us here were hardly broken in. Sgt. Riley calls them spirited. Most of us are finally over the aches and pains we got learning to ride them. We are getting pretty good, actually.

We are going on maneuvers in a couple of days to somewhere near Lake Michigan. It should be fun. Father Engle from St. Mary's Church has been saying Mass for us every Sunday. I think there are more Catholics here than any other. Lot of Methodists, too, I think.

I hope the crops are coming along, Papa. Have you had much rain lately? We haven't had much here the last two weeks. Food is getting better, Mamma. Not at all like yours, of course. But I'm getting enough. It will surprise you that each of us takes turns cooking. Even I have to take a turn. Can you believe that? Please continue to write.

Love,

Michael

***

One thousand mounted men and a dozen wagons left the Grand Rapids encampment at dawn on October 5. The morning sun was just peeking over the horizon, and dew still covered the ground. In columns of four, the twelve hundred cavalrymen of the 6th Michigan Regiment mounted their horses and rode west toward Lake Michigan.

From the Regimental flags in front of the formation to the last wagon in the rear, their column stretched almost a mile.

They rode at a walk, forty-five minutes of each hour, and led their mounts the other fifteen minutes. This way, they would likely travel three miles each hour.

At this rate, they would make their first camp by three in the afternoon. Then, if they were in the saddle the next morning at dawn, they would reach their Lake Michigan training area late in the afternoon.

Marching and setting up camp were part of the training, too. This was the first opportunity for the men of the 6th Cavalry to ride in formation for such a distance with all their gear, as well as set up and break camp while on the move.

Once at their Lake Michigan encampment, they would conduct regimental, squadron, troop, and platoon drills and patrols. They would even have mock battles. Referees would judge each unit's performance. Awards would then be given at the end of each day in front of the entire Regiment. The competition was expected to be fierce.

"All of ya, listen up," ordered Sgt. Riley. "Lieutenant Thomas is going to tell yas the orders for today."

"Today, we are working against Second Platoon of G Troop," Thomas revealed. "They are somewhere within ten miles of our camp. Our assignment is to find and capture them.

"Our platoon has done very well so far. There is no reason we cannot accomplish our mission today, as well. Squad leaders report to Sergeant Riley. He and I will give you your orders. We leave in one hour, Sergeant."

"Platoon, attention," shouted Sgt. Riley. "Squad leaders remain with me. Platoon dismissed."

"Gather round boys," Riley told the squad leaders. "Smoke if ya like." He spread a map on the ground as the squad leaders knelt in a circle around him. Two of the four squad leaders hastily packed and lit pipes.

"We think the enemy should be in this area. But to take no chances, we will send out scouts in all directions as we move northerly, keeping the big lake ta the west, on our left.

"Drieborg, yer squad will take the point first," Riley directed. "Ride at a walk, with two troopers out front one hundred yards from yer position. Put another one out a hundred yards east, with another one west the same distance. Stay in the center with a mounted trooper to relay messages. Any questions Drieborg?" Hearing no response, Riley snapped,

"I asked a question, trooper. I want a response!"

"I understand your orders, Sergeant Riley," responded Drieborg.

"That's better. The First Squad will remain in the center two hundred yards behind Drieborg. This is where the lieutenant an'me will be. Third squad, you will send out a picket line, three a' yas a hundred yards to the west a' me, an' three Troopers one hundred yards to the east a' me. Do any a' yas have any questions?"

This time, the squad leaders responded quickly and loudly.

"No, Sergeant."

"All right, Drieborg, take the other copy a' this map," he ordered. "If'n the targets not found in an hour or so, First Squad will relieve Drieborg's squad on the point. Jus' look to me for any such changes.

"As for equipment, leave the sabers in camp. We don't need the noise. Each trooper can have one ration an' a cup in his haversack. Make sure every man's canteen is full a' drinkin' water, too. Check yer men careful. I don't want to hear any rattling noises. Don't let any'a yer men forget their rain ponchos, either. Off with ya now. I want yer squads to be ready for inspection in thirty minutes."

"Isn't that Bacon's platoon we're looking for, Mike?" said Bill.

"Would sure be nice to bag him and his platoon," Stan added.

"Let's make him an' his men walk all the way back to camp. Wouldn't that be getting even for rousting us out in the middle of the night back in camp?"

"Yep, that would be nice to see," Mike agreed. "Make the men of his platoon walk behind us and eat our dust. Lieutenant Thomas probably won't like it, though. But if his men's horses would run off for some reason, they'd have to walk then, seems to me."

Stan chuckled. "Could probably be arranged, Mike."

At dawn, the Second Platoon of G Troop moved out. Moving within a ten-mile radius, they were to evade capture by the First Platoon of I Troop. They could use any evasive maneuver they chose. In fact, they could even attack I Troop if they chose.

Two hours later, I Troop's First Platoon under Lt. Thomas left camp in pursuit. He had divided the ten-mile area into zones. With riders to the front and to the east, the main body of his platoon moved south along the shore of Lake Michigan. Within an hour, he knew the target was not in the zone south of the main camp. Swinging east and north, he had his squads examine the zone east of camp with the same result. Unless his men had done a poor job, thus far he decided that the target platoon would be found north of camp.

"Sergeant Riley," Thomas said. "Swing the squads north now. Have them on alert. Bacon's platoon has to be north of the main camp."

"Yes, sir," Riley replied. "I'll send a rider to each squad right now, sir." As each squad was informed, they swung north. Before long, the lead man on the point squad rode back with a report of an encounter with a traveler. The man told him of a Troop movement that morning along the shoreline.

"Are you sure the man said he sighted them to the west of this road? The one we are on right now?" asked Lt. Thomas.

"Yes, sir," replied Cpl. Smith. "The man was very sure about it. In fact, he described the officer leading the mounted troopers very accurately. The only officer I know who wears a red sash and a big yellow feather in his cap is Lieutenant Bacon."

"Thank you, Smith. Good report. Sergeant, I believe we should finish our search in this northeast section, just to be sure. After that is completed, we can swing south along the lake's shore."

"Yes, sir," Riley agreed.

"Assign Smith's squad to patrol the south of that last zone along Lake Michigan. We wouldn't want Bacon to slip by us and get back to camp. That would be embarrassing. We'd never live that down."

"Yes, sir," responded Sgt. Riley. "An' I'll tell that squad leader to avoid contact with our target should he see them a'fore we do. He can send a rider to tell us if he spots them."

"Good, Riley. That'd work well," Thomas agreed. "Let's get on with it."

It wasn't long before they were assured the area to the south was clear.

While Riley and Thomas were waiting, a scout reported sighting a group of troopers along the Lake Michigan shoreline.

"The point man of Second Squad sighted a group of troopers just about a mile due west of this very position, sir," the trooper reported. "We weren't close enough to recognize anybody, but it was a group about the size of a platoon."

"See any sentries, trooper?" asked Sgt. Riley.

"No, sir," he responded. "Matter a' fact, the troopers in that platoon were all jus' milling around. We saw no sentries, either."

"What about their horses?" Riley asked.

"They weren't tethered, Sergeant," the scout continued. "In fact, the horses were pretty well scattered along the beach, just like the troopers."

"Good report, Private," complimented Lt. Thomas.

"Sergeant Riley, have this man lead us to their position. We can better decide our plan of attack from there."

"Yes, sir," responded Sgt. Riley. "If'n you don't mind, sir, I'll bring the troopers at the point in some but keep the troopers on our flanks out for a while yet."

"That'll be fine, Sergeant," Thomas agreed. "Proceed."

Moving cautiously, the movement toward the lake took almost forty minutes.

"My squad should be just beyond that big dune, sir," related the scout.

He then led Lt. Thomas and Sgt. Riley to his squad's position.

"First things first, men," began Lieutenant Thomas. "We must prevent any troopers of the target platoon from escaping once our attack begins. So, Corporal Williams, take your squad and form a skirmish line along the shoreline to the south of the target. Corporal Andrews, you move your squad to the north of the target and form a skirmish line there along the shoreline. When you hear my pistol shot, you will know the attack has begun. Then, each of you will move your skirmish line at a trot toward the target. Do you want to add anything, Sergeant Riley?"

"No, sir, I believe ya covered it nicely, sir."

"You squad leaders," Thomas asked. "Do you have any more questions or have anything you want to add?"

"No, sir!" responded the two squad leaders.

"Fine. The main body will attack in twenty minutes, but wait for my pistol shot. Move out now, William. You head out too, Andrews."

Turning to Drieborg, he continued, "Now, as for you, Drieborg, you will take charge of the First and Fourth Squads. Without being detected, you will move as close to the eastern flank of the target as you think safe. Once I fire my pistol, the target should be alerted. I would suggest you be no more than thirty or so yards away, mounted and ready to charge. I would also suggest that you position yourself between that big dune and the smaller one beside it." Thomas stared intently at Drieborg.

"You have the main responsibility in this attack, Drieborg. Can your squad handle it, Corporal?"

Without hesitation, Drieborg responded, "We can sir, absolutely."

Thomas turned and faced the last squad leader in his platoon. "Corporal Smith, you trail Drieborg's squad by about twenty-five yards. When you hear my pistol shot, you will charge the target, too. Three of your men will gallop to the right flank of Drieborg's force. The other three of your men will go to Drieborg's left flank.

"Tell your men they have a vital objective," Thomas continued. "It is to capture the horses. Our scout told us that they were not tethered, but were scattered all over the beach foraging. Once the noise of our attack begins, I expect them to spook some. It probably won't be an easy assignment, Smith. But I expect your men to gather the horses up and drive them south along the beach toward the Regimental camp. Do you have any questions?"

"No, sir," Smith responded.

"Then move out, Corporal," concluded Lt. Thomas.

"Sergeant Riley. Did we overlook anything?"

"No, sir, I don't think so. I think it tis a good plan, sir; an' your orders were clearly given. All we can do now is trust that our troopers will carry them out. I believe they will, sir."

"Very well, Sergeant," said Thomas. "We will see if you are correct. At any rate, I will fire my pistol in twenty minutes. One of the Regimental referees is with Drieborg's unit, and another is with our target. These observers will decide whether or not our plan and its execution succeed. You and I will move out now, Sergeant. I want you close by when the attack begins."

Fifteen minutes later, Lt. Thomas and Sgt. Riley dismounted on a high sand dune.

"I think this is a good position, Sergeant Riley," Thomas decided.

"From this position, we can see Lake Michigan, the troopers under Drieborg's command as well as the squad led by Corporal Smith. We also have an excellent view of the attack area."

"Looks like the men are in position jus' like ya wanted, sir," commented Riley.

"Yes, they are, Sergeant. Well, no sense waiting any longer. Hopefully Williams and Andrews have their skirmish lines in place, too." Thomas raised his pistol and fired.

The twelve troopers Drieborg led spurred their mounts to a gallop and charged around a sand dune, screaming at the top of their lungs. Smith's squad of five men joined the attack.

Some of the men in the target platoon had been lounging on the sand in small groups. Others were just walking around. All of them were startled.

Their horses scattered at the noise created by the attacking mounted men and galloped about in confusion. Mounted troopers seemed to be everywhere.

Within minutes, the attackers had rounded up the troopers of G Troop's First Platoon. The mounted men used their mounts to force the captives into a tight circle.

Smith's squad rounded up the scattered horses and, as ordered, drove them south down the beach toward the main encampment.

"I think we've rounded up everyone in Bacon's platoon, Mike," reported George Neal. "But I don't see Lieutenant Bacon anywhere."

"Sergeant," Mike asked the platoon sergeant from G Troop, "do you know where Lieutenant Bacon is?"

"Last I saw him he was running toward that patch of bramble bushes over there." The sergeant pointed north toward another sand dune.

"Best go and take a look, Sergeant," Mike suggested. "After all, he is your platoon leader. It sure is not my responsibility to look after him."

With that, the sergeant walked up the beach.

"Corporal," he shouted back, "Lieutenant Bacon is back in the dunes." He pointed east, away from the shore. "I believe he's over that way."

Mike rode over to the sergeant. "My orders are to move your men toward the main camp. I expect you know the way back to the camp. Bacon is not my responsibility."

But before Mike could ride away, he saw Lt. Bacon running toward him, shouting loudly,

"Drieborg, this is your doing. I'll get you for this, just you wait."

"Where is my horse?" Bacon shouted at his platoon sergeant.

Mike interrupted. "Another one of our squads rounded up your platoon's horses, sir. Lieutenant Thomas ordered that squad to drive them back to the main camp. Your mount is probably in that bunch and back to camp by now, sir."

"Walk? You expect me to walk?" Bacon whined.

"Not up to me sir," teased Mike. "I'm just a corporal. You can figure it out, sir. You're the officer here."

Mike wheeled his horse around and galloped south along the shoreline to rejoin his platoon as they rode toward the Regiment's camp.

He could hear Bacon shouting, "Don't think this is over, Drieborg. You'll regret this day."

***

Long before Bacon's men returned to camp on foot, the men of Sgt. Riley's platoon had taken care of their mounts and had joined Sgt. Riley to review the day's events.

"Are all the mounts taken care of, Swede? Never forget, they come first, eh? Well, I'll let ya go to yer food in a minute, boys.

"I'm proud a' ya men," he continued. "This platoon is the best I've seen in this here whole darned Regiment. Two days of patrolling an' all, and we've won all the awards there is so far. And Captain Hyser wanted me to tell all a'ya in this platoon how pleased he is too. I specially liked what ya did jus' did capturin' that Lieutenant Bacon's platoon from G Troop. He's the officer who was behind getting' Drieborg's squad out of the sack in the middle a' the night. Remember? Well, I don't forget that kind'a crap.

"We captured his platoon proper," Riley reminded his troopers. "The Regimental referee reported that our ambush was a complete success. An' to top it off, ya found him hidin' behind a sand dune, too. Don't that beat all."

Riley stomped the ground and laughed aloud. His men laughed heartily, too. "Was terrible bad luck that you guys scattered their horses when you attacked." Riley continued leading his men in laughter.

"Them troopers havin' to walk back to camp following a trail of drippings from their own horses, is truly a shame, an' Bacon walking, too. Poor lads. But worse was ya laughing so loud at 'em, boys. They won't forget that soon, I'm betting; especially that Lieutenant Bacon.

"He could still have a mind to cause problems," Riley warned. "Unless I miss my guess, he'll try ta get even somehow. He's seems especially angry with Drieborg; but maybe with all'a the platoon, too. So, watch out wanderin' away from our area. Ya all best go in pairs until we break camp.

"And, I gotta admit yer squad surely stands out, Drieborg," Riley praised.

"Put ya in a contest, an' offer a prize, an' it's the devil to beat ya. Yer men sorta catches the fever, too, seems to me. But a'fore you get too big a head, Mike, remember that the Swede keeps our horses in the best a' shape. All of ya would be walking like infantrymen without his help. An' that's the truth.

"After ya eat, Swede, give the men of third squad a hand with their mounts, if ya please. Ya'd think they never heard me talk 'bout taking proper care a' their horses."

Riley turned to the rest of his platoon. "We got two more days of maneuvers a'fore we return to our training camp at Grand Rapids. An' every Troop is a'lookin to best us before we do. So, be on ya toes, boys. Get on with yas now! Eat an' relax. Ya all earned it."

***

Lt. Thomas was not present when Riley reviewed the events of the day with his platoon. He was riding around camp leading Lt. Bacon's horse by its halter. He was looking for his friend so he could return his horse.

When he did, Bacon was in no mood to appreciate it.

"I don't care for your damned excuses, Thomas," Bacon heatedly shouted. "You were not supposed to capture my platoon. I certainly paid you enough. We had a deal, didn't we?"

"Yes, we did, Carl," Thomas admitted. "But you made your position so obvious it was simply not possible to avoid finding you. And with the referee attached to my platoon, he would have easily known we were missing you on purpose."

"I don't care what he thought," Bacon protested. "You could have let us escape or something."

"Carl, you didn't even have guards posted," Thomas reminded him. "Your men were just lying around. Besides, even if your platoon had been warned, you didn't have your horses tethered. They spooked right off. So, your men couldn't have gotten a hold of their mounts if we'd given them five minutes warning. You made it almost impossible to botch that attack."

"You've got to make this up to me, Thomas," Bacon whined.

"You owe me too much to just let this go."

"All right, Carl," Thomas responded. "Let's stop arguing and come up with something."

The Attack On Drieborg

Lt. Thomas was standing in the doorway of his tent.

"Sergeant Riley!" he shouted.

"Yes, sir," responded Riley, hurrying over to him.

"Have Drieborg and Neal report to me immediately."

"Right away sir." Instead of saluting and doing an about-face to carry out this order, he paused. "But, begging the lieutenant's pardon. If there's a problem, shouldn't I be taking care of it now?"

"Sergeant," Thomas responded angrily, "I need not explain anything to you. Just do as I say. Understood?"

"Yes, sir." With that, Sgt. Riley saluted, turned and walked away. Once he found the men, Riley shared his concern.

"Now ya boys listen to me. I don't like the sound a' this, not at all. I don't know what he has in mind for yas. But keep yer mouth shut an' move careful. I fear there's trouble afoot. That Bacon fella in G Troop might have something to do with this. Off with ya now."

"Corporal Drieborg and Private Neal reporting as ordered, sir," shouted Drieborg, both men at attention in front of Lt. Thomas's tent.

"Yes, I did Drieborg. Good action today, men," Lt. Thomas told them. "But, you carried it a bit far, though, don't you think, Corporal? You scattered their horses and made the captured troopers walk back to camp. Had I been immediately present I would not have allowed such treatment of our fellow troopers."

"But sir," Mike interrupted, "we were just following your orders."

"You are at attention, Corporal," reminded Thomas. "You are to hold your snotty tongue until I ask for you to speak."

"Yes, sir."

"It has also been reported to me that you in particular, Drieborg, took great delight in their plight, and you made their platoon leader, Lieutenant Bacon, walk as well. It appears you have little respect for your betters, Drieborg. I think it best that this gap in your education be corrected as soon as possible.

"We will start this very evening. You two will carry water from the lake to the water trough of the G Troop platoon you mistreated. Use that device where you carry a bucket suspended from each end of a wooden bar carried over your shoulders. A yoke, I think it's called. Lieutenant Bacon and the men of his platoon are looking forward to seeing you again. I suspect that you are of particular interest to them, Drieborg. Are my instructions clear, Corporal Drieborg?"

"Yes, sir."

"Fine," Thomas concluded. "You will proceed directly from here to carry out this order. You will not return to your tents or inform any member of your platoon of this assignment. You are dismissed."

Neal and Drieborg turned and headed for the area used by G Troop to pick up four canvas buckets for the water and two shoulder yokes.

"What is this crap all about, Mike?" complained Neal.

"We're carrying water for that outfit? I never heard of such a thing! And for what; besting' them today? Wait till the boys and Riley hear about this. Thomas is carrying this Bacon's hate of you too far. Why, I'll bet the Captain will tan Thomas's hide when he hears about it."

"You're probably right, George. But for now, we can't do anything about it. Just keep your lip buttoned when we get to their area. Some of those guys would like nothing better than for us to give them an excuse to mix it up. Remember what Riley told us? Keep a sharp lookout for any funny business on their part. I can't imagine Bacon would let an opportunity like this pass without making it worse for us somehow."

"I know what you're saying, Mike. So, let's get this damn thing over with. That Thomas sure boils my blood, though."

They arrived at the G Troop area and asked the first Trooper they encountered where they could get the water buckets.

"Well lookee here, boys," taunted a trooper. "If it ain't the high an' mighty I Troop champion hisself an' his sidekick, too. It's nice of you water boys to fill our horse trough. You'll find the buckets and yokes right by the trough."

Mike and George headed for Lake Michigan forty yards or so past the sand dune area to fill their water buckets. It was about an hour until nightfall, just enough time to fill the horse trough before nightfall, if they hurried.

The same trooper continued to rag on them as they returned to the lake with the empty buckets. He was now joined by a few more from G Troop.

"We sure do 'preciate you boys helping us out this way. But you being such a champion shouldn't take you long at all."

It was getting darker now. The loudmouth was no longer hanging around. In fact, the area was deserted. Four more trips would finish the job. With just another few buckets of water to haul, they found the ground wet and the trough empty.

"What the hell, Mike!" George cried out. "Those guys dumped the water out. Crap! We'll never finish this job at this rate."

"We only have three more loads, George," responded Drieborg. "If they chose to dump it out, that's no concern of mine, or yours. Come on. Let's finish as fast as we can."

Carrying their last load, they trudged in the soft sand toward the camp. It was quite dark now, but there was a harvest moon out. They could at least see each other and the trail in front of them rather clearly. But they were very tired and getting sore now, and they moved with backs bent under their load, with their heads down, eyes on the ground before them.

"What?" George shouted.

Mike looked to his right and saw George lying on the ground. Two shadowy figures loomed over him with what looked like tent stakes in their raised hands.

He saw a man rushing at him as he felt a blow from behind on his left shoulder. The yoke on his shoulders took the force of the blow. However, he was still driven to one knee. As he fell, the buckets of water came loose from the yoke. Freed of that weight, he swung the pole, using it as a weapon.

His pole struck the man behind him on the side of his knee, knocking him to the ground. Mike swung around and hit the ribs of the man attacking him from the front.

His attackers were surprised by his sudden response. Again, and again, Mike struck them with the pole. He knocked one man unconscious with a fierce blow to the face. Blood spurted into the air. He hit the other attacker in the ribs again. Both of his attackers were now on the ground. Mike turned his attention to George.

George was curled up on the ground, protecting his head with his arms and hands. His attackers were pelting him on his back and arms. Mike hit one attacker on his back with the yoke.

Enraged, Mike jumped at the last of the attackers. He hit him in the midsection, then the jaw. Before he could land any more blows, the man tried to scramble away.

Mike caught him by his boot and dragged him back toward the water. Mike raised his fist to continue the beating.

"Please, stop! Please!" he pleaded, holding his hands over his bloody face. "This weren't my idea."

"Tell me who put you up to this, or by God, your own mother won't recognize you when I've finished," Mike threatened.

"Bacon, he ordered us to do it," the terrified trooper confessed.

"None of us thought of it. He told us we had to, or he'd make life so hard, we would desert. He said you were gonna be sent to fill our water trough. We were ordered to attack you two after it got dark."

"You swear that to my sergeant?" "Yes, yes! Jus' don't hit me again."

Mike took the man's own belt and tied his hands behind him. Mike then half-dragged him back down the Sunday slope to where George still lay moaning.

"Can you get up, George?" asked Mike.

George moaned. "They got me good on the back'a my head, Mike. They hit my hands, too. I think my fingers might be broken. I can't move 'em without a lot a pain."

"Don't move then, George," Mike told him. "Just lay still. Riley will get the boys to carry you over to the surgeon's place. Fix you up in no time. I hate to leave you, but I gotta get you help. Riley doesn't know where we are. Can I leave you for a few minutes?"

"Sure. Go ahead. But hurry, please," George pleaded. "I hurt a lot." As Mike rounded a nearby dune with his prisoner, he met Sgt. Riley and six men coming from the other direction.

"Drieborg, are ya all right, lad?" asked Riley.

"I'm fine, Sarge, but George is hurt bad. I think he needs to be carried to the doc right now."

As they hurried toward the injured man, Riley asked, "Who's this one?"

"He will explain the whole thing to you, Sarge," Mike said.

"You'll tell my sergeant who sent you to beat up on us, won't you, trooper?" With that, Mike gave the fallen man another blow in the ribs with his fist.

"Yes, yes!" he moaned. "Jus' don't hit me again."

"Come on, trooper," ordered Riley. "Either ya walk on yer own, or I'll plant me foot in yer hind side till ya do."

As they walked toward Neal lying unconscious nearby, Mike told Riley, "That trooper told me Bacon ordered them to beat us up. I left another attacker unconscious lying near George. The other two who attacked me got away, but they won't be hard to find with all the broken bones and the bloody faces I gave them."

The men reached George Neal quickly.

"Easy, boys," urged Mike. "His arms and hands are pretty bad. I think he has a bad cut on his head, too. Carry him gently."

Riley kicked one of the attackers who lay near George. "Get up, ya lout," he shouted. "Swede, drag this piece a' trash along."

The Swede wasn't too gentle with the groggy man, either.

"I'm takin' yer sorry ass with me too," Riley told the other trooper who had attacked Geroge, "yer going with me to my Troop commander. Any trouble outta ya an' I'll finish the job Drieborg begun. Got it?" he shouted.

"Speak up man." He slapped the across the face. "Answer me, now! Da ya want more a' that?"

"No, please. I'll tell him the whole thing," he promised.

"An'give him the names of the others, too, right?" He slapped the trooper again. "Right?"

"Right, Sarge," he responded. "Anything you say." "Swede," Riley asked. "Got that other one?"

"Ya," responded Swede. "But I tink he fell a few more times already, though."

"Is he going to tell the Captain who it was who ordered him to attack Drieborg and Neil?"

Swede grabbed the man he had brought from the beach area. "Vell?" he asked. "You heard da question. Vhat about it? Do you and I take anoder walk to da beach?"

"No," the man moaned. "I'll tell ya everything."

More men of Riley's platoon joined him.

"You two, stay with Neal," he ordered. "Smith, you run to the Regimental hospital and bring a couple a' orderlies down here with a stretcher for Neal. Off with yas now!"

He turned to Mike. "Drieborg, we're going to get First Sergeant Williams. You bring this fella, and Swede, you bring the other one."

Riley led them to the tent of I Troop's First Sergeant Williams. After listening to what the captives had to say, he ordered Riley, Drieborg, Swede, and the two prisoners to wait there for his return.

***

Captain Hyser was enjoying the pleasant Indian summer evening having a smoke. He sat just outside his tent, both flaps tied open.

Williams came to attention in front of his Troop commander.

"Sir, excuse the interruption at this hour, but we have a very serious problem that needs your attention."

"Very well, Sergeant. What is it?"

"Two of Sergeant Riley's men have been attacked by men from G Troop, sir," explained Williams. "We have two of the attackers outside, sir."

"If this is in the nature of a soldier's quarrel, Sergeant," he asked, "why have you brought this to me? Shouldn't you be settling this with the First Sergeant from G Troop?"

"Normally, he and I would do just that, sir," Williams responded. "But this attack was ordered by Lieutenant Bacon of G Troop. And the attackers we have in custody insist that Lieutenant Thomas was involved."

"Oh, my Lord!" Hyser jumped to his feet. "Where is Riley now, Sergeant?"

"I ordered him to remain with his prisoners at my tent until I spoke with you, sir."

"All right then, First Sergeant," Hyser commented. "Let's start with Riley. Get them over here now."

It took only a few minutes for Sgt. Riley, Drieborg, Swede, and the two prisoners to report to Captain Hyser's quarters.

"At ease, men," directed Hyser. "Riley, are any of your men hurt?" "Neal is over at the hospital now, sir," Riley answered.

"We think he may have broken bones in his hands. He took a beating from these two men. They used tent stakes on him. Drieborg has no injuries, but he sure is boiling mad, sir."

Riley looked at Drieborg, who stood there without his cap and the front of his shirt torn open. "Are ya all right Mike?"

"I'm still pretty riled up, Sergeant," he responded. "But I'm not hurt, if that's what you're wondering."

Captain Hyser broke in. "How was it you were down on the beach after dark anyway, Corporal?"

Mike told him of the order from Lt. Thomas that he and Neal had to fill the water trough for Bacon's platoon over in G Troop. Once it became dark, they were attacked by men with tent stakes.

"It would appear that Lieutenant Thomas had a part in this business," said Hyser. "Do you agree with that assessment, Riley?"

"Yes, sir," Riley replied. "An hour or so before retreat, the lieutenant ordered me to send Drieborg and Neal to his quarters. An' I did, sir. That's the last I saw of my two men, sir.

"Shortly after retreat, they were still not back. So, I took some men to look for 'em. We came upon Mike beating on this fella here and George lying on the ground nearby, barely conscious. Another trooper, the one Swede is holding here was lying near him."

"Are those the two troopers you have with you now?" asked Hyser.

"Yes, sir," Riley said with a dark look about him. "One man is just coming around, so to speak, sir. The other one is battered a bit. But the both a' them are eager to talk to ya, sir, about how they come to be hitting Drieborg and Neal with tent stakes. Swede an' a few a' the boys are keeping them safe from Drieborg at this very moment just outside the first sergeant's tent, sir."

"Let me hear what those two have to say, Riley. Take me to them right now."

Hyser approached the men. He went first to a hatless Trooper who was standing in the center of the group with his hands bound behind him. His face was covered with blood, his nose was bleeding, and his lips were freshly split.

"Trooper," Hyser asked, "What do you have to say about this?"

"Captain, please don't let that Drieborg guy hit me again," the frightened trooper whined. "He broke my nose for sure. I lost a tooth, too, sir."

He paused and then blurted out, "Lieutenant Bacon put us up to this. He ordered us to jump your men. He threatened to make it bad for us if we didn't. He said it was all set up with an officer of I Troop. A Lieutenant Thomas, he said. That's all I know, Captain."

"Sergeant Williams," Hyser directed, "in my tent you will find writing paper, ink, and a pen. Sit down there and write down this man's statement. You will sign it, won't you trooper?"

"Yes, sir. I can write my name. An' I can read, too, sir. Can you get me out of G Troop, sir? That Bacon's a bad one, sir. He's sure to take this out on me."

"I'll see what can be done, Trooper," Hyser promised. "Williams, make sure he includes the names of the other two G Troop men involved in this. And that trooper who

Swede is holding up, give him a choice; sign that statement, too, or you'll let Drieborg take him for a private walk."

"I'll see to it, sir," promised Williams, smiling.

"As soon as you obtain those signed statements, Sergeant, I'm going to take a walk over to the G Troop area for a little visit with Captain Smith. You and two of our troopers will accompany me, Sgt. Riley.

"Sgt. Williams, have Drieborg write a statement, too. Have him describe his orders from Lieutenant Thomas and the events that followed. Have him and Neal, if he is able, sign it as well."

"Yes, sir."

"Oh, yes. Riley, before we go to G Troop, find out for me if the other two assailants can be identified in any way other than their names."

"I already done that, sir," Riley responded. "Drieborg says one should have trouble walking on a badly bruised leg and have some very bloody face cuts. The other trooper, he says, should be having sore or broken ribs, sir, and maybe a tooth missing."

"Thank you, Sergeant. That should be enough for Captain Smith to identify the other attackers."

The statement completed, both prisoners signed it without question. Captain Hyser then wrote a short order and gave the document to First Sergeant Williams.

"Sergeant, take two men to the hospital. Then, find Lieutenant Thomas, read him my order for him to remain in his tent until I return.

"Have two troopers stand guard to see that he stays there. Any questions so far, Sergeant?"

"No, sir.

"Then take this note to Colonel Copeland at Regimental headquarters," Hyser continued. "Bring his response to me. You will find me with Captain Smith. I intend to settle this matter tonight. And yes, Williams, when you pass the hospital, get a report for me on Private Neal's condition."

"Yes, sir."

An hour later, First Sergeant Williams found Captain Hyser. He came to attention. "Sgt. Williams reporting as ordered, sir."

"At ease First Sergeant," directed Hyser. "Please be seated. You can use that camp chair over there."

"Thank you, sir," Williams responded, seating himself across from his Troop commander.

"Light up your pipe if you like, First Sergeant," Hyser told him.

Both men lit their pipes and sat quietly for a few moments, content with their own thoughts and their pipes.

"Thank you for chasing me down, Sergeant. My business with Captain Smith of G Troop was concluded more quickly than I expected," Hyser informed him.

"The Captain took immediate action. Bacon is under arrest, awaiting a military court-martial. The other two attackers were easily identified. They, too, signed the statement and are at the hospital receiving treatment."

"How is Neal?"

"The doctor believes he has a few broken fingers and a deep bruise or two on his right arm," Williams informed him. "He should be well enough to ride in a few days, sir."

"Good. Glad to hear it."

"Captain Smith told me he was glad to be rid of Bacon. He believed him to be a troublemaker and worthless as an officer. Remember when you and I were told that Drieborg was the bad apple?"

"I remember that now," Hyser responded. "Wasn't it Bacon who told us that?"

"Yes, sir, he did," Williams agreed. "When Riley and I confronted Drieborg, he insisted otherwise. In fact, he told us that Bacon was the rotten one. He was right. That Drieborg boy has leadership written all over him, sir."

"The Lord knows, we need that type of man if we are to win this war, eh Williams?" Hyser reflected. "What we don't need is men like Bacon or Thomas. What they did is most distasteful to me, Williams. Enlisted men should be able to trust that their officers will look after their welfare and be fair with them at all times.

"A military court will hear their case in the morning. I am confident that both officers will receive the severest punishment allowed. Have Drieborg and Riley available to give testimony should it be required tomorrow. Thank you for your help tonight, Sergeant. Let's both get some sleep. Tomorrow will be a trying day."

Court-Martial: October 1862

The maintenance of discipline in the various branches of all land and sea military organizations has been essential to their successful operation. Over the centuries, rules necessary for the accomplishment of that end have been identified and written down. In the United States, the actions of all military personnel are covered in what is called The Universal Code of Military Justice.

On a daily basis during the Civil War, soldiers were punished for all sorts of transgressions. An example might be late reporting for duty. Intoxication was not tolerated either and was therefore punished; so was cheating at cards. Most of these transgressions were punished by the Troop commander, or one of his officers or noncommissioned officers.

Extra cleanup duty was most often used as a punishment for such things. Cheating, stealing, and fighting were offenses treated more harshly. Wearing leg irons, standing outside in the stocks, loss of rank, and even short-term imprisonment were punishments reserved for these more serious infractions.

During wartime, few transgressions went unpunished. Some, like falling asleep while on guard duty, desertion, and even sassing an officer, were punished quickly and harshly.

The commander of the 6th Cavalry Regiment decided that the enlisted men who had attacked Drieborg and Neal would be punished by their Troop commander. He came to this conclusion because the attackers from G Troop were following the orders of their platoon leader, Lt. Carl Bacon III, also of G Troop.

But officers Thomas and Bacon had joined together in the planning and had ordered the attack on the two enlisted men. Therefore, the charges against them were much more serious and would be heard by a military court-martial.

The Regimental commander, Col. Copeland, and two other officers would hear and judge the case against Lt. Bacon first. Then they would hear the case against Lt. Thomas.

In the field, the officers took their meals in an open-air mess tent. The tent was twenty feet by twenty feet, and it contained enough covered tables and chairs to serve seventy or so officers at one time. This is where the court-martial would be held.

Behind a table at one end of the covered area sat the three officers who would judge the case. The defendant sat on a chair alone in front. Officers representing the court and the accused were behind them, along with witnesses.

Sgt. Riley, Mike and even the injured George Neal were among the witnesses. The four troopers from G Company were in leg irons awaiting their opportunity to testify against Lt. Bacon.

"Let this military court-martial in the case of Captain Harvey Bacon III, come to order," stated Col. Copeland.

The charges against Lt. Bacon were read. Captain Watters from A Troop had been appointed prosecutor. He then presented the evidence in support of the charges against Lt. Bacon.

The first witness for the prosecution was Cpl. Drieborg. Once sworn in, each told the court what had happened to him. Pvt. George Neal was brought from the field hospital on a stretcher, sworn in, and then questioned about the incident. He supported Drieborg's testimony.

Then, one at a time, each of the G Troop soldiers who had attacked Drieborg and Neal was sworn in and gave his testimony. Each one of them told the same story. They had been ordered by their superior officer, Lt. Bacon, to attack Drieborg and Neal. The written statements they had previously signed were given to the court as evidence as well.

"The prosecution rests, sir."

"Does the defense have anything to say at this point?"

"Yes, sir," stated Captain O'Malley of C Troop. He had been appointed to represent the defendant. "Lt. Bacon wishes to take the stand in his own defense."

"Very well," Col. Copeland said. "Swear him in and proceed."

Bacon appeared very much shaken. His hand shook as he was sworn in. Despite the cool temperature, he was sweating noticeably.

"It's all lies," he began. "Drieborg has been after me ever since we were in primary school together. He put my men up to it. I never ordered my men to attack anybody. All these Troopers are just sticking together to get an officer in trouble. They are lying for Drieborg."

"Allow me to remind you, Lieutenant, that every one of the troopers from your platoon gave the same testimony independently of one another."

"That's all I have to say," Bacon concluded.

"Does the prosecutor wish to ask anything of Lt. Bacon?" asked Col. Copeland.

"No, sir."

"Very well," the Colonel said. "You will all remain here while this military court considers the case."

The president of the court, Col. Copeland, and the other two officers of the court conferred quietly. It was a very brief conversation. They returned to stand behind the court's table.

"This court will come to order," Col. Copeland began. "The prisoner will rise to hear the verdict."

Bacon stood at attention in front of the court's table.

"Second Lieutenant Carl Bacon III, this court finds you guilty of all charges," the Colonel declared. "You used your rank in an illegal and scurrilous plan to do bodily harm to enlisted men. You have thusly abused the rank entrusted to you and destroyed the trust enlisted men must have in their officers.

"Therefore, it is our decision that you appear before the entire Regiment and there be stripped of your rank. In addition, you will be dishonorably discharged from service in the Army of the United States. You will then be taken from this place by the most direct route available to the military prison in Detroit, Michigan. There you will serve a term of one year.

"This judgment will be made a permanent part of your military record. And lastly," Col. Copeland concluded, "the newspaper serving this area, the *Grand Rapids Eagle*, will be informed of the action taken here this day. The defendant is bound over to the Regimental Provost Marshal. That officer will see to it that this sentence is executed. This court stands adjourned."

Throughout the reading of the sentence, Bacon was standing at attention in front of the court's bench. "No!" he shouted and rushed toward the front table. Hands on the table in front of Col. Copeland, he leaned toward the Colonel. "You can't do this to me. My father won't allow it. He paid for this commission. I didn't do anything wrong!"

"Take this man into custody," thundered Copeland. "Do it now!" Guards rushed forward and grabbed Bacon by the arms. He continued shouting as he was dragged from the courtroom to the field stockade.

"I'll get you, Drieborg," he yelled. "Just you wait. Your whole family will pay for this!"

***

Once order was restored, the court-martial was convened once again. This time Lt. Thomas from I Troop was on trial.

The result was the same. He was found guilty as charged and the sentence was the same as Bacon's. But Thomas allowed himself to be led off quietly after the sentence was pronounced.

In the small audience of witnesses and spectators, Captain Hyser spoke to Sergeant Riley. "You know, Sergeant, it's truly a shame. That young man Thomas had the makings of a good cavalry officer."

"Maybe sir," responded Riley. "But something just wasn't right with Thomas, if a weakling like Bacon could get his hooks into him like that. We're better off finding out now, not in battle."

"I missed seeing that weakness in him, Riley," Hyser decided, "but you didn't. I'm fortunate to have you in my Troop, Sergeant. Your men are, too."

***

On Wednesday, the 6th Cavalry Regiment had returned from the two weeks of maneuvers at the Lake Michigan encampment to their training site in Grand Rapids.

By Friday, the troopers were once again comfortably in the routine of training camp. The barracks and their bunks were also welcome after all that time sleeping outside on the ground.

The men of Sgt. Riley's First Platoon had just finished taking care of their horses. Feeding and watering were followed by an exercise period, when each man walked and rode his horse. It was only after this that the men were allowed to prepare their morning meal.

At nine that morning, each trooper and officer in the Regiment received their monthly pay from the Regimental paymaster. By ten o'clock, most of the men had received their passes and headed down the Fountain Street hill into the downtown area for the remainder of the day. The troopers of Riley's platoon, however, knew it wouldn't be that easy. Not with Riley in charge.

First off, Sgt. Riley thoroughly inspected each man's horse.

"Yer horse comes first," he had told them time and time again.

"Remember, without yer horse, yer're not a cavalryman. There'll be no pass for anyone who has not taken proper care'a his horse."

"If any a' ya has a bridle, girth strap, reins, or any other piece of leather not in good repair, ya'll be staying in camp today until ya fix it."

The platoon barracks had to be spotless, too, before anyone received a pass to town. Lastly, Sgt. Riley inspected each man's bunk area.

"If yer personal things, like clothing, are not clean and kept organized, ya'll be a sloppy cavalryman, too," he reminded them. "Sloppy troopers cut corners caring for their horse an' gear; they don't pay attention during training exercises; they are not sharp. So, when it really counts in battle, that trooper can't be depended upon. They are a danger to themselves and us all. I won't have that kind of man in my platoon. I'll run him off fer sure."

As a platoon sergeant, Riley had a unique way of making his point and getting each squad of six troopers to pull together.

"If any squad has a trooper in it who does not pass inspection this morning, the entire squad stays in camp."

No one in Drieborg's squad was denied a pass. Of course, they had the Swede to help them properly care for their horses.

***

"Can you believe it, Stan?" exclaimed George. "The first squad is staying in camp until that one guy repairs a horse bridle."

"Just like we would have lost our pass last month," Stan replied. "Remember that?"

"Oh, you mean the time you and Dave got me riding my horse." "Can you imagine what those guys in First Squad are doing to their bad apple?"

"I wasn't a bad apple," protested George.

"Maybe not," interrupted Swede. "But if you had not ridden dat horse, und we lost our passes for it, Stan or me vould have taken you to da back a' da barracks, alone."

"Not you, Swede. Maybe Stan would have tried to rough me up, but not you."

"Goot ting we not lose our passes back den, George. You find out den, for sure."

The downtown area of Grand Rapids had not changed since the men of the 6th Cavalry Regiment were last there. Townspeople and farmers, in town for their normal Saturday activities, were still a bit leery of these men in blue. But the soldiers behaved better this time.

"I don't remember that five-story building the last time we were here," Mike commented. "What is it for, George?"

All six of the men stood on the Monroe Street sidewalk and gawked at the tall structure.

"Been here a long time, guys," George explained. "It's called the Pantlind Hotel. It's the tallest building in town. Pretty fancy inside, I was told. They have a fancy dining room there, too. Want to eat there?"

Bill Anderson took his pipe out of his mouth. "Not for me, guys. That's officer country; too rich for my blood. Ever eat there when you lived in Grand Rapids, George?"

"No, I didn't."

"Why didn't you?" Stan asked.

"Costs too much," George told him. "Besides, I didn't have the right clothing for that place."

"You still don't. I think Bill's right," Stan agreed. "That place we ate at the last time we were here wasn't all that fancy, but I felt welcome there. It had good food, and a lot of it. I'm for heading there again."

That's just what the men did. They had a relaxing meal of ham with all the fixings. Apple pie and coffee topped it off.

A trip to the Old Kent Bank and a bit of exploring new parts of downtown took up most of an Indian summer afternoon. While they were resting on the grass of Campau Square Park, George brought up a subject that startled even the most relaxed of his comrades.

"Any of you guys been to a brothel?" he asked.

"Well, I'll be," exclaimed Stan. "What do you know about such places, little fella?"

"I do know there's one down by the railroad station in a private house. At least, there used to be. I've never been there, actually. But I heard about it when I worked in town."

Swede stood up. "You show me, George, ya?"

"Anyone else?" asked George as they started walking toward the railroad station. Only Stan joined them.

An hour later, the three men returned. No one said anything for a while.

"Don't you want to know what happened?" George asked excitedly.

"Not something a real man talks about, George," commented Swede.

"It was a dump," Stan told them. "A man would be better off in a barn, seemed to me. I left and just waited outside for these two."

Dave pulled his pipe out of his mouth and said, "I miss my Clara a great deal. We enjoyed our marriage, all of it. And even though she is gone, nothing could get me to betray the promise I made to her when we married years ago. I'm not judging you or criticizing you boys, I just couldn't go to the place you just went to."

No one said another word.

Thanksgiving at Home

As the Indian summer days of October faded, Sergeant Riley drilled his platoon day after day. Hour after hour, his troopers repeated maneuvers on horseback. Turns to the right, to the left, at the trot or at the gallop, he drove his men and their horses. They learned to control the horse while attacking with a saber. Dismounted and mounted, the troopers learned to respond to bugle commands. They were also surprised to learn that cavalrymen were expected to do most of their fighting dismounted.

By the end of the month, the men of Riley's platoon had become quite accomplished. They had learned to control their mounts, and in so doing had formed real bonds with them. Their confidence grew as their ability to control the horse increased.

Everyone knew the training was near its end. They were needed in the war, and they were ready to move on. An assignment in one of the war zones was surely expected.

Sgt. Riley had his platoon in mounted formation. They had just completed another rigorous exercise. They had taken care of the mounts, and their supper awaited them. Rumor had it that they would break camp very soon and move to one of the war zones. In fact, there was a betting pool going on about it. The big money was on joining General Grant for the attack on Vicksburg, a major port on the Mississippi River. Others wagered that the destination would be General Hooker's Army of the Potomac in Virginia. Some thought their Regiment would be sent to reinforce the defenses of Washington, D.C. A fourth destination might be the army fighting in Tennessee.

"Before I dismiss the platoon," Riley began. "I want to remind each of ya to write home tonight. When ya do, tell 'em that ya'll be coming home on leave a week from this Friday. I expect ya to be back here the Sunday after Thanksgiving, afore three in the afternoon.

"Each of ya will sign the leave roster and write down where ya'll be during yer leave. Squad leaders will turn that list into me by this Sunday at noon. You will be responsible for all yer gear, saddle, and your horse tack, too. None'a ya will leave anything in the barracks. As soon as I get the leave roster, I'll arrange train travel for those a' ya who need it. That's right, Killeen. No need to look at Drieborg; ya will take yer horse with ya; all your gear too.

"Squad leaders," he concluded. "Get me a letter home from each member of yer squad. There will be more information coming, but that's all for now. Platoon dismissed."

During their supper, the men talked of nothing else but the upcoming leave.

"What are you guys going to do during your leave?" asked Mike to no one in particular.

Each of the men began to think out loud.

"Well, I'm headed for home in Newaygo," said Dave. "I got a lot of fixing up to do before winter, wood to cut, and pigs to slaughter. I should get a couple of deer smoked, too."

"I'm going to spend some time with my daughter and her family at their farm," Bill told them. "I'm sure they could use a little help getting ready for winter, too."

"What about you three?" Mike asked the others. "You and Swede don't even have a home to go to, do you, George?"

"I don't have a home, but I do have some friends in Grand Rapids," George said. "I think I'll just visit them. I've got some money in the bank, so I could even stay in a boarding house, too. It might be fun. I can put my horse up at the livery and come up here to work him out now and again."

"That sounds sensible," Mike commented. He was sitting on his bunk about to write home. "Say, Swede, how about going home with me? My family would love to have you."

"Fine mit me, Mike," Swede responded quickly. "How about Stan coming mit us, too? Vould dat be too much?"

"As long as he is willing to do some farm work with us each day, and sleep in the hired man's barn room, I'm sure my folks would welcome you both."

Stan joined the conversation. "I haven't decided, Mike. I must admit that I don't look forward much to traveling all the way up north to my folk's home just to do farm chores. Besides, my older sisters are something to live with. Why do you think I worked in the Upper Peninsula cutting trees the last two winters? They drove me out of the house, if truth be told."

"Why don't you join me, then?" offered Dave. "I admit it's a bit of a ride to Newaygo. But you would be welcome. Besides, I need some help setting my wife up for winter. You could really be a great help. What do you say?"

"Sounds good to me," Stan answered. "You sure it will be all right with your wife?"

"She won't mind. Then it's settled. Right, Stan?" Dave concluded. "It's fine with me Dave" Stan responded. "But, write your wife about it first. Let's give her some warning at least."

***

Two weeks before Thanksgiving, Mike and Swede set out for Lowell on horseback. They carried all of their gear with them too. It was quite chilly, a light wind swirling snow about them. Each rider's fatigue cap was held on by a scarf tied under their chin, and the high collars of their greatcoats protected their faces from the wind and cold. They had been training in this type of weather for the last ten days, so the men and their horses were somewhat used to it. They hoped to arrive at the Drieborg farm in time for noon dinner.

They talked some as they rode their horses at a walk.

"You will really like Mamma's cooking, Swede," said Michael.

Swede smiled. "I could use some good food, I bet your papa vill vork it off us soon enough."

"You have that right, my friend," Mike assured him. "But, this time of year, it's mostly animal care, chopping wood, slaughtering animals, and smoking them. Mamma and the girls can chicken, too. I just remembered, though… In Susan's last letter, she told me Papa and my brother Kenny are helping out on some of the farms near ours. The men are off fighting, so the women are alone and need help. I expect we will be doing some of that, too."

"Dat's fine mit me, Mike. I'm glad to help."

***

Michael and Swede arrived at the barn and went through a practiced routine with their horses. Saddles and gear removed they led their mounts into stalls. A leather bucket full of water hung from each horse's head as the two troopers wiped down their horses. Each horse was fed some grain next. Before they were finished, Swede and Mike examined each of the horse's hooves, too. Sergeant Riley had trained his men well. They would not skip any step, in horse care, good meal waiting or not.

If truth be known, however, they did rush it a bit. As soon as they finished, they washed up and hurried to the house. Once in the enclosed entryway, they hung up their greatcoats and cleaned their muddy boots.

They entered the warm home. "Hi everybody!" shouted Michael. His two sisters rushed to hug him.

"This is the man you've been writing to, Susan," Michael told her. With that, she curtsied and blushed some.

"Nice to meet you, miss," Swede responded.

Michael hugged his mother. His young brother hung back. Feeling grown up, he wasn't sure if he should hug his brother or not. Mike solved his dilemma by extending his hand. When Little Jake gripped it, Mike pulled him close for a hug. The young brother responded with a little pressure of his own, embarrassment aside.

"Come boys," ordered Jacob Drieborg. "Sit. It is time to eat. Michael, you say da prayer."

Afterwards, Jacob began to pass the food. Roasted chicken, mashed potatoes with gravy, freshly baked bread, applesauce and cooked corn were in evidence on Michael and Swede's plates. Fresh milk and apple pie were served, too.

"Well Papa," began Mike, "what do you and Little Jake have in store for us?"

"Before I answer da question you asked, Michael," his father responded, "what are you willing to do mit us during your stay, Swede?"

"I expected to help, Mr. Drieborg," the Swede answered. "I never milked a cow, but I can help with da animals, repair da tack, and cut wood."

"Swede is a good worker, Papa," Mike interrupted. "He and I will help with chores here, and with the neighbors who need it, too."

"Fine," Jacob said. "Right now, Michael, you can stay around the house mit da girls und Mamma. Swede, you can come mit me. I will show you around da barn und da rest of da farm. Michael will join me with da milking later today. Is dat fine mit you, Mamma?"

"Yes, Papa," his wife Rose responded.

"Goot," Jake concluded. "Come, Swede. We will have hot coffee after we are done."

***

Over the next two weeks, both men helped a great deal on the farm. Swede learned how to milk cows. The men cut wood every day, helped with repairs on the buildings, and helped dig stumps to clear more land for spring planting.

Sergeant Riley had told them they must work their horses daily. They made sure they followed his instructions. They spent time in the morning and again in the afternoon drilling their mounts. They practiced all the basic maneuvers, directing the horse's movement by leg pressure. They trotted, galloped, and walked their horses as well. In addition to drill and exercise, they fed and groomed their mounts carefully.

They also visited Lowell. Michael remembered more people in town on a Saturday. The November weather probably kept many home. He ran into the Justice of the Peace one Saturday.

"Good morning, Corporal Drieborg," Joseph F. Deeb greeted, hand extended. "I assume you're home on leave?"

"Yes, sir," Mike replied, "and it's great. I believe this leave means we have finished our training."

"I expect, then, you will be sent off to the war very soon," Deeb predicted.

"Probably soon, sir," Mike agreed. "That's what we all expect. Tell me, sir, if you can, what of the Bacon kid? Is he still in prison?"

"Quite a story around town," Deeb informed him. "There was a very detailed report of the entire affair in the *Grand Rapids Eagle* last month. They printed the details of his offense and his court-martial and sentence. As far as I know, he is still in a military prison. But his father has hired lawyers who are trying to get the conviction set aside or modified. He has made it pretty clear that all of it was your fault."

"As you probably read, he brought it on himself. As an enlisted man, I left him alone. He was the officer who abused his authority in his several attempts to harass me. I had no power. How can his father blame me?"

"I understand that, Mike," Deeb agreed. "Most people around here do, too. You know no one can change Mr. Bacon's mind about anything. Well, it's good to see you, Mike, but I have to go. I have a client waiting for me right now. God bless you, young man. Come back to us safely."

"Thank you, sir," Mike responded as they shook hands again and went on their way.

At the general store, Michael was greeted warmly by Mr. Zania. Later, he called on Mr. King at the King Elevator. His first visit to Lowell since August felt very comfortable to him. Even the librarian remembered his Saturday morning visits. Swede wasn't much impressed with the town after his two visits to Grand Rapids. Besides, it was very cold, and he was anxious to return to the farm and the noon dinner.

When Mike's father had no more chores or stumps to dig, they worked on other farms in the area. Up at five-thirty in the morning, they worked most of the day, cold or not. Cutting wood, animal care and building repairs were always needed. Under the direction of Mike's father, they slaughtered pigs at home, as well as for the neighbors. They got pretty good at it, too. They hunted deer, rabbits and fowl, too. So, the smokehouses of the area were busy with the game they shot and the animals they slaughtered. As always, they spent time each morning and afternoon working with their mounts.

***

The time passed all too quickly, though. Before they knew it, their leave was over. After he and Swede had saddled their horses, his father had held him at arm's length.

"God go mit you, Michael," he said. "Mamma und I are proud of you, son. And I know you will keep your promise to me." With that, Jacob hugged his son tightly before walking out of the barn.

Mike thought he saw tears in his father's eyes, but Jacob had turned and left the barn before he could be sure.

***

Two days after the two men returned to their Grand Rapids training camp, they were told that the Sixth Michigan Cavalry Regiment was assigned to the defenses of Washington D. C. Their movement toward that city was to begin immediately. First, their horses and gear were loaded on trains and sent ahead. Then, at midnight on December 1, 1862, Mike and his comrades formed outside their barracks in Grand Rapids for the last time. They stood at attention under a full moon. Each trooper had his personal gear in a canvas bag slung over his shoulder. The order to move was given.

"Troop — Attention!" All the men in ranks snapped erect. "Right — Face! Forward — March!" The entire Regiment moved toward the railroad station.

As the men tramped in formation through the deserted streets of the city, all Michael could hear in the silence was the crunching sound of their boots on ice-covered snow and the roar of the nearby Grand River.

"Will I ever see this place again?" He wondered.

The train pulled out by three a.m. for Lansing, the state capital of Michigan. The train's wooden bench seats and chilly compartments did not encourage sleeping. Besides, Michael was too excited. He had never been more than a few miles away from home and had never been on a train. So, as the train sped along, he just sat quietly and looked out of the darkened railroad car window at the winter landscape.

He was surprised that, despite the early hour of their arrival in Lansing, the state capitol, Governor Chase and many other dignitaries were on hand to greet them. After several speeches and a warm meal, the train pulled out for the city of Detroit. The en-thusiastic greeting was repeated in Detroit later that same day; this time, a band and a much bigger crowd met them. There, they heard more speeches and were given even more food before they left the Detroit railroad station. Cleveland and Pittsburgh were next. At each of these stops, the greeting was warm, with many shouts of "God bless you, boys." It seemed to Mike that the entire nation supported the war.

At 2:30 p.m. the next day, they got off the train in the third largest city of the United States, Baltimore. A year earlier, much of the city's population supported the South. Hostile crowds met the first Union troops to arrive. In spite of still being a city of divided loyalties in this war, the Michigan men were greeted with cheers from many citizens.

Their first night in Washington City, was spent sleeping in the corridors of a military hospital.

Washington, December 8, 1862

Dear Family,

I hope this letter finds you all well. I am fine. Yesterday was our first day in Washington, D.C. The train trip here was exciting. I did not sleep much because I did not want to miss anything.

Our country is so large, and the cities are so big. I am still amazed by it all.

All along the way, people cheered us. It didn't seem to make any difference what time of day it was. Crowds greeted us at every stop with food, bands, and well wishes. Even at train stations where we did not stop, crowds and bands greeted our passing.

We marched to our permanent camp area yesterday. It is located on the northwest edge of the city. The land is almost bare. There were just a few small trees. It is twenty acres of well-drained land that would be good for either wheat or corn, Papa.

Instead of crops, the men of our Regiment covered the land with almost two hundred tents in just a few hours. I was surprised the ground was not frozen, like at home. We have been told that the temperature will seldom drop below freezing, and then only for a few hours.

Good thing for us, because Sgt. Riley had us do a lot of digging before he allowed us to erect the five tents needed for our platoon. First, each of the five squads drove a stake in the ground. We then attached a rope four feet long to each stake. With this rope, we marked the border for each tent, a circle eight feet from side to side. Then he made us dig out each circle to a depth of two feet. We lined the outer edge of the circles with logs, stones, and hay. We then raised the tents over each circle using several poles to support the canvas.

My squad now has a dry home to protect us from the cold wind, rain, and snow. A fire pit is in the center of our tent. Here we cook our meals and dry our clothing. We also line up our boots around the fire pit and sleep with our feet to it, too.

It is not as snug as our home, Mamma, but it is dry and warm. This morning we will be issued our revolvers. They are called side arms. This afternoon we will get our horses back. Tomorrow we will be issued our carbines to complete our equipment issue.

Then our training will resume and patrol work will begin, too. I truly do not know the kind of schedule we will be given. So, I can only promise to write when things settle down.

Now that you know where I am, you can send me some of your cookies, Mamma. And, my dear sisters, if you could knit me some socks, mittens, a stocking cap, and a scarf, it would be greatly appreciated.

By the way, girls, you know Swede and George still have no one back home. So, maybe some of your girlfriends would knit for them.

Love to you all,

Michael

Winter in Washington City

Between patrols, most of the men in Michigan's 6th Regiment took every opportunity to visit downtown Washington. It was only a two-mile walk from their encampment.

"I don't care how much fun Swede had yesterday," Mike told George. "Get him to go with you to the brothels if you have to go. Besides, we haven't seen the Smithsonian Institute like we planned today."

"You're just afraid to be with a woman," George accused him. "Besides, we can always look at an old building. We should go and have some fun for a change. Come on."

"Darn right, I'm afraid," replied Mike. "You were with us when the Captain marched us through that hospital ward the other day. That doctor showed us those guys who got diseases from women down in Hooker's division.

"Remember? He told us that the doctors don't know how to stop men from getting the infections, or how to cure anyone once they got it. Didn't you take a whiff of that terrible medicine they make those guys swallow? Weren't you paying attention, George?"

"Yeah, I was," George admitted. "I'm going down there one of these days, anyway. You will too, I bet."

"No thanks, George. Let's finish our tour. Remember, we have to get back to camp for picket duty tonight."

Reluctantly, George went along with Mike. *"I'll find someone else to join me when I return here after our patrol."* George thought to himself.

December 12, 1862

Dear Family,

I hope this letter finds you all well. I am fine. Now that we have our camp all set up, I have more time to write. We have been doing quite a bit of mounted drill in preparation for picket duty. That is where we are assigned an area to patrol on horseback.

We will be on this duty for 24 hours, followed by 48 hours back in our camp. This is probably not very comfortable duty this time of year, but we will see. I will write you about it soon.

I bought this paper, a pencil, and a stamp right here in camp. It seems that at every Regimental campsite, a merchant, called a sutler, is allowed to set up a store. There, we can buy most anything we want. Even food is for sale there. I looked over the clothing there,

Mamma. The socks were so thin, I just know they would not last very long or be very warm, either.

The wool ones you will knit for me will be perfect. Most everything at that store seems to cost a lot, too. Sgt. Riley told us to wait a few days, and other merchants will set up stores just outside of camp, too. He promised that we will see prices coming down then. Whiskey is for sale, too, Papa. But do not worry. I will keep my promise and not take up drinking. Besides, Captain Hyser will not allow it in our camp. Anyone reporting back to camp drunk has been severely punished. Besides having to dig latrines, the drunk has to wear a sign pinned to his uniform saying, I AM A DRUNK. No one in our platoon has had this misfortune. I feel sure Sgt. Riley would add other punishments, too. No one in our squad wants to be the first to find out.

I'm sending you my November pay, Papa, for my land payment. I kept four dollars for supplies and a meal when we go into town. We have a Priest from the city every Sunday for confession and Mass. I don't know what will happen if we are in the field on patrol some Sunday. Cross that bridge when I come to it.

David, the sheep farmer from Newaygo, just got a package from home. Of course, he shared the food. Oatmeal cookies with dried cherries were very welcome. Were they good. His wife knitted him socks and a scarf from their own wool. How are our sheep doing, Papa? Will it be spring before you harvest any wool from them?

I promise to write again soon. You write too, please. Tell me all the news.

Love you all,

Michael

***

Winter in Washington City was much like November in Michigan. It seemed damp and chilly, with a mix of rain and snow falling on and off all the time. Not a comfortable time of year for man or beast.

But the men of the 6th Cavalry were rather well prepared. Their wool uniforms, boots, and heavy greatcoats kept them warm, and their rain-repellant ponchos kept them dry. Sgt. Riley was always after the men of his platoon about keeping their feet dry.

"Carry dry socks in yer haversack," he would insist. "Are yer feet wet, boys? Have ya changed into yer dry socks yet today?" he pestered.

He expected each man to change socks at least once during their twenty-four-hour picket duty. "Keep a spare dry pair in yer sack, too," he would order. The tent used by his men stank with the smell of wet socks drying on a line over their fire pit.

Boots earned special attention from him, too. "Put'em close to the fire pit and grease them up really good an' often. That'll keep the water out. And while yer at it, sleep with yer feet to the fire," he repeated.

The men did what he directed. It was more like an order, anyway. It seemed he harped at them more about staying healthy than about the fighting part of the job. He reminded them that they would be of little use to the Union if they were sick. So, his men cleaned their cooking and eating gear carefully, always boiled their water, and threw out their straw bedding every few days.

It certainly seemed to be effective. The men of his platoon seldom reported for sick call in the morning. Nor did his men miss picket duty, either. Even if one of them didn't feel well, his men remembered what Riley had told them.

"If yer unable to report for duty, lads, it better be 'cause of something the Rebs done to ya, or I'll see to it ya wished they had."

Eventually, the Captain adopted Riley's suggestions for the entire Troop. The results were similar with the other seventy men. Diarrhea, a common and serious medical problem, stopped, and the common cold and flu bugs seldom kept any man from his duties.

The only battle they were to lose was with lice. Called Graybacks, lice seemed to be part of life in every army camp. They followed the men everywhere. So, despite the winter weather, Riley had his men clean out their shelter every few days. He even had them boil their clothing and blankets in a strong concoction he brewed every now and again. The battle with the Graybacks was constant and never won.

All the men were sitting around the hot wood in the fire pit of their quarters. They each were holding a set of long underwear on their lap, examining the cloth very closely and occasionally picking off a louse and dropping it into their heated tin drinking cup. When it hit the bottom of the hot cup, Mike could hear a sound like spit hitting a hot piece of metal.

"Who's found the highest number of lice so far?" Stan asked.

"This is the most disgusting contest I ever heard of, Stan," Mike said. "Let's just throw this clothing into that pot of foul-smelling stuff Riley fixes up. That'll take care of these lice."

"No fun in that," joined in George. "'Sides, we all chipped in ten cents for the winner."

"But who would want to admit having the most lice on his underwear?" Mike asked.

"For sixty cents, it wouldn't bother me a bit," George said. "Last time, Bill won. It didn't seem to bother him much."

Bill chuckled. "I gotta admit, I never thought I would be doing this, much less admitting it. For fun and profit, though, what the heck?"

Bill won again.

***

The Second Platoon of I Troop was directed to patrol a five-mile stretch of countryside on the southwest border of Washington. Each six-trooper squad was assigned an area within this five-mile stretch. In pairs, the troopers rode in circles one mile across. Thus, the six men riding in three interlocking circles could patrol an area thoroughly.

It was just after sunrise. Swede and Mike had been in the saddle for two hours. Mike noticed how the heavy snowfall had accumulated on Swede's broad-brimmed hat and on the shoulders of his greatcoat. He could feel the bite of the cold wind on his face. It chilled him despite the woolen uniform, greatcoat, scarf and riding gloves. Suddenly, through the snowfall, he saw a brightly lit window not twenty yards in front of him. Moving a bit closer, he noticed smoke from a farmhouse chimney, too. He directed his horse toward the light. Swede followed close behind.

Then, Mike saw a man standing between them and the house. He was waving to them in greeting. He was about five-foot-seven inches tall and looked a bit portly under his winter coat and hat. Moving closer and still seated on his horse, Mike looked down at the man. He noticed his rosy cheeks and bright smile." He *looks just like pictures I've seen of Santa Claus.*" thought Mike.

"Velcome, boys," the farmer said. "Step down und take a minute to stretch your legs. I'm Ruben Hecht. I'm jus' done mit da chores and am going to have something varm to drink. My wife Emma, vill have hot coffee and cornbread ready for me. Der should be enough for you, too. Tie your horses in da barn over der. Vater und feed dem if you vant."

"We can't stop for long, sir," responded Mike. "But hot coffee sure sounds good. And our mounts could use a wiping down and some water, too."

After taking care of their horses, the three men stomped the snow from their boots in a sheltered entryway. As they came through the front door, a warm room brightly lit by the fireplace greeted them. It was a typically built farmhouse with the fireplace at its center. It was where all the cooking was done too.

As they entered the central room, the heat generated by the fire immediately warmed them. A metal pot hung from a crane on the right of the central fire. A smaller metal pot lay on a grate to the left of the main fire. Such pots were typically used to bake bread, pies, biscuits, stews, and casseroles. Meats and poultry were sometimes boiled this way for canning, too. Such foods were also fried on grates for immediate consumption.

"This is just like my home in Michigan." Michael thought.

"Mamma, dis is Corporal Drieborg, and dis is Private Bjourn. Dey are from Michigan. An' dey are cold like me. Have you some hot coffee for us?"

A stout lady, slightly shorter than her husband, greeted them with a bright smile. "Please sit boys. We have plenty, and some warm cornbread, too." Mrs. Hecht poured some coffee for Drieborg. "Your name sounds German, Corporal."

"No Mrs. Hecht, my parents came to this country from Holland," said Mike. "They were living on a farm in the Catholic part of Holland near the Belgian boarder. I am the oldest and was born in Michigan. My family has a farm of some one hundred eighty acres. It's near a small town called Lowell."

"And you, Private Bjourn, where do you come from?" Mrs. Hecht asked, putting some warn cornbread in front of him.

"Und call me Svede, missus," he responded. "I come from Sweden a year ago. I was a contract vorker in da copper mines of northern Michigan. That's in der north part. I took care of da mules and horses for da mines. I paid the company back the passage money ven I got bounty to join da cavalry in Grand Rapids. Tank you for da coffee and cornbread, missus."

"You are both very welcome boys," Mrs. Hecht told them. "Papa and I came here from Germany twenty years ago. Der are many German families in dis area. A cousin helped us get here. We worked on his farm until we could get our own place ten years ago or so. We are Catholic, too, Corporal.

"Ah, we have forgotten our manners, Papa." Mrs. Hecht turned toward a beautiful young woman sitting by the fireplace. "This is our oldest daughter, Eleanor. She married a neighbor boy who was in da Union Army. She is staying mit us with her son Robert."

Eleanor stood up and nodded a greeting to the two men with a smile. She was taller than her parents. She was slender, with blue eyes and long blond hair braided down her back. "*A very pretty woman,*" Michael thought.

She sat down again, and her son stood by her side, hanging on to her skirts with his head on her lap.

"Robert is still very shy," Mrs. Hecht told them. "He is only one year old now. His father has not seen him, even. And dis is our younger daughter Julia and our son Kenny. Dey are home today because school is out for da Christmastime."

Julia was pretty like her sister, but a bit shorter. Kenny stood taller than the other members of the Hecht family, even at thirteen years old. He seemed to have the outgoing nature of his parents, though.

Both troopers stood during the introductions. "Nice to meet you all," responded Mike. "I always loved vacations from school, even though it meant more work for me at home. Is it the same for you, Kenny?"

"Really Mike," Kenny responded. "I love not having to go to school. I would much rather work around here with Papa."

Mike looked at Eleanor. "Where is your husband stationed, Eleanor?" She looked at Mike as though surprised by the question. She buried her face in her hands and began to cry. She picked up her son and fled to another room, slamming the door shut behind her.

"Eleanor's husband was reported killed last May," Mrs. Hecht told Mike and Swede. "He was in a battle someplace in Virginia."

"I'm so sorry for upsetting your daughter, Mrs. Hecht," Mike apologized.

"She vill be all right, Corporal," Ruben interjected. "Every now and den she cries. You had no vay of knowing."

"What do you grow on your farm, Mr. Hecht?" asked Mike, changing the subject.

"Ve have one hundred sixty acres, one hundred ten acres cleared. Corn, wheat, and hay we plant, mostly.

"Ve have two milking cows, some pigs and goats, a big vegetable garden and a large poultry flock. So, ve sell grain and some eggs in da town nearby, too. Vhat does your papa plant on his farm?"

"Before I joined the Army in September," Mike responded, "we had about one hundred acres of corn. It looked really good, too. My father purchased harvesting equipment last fall and was able to bring in the entire crop alone. We also had sixty acres of wheat this year. With me gone, my young brother and even my two sisters had to help with that harvest. And last spring, we added a small flock of sheep.

"My sister Susan wrote me that our papa got a dollar twenty-five a bushel for his corn and a dollar eighty-three for his wheat. These prices are three times higher than last year. The war, I guess. Even the price they got for our first wool harvest allowed my father to pay for the sheep already, and he expects his flock to double in number by spring."

"It is da same here, Corporal. Ve get goot prices, too," explained Mr. Hecht. "But da war is so close, ve vorry. Deir have been Rebel raids in dis area. So, ve are glad to see you boys around here, eh, Mamma?"

"Yes, Papa," she agreed. "Can you boys stay for supper?"

"Thank you, Mrs. Hecht," responded Mike. "We would love to, but we have to move on, or our sergeant will have our hide. We were told to stop and talk with the farmers in our patrol area. But we have to get back. Thank you for the coffee and cornbread. The other troopers will really be jealous."

"Tank you missus," added Swede.

"You boys come anytime," she told them. "You will always be welcome here."

"Mamma is right," said Mr. Hecht. "You come here und stay longer. Eat mit us too. Can you do dat?"

"We sure could, but only if you let us help with the chores or something," Mike offered. "I'm sort of out of practice, but I would like to help if you'd let me. And Swede is awfully good with animals."

"I vould like to come mit Mike," said Swede. "Vould you let me help out, too?"

"Den dat settles it, eh, Mamma? Dey come back, und we let dem help around da place." Mr. Hecht slapped his right thigh. "Maybe you can come for Christmas, too?"

They agreed to return after their tour of picket duty.

The Hecht Farm

Once again in the saddle, Mike and Swede leaned into the wind and snow as they rode back to camp. The wind gusted so hard that they had to tie scarves under their chins and over the crown of their broad-brimmed hats to keep them from blowing off their heads. After two hours of riding, they found their encampment.

First, they unsaddled their horses. They rubbed them down, examining them for cuts or sore spots. Then they gave the animals feed and water. After checking the hooves for stones or loose shoes, Mike and the Swede covered each with a blanket.

Swede could not resist inspecting the other mounts in their squad before they reported to Sgt. Riley.

"Give me a hand here, Mike, vill ya?" he asked. "Ya know Riley vill skin us alive if any of da squad's mounts are not well taken care of."

"Sure," Mike agreed. "But let's get on with it, will ya? I'm tired, hungry and cold."

Finally finished, they found Riley by a fire, talking with some other Troopers.

"I was about to send out a search party for yas," he said. "Any trouble, Drieborg?"

"None at all, Sarge," Mike responded. "We were following orders about talking with friendly farmers, and we met one a few miles back. A man named Hecht and his family. Time sort of slipped by on us, I guess.

"He told us that he would keep an eye out for any Reb activity, but he hadn't seen any for a few weeks."

"Get something in yer belly, an' some sleep, too. Both a' ya are back in the saddle in four hours. Don't forget to change yer socks a'fore ya go out on the next patrol. Off with ya, now. I'll talk to both a' ya later." He paused.

"Oh, Swede. Did you look over the mounts when ya got back?"

"I did, Sarge," he assured him. "Mike, he helped me, too. They look fine."

"Let me know if ya see any saddle sores or hoof problems really quick," Riley directed. "It's easy to overlook such things when we're out on patrol."

When in the field on patrol, the soldiers of I Troop erected dog tents. Riley liked such an arrangement best during the winter for the added warmth and protection against the elements it provided his men.

Each man was issued a ground tarp half. This was then buttoned to another such tarp, forming a two-person tent called a dog tent. Each man's poncho was then put on the ground over pine needles, leaves, grass, or straw.

Troopers usually slept in their clothing when in the field, sometimes with their boots on. Each man also had a blanket and a greatcoat for warmth and their saddle for a pillow. This usually provided a warm and dry sleeping arrangement. But it could be a bit crowded for some troopers.

Mike and Swede shared a dog tent. But, because they were both broad-shouldered, they were crowded in their tent. On top of that, Mike was six-foot-two inches tall. Without curling up, he found it hard to keep his feet inside the dog tent. Swede had no such problem with the size of the tent since he was much shorter than Mike.

This was one field problem Sgt. Riley couldn't do much about. Right now, Mike and Swede were too tired to care about it.

Two days later, the men of I Troop returned to their permanent camp on the outskirts of Washington City. Their first day back would be a day of caring for their mounts, cleaning their weapons and clothing, and repairing their gear. Being back in their warm and dry shelter was most welcome. The mail and the packages that awaited them were welcome, too.

***

The following week, Mike and the Swede returned to the Hecht farm. There, they spent a full day helping Ruben and his son Kenny clear a field for spring planting. That meant digging up several tree stumps. Despite the December cold, they worked up a sweat swinging a pick to loosen the dirt around the stump, shoveling out dirt and severing the exposed roots.

The physical nature of the work pleased them both. Of course, the Hecht home was a welcome relief from army life, and the food was the best they had since last Thanksgiving at Mike's Lowell home. After staying a second night, they had to leave. Before they did, however, the Hechts invited them both to return and celebrate Christmas at the farm. They quickly accepted the invitation.

***

Once back in camp, Michael found that he had a letter from home.

Dear Michael,

How are you? Everyone here is in good health. I hope you are still well, too. Ann and I are working on socks for you. We finished the mittens and scarf you asked for. We added them to the package we just sent you. Ann has also been working with Papa in the barn and with the sheep flock a lot.

With so many of the men gone to the war, most of the farms are in need of workers. If Papa was gone, I know we would have trouble, too. Without help, Papa says the bank would take many of the farms because the farmers could not make their note payments. So, Papa and some other men have been helping our neighbors. Papa was very grateful for the help you and Swede gave the neighbors when you two were here at Thanksgiving time.

So, Michael, we all have to do more here at home. Good thing we have that new plow and harvester. The bank owner, Bacon, would not loan Papa the money to buy them because he still blames you for his son's troubles. But the Harvester Company will not expect payment until after the next harvest. Papa will let our neighbors use the equipment for a share of their crops. That will help him pay for it.

Mamma is so happy you have found a nice farm family to spend time with. And Catholic, too! She wanted me to remind you to take a gift for each member of the family. Papa suggested an axe for Mr. Hecht. Mamma said to get a wool blanket for Mrs. Hecht. I think you ought to buy some nice cloth for each of the two girls so that they can make themselves a dress. Wool is best this time of year. Three yards should do. The boy might like a knife, Little Jake suggested.

Write and tell us all about the daughters. Ann and I want to know how pretty they are, and if they are nice. Oh, yes, and what are their names?

Papa says you should offer to help Mr. Hecht with his farm work if you can.

Take care of yourself, Michael. We miss you very much.

Love and Merry Christmas from everyone here,

Your sister, Susan

***

"Swede," Mike urged. "Don't worry about the presents we bought. They are just fine."

"I never have been to a real Christmas before, Mike. Are you sure?"

"If you're going to keep worrying about this, you won't enjoy Christmas at all. And I'll just end up worrying, too. Didn't my mother and sisters tell us what to buy from the sutler's store for the Hechts?" Mike snapped at him.

"I know. I vill stop talking 'bout it, Mike," Swede promised.

Since they left their camp in Washington, D.C., the temperature seemed to have dropped several degrees. A soft snowfall replaced the chilling rain that fell as they left camp. It began to look to Michael like a Michigan white Christmas.

The Hecht family farm was only sixteen miles west of the city. Mike calculated that if they rode their mounts at a walk, it would take about three hours to reach the farm. At a trot, they could cut the travel time by more than an hour. But he knew that they needed to watch for rebel raiders, as well as Union cavalry pickets who might mistake him and Swede for rebs.

They certainly didn't want to ride up on either unexpectedly. They could be captured by one or shot by the other. Either prospect was not how they wanted to celebrate Christmas.

"Did you say that E Troop had picket duty in this area today, Swede?" Michael asked.

"Dat's vhat Sergeant Riley said when I told him vhere ve go today. He said to be careful, too. No telling vhat our own trigger-happy troopers might do. Mistake us for rebel spies maybe."

"You won't have to worry about that possibility much longer, Swede," Mike promised. "The good road we spotted the other day when we were on picket duty is just over that rise ahead of us. Then we can move at a trot and be at the Hecht farm in another hour. Does that sound good to you?"

"Ya, I guess."

Once on the new road, they spurred their horses to a good trot.

"I'm going to drop back ten yards or so, Swede," Mike told him. "I'll look toward the field to our right. You look toward the woods on the left. Okay? Sarge was right; we can't be too careful."

Without any problems, they arrived at the Hecht farm in less than an hour. On a rise, they paused to look down at the farmhouse. The snow was falling harder now, blown by a strong, cold wind. Nevertheless, each was warm in his greatcoat, with its large collar forming a hood when buttoned. Thus, they were well protected from the cold wind and the blowing snow.

Before long, they saw smoke from the Hecht farmhouse chimney. It promised a warm kitchen, and probably a great meal, too. They could see a light in the barn.

"You tink Ruben und Kenny are milking da cows now Mike? Swede asked.

"Probably Swede: we'll soon see."

They urged their mounts along the road. Snow was blowing off the fields surrounding the house. They could still see yellowed cornstalks and other remains of the fall harvest standing stiff and tall, reaching for the sky through the drifting snow.

Both men dismounted and led their houses into the barn. As they thought, Ruben Hecht and his twelve-year-old son Kenny were inside.

"Mr. Hecht, good afternoon," Mike shouted out. "I hope we haven't arrived too early."

"Hello, boys," Ruben greeted them. "No, you are just on time for Mamma's special Christmas supper. Come, und bring da horses into da barn. Kenny, show dem da place you fixed for der horses. Wipe um down good, boys. Kenny has some special feed and water for dem, too. And den we will vash up for supper, eh?"

It was another half an hour before they had finished taking care of the horses and washed up for dinner.

Ruben Hecht led the way toward the house. He burst into the warm dwelling.

"Look who's here, Mamma," he announced. "Mike und da Swede. Come, girls, take da caps and da big coats. Sit, boys, sit by da fire. Dey been riding for tree hours almost, Mamma. Imagine."

"For your company and one of your meals," Mike assured her, "we'd ride twice that distance, even in this kind of weather."

"Thank you, boys," she responded. She moved toward them, wiping her hands on her apron. And, to their surprise, she gave each of them a big hug.

"Where can we put these presents, Mrs. Hecht?" Mike asked. He had several packages in a canvas sack he had carried into the house.

"You didn't have to do that, boys," she responded. "You can put them under the Christmas tree, Michael. Excuse Papa, boys. He has been waiting for you since early this morning. He's so excited that you are finally here. We all have been looking toward your visit. Haven't we, girls?"

Julia flushed in embarrassment. "Oh, really, Mamma," she exclaimed. "Julia, bring da hot cider for us here," interrupted her Papa. "Dis will warm us up."

The hot drink was served in wooden mugs.

"For Kenny, too," insisted Ruben. "'Remember da tree stumps you helped us dig out last time you vas here?"

"Sure do," Swede responded with a smile. "Your trees have deep roots here, by gum."

"Well, Kenny und I dragged dem out to da road you just came in on," Ruben continued. "The stumps make sort of a marker for our property, I tink. Only six more stumps to dig out, und we can plow dat field dis spring."

"Could you use any help with that, Mr. Hecht?" Mike asked. "I don't know how soon we'll get time off again. Can't be more than a week or so from now. What do you say, Swede? Are you up to digging a few more stumps?"

"Sure enough. I do just about anything for more of your cooking missus'."

"You don't have to work like that for a meal here, boys," Mrs. Hecht responded. "You will always welcome here."

"Thank you, Mrs. Hecht. But actually we don't get much real exercise," Mike told her. "As we told Mr. Hecht last time we were here, we're either in the saddle or in our tents this time of year. We enjoy getting out and swinging an axe. Besides, the blisters I earned last time I was here are pretty near healed. My hands need to be toughened up more." He smiled.

"Dat settles it, Mamma," concluded Ruben. "You boys get back here as soon as you can. Den we clear dat field and Mamma will feed us all goot. Oh, und boys, please call me Ruben; I vould like dat."

"Fine, Papa," Mrs. Hecht added. "But right now, we are going to have dinner. Girls, show our special guests to the table. Take your cider with you if you want, boys."

The men and Mrs. Hecht took their seats while Eleanor and Julia brought the food to the table: sweet potatoes, cranberries, applesauce, hot bread, buttermilk, dressing, gravy, and a good-size turkey. The turkey was set down in front of Ruben for him to carve.

"Does everything look good to you, Mr. Swede?" Mamma teased.

"Yes, it does, missus. And, please call me Swede, missus," he urged her.

"May I call you Gustov instead?" she asked. "After all, it is your given name, isn't it?"

"Ya, missus, it is."

"Before you start to carve, Papa, let us offer thanks to God for all His blessings," said Mamma. "Would you do that for us, Michael?"

"Thank you, Mrs. Hecht," Mike responded. "I would be happy to." He bowed his head.

"Dear Lord, thank you for the many blessings you have bestowed upon all of us here today. Thank you for the hospitality the Hecht family has shown Swede and me. Please continue your blessings for them this coming year. Look after Eleanor's child. And, Lord, bring this war to a speedy end. Amen."

"Thank you, Michael. That was very nice," said Mrs. Hecht. "Now, Papa, you can carve the turkey."

Once Ruben cut off the legs and wings, he began to slice the white meat for each plate.

"Kenny likes a turkey drumstick. Anyone else? Or a ving maybe?" he asked.

"Fine. Now pass da other dishes around da table," Ruben directed.

"You first, Mrs. Hecht," insisted Mike.

"Thank you, Michael. But just take what you want when the dish is passed to you, there is plenty. I will not go hungry tonight. Go now, take what you want. Then pass the dish on."

"What is your army food like?" asked Kenny.

"Tell him, Swede," urged Mike.

"Ve take turns cooking our food, Kenny. Ve call our group a mess. Six men live together in one shelter. Ve are lucky to have George Neal, who was a baker back in Michigan. So, ve get bread, biscuits, und other good tings from him. Ve eat stew a lot, and George's biscuits with gravy are very goot. Ve find wild onions or buy dem from da sutler store. Und potatoes, too. Each of us takes a turn cooking. Ve like da stew best I tink."

"When we are on picket duty," Michael added, "because we spend most of our time either in the saddle or sleeping, we seldom cook much. Instead, we prepare the meat and bake the bread in advance. Then, we eat out of our haversacks and brew coffee whenever we can."

"Sounds exciting," concluded Kenny.

"Not as goot as dis," insisted Swede. "If it veren't for Sergeant Riley, making us take care of our pots an' such, and vatching how we cook our food, ve vould be sick most a' da time like a lot a' troopers."

"Is there a lot of that kind of sickness, Mr. Swede?" asked Eleanor.

"Yes, miss," Swede answered. "Sick call in da morning is full of men mit sickness like dat. Sergeant Riley tells us tings I should not talk about at da dinner table. Mike, you tell her."

"Eleanor," Mike began. "When you don't clean your cooking gear properly after you use it, you take a big chance of getting ill. Most of the time, it passes quickly after a few days of not being able to hold down any food and being very weak. Sometimes, though, men have died because they have lost so much liquid or so weak that they have caught a cold and have died from that. In our Regiment, we have already lost several men. They died or were discharged because of such illness."

"Good thing we don't have that kind of problem in our house," exclaimed Kenny.

"Well, of course not, dummy. You don't live in a barn, you know," Eleanor sharply reminded him.

December 28, 1862

Dear Family,

Merry Christmas! I hope you had a good one. I miss you very much. Swede and I rode to the Hecht farm the day before Christmas. We had a big dinner Christmas Eve before we went to church with them for evening Mass.

The meal was fine, and they cooked most of the same things you usually do, Mamma. As good as it was, I don't suppose anyone can beat yours. But most anything beats Army food. So, you can believe I ate a lot.

It was a five-mile ride to the Catholic Church. Mass began at ten o'clock. The weather was chilly and a bit snowy. But the road was firm and easy going. We didn't return to the farm until after midnight. Just like home, they open presents when they get up Christmas morning. They liked the gifts we had brought. Thanks for your suggestions, ladies. And guess what, girls? They gave us each a nice scarf and a pair of wool socks. Please, though, don't stop knitting more for me. I need more. So, does Swede.

We didn't have to be back until the day after Christmas, so we spent the day helping Mr. Hecht and his son Ken around the farm. It was nice to get the feel of doing farm work again. We worked with their two cows, chopped firewood, and did some other farm chores. Of course, we ate leftovers. Just like at home.

We talked about farming a lot. It was interesting to find that they have the same kind of troubles as farmers in Lowell have, and they are getting good prices here, too. After I told them of our new flock of sheep, and the price of wool, Mr. Hecht said that they just might start a flock, too. The more I enjoyed my visit, though, the more it reminded me of home and made me homesick.

For your information, girls, Eleanor Hecht is a widow with a twelve-month-old son. Her married name is Bierlein. She is tall and very pretty. Blond hair and blue eyes, too. Her younger sister, Julia, is sixteen with brown hair and brown eyes. Their brother is twelve. He reminds me a great deal of Little Jake.

We hated to leave, but Swede and I will return in January to help with removing some tree stumps. Blasting supplies are hard to obtain now, so we use the axe mostly.

Love you,

Michael

A Chance Encounter: January 1863

Swede and Mike Drieborg were walking down E Street in downtown Washington late one afternoon, heading back to camp.

As they paused on the curb, they saw a well-dressed lady crossing the street coming toward them. She held her head down and used an umbrella as a shield against the light rain.

As she reached the middle of the muddy street, a wagon drawn by two horses swung wildly around the corner and headed right toward her. Her umbrella blocked her view, so she could not see it coming.

"Mike, look!" shouted Swede. "Dat vagon is going to run over dat girl."

"I see it," Mike shouted as he jumped from the curb and sprinted toward her. The horses were almost on top of them as he hit the petite woman full-force with his shoulder. He sort of ran through her, lifting and carrying her out of the horses' path.

She and Mike lay in the muddy street, dazed. As others ran to help them, the girl tried to get up without success.

"Are you all right, soldier?" someone asked.

"Yes, I think so," Mike said as hands helped him to his feet. "Give me a minute to clear my head, though. Is she, all right?" He turned to the woman, a young girl, actually. "I hope I did not hurt you, miss."

Holding her head, she weakly asked, "What happened?"

"This soldier saved you from being run over by two runaway horses pulling a wagon, lady," someone answered. "If he hadn't knocked you out of the way, you would have been killed for sure."

"She wants to know your name, soldier," stated another. He told her his name and unit.

"My wife here will help her home. She lives just up this street. We'll take care of her, young fella."

Swede and Drieborg headed off for camp.

"Dat was some ting you did, Mike," said Swede. "You all right, fer sure?"

"I'm fine, Swede," Mike responded. "I have my wind back. But I'm sure that little lady will have some sore ribs for a while. I'm afraid I hit her pretty hard with my shoulder.

I sort of landed on her, too. The mud probably helped soften the landing some, but I know I knocked the wind out of her, at least."

***

Back in their shelter, Mike was trying to clean all the mud from his clothing when Sgt. Riley burst in excitedly.

"Mike, are ya all right? A trooper told me ya saved a girl from being run over in town. What exactly happened?"

"It was nothing more than that, Sarge. I just pushed her out of the way of a wagon, that's all."

The Swede was more descriptive. "I never seen a person move so fast as Mike. Von minute we were standing der by da side of da road. Da next ting, he was lifting dat girl on his shoulder out of da vay of da horses. She vould have been run over for sure, Sarge. Killed probably, too."

"Maybe ya should see the doc, Mike," Riley suggested.

"I'm fine, Sarge. Really, I am. I hit that girl pretty solidly, though. She is probably going to find herself black and blue in the morning."

"Maybe, but I'm worried about ya. So, report to me first thing in the morning. Jus' to be sure."

***

Late the next afternoon, the commander of I Troop, Captain Hyser, was resting in his quarters. Someone outside called his name.

"Captain Hyser?"

He opened the makeshift door. "Yes, Lieutenant, what can I do for you?

"Sir, the Colonel would like to see you at Regimental headquarters, sir. As soon as possible, he said."

"Thank you for the message, Lieutenant," Hyser responded. "You can tell the Colonel that I will be along shortly."

"Yes, sir!"

Hyser pulled on his boots, donned his tunic, grabbed his hat, and was on his way. He buttoned his greatcoat as he walked. He arrived at Regimental headquarters only a few minutes after receiving the summons.

"Captain Hyser, you remember Congressman Kellogg. He introduced us to President Lincoln the other day at the White House."

"Yes, of course, Congressman. I much appreciated the opportunity to meet Mr. Lincoln. Thank you."

"You are most welcome, Captain," Kellogg said. "I am proud of the men from my district in the Grand Rapids area. You gave me a great opportunity to show off for the President. I had a little something to do with raising the Sixth, you know.

"But that's not why I asked to talk with you, Captain. I understand a Corporal Drieborg is a member of your Troop. Did you know that he saved my daughter from being killed yesterday? Very brave thing he did, in my opinion. He risked his own life, from what I am told. I'd like to know a bit more about him."

"Well, sir," Hyser responded, "The young man is a born leader. His determination to be the best infects those around him. They follow him without question, and they like him, too. I wish I had a dozen like him. He's a fine young man, Mr. Kellogg. I wasn't surprised when I heard the report from his platoon sergeant. What I didn't know was that the woman he helped was your daughter.

"But more about the corporal. He comes from a Lowell farm family. He graduated from grammar school. He would have enlisted sooner, but he obeyed his parents and stayed on the farm the first year of the war. He's a Catholic and attends church every Sunday. Michael doesn't drink. And he is probably one of the few unmarried troopers who have not been down to Hooker Street. The men ask him to read in the evening, and he helps them with writing letters, too. I'm proud to have him in my unit, sir."

"I'm glad to hear such things about Drieborg, Captain, because I'd like to talk with him about becoming my military Aide," stated Kellogg. "It would mean a promotion to lieutenant for him, too."

"Well, sir, that sounds like a fine opportunity for the lad. Even though I'd hate to lose him, I'll not try to influence him one way or another. In fact, I will suggest that he accept the position. But Congressman, it wouldn't surprise me if he refused your offer, promotion and all. They're such a tight bunch, these men, and Drieborg is their leader, even if he doesn't realize it at this point. I doubt if he would leave them."

"I hope you're wrong about that, Captain. But with your permission, I would like to ask him."

"I will not stand in your way, Mr. Kellogg. When would you like to talk to Corporal Drieborg, sir?"

"Would you be willing to bring him to my home this Saturday evening? I'll be having a dinner for several guests, and we would be pleased to count you and Drieborg among them."

"Thank you, Congressman," Hyser replied. "But neither Drieborg nor I have a dress uniform handy. I'm afraid we would be out of place at such an event."

"Nonsense, Captain," Kellogg said quickly. "Tell you what. I will inform my other guests that no dress uniforms or formal wear will be allowed. Of course, we wouldn't want to prevent the ladies from doing their best to impress one another. Will that do?"

"That would be fine, Mr. Kellogg," Hyser replied. "I accept your invitation for myself and Corporal Drieborg."

***

Captain Hyser had told Mike to meet him at five o'clock, mounted and ready to leave for the Kellogg home in Georgetown.

It was already dark when they began their three-mile ride into Washington. A light drizzle fell as they rode.

Mike asked his commander, "Have you ever been in one of these Washington homes, Captain?"

"Can't say that I have, Mike. But it would surprise me if a Congressman's home wasn't large and very richly furnished."

"If this Congressman just wants to thank me, couldn't he have done that when he talked with you back at our encampment?" Mike wondered aloud.

"I suppose so," Hyser answered. "But, remember, this man is our Congressman from Grand Rapids. Besides, we're in Washington. They do things pretty big around here, I suspect. He probably wants to thank you in front of other important people."

"Whatever, we'll find out soon enough," Mike concluded.

The two men finally arrived at the Kellogg residence. They dismounted and tied their horse halters to the hitching posts. There were several carriages already in front of the home. At the doorway, they were greeted by an elegantly dressed Negro servant. White hair covered his head, and he was tall enough to look Michael directly in the eye.

"Good evening, gentlemen. Please come inside." As soon as he closed the door behind them, he held out his white-gloved hands. "My name is Adam. May I have your over-coats, please?"

Once Adam had hung their greatcoats in a large closet just off the front entrance, he showed them where they could clean the mud from their boots. When they finished, he then led them into the main hallway of the home.

Michael had never seen such a large room, which seemed to serve no other purpose than to house a wide, winding stairway to the second floor. A large and brightly lit glass chandelier hung from the very high ceiling. There were several closed doors on this main floor, as well.

"Now gentlemen," Adam asked, "may I tell the Congressman who is here?"

"Captain William Hyser and Corporal Michael Drieborg," responded the Captain.

"Thank you, sir. Please follow me." He turned to their left and opened the double doors.

He led them into a large brightly lit room. A large candle-holding device sat on a grand piano in one corner. Several high-backed chairs flanked a fireplace and faced a low table holding a silver decanter surrounded by silver cups.

Candles on end tables burned brightly at each end of two red velvet couches. Silver oil-burning lanterns also were attached to each of the room's walls. Their light cast a hazy shadow over walls covered with a sky-blue velvet covering. Completing the room's illumination was a large circular fixture hanging from the ceiling at the center of the room. Several kerosene lanterns rested on this device.

"Captain Hyser and Corporal Michael Drieborg, sir," the servant Adam announced.

They remained standing in the wide doorway, waiting to be greeted before entering the room.

"Thank you, Adam," said Congressman Kellogg, stepping toward them in greeting. "Good evening, gentlemen. You honor my home."

"It is our pleasure, Congressman," Captain Hyser said. "Allow me introduce Corporal Michael Drieborg, recently from Lowell, Michigan. He is presently a squad leader, Second Platoon of I Troop, Sixth Cavalry Regiment."

"Welcome to my home, Corporal," Kellogg enthused, pumping Drieborg's somewhat limp hand in both of his.

Looking directly into Michael's eyes, the Congressman spoke with great emotion. His eyes teared up some, and his hands never relaxed their grip on Michael's right hand.

"I owe you a great debt, Michael," he said. "You gave me the best Christmas present a father could receive when you saved my daughter's life. We lost her mother several years ago. Without Patricia, my life would be empty of meaning. Thank you."

"You're welcome, sir. I am pleased I could be of help. But I am sure others on that street would have tried to assist her. I just happened to have jumped a bit more quickly."

"That may be true, son, but this was my daughter's life you saved. I am most grateful," insisted Kellogg, still holding Drieborg's hand.

"I'm glad I was there to help," Drieborg repeated.

"Now, let me properly introduce you to the young lady whose life you saved. Patricia, dear, this is Michael Drieborg."

With that, Patricia stepped forward and took Michael's hand from her father. The touch of her right hand warmed his palm, and when she brought her left hand to cover his, he couldn't remember feeling anything so soft and smooth.

A girl of not much more than five feet two or three, she was almost tiny. Her white dress, buttoned clear to her throat, did not hide her shapely figure. Her brown hair was swept back and held in place by a gold ribbon. Michael blushed a bit, remembering how close he had held her as he carried her out of harm's way the other day.

"*She wore the same perfume then too; nice.* He thought. *What a dazzling smile. Is that a twinkle I see in her eyes?*"

"You look much better Corporal Drieborg, without all that mud covering you."

Recovering his senses, Michael looked down at her with a smile. "The last time I ran into you, Miss Kellogg, you weren't smiling. It is a nice change. A very nice change."

"Come, you two, you can talk later," her father interrupted. "Patricia, let us introduce our guest of honor around the room."

Patricia smoothly slipped her right arm through Michael's left and led him into the parlor.

"Corporal, this is General Scott," said Kellogg, smiling. "He directs this war for Congress and the President. That would make him your boss, I think."

General Scott was seated on a loveseat that normally could hold two people comfortably. However, he was so large that he took up the entire seat. His white sideburns went all the way down to his chin. He looked up at Michael and smiled.

A bit confused, Michael snapped to attention, somewhat startling Patricia, who was still holding his arm.

"General Scott, may I present our guest of honor this evening, Corporal Michael Drieborg."

"Rest easy, young man," Scott ordered with a smile. "You do not have to stand at attention here. You did a very daring thing the other day, according to what I'm told.

Your Troop commander, Captain Hyser, told the Congressman that he wasn't surprised at all by your action. He says you are a born leader who does not hesitate to lead and that the men follow you without question. Wish we had a few generals like that, eh, Kellogg?

"Are you a leader, Corporal?" Scott asked.

"Sir, I don't know what to say," responded Michael, still standing stiffly in front of the General. "All I know is that I am the oldest in my parents' home. They expected me to take charge when something needed to be done. My father would be very disappointed if I hadn't helped Miss Kellogg the other day. He taught me that if something needs to be done, just do it. If that's being a leader, I'd be thanking my parents for being one."

"Well said, young man," interrupted Kellogg. "Now, dinner is ready. Patricia, will you escort Michael to the dining room?"

Fourteen people gathered in the Kellogg dining room. The four men in uniform included Drieborg, his Troop commander, General Scott, and his Aide. In addition to Congressman Kellogg and his daughter Patricia, four couples representing Washington society were present.

This would-be Michael's first formal dinner. He had learned good manners at his mother's table, but he was still quite nervous as he surveyed the ornate dinner setting. He watched the other men hold chairs for the ladies standing to their right, so he followed their example and helped Patricia Kellogg be seated.

"Corporal Drieborg," asked the wife of a guest whose name he had forgotten, "I've never had a chance to talk with an enlisted soldier. Would you mind if I asked you something?"

"No mum," Michael responded. "What would you like to know?"

"My husband tells me men join up to fight because they get caught up in the excitement of war. Others join because all their friends and neighbors join. They get carried along in the enthusiasm. Is that what happened to you?"

Michael paused just a minute, setting down his fork. Swallowing the last of the food in his mouth, he answered,

"My parents were born and raised in Holland. They came to the United States to escape what seemed to them constant warfare in Europe and to obtain land of their own. So, they were against my joining this fight. I honored their request to remain at home. Besides, we all believed the issues would be settled and the war over quickly. That was in April of 1861. But in August of 1862, the war had not ended. Actually, it seemed that our side was losing. And from what I read in the *Grand Rapids Eagle*, there didn't seem to be any end in sight, either.

"So, I expressed my feelings to my father. I told him that I felt we should do something to keep our country whole. I told him that I believed our family had a debt to the United States for taking them in and offering them opportunity. I told him that I believed I should respond to our President's request for help. And, yes, mum, I did feel guilty staying safe at home while many boys I knew were fighting. Some had even died, too."

"What did your father say?"

"When I told him how I felt, we were in the barn working with the animals. We were milking our cows, in fact. My father doesn't talk a great deal. But he listens. Doesn't miss much, it seems to me. He was in the next stall, and he stopped milking. I could tell because the sound of milk spraying into the bucket as he worked the cow's teat, excuse me, mum, stopped. It was real silent for what seemed like a long time. Then he said,

'After harvest, Michael. We will talk to Mamma, den.'

"The sound of milk landing in the bucket resumed, and we didn't talk about it again."

"But you joined in September. Had you already harvested your crops? Excuse me, Corporal, I know nothing of farms or crops," protested the lady.

"Well mum," responded Michael, somewhat cautiously, "actually, I had to join or go to jail."

The room suddenly became silent. The woman looked stunned. Even the men seemed uncomfortable. Recovering from her surprise, Patricia put her hand on Michael's arm.

Captain Hyser broke the silence.

"Excuse me Congressman, may I interrupt?" "Certainly, Captain."

"When Corporal Drieborg was assigned my Troop, I knew he had volunteered, as had every other trooper in my command. I also knew the choice he had been given by the Lowell Village justice of the peace. So, I checked it out with that official. It seemed that the son of the village banker held a purchased commission in our Regiment. I wish you would stop that practice, General. Usually turns out badly, you know. Anyway, this fellow was in town on a Saturday morning in full uniform, sort of parading around and showing off, I was told. He had not been very well regarded by his peers or adults in town as a young man. He was thrown out of the University of Michigan, too.

"It seems that some small boys were teasing him about how he looked in his uniform and how he got it, when he started beating one of the boys with his riding crop. Michael came along, stopped the beating, and dunked the fellow in the street's horse trough, new uniform and all, much to the amusement of the boys and a good-sized crowd.

"The result was that assault charges were filed against Michael. The Justice of the Peace chose to give him a choice: join up or go to jail. He chose to join up. I still might have refused him, but he and his family are very well regarded in Lowell; except by the local banker, I would guess. I have not regretted my decision."

"And I, for one," interjected Congressman Kellogg, "am most grateful for your decision, Captain. It seems, Michael, that you make a habit of rescuing people in distress. Let me propose a toast, ladies and gentlemen, to Corporal Drieborg and the men of Michigan's Sixth Cavalry Regiment. May God protect them from harm and grant them victory over our enemies!"

"Hear, hear!"

"Congressman, would I be pushing the bonds of hospitality if I asked our guest of honor another question?" asked Congressman Roberts of Illinois.

"I'm not sure I could stop you if I wanted to, Tom," responded Kellogg. "But it's up to Michael, surely."

"Michael?"

"Certainly, sir," he answered.

"Do you think this war is about slavery, Corporal?" asked the Illinois Congressman.

"It might be for some, sir. It's not my reason for fighting," Michael responded. "And, I haven't heard any of the five troopers in my squad talk much about slavery. For that matter, no one in my entire Troop has talked about it at all.

"I don't think any of us had ever seen a Negro before we came to Washington. So, even though there may be other reasons for joining, all of us think we are fighting to preserve the Union, like Mr. Lincoln said. But sir, I personally think slavery is wrong. I sure wouldn't want slaves in Michigan. Even if what I read in that book *Uncle Tom's Cabin* is made up, the very idea of slavery just bothers me."

"Are books widely circulated in Michigan Corporal?" asked another guest.

"Well, I can't speak for the entire state of Michigan, but we have a nice library in Lowell. My mother insisted we stop there on our Saturday morning trips to town. At home, each of us took turns reading most every night. Usually we read the Bible, though."

Captain Hyser spoke up. "Readers, musicians, storytellers, and singers are in great demand in our camp, mum. Michael happens to be an excellent reader. He is often called upon to write letters for those troopers who cannot do so very well. That said, I must tell you that most all of my men are literate. Still, you can find groups listening to readers throughout camp most every night. The novels of Dickens are the current favorites, after the Bible."

The guests were served the main meal, followed by dessert. While they ate, they visited quietly. Michael and Patricia continued to get acquainted.

"Will I see you again, Corporal?" she asked him very quietly.

"I would like that very much, Miss Kellogg. I am at somewhat of a disadvantage, being a lowly enlisted man with a war going on. What would you suggest?"

"Possibly, I could join you when you visit one of those buildings you told me about," she suggested. "I live here in Washington and have not even been to the Smithsonian. That's the one you told me about, I think. Could you show it to me sometime?"

"It would be my pleasure," he answered. "But on one condition."

"What's that?"

"That you immediately start to call me by my first name, Michael." She smiled.

"I accept! But you then will have to use my first name, Patricia."

"That's fine with me. But before dinner is served, Patricia," Mike asked, "could you tell me what all these spoons and forks are for, please? We eat with them at home, of course, but only one of each. I've never seen this many at one meal for one person."

Patricia held her hand up to her mouth to hide her quiet chuckle from the other guests at the table.

"Young woman," Mike chided, smiling, "are you laughing at me? And here I am, suffering in ignorance and fear."

"Fear?" Patricia said, pretending to be shocked. "I can't imagine a brave member of our Michigan cavalry is sitting at this table, in fear."

"Well, maybe not fear. But I'm afraid of making a mistake."

"Excuse me Michael, I forgot my manners. Each of these spoons and each of these forks are used for a different dish being served tonight. First, we will be served soup. So, we will use the somewhat larger spoon on the outside. As the meal progresses to a salad served on its own plate, we will begin to use the forks. Pick up the one on the outside first."

She covered his hand with hers. "I know. Just follow my lead. Wait for me to pick one up, and do the same." She returned his intent stare with a bright smile. "Will that be all right?"

"Thank you, Patricia," Mike responded, staring into her blue eyes. "That would be fine."

And it was. From the soup and salad to the main courses of fowl and pork with the side dishes of cooked vegetables, Patricia patiently led Michael through the utensils.

Even when wine was poured for each guest, she led him by sipping small amounts throughout the meal and after each toast. Michael hoped his father would understand why he had broken his promise not to drink alcohol.

The last of the forks was used for chocolate cake; and the last of the three spoons was used for stirring cream and sugar in their coffee.

"Gentlemen, let us have our cigars and brandy in my library," suggested Kellogg.

Before the men left the dining room, Captain Hyser addressed the Congressman. "Sir, General Scott, gentlemen, and ladies, I must ask to be excused. The corporal and I must report for picket duty at dawn tomorrow. So, with your permission, we regretfully must leave."

Thanks, were expressed, and goodbyes given to all.

"Remember your promise, Michael," Patricia whispered, walking him to the door.

"What promise was that, Patricia?" He looked at her, a bit puzzled.

"You promised to take me to the Smithsonian Museum."

"Oh, yes," Mike said, somewhat embarrassed. "I didn't actually forget Patricia. But I'm just so dazzled by your beauty that it flew out of my mind for the moment. Out on patrol duty tomorrow, in all that snow and danger, I would have thought of you and remembered my promise then."

"Such nonsense! You had better leave, Corporal, before I give you a good sock," Patricia said in mock anger.

After Captain Hyser and Corporal Drieborg left the Kellogg residence, the other dinner guests followed the Congressman into his study for cigars.

"A well-spoken young man, Kellogg," General Scott commented.

"Captain Hyser is correct in regarding him highly. If you don't make him your military Aide, I might steal him from Hyser myself. Lord knows, I could use his freshness, honesty and leadership around my office."

The Drieborg Family Debt

As the two men rode out of the city to their Regimental encampment three miles away; a light rain was trying to become snow. Since their ride to the Kellogg home three hours ago, the temperature had dropped, and a brisk wind blew at their backs. Nevertheless, they were both warm in their greatcoats. Turning in his saddle, Mike could still see the street lamps of Washington behind them.

"I wonder; will I ever see Patricia again?"

"Well, Drieborg, what did you think of this evening's experience?" asked Captain Hyser.

"Sir, I haven't quite sorted it all out yet," related Drieborg. "Everything was such a new experience for me. I was sort of overwhelmed by it all, and still am a bit. One thing is for sure. Patricia Kellogg looks a whole lot better without all that mud on her. She's not only beautiful, but a very nice person, too. She took my arm and escorted me to each guest during the introductions. And at the supper table, she quickly noticed how confused I was by almost everything there. I had no idea which utensil or glass to use next, or how to handle the wine drink they served. She guided me by example through the entire meal. Without her help, I would have made a fool of myself."

"It seemed to me, Corporal that you handled yourself very well. Your responses to the questions of General Scott and the guests at the dinner table were excellent. I was proud of you, son."

"Thank you, sir. And thank you for explaining how I came to enlist in the Regiment. They seemed shocked when I told them it was either enlist or go to jail for assault. Do you think your explanation took care of it?"

"Yes, I do. They were surprised when you told them about the choice you were given. They were shocked too, probably. But when I told them the circumstances, I believe they were satisfied. In fact, I feel their respect for you increased, not diminished."

"Patricia Kellogg asked me to call on her, too," Michael revealed. "That was terrific to hear. I'm not sure how to arrange that properly, but I intend to find out."

"I might as well tell you something else, Hyser continued. "Congressman Kellogg has asked my permission to talk with you about becoming his military Aide. He has taken a shine to you, Drieborg. Your conduct tonight, and the obvious approval of his daughter, I might add, should only increase his interest in you for that position. It would also mean a promotion to the rank of second lieutenant. What would you think of his offer, Corporal?"

"I don't know what to say, sir," responded Michael. "I think that his offer is a big compliment. I was surprised to even be invited to the home of such an important man. But this! My mother would sure like to see me safe in Washington instead of on a horse fighting rebs. But I don't know if I could leave the men of my squad or Sergeant Riley and the platoon, just when we are about to fight for the first time. Well, anyway, those are the first things that come to mind, sir. What do you think I should do?"

"Well son, first off, I suggest that you don't talk to anyone about this possible offer just now. He hasn't asked yet. If and when he does ask, he will do it in my presence. Listen respectfully of course. If you're not ready to give him an answer right off, you could ask him for some time to think about it. Then, if you wish, discuss the matter privately with Sergeant Riley. I believe him to be a wise man. I know you have great respect for him, too. Of course, you can discuss the matter with me as well."

"Thank you, sir."

***

By the time, Captain Hyser and Michael returned to the encampment, it was almost midnight. They would be on Picket duty very early in the morning.

Once inside his squad's darkened quarters, Michael struggled to find his sleeping area. In the murky light of the fire pit, he stepped on someone.

"Hey. Is that you, Drieborg? Get off me, for crying out loud!"

"I'm sorry, George," Mike whispered. "I tripped in the dark. Shush. You'll wake everyone."

He shed his greatcoat and boots, but decided to sleep in his clothing. He was just too tired to bother taking them off. He would live in them for the next two days, anyway. He found an empty spot, lay down and pulled his blanket over himself. He had no trouble falling asleep that night. Six house later, the bugler sounded reveille.

"Can't be time to get up already," Michael moaned. But the sound of the bugle continued.

"Well, well, what have we here?" Stan said in a mocking tone of voice. "The party boy found his way back. We thought they might have kept you all for themselves. What time did you stop hobnobbing with the rich and powerful last night?"

Mike sat up, still half-asleep. "I'll tell all you about it later. Right now, I'm still too tired to even think. You guys had all of last night to get your stuff ready. I only have a few minutes, so get out of my way, Killeen."

"Well, excuse us," retorted George. "Aren't we cranky this morning?"

***

Two hours later Mike's Troop arrived at their assigned area. He and Swede were on patrol for the first two hours. Back in camp for four hours, they set up their dog tent, ate, and got some rest. Before the first day ended though, Mike took advantage of a break to write home.

Dear Family,

I hope this letter finds you all well. I am fine. I am writing this letter while on patrol duty. The water spots on this paper are from the wet snow. Winter here is warmer than in Lowell. A lot less snow, too. What snow we do have melts fast. So, we mostly have mud all the time. Think I'd rather have the ground frozen like back home.

I can't remember if I told you, but when Swede and I were in town last week, I saw a wagon bearing down on a girl crossing the street. I ran out and pushed her out of the way. Turns out, she is the daughter of our Congressman, a man named Kellogg. Well, he told Captain Hyser to bring me to a dinner last Saturday at his home.

What a house! It was huge. Ours would fit into their living room alone. We cleaned our boots in a little room by the front door called a foyer, but I still hated to walk on the beautiful carpets. There, I met General Scott. He commands all the Union forces. That was sure a surprise. At the dinner table, several other important men were present with their wives. Patricia, the Congressman's daughter, helped me figure out which fork or spoon to use with what food. The food was not as tasty as yours, Mamma, and not very filling. But I enjoyed Patricia's company a lot.

They served wine with the meal, Papa. I hope you won't be mad, but I followed Patricia's example and just sipped a little as I ate like she did. I only did it to be polite. The wine tasted a bit bitter, actually. I mostly drank water with my meal.

I will write you about the rest soon.

Love to all,

Michael

***

After I Troop returned from patrol, Mike was summoned to Regimental headquarters.

"What in heaven's name could they want with me?" Michael wondered. *"Would the Colonel want to see me about that congressional aide business*

"Captain Hyser mentioned to me on our way back to camp from Congressman Kellogg's home? I'll soon know."

"Sergeant Drieborg reporting as ordered sir." He announced to the staff officer.

Mike was quickly ushered into his Regimental commander's office. There he found his Troop commander, Captain Hyser, his Regimental commander, Colonel Alger, and Congressman Kellogg.

He stood at attention.

"At ease Sergeant; please be seated," directed Colonel Alger. Mike took a chair opposite the three men. "I think you have met the Congressman, Sergeant. Of course, you know Captain Hyser. The Congressman has something to ask of you."

"Thank you, Colonel," Kellogg began. "First, let me congratulate you on your promotion to the rank of sergeant. I am really here to ask you to accept a position as my military Aide. This appointment would mean a promotion to second lieutenant and a considerable increase in pay, too. I need an Aide upon whom I can depend. I think you are that man. It would mean that you will be stationed here in Washington City and work in my offices here. What do you think of the offer, Sergeant?"

"Captain, do you think I should accept?" Mike asked.

Captain Hyser nodded. "It is a fine opportunity for you, Mike. Even though I would hate to see you leave my Troop, I do recommend that you accept."

Colonel Alger agreed with him.

"Thank you, sir," Mike responded. He turned his attention to Congressman Kellogg. "I appreciate the offer. However, if I accepted, it would be like deserting the men of my squad just as we are to meet the enemy. I can't do that, sir."

The Congressman stood and faced Michael, who stood in front of his own chair. The two men shook hands. "Is that your final decision, Michael?" he asked, still gripping Drieborg's hand.

"Yes, sir. It is."

"That's too bad. I believe you to be a young man of fine character. I regret your decision, but I respect it. God bless you, son."

"Thank you, sir," Mike responded.

Colonel Alger ended the interview, "You are dismissed, Sergeant."

***

Mike left his Regimental commander's office and returned to his squad's quarters.

"What's this business of you visiting the high and mighty again, Mike?" chided Stan. "First you get invited to a congressman's fancy house, then you get promoted to sergeant. And now you go visiting the commander of the whole Regiment. A'fore you know it, we'll have to call you 'sir.'"

"I'm just as surprised about all of this as you are, Stan," Mike responded, sitting down by the fire pit. "Anyway, you might just as well hear the whole thing from me, first."

Mike explained the entire business to them, including his refusal.

"Let me get this straight Drieborg," interrupted Killeen. "You turned down a big promotion and a cushy job here in Washington because you thought we needed you?"

"Not actually need me, Stan," Mike said defensively. "But it did make me feel like I'd be deserting the squad, just as we got close to the Rebs."

"Well, well," Stan cut in again. "I can't say that I feel safer knowing you will hang around. Actually, I think you're a damned fool for turning it down. That's what I think."

All the squad members began to chime in. Most were thankful that Mike was sticking around, even though they all thought he should have accepted the offer.

"Well," Mike concluded, "it's too late now. I refused, and you're stuck with me."

***

That night, during their evening meal, Congressman Kellogg told his daughter Patricia that Michael had refused his offer of the Aide appointment.

"Why did Michael refuse your offer father?" asked Patricia.

"He has the idiotic notion of loyalty to his squad. He believes they need him or something. He thinks they depend upon him. He feels that by accepting my offer he would be deserting them. Colonel Alger told me after Michael left that such a bond between soldiers is common and very essential to the men's fighting spirit.

"It didn't help that Captain Hyser made him a sergeant. Whatever Michael's reason, it is misguided. I don't intend to allow him to make such a mistake. Besides, I usually get what I want, and I want him as my Aide. The War Department could be made to assign him to me. But I want him to volunteer for this assignment. I'll find a way. It may take some time, but I will have him."

***

"Patricia, remember our conversation a few weeks ago about that Drieborg boy refusing to become my Aide?" asked Congressman Kellogg.

"Yes, Father. I also remember that you said he would eventually accept your offer. Has he?"

"Not yet. But I have information that will change his mind. When he was our dinner guest, his Troop commander explained to us the circumstances of his enlistment. You remember? He was told by the Justice of the Peace, enlist or go to jail for assault. Anyway, the assaulted person is the son of Herbie Bacon, owner of the Lowell bank. It seems his son was an officer in the same Regiment Drieborg was required to join. Bacon carried over his bad feelings toward Michael to their Regimental training area in Grand Rapids.

"Eventually he ordered some of his men to assault Drieborg. An officer from Drieborg's Troop helped set the whole thing up. As you might guess, Michael beat them off. The Troopers involved testified against the officers at a military court-martial.

"The court-martial was justified in its decision to dishonorably discharge Bacon's son and the other officer. I'm told that the repercussions in Lowell were quite severe.

"It seems that Bacon had often used his power as bank owner to dominate farmers and townspeople. And the son had been a problem in the community for years, too. So, the people of Lowell took some pleasure seeing young Bacon get into trouble from which his father could not rescue him. The kid was given a dishonorable discharge and a year in the military prison at Detroit.

"Bacon bought his son an early release, and now the kid is a drunk and a continuing embarrassment to his parents. I am told they blame Michael for all of it. So, Bacon had his bank demand the full payment of the Drieborg's farm mortgage. Now, instead of an annual payment, the entire amount of the note is due before the next harvest. Consequently, Michael's family will probably lose their farm.

"My people tell me that Bacon is not interested in the money. It's revenge he's seeking. By doing this to the Drieborg family, he can also remind everyone just what can happen to them if they displease him."

"Why are you telling me this, father?" Patricia asked. "What has it to do with Michael becoming your Aide?" Patricia considered her father's words for a moment.

"Oh, Father! How could you? You intend to use their problem to your advantage!"

"Now look young lady. Michael's parents are going to lose their farm.

"I have checked all of this very carefully. Despite Mr. Drieborg's reputation as an excellent farmer, even a good crop bringing wartime prices will not supply him with the funds he needs to pay the balance of the bank note by the time it's due. And no other banker in that area will lend money against another banker's wishes.

"I want Michael as my Aide. I am sure he wants to help his parents in their time of need. So, I will lend him the funds his father needs. He remains my Aide until the note is repaid. We both get what we want. What is so terrible about that, Patricia?"

"The way you put it father, nothing," his daughter admitted. "But it just seems you're taking advantage of him somehow."

Dear Michael,

Everyone here is in good health. I hope you are, too. Little Jake is doing well in school and will be helping Papa with the planting come spring. I am helping Papa with the milking. Can you just see me? Ann is working on another pair of socks for you. She is also helping with the sheep a lot.

At Sunday church, the pastor read an article from the Grand Rapids Eagle to the entire congregation about how you saved the Congressman's daughter. To one of the other men, I heard Papa say, "Well, he is a Drieborg." We are all proud of you Michael.

Did you get the package we sent you? Easter is early this year. I hope it will get to you before Easter Sunday. Papa is working hard as usual. I know he misses you very much, Michael, and he worries about you, too. We all do.

Papa would not ever tell you, Michael, but you are the oldest and a man now, so you should know. Mr. Bacon, at the bank, has told Papa we have to pay off our loan from the bank this fall. Papa has made the payments for ten years now. All of them have been on time. Papa has not told me how much we still owe. But even with the higher prices and a good harvest of wheat, corn, and wool, Mamma says they cannot pay the note off by this fall. Then the bank will take the farm. We would lose everything.

Mr. King at the elevator told Papa that the banker is getting even for his son. You were not here, but when his son was kicked out of the Army, it was a big disgrace here in Lowell. And Bacon's father blames you.

Papa cannot go to another bank, either. No bank outside of Lowell will lend money to anyone here. Bacon has seen to that. Mamma is very upset about this. Do you have any ideas of what we can do? Sorry about this bad news. We love you and pray for you.

Love,

Susan

Life as a Congressional Aide

Mike and Stan were alone in their quarters.

"Listen to this, Stan," Mike asked. "Congressman Kellogg's Aide, a guy by the name of George Krupp, asked me to come to his office to discuss a possible solution to my family's debt problem. What do you think that means? How does he even know about it?"

"Beats me," Stan replied. "Probably wants to offer to throw that Lowell banker in front of a runaway wagon. Sort of like repayment for you saving his daughter from a runaway wagon here in Washington."

"That's very funny Stan. I can't say I would be sorry for that to happen, though."

"No time to check it out now anyway," Stan reminded him. "We're due on picket duty in a couple hours, and we're gone for the next two days."

"I'll check it out when we return."

Three days later, Mike's squad had time to go into the city, so he was at the Capitol building early, looking for Congressman Kellogg's office.

A uniformed soldier sat at a desk just inside the building's entrance. Mike approached the seated man.

"Can I help you, Sergeant?" the man asked.

"Yes, you can. My name is Michael Drieborg. I was asked by Congressman Kellogg's Aide, George Krupp, to see him here. Could you direct me to his office?"

"Wait here, please. We have to be very careful nowadays. The capital is full of southern sympathizers, it seems. I'll send someone to tell Mr. Krupp that you are here." With that he passed a note to another soldier and then motioned Mike to a row of chairs.

Shortly thereafter, the messenger returned with another man in civilian clothing.

"Sergeant Drieborg," the man said, "it's nice to see you again. You might remember that we met at the Congressman's home."

"Yes, Mr. Krupp, I remember." Mike took the man's outstretched hand.

"Let's go to my office, Sergeant," he suggested. "It's right down this hallway."

Once seated, Mr. Krupp began, "I'm sorry the Congressman is not here today. But he asked me to talk with you about his interest in helping your family with that note the Lowell Bank has called in. Is that all right with you, Sergeant?"

"Yes, it is," Mike responded. "I haven't heard from my family this week, so I assume the problem is still unresolved."

"You are aware of the Congressman's gratitude for saving his daughter's life," Krupp continued, "so this is not too complicated. He would like to help you help your family. To do that, he is willing to lend you the money you need to pay the note. What is your reaction to that offer?"

"That would certainly solve the debt problem my parents have, Mr. Krupp. But it would create another debt. How could I possibly repay the loan on a sergeant's pay?"

"You certainly go right to the heart of the matter, don't you?" Krupp chuckled. "Your observation is correct. It would be very difficult on a sergeant's pay. But, not so hard on a second lieutenant's pay."

Both men sat silently.

"The Congressman usually gets what he wants, doesn't he?" Mike commented.

"Yes, he does. Does that bother you so much that you would pass up this opportunity to save your parents' farm?"

"It doesn't bother me at all. Almost non of this troubles me, Mr. Krupp. If I recall correctly, the rank of second lieutenant comes with the job of aide to a Congressman. So, you best tell me what my duties as an aide would be."

"So, am I correct in assuming you will accept both the job as the Congressman's military aide and his offer of a loan sufficient to pay your parents' debt?"

"Yes, on both counts."

"Fine, Mike," Krupp told him. "I know the exact amount of the mortgage your parents owe. You will be given that amount when you sign a personal note which the Congressman will hold until you pay it off. You will not be charged any interest. After you get settled here in Washington, you will begin to pay fifty dollars a month on the debt. As far as your reassignment and promotion are concerned, we will take care of the details. You can plan on reporting here two weeks from today. You will be expected to be in be in proper uniform then. Is that all clear?"

"Whoa. Slow down here," Mike almost shouted. "For starters, I'd like to explain all of this to my Troop commander and the men of my squad, if you don't mind. And how am I supposed to pay the note in Lowell with me here in Washington? Where do I get the proper clothing; and housing, too? I don't know that much about this town."

"Sorry, Mike, I probably was going a bit fast on this," Krupp admitted. "We can do this more slowly. But the Congressman wants you to begin as soon as possible. So, let's go over each step one at a time, together. And call me George, now that we are going to be working together."

***

Mike did not want to leave his platoon, especially not his friends in the squad. Telling them was the hardest part. He met with them in their winter shelter. Everyone in the squad was there.

"Let me get this straight, Drieborg," Stan Killeen began. "You're going to leave us to become an officer. Do I have it right so far?"

"Yes, you do," Mike allowed.

"You're doing that because Bacon's old man is calling in your father's note at the Lowell Bank. The Congressman is loaning you the money to pay this debt. And, in exchange, you agreed to become his military aide and look after his beautiful daughter, who you saved from getting killed by a runaway wagon. Is that it?"

"Yes, that's it," Mike answered.

Bill Anderson broke the sudden silence. "Mike, you had no choice, in my opinion. Your folks would have lost everything, otherwise. Actually, I think it was fortunate that the Congressman was willing to loan you the funds to save your family. I'll sure miss you. But I understand, and I wish you well."

"You wouldn't need an assistant, would you, Mike?" asked George Neal. "I never did like riding horses much."

"God bless you, Mike," Dave added. "You watch out for these Washington types. I think I'd rather face the Rebs than face the crowd of vultures I read about who prey on each other here in Washington."

Mike stood and shook hands with each of the men. Before leaving, he said, "I hope you all believe I would never have agreed to this if it had not been for what Bacon threatened to do to my folks."

"Will you look after my horse Swede?"

"Sure Mike, don't vorry about it," he assured him. "I vill miss you fer sure."

As he was gathering his gear, he heard a familiar voice.

"Ya weren't going to leave without having' a word with me, were ya Lieutenant Drieborg?" Sgt. Riley said from the doorway of the shelter.

"Wouldn't think of it, Sergeant," Mike replied, turning around. "I hope you know how much I hate leaving."

Riley shook Mike's hand. "A' course I do, laddie. If the Rebs knew about ya, they'd be paying the Congressman to pull ya out of this fighting unit. We'll be missing ya for sure."

"Thanks, Sarge," Mike responded with a smile in spite of his sadness. "I appreciate all that you have done for me."

"Watch yer back in this town, lad," Riley concluded, still holding Mike's hand. "It has been a pleasure watching ya lead your men."

***

Congressman Kellogg's office in the nation's Capital was somberly decorated to suit the times. Dark walnut wood and gray painted walls were not intended to lift one's spirits. Nevertheless, a table in the broad hallway was filled with food and good wine.

The occasion was the introduction of Michael Drieborg, recently made a second lieutenant, as Congressman Kellogg's new aide. Other congressmen and their staff members had been coming by for some time to meet the newcomer and to sample the food and drink.

"Well, Michael, how has your first day gone?" asked Kellogg.

"Fine sir. Mr. Krupp has introduced me to more people in one day than I have met in my entire life. As the person in charge of your office here, I assume he will be directing my work, as well."

"That's correct. Each morning he will give you your assignments for the day. You will also be working on projects that will require days and even weeks to accomplish. He will supervise that, too."

Kellogg drew Michael aside into his private office and shut the door. "There is another responsibility I want to ask you to consider accepting that George will not direct," the Congressman began. "Let me first give you a little background.

"As you might know, Patricia's mother died several years ago. Now that she has grown some, Patricia acts as my hostess for the social events at our home and accompanies me to some social events that I must attend outside my home. Now that she is sixteen, I want her to take an even more active role in this regard.

"You have also noticed, I'm sure, that Patricia is a beautiful young lady. She is also very intelligent. But she has yet to be in the world outside our home much. I hesitate to allow her to be escorted by the type of men I see around this town. Washington City is full of ambitious men who would try to use her in an instant if they thought it would help their career. I can't allow that. Can you understand that, son?"

"I think so sir. My parents depended upon me to look after my two sisters all the time. I think I understand your concern."

"Good. The other part of my concern is that I don't want to isolate Patricia from society just because I'm afraid for her. She needs to get out and learn of life outside my home. So, I need a man who I can trust, a man she can trust, someone who will look after her. I need a man who will be her escort at social events, both at our home and around the city.

"I know that you accepted the position as my military Aide only to save your parents' farm, Mike. And, I know that you have no interest in a Washington career or the power I have. I also feel that you would much rather be with your unit fighting the Rebs. So, I trust your motives. Everything I have come to know about you tells me that you are an honorable man, too. Are you the man I can trust Patricia with, Michael?"

"Yes, sir. You can, without any question."

"Then will you accept this responsibility, too?"

"Yes, sir. I will."

"Now, with that settled, let me introduce you to a few very important people. They need to know how much I think of you, and I want them to hear it from me."

They left the privacy of Kellogg's office and returned to the wide hallway and the guests.

"Congressman Smith, let me introduce you to my new aide, Michael Drieborg."

"It's nice to meet you, son. I hear you hail from the same community as your new boss. A cavalryman, too, I see. Welcome to Congress."

"Thank you, sir."

"This is another George for you to meet, Michael," the Congressman told him. "He is Congressman Smith's aide. I have asked this George, George Kelley, to show you around the capital and help you get settled in a room here in town."

"Nice to meet you, Mike," George broke in. "If you don't have a place yet, you can bunk with me temporarily. We could move your gear this afternoon and start your education here tomorrow. Sound okay?"

"That's great, George," Mike answered. "I should check tomorrow's schedule with Mr. Krupp first. But it sounds fine to me."

"You had better check your schedule with me as well, Lieutenant Drieborg, if you know what's good for you," interrupted Patricia, who had silently come up behind the men.

"Guess I have more than one boss around here," Mike retorted. "Can I get something for you to drink, Patricia? Congressman, may I refresh your wine glass, sir?"

With that, Mike retreated to the wine table. He returned with fresh glasses of wine for each member of the group except Patricia. He handed her a glass of punch.

"Where is my glass of wine, Lieutenant?" she asked.

"I'm just following orders from the Congressman," Mike responded politely. "He has given me direct orders to protect you from demon rum. In this case, wine."

"Father!" she fumed.

"I did tell him that. And he is right."

"Allow me to offer a toast," suggested Congressman Smith. "Wait. Where is your wine, Lieutenant Drieborg? Don't tell me Kellogg has brought a teetotaler into our midst?"

"Don't worry sir," said George Kelley. "I'll educate Mike properly on that score before long."

"Be careful there, George," cautioned Congressman Kellogg. "I sort of like this young man just as he is."

Congressman Smith raised his glass. "A toast to the beautiful Miss Patricia Kellogg and to the new lieutenant, Michael Drieborg."

Meeting Captain Hayes

Now that Michael was formally appointed to Congressman Kellogg's staff as his military Aide, it was necessary for him to report to Captain Hayes, the staff director for the Joint Committee on the Conduct of the war.

Standing five-foot-ten inches tall and weighing one hundred and ninety pounds, Hayes was a dark-haired Ohioan with fashionable pork-chop sideburns which disappeared into a bushy mustache. Despite a bit of a pot-belly, he was well groomed and carried himself well.

"Watch out for that guy Hayes Mike," George Krupp had confided. "I've been in charge of this office for three years and have seen a lot of shady characters around Congress. Hayes is definitely in that category. Political pull from someone in his home state of Ohio got him appointed to the committee right after the war began. Since he has been in charge, he has used his rank to abuse those under his command and earned a reputation as a carouser and a liar. Don't trust him, Mike."

Within a few days, Lt. Drieborg went to the offices of the armed services committee. He knocked on the door of Captain Hayes.

"Come in," he heard. Once inside the office, Mike introduced himself and stood at attention in front of the Captain's desk. Hayes stood up, unsmiling.

"So, you're the new guy," snarled Hayes. "Up front, farm boy, you best know one thing for sure. I am the hardass you must deal with around here. Screw with me, and you will be dead meat at the front lines fighting Rebs. Understood?"

"Yes, sir," Mike responded, still at attention. "Can I have the committee schedule I was sent to get, sir?"

"Don't get smart with me, kiddo." Hayes picked up the paperwork Mike requested. "Here's the committee schedule. By the way, all the committee's military aides are taking me to supper at Molly's this Thursday. It's a place on Hooker Street. Ask the other aides for directions. You are expected to be there at seven sharp. Bring some money with you. For now, Drieborg, you are dismissed."

Returning to Kellogg's offices, Mike went directly to Krupp.

"Wow!" Mike exclaimed. "You told me not to trust the man. But, is he always such a bastard, too?"

"Now you know, Mike," responded Krupp. "He's an all-around bad apple. Did he tell you about his famous suppers?"

"Yes," responded Mike. "What is that all about?"

"It's just his way to get you to pay for his night out and intimidate you at the same time. Remember, be careful of him."

"Well, I think I have a problem with him already. The night he ordered me to join him and the other aides, I am to escort the Congressman's daughter Patricia to an evening dinner party. How do I handle that with Hayes?"

"I'll take care of it this time. Hayes will soon get the message that you have evening duties, and that he's not going to use you the way he does the others."

***

Michael was at the Kellogg residence working with Patricia Kellogg on the final arrangements for a reception to be held in their home. The routine they had developed over the last few weeks had them working in a room off the front hall with the door open. They sat on opposite sides of a small round table close to high windows on the street side of the room. There was good natural light there. They had finished the invitations for a dinner party the Congressman planned to hold in his home soon. Patricia surprised Michael with a question about Captain Hayes.

"So, Michael," she asked, "what do you think of the captain inviting me to attend a play with him?"

"Patricia, you're not really going to accept this guy's invitation, are you? I know he is well groomed and is pretty good looking and all, but I've seen him operate. He uses his authority to bully others of lesser rank. George Krupp told me that the man drinks a lot, spends time down on Hooker Avenue, and is generally considered of poor character."

"Michael you're just jealous because I might prefer that he, not you, escort me to a social event," responded Patricia with some vehemence. "And yes, I think he appears a gentleman. I met him at a social luncheon before you became my father's aide. He made a good impression. I like him. Maybe a lot."

"I must admit that it would be easy to become jealous where you are concerned, Patricia."

"Then why haven't you done anything about it?"

"Because your father asked me to look after you, not date you. To me, there is a big difference."

"Michael," Patricia fumed, "I am so sick of your attention to me being the result of an order from my father, I could just scream."

***

A few days later, Mike was walking down the wide hallway of the congressional office building. Captain Hayes noticed him. "Drieborg, I want to see you in my office."

Mike followed Hayes down the hall. "Yes sir," he responded as he entered the office used by Captain Hayes.

"Close the door. Sit and relax, Drieborg. We might have gotten off to a rough start, so I just want to talk a bit, get better acquainted. You have a problem with that?"

"Not at all Captain." He sat as directed in front of Hayes's desk. He did not feel at all comfortable with the door closed, but he had little control when ordered by a superior officer.

Hayes came around from behind his desk and took a chair a couple of feet from Drieborg's. He leaned forward, elbows on his knees.

"You're pretty close to the Kellogg family, I suppose," Hayes commented. "You rescued his daughter from certain injury, possibly death. So, the Congressman trusts you, it seems. He trusts you enough to allow you to spend a good deal of time alone with Patricia, his daughter. Tell me, Drieborg, how is she in bed? Is she as hot as she looks?"

Drieborg was immediately out of his chair, his face up to Hayes's. "You, sleazy bastard," Mike hissed at him. "Stay away from Patricia Kellogg, or you will live to regret it!"

Hayes leaned back in his chair, smiling. "I'm not only going to find out just how good she is in bed, farm boy, I'm going to marry her," he said with a chuckle. "I'll have her and her daddy's power, too. And there is nothing you can do to stop me." With that, Hayes began to laugh.

Drieborg straightened up and stepped back.

"*Remember the promise you made to your father*," Michael thought. *Control your anger.* " Fists at his sides, Michael took a deep breath.

"You are baiting me to hit you, aren't you Captain?" Mike said, in control of his emotions now

"You'll not get a rise out of me that easily. Besides, even you must realize that there is probably a good reason you have not been invited to the Congressman's home. Nor have you been allowed to even present your card to her. Your Hooker Avenue reputation is so well known around this building that the only female you could get close to would probably have to be paid to do it. You can't believe Congressman Kellogg would allow his daughter to be seen in public with you, much less marry you. So, boast all you want, Captain. Those wild dreams of yours will never be realized."

Hayes's face showed his anger now. His hands gripped the arms of the wooden chair in which he was sitting. But he soon regained control of his emotions.

"We'll see Drieborg," he hissed. "You can be sure of one thing. Before you have that young lady for yourself, you'll be pushing up daises in some battlefield. I'll see to that. Now get out of here."

***

At breakfast, Patricia Kellogg brought up the subject of her being escorted to Washington, D.C., social events without her father.

"I thought you wanted Michael Drieborg as your military aide, Father."

"Yes Patricia, I did. And he is. What is the point of your question?"

"With all the time he spends working with me planning your social events, and with all the time he spends escorting me around to other social events, when does he have any time to be a military aide?"

The Congressman stopped eating his morning meal and sat back in his chair. "Do you object to Michael's help, Pat? Do you object to him as your escort?"

"No," she quickly responded. "But it seems like a job to Michael. It would be nice for a change if the person who escorts me is not ordered to do so but actually really wants to take me out."

"Have anyone in mind?"

"I met a captain recently at a luncheon who seemed nice. Yesterday, he sent me an invitation to attend a play at Ford's Theatre with him. Unlike your Aide, Michael, this captain actually wants to escort me. That would be nice for a change."

"Who is this nice captain?"

"His name is Captain Hayes. From the few minutes we spent talking, I observed him to be well groomed, good-looking, and well mannered."

"I see. Is this the same officer who works for my war committee, Patricia?"

"I believe he is, Father."

"This Captain Hayes you met briefly is a good-looking and well-groomed young man," he agreed. "But the Captain Hayes I know very well is definitely not a man of good character. So, young lady, you will not accept his invitation. And further, he will be informed that any future contact with my sixteen-year-old daughter will be most un-welcome."

"Father," Patricia angrily retorted, "when will you see that I have become a woman? I should be able to pick out my own escorts."

"And you will, my dear," her father assured her. "That day will come sooner than you believe. But you have not yet reached that day, and even when it comes, the escort will not be Captain Hayes."

***

When Michael reported for work the following day, he was told of some verbal fireworks the previous afternoon at a closed session of his committee.

"Good morning, Mike," George Krupp said. "Good morning to you, George."

"Since you were out of the office yesterday, you probably haven't heard the latest with Captain Hayes?"

"No, I haven't. What happened?"

"More reason for you to be careful of Hayes, I'm afraid."

"Why?"

"In front of the members of the War Committee, the Congressman told Hayes to stay away from his daughter. He told Hayes that if he made an attempt to contact her in any way, he'd find himself joining Grant's army in the West.

"Afterwards, Hayes let it be known through one his lackey aides that you probably influenced Congressman Kellogg to embarrass and threaten him. There's not much you can do about it at this point."

"Thanks for the warning, George."

***

Despite Patricia's resentment and frustration with her father's refusal to allow other men to take Michael's place as her escort, she and Michael continued to work together regularly and cordially at the Kellogg residence.

She was maturing into a beautiful and socially accomplished woman who wanted to see and be seen on the Washington social scene. As

Michael, her strikingly handsome escort, became more comfortable in Washington society, he began to enjoy rather than endure his escort duty. As a result, they both began to relax and enjoy one another's company.

The Congressman, ever worried about his motherless daughter, was very comfortable with Michael as her escort. So, he made working with his daughter and escorting her to social events an integral part of Michael's duties as his Aide.

For Michael, this had become very pleasant duty.

***

One afternoon at the Kellogg home, Michael was helping Patricia work on the invitation list and arrangements for an upcoming dinner party the Congressman was planning.

Working at their customary small table in the front sitting room, they sat across from one another. Patricia looked up at Michael.

"Michael, don't you think I'm pretty?"

"Of course, you are, Patricia. Actually, you're a beautiful girl," Mike responded with some surprise. "Why would you even doubt that?"

"I happen to be a woman, Michael, not a girl. And if I'm so beautiful, why do you act so standoffish toward me?"

"Standoffish?" Mike sputtered. "What in heaven's name does that mean?"

"It means that as often as we have been here alone or ridden side by side alone in a carriage, you have never given even a hint that you found me attractive or desirable."

A little too hotly, Mike said, "Let me tell you something, young lady, you are very attractive and desirable. So much so, that it is very difficult for me to even be around you like this. But I promised your father to look after you. So, how can I show my feelings for you and keep my promise to him? Answer me that, Pat!"

"Look here Michael Drieborg," Patricia snapped, sitting up straight with her hands on the table. "I know my father is your boss. But you let me take care of him. You just treat me as the desirable woman you say I am. Is that clear?"

Michael stood. He took one step toward Patricia and reached out his hand. She gripped it and was in his arms before he realized it. Despite his height, her lips were quickly upon his, and he pulled her body tightly to his chest.

The last time he had held her in his arms was several months ago. That was when he had roughly grabbed her and carried her out of the way of a runaway wagon. On that occasion, he landed in the muddy Washington street still holding her close.

Then, his heart beat wildly because of the excitement of the moment. This time, his heart seemed near to bursting with excitement caused by her lips and the feel of her warm body against his.

Patricia held his lips to hers with her hand behind his head. She had Mike hot with excitement. When she moved her hips against him, he was sure that she could feel his arousal. He felt his face flush in response to the touch of her hand on his neck, the smell of her perfume, and the pressure of her body against his. He didn't want it to end.

Then, he heard the kitchen door slam shut.

Evidently, Patricia heard the noise, too. Startled, they both broke their embrace. Patricia slipped back to her chair and looked down at her hands folded in her lap. Michael, still standing, turned to face the parlor door, expecting it to open. When it did, the cook, Mable, entered the room.

She was a stout, round-faced Negro lady who had helped raise Patricia from infancy. Now, she ran the Washington household along with her husband Adam, the butler. The way she paused in the doorway and looked at him, Michael felt certain she could see his startled expression and flushed face. He looked at Patricia sitting at the table and saw how red her cheeks were, too.

"You children may not realize it, but it is near suppertime," Mable announced. "The Congressman told me to have supper on the table by five o'clock sharp. So, I expect him any minute. Go wash up now. I'll not disappoint him. Go on now."

She was used to being obeyed in "her" house. So, she waited by the door and watched as Michael and Patricia obediently filed out of the sitting room.

Patricia went up the stairs to her second-floor bedroom. Michael headed for the main floor washroom. Once there, he splashed cool water on his hot face. It helped some. He just knew that Mable had noticed his flushed face.

Later, when he sat next to Patricia during the meal and noticed her perfume again, all the excitement of their embrace in the sitting room returned. He felt his face flush all over once more.

While Mable served the meal, he thought she looked suspiciously at him and Patricia several times.

Once the meal was finished, they talked with the Congressman about the dinner party plans they had been working on earlier that day. Michael yearned to spend some time with Patricia without Mable's interruption before he left for the evening. However, her father had other plans.

"I don't mean to rush you off this evening, Michael," he said, "but I need to go over some things tonight with Patricia. We have to discuss our annual Easter trip to Grand Rapids. I'll see you at the office tomorrow."

"Of course, sir, I understand," Mike responded respectfully. He stood behind his chair and turned to Patricia. "Good night, Patricia."

"Good night, Michael," she responded softly. "I enjoyed working with you this afternoon. Thank you for your help."

Her words got him thinking about what had actually happened that afternoon all over again.

"*What beautiful blue eyes she has,*" Michael thought as he left the house. "*That perfume of hers drives me crazy. It was probably just as well I had to leave before seeing her alone again tonight. The Congressman doesn't realize that the man I'm supposed to protect his innocent daughter from is me.*"

Before Patricia and Michael could see one another alone again, the congressional session had ended, and Patricia left Washington with her father for the Easter recess. They would not return from their home in Grand Rapids, Michigan, until the middle of May.

Bacon Returns: May 1863

Easter Sunday had come and gone. Congress was still in recess, so the workload for Aides like Michael had tapered off considerably. Reading military dispatches and checking contracts for military supplies was not very exciting.

He had spent a great deal of time with Patricia before they left for Michigan. He missed her. She and Congressman Kellogg would not return to Washington for another week or so.

This morning he was ordered to report to Captain Hayes. Not even George Krupp knew how Hayes had gotten his current assignment. He told Mike that it was probably in the early days of the war when everything was in chaos. *He's a good-looking fellow*, Michael thought. He had probably gotten his reddish complexion from all the whiskey it was rumored he drank. It was partially hidden by a bushy mustache.

Michael stood at attention in front of the very large desk the Captain sat behind.

"Lieutenant Drieborg reporting as ordered, sir."

"Took you long enough, Drieborg," Hayes retorted, sitting in a high-backed chair and facing Michael across the wide desk.

"Tonight, you are going to join me and the other house committee aides for dinner and a little fun. I've checked your schedule, so don't give me any crap about having to be at your congressman's house or something. They are out of town. You will meet me and the others in this office at five sharp. Do you have any questions?"

"No, sir."

"Good decision. You may be learning how to survive around here after all, Drieborg. Don't forget to bring some money. The aides pay, you know."

***

Early that evening Michael found himself with several other Aides. "Follow me, gentlemen," ordered Captain Hayes.

Hayes led the group of junior officers out of the building housing the congressional offices. Trailing him along the Hooker Avenue boardwalk, a fellow aide, Mike's current roommate Bill, asked, "Have you ever been to Hooker Avenue, Mike?"

"No, Bill, not my style," he responded. "Have you?"

"It can't be avoided if Hayes gets his hooks into you. So, yes, I've been there. If we don't go with him, and pay his tab, too, he threatens us with a transfer to a combat unit. I don't know if he could actually do it, but I'm not going to test him. You've been fortunate, Mike. Kellogg keeps you busy most evenings. That's not bad duty, either, with his beautiful daughter."

"My good luck ended with the congressional recess. The Congressman and that beautiful daughter of his are back in Michigan, so here I am."

The street they were on had been named after a rather famous Union General, Hooker. Dozens of houses lined both sides of the street where ladies of the evening entertained. The word was that in a few of these houses, the best food in Washington was served.

"Hayes usually takes us to Molly's place," Bill related. "Got to admit, the food is excellent. The girls are better looking than any I've seen in Ohio, too. Of course, they wear clothes back home."

As predicted, Captain Hayes led them to his favorite, Molly's. They were taken to a private room on the second floor. The only window was hidden with red drapery, and the walls of the room were covered with gold-colored paint and paintings of naked women. Gas-burning lights hung over each of the room's four tables.

Steaks were served with biscuits, potatoes, and gravy. The apple pie was tasty, too. Water was not in evidence, so most of the men in the room drank whiskey or beer with their meal. Mike had to agree with Bill. The food was very good.

Michael nursed a glass of wine. He had learned to handle a glass or two at the dinners held in the Kellogg home.

After the table was cleared, the women who had served the drinks and the meal reentered the room. This time, though, each girl wore only an unbuttoned, colorful knee-length shirt over her stockings and shoes. They gave a cigar to each man as they sat on his lap to light it. Michael did not take a cigar, but he did get a girl in his lap just the same.

She was a tall girl who easily filled her nightshirt. She had long reddish hair tied up on top of her head. Her very pale skin sported some freckles, too. Her green eyes sparkled with devilment, and her wide smile showed off her white teeth. Much to Michael's embarrassment, she threw her arm around his neck. Her shirt was open to her waist. Snuggling close, she pressed close to his chest and planted a kiss on his mouth.

"Drieborg!" shouted Hayes across the room. Breaking the kiss, Mike responded, "Yes, sir."

"Isn't that girl a beauty?" Hayes teased. "Her name is Janie. I think she likes you. She's enough to curl your socks, boy. I hardly had the strength to go into the office the next morning. Where's your cigar, boy?"

"I never developed a taste for tobacco, Captain," Michael responded while he attempted to hold Janie at bay.

"I thought all you farm people used chewing tobacco."

"People around our town need all their cash to pay their farm notes and buy supplies, if they gave the issue any thought at all. Farmers I know would consider tobacco an unnecessary luxury."

"Well, doesn't that beat all. Who knows what else we might learn this night? By the way, boys,"

Hayes announced, "You all will be pleased to hear that you won't have to pay for tonight's festivities. Even the cost of the girls has been taken care of."

"All right!" one of the aides shouted. The rest began to clap in appreciation.

"Actually, men," explained Hayes, "you can thank Drieborg for tonight's treat." He looked at Mike. "Puzzled, boy? It seems you have an admirer from your hometown in Michigan who is paying for our fun. Can you guess who that might be?

"Janie, why don't you go and ask Drieborg's friend to join us," Hayes directed. "Come right back, though. I think your farm boy here has developed a liking for you."

She left the room. When she reentered the room, she was holding the hand of Carl Bacon III.

"You should remember Mr. Bacon, your old buddy, don't you, Drieborg?" taunted Hayes.

Mike was stunned. What was happening here? He wondered how Carl had tracked him down.

"It seems you have been something of a hero back in your town. The local paper wrote all about you saving the Congressman's daughter. They also wrote about your promotion and your appointment as Kellogg's aide. Carl Bacon here was most interested in your progress. He visited me after your appointment and told me how you had mistreated him. He has been looking forward to this evening ever since. He even volunteered to pay for our fun tonight. He was doing it out of his regard for you, he said."

Mike stood up by his table, hardly hearing Hayes. Everyone in the room looked at the girls who were bringing Bacon to Hayes's table.

Janie returned to Mike's side. She held his arm and brushed against him. His face reddened in anger. It certainly was not passion.

"Come in, come in, Carl. Take a seat at my table here," Hayes suggested. "After all, you are the host of this party. Sit down, Drieborg. It's not polite to stare like that at our host."

Bacon finally spoke. "I told you I could get to you anytime I chose, farm boy," he boasted. "Believe me, I'll be on your back until the day you die."

"Gentlemen," Hayes said, rising from his chair. "Let us raise our glasses in a toast to Mr. Carl Bacon, our host."

Seated again, Mike tried to calm himself.

"What is this all about? The entire evening seems to be focused on me. Has Bacon been behind my problem with Hayes all along? What have they planned next?"

"Wait, Captain," Bacon interrupted. "Lieutenant Drieborg doesn't have a drink."

Michael had regained his composure. "I had my fill of wine with my dinner, thank you. But if they have cider here, I'll have a mug of that."

"The pretty young girl sitting in your lap, Drieborg, will fetch a cider for you. Won't you, Janie?" offered Hayes. "We can't have anyone here without something to drink."

With that, Janie slid off Michael's lap, but not before she gave him another quick kiss.

While she was gone, Michael noticed that the other girls were kissing their lap partners, too. Cigars had been long forgotten.

"Bacon has put Hayes up to something." Mike wondered *"How am I going to get through this night?"*

Sooner than he thought possible, Janie returned to his lap with a mug of warm cider.

"Have a drink, sweetie," she offered, putting the mug to his lips. Defensively, he took a swallow.

"Now gentlemen," Hayes directed. "Take a moment away from your companions. Let us offer a toast to Mr. Bacon. Don't forget that he is paying for your pleasures tonight."

With that, everyone raised their glasses and shouted, "Hear! Hear!" Everyone, including Mike, took a drink before sitting down.

"That a'way, honey." Janie said to Mike.

Michael tried to recoil, but the tall-back chair and Janie's hand behind his head prevented him from avoiding her offer without spilling his warm cider or dumping her on the floor.

"Come on, Drieborg," taunted Captain Hayes. "Don't be shy. Surely you farm boys know something about women. At least accept what our host Mr. Bacon has provided. Maybe you prefer the barn animals back home?"

Mike was able to jerk his head away from Janie for a moment. "No Captain," Michael responded. "Women are preferred, hands down. But I never have had to pay for a woman's attention."

With that, Michael pushed Janie completely off his lap.

She stood by his chair, hands on her hips, quite angry. "Hey, what's the matter with you anyway, buster?" she shouted.

"Don't take it personally, Janie," Carl Bacon interjected. "Drieborg here is considered sort of a saint, don't you know? But I suspect he has his hands full with that pretty girl he spends so much time with. She hot, Drieborg?" Bacon taunted him."

"With all due respect, Captain, for your host here," Michael said angrily, "Mr. Bacon should watch his mouth. It just might get him in trouble again."

"Are you threatening me, Drieborg?" asked Bacon, laying a pistol on the table in front of him.

"Now, now, Lieutenant, no need to threaten our host," Hayes said. "No need for you to feel uncomfortable, Mr. Bacon. I'll take care of Drieborg here."

Before Michael could respond or get up from his chair to challenge

Bacon, he suddenly felt dizzy and unable to move.

"It appears that Saint Drieborg can't hold his cider," commented Captain Hayes. "You will have to excuse the conduct of your friend Drieborg, Mr. Bacon. His lack of hospitality is only exceeded by his inability to stay sober."

"Or, maybe Janie got him too excited," laughed Tom, one of the aides at Mike's table.

"Could be Tom," observed Hayes. "You and Bill help Janie find a place for Drieborg to sleep it off. Here boys, give them a hand with the poor drunk. Excuse us, Mr. Bacon. All part of Drieborg's education, boys. But we will keep what happened here tonight inside our little group, won't we? If his drinking problem became known, it might land him back on a horse fighting Rebs. Look out it doesn't happen to you. Now, let's get back to the girls, eh boys?"

***

Michael awoke with a thunderous headache.

As he slowly sat up on the bed, he noticed he had no clothing on. Neither did red-headed girl, Janie, who was asleep beside him.

Holding his head, he wondered how he had gotten there last night from the private dining room. He swung his legs off the bed and sat there for a moment.

"I would remember undressing, wouldn't I? I certainly would remember being in bed with this girl! I can't remember either. Bacon and Hayes had taunted me about Patricia Kellogg. In anger, I pushed Janie from my lap and stood to confront them. From that point on, I remember nothing."

He slowly moved across the room to the dressing cabinet. He poured water from the room's pitcher into a basin and splashed water on his face. Then he dressed and headed to his quarters.

Mike discovered that he still had his money and pocket watch. He saw that it was five in the morning. At least he had three hours to rest and wash up before he had to be at work.

"My roommate Bill was at last night's affair. I'll ask him."

Confrontation: June 1863

The Congressman and his daughter Patricia were seated at their dining room table. There was quite a stack of mail piled in front of each of them. His office manager, George Krupp, had sorted it and delivered it upon their return from their Easter trip to Grand Rapids, Michigan. They had divided it between them this morning and were busy opening envelopes. Most of it involved an upcoming dinner party they were hosting. It would be their first since Congress reconvened.

"Oh, my goodness," Patricia exclaimed. "Look at this, Father." She was visibly upset and flushed.

"What is it?" her father said as he picked up the letter she had dropped in front of her.

He read without comment.

Finished, he looked at Patricia. "I wouldn't take this too seriously, sweetheart," he said softly. "If I paid attention to every crank letter my office received, it would drive me crazy. I have enemies, too, you know. I'm happy you don't hear what they say about me behind my back. It's pretty terrible. Most of what they say are lies, I am pleased to report. But look, the letter is not even signed."

"I'm sorry, father," she replied. "I just can't dismiss the thought of Michael carousing on Hooker Street. It would appear he ran down there as soon as we left town. How could he?"

"I'd give him a chance, if I were you," her father advised. "At least hear him out."

"I don't know, Father," she said angrily. "Please keep him away from here for a while." She stood up and left the room in a huff.

The Congressman returned to the stack of unopened mail in front of him.

***

It was shortly after ten in the morning. The sitting-room windows were open to a gentle breeze and a bright sun. Patricia could hear the birds singing from their perch on the front trees. She was working on some correspondences with friends back in Grand Rapids, Michigan.

Her work table was the same one she and Michael had used when they last worked together. That was just before she and her father had left for the Easter recess. She and

Michael had kissed passionately that afternoon. She thought Michael loved her. *How could he have gone down to Hooker Street as soon as I left Washington?*

She heard the front door bell.

Shortly thereafter, Adam the butler softly knocked on the barely open door of her sitting room.

"Yes, Adam," she responded softly. "What is it?"

"There is a Captain Hayes to see you, miss. This is his card."

She took it from him. It identified the captain as being assigned to one of her father's congressional committees.

"Are you sure he wants to see me, not my father?" she asked. "Yes, miss."

"Show him in. But I want you to stay in the room with me until he leaves."

"Yes, miss."

Adam followed Captain Hayes into the room and left the door open. "Please be seated, Captain," Patricia directed. "How may I help you?"

"I only came to apologize for the member of my staff who sent you an unsigned letter telling you about Lieutenant Drieborg's consorting down on Hooker Street while you were out of town," Hayes began.

"Having nothing but respect for the Congressman, he did not want to see you misled and hurt by Drieborg's other side. His dark side, as it were. But after the man sent the letter, he was so worried he had hurt you instead, that he asked me if I would apologize for him."

"Whatever do you mean, Captain, by consorting? The letter told of being drunk. Was there more that this aide did not reveal?"

"Oh, my!" Hayes feigned regret. "Now I've done it. I went too far. You haven't seen these photographs, then. I thought he included them. I'm so sorry." Hayes passed two photographs showing Michael in bed with the prostitute Janie.

Patricia glanced down. She stiffened, and her cheeks flushed. She raised a handkerchief to her face. "You'd better leave, Captain," she directed in a hushed voice. "Adam, show the captain out."

***

Michael stormed into the office of Captain Hayes. He slammed the door shut behind him and faced Hayes across his desk.

"What the hell do you think you are doing?" he demanded.

"Whatever do you mean Michael?" the captain responded. "Calm down, boy, and have a seat."

Michael ignored the offer, leaning against the desk as though it was the only thing keeping him from physically attacking Hayes.

"I don't want to sit or be calm, damn it. What were you doing at the Kellogg house?"

Hayes chuckled. "I'm just trying to help out, boy."

"Help my ass! You told her I got drunk at that dinner you ordered me to attend," Mike shouted.

"I think she was disappointed in your conduct that night, boy. Not able to hold your liquor, and all."

"Hold my liquor? I don't drink. I was drugged, and you know it, Hayes."

"Maybe so, boy," he taunted. "But you'll never be able to prove it." Hayes sat back in his chair, hands folded on his lap, and smiled smugly

"What is important is that she believes you got drunk. And that is hardly like the saintly image you have presented to her, is it boy? She could probably forgive you that. But when you chose to take a whore to bed instead of her, well, I'll bet that is another matter. I would guess she's finding that very difficult to forgive."

"Chose?" Mike almost shouted. "What are you talking about? Even you have been telling the story that I passed out and that you had me put to bed to sleep it off."

"That's true Drieborg. But what happened after I left you could be another matter, eh? So, when Miss Patricia received another little present, I imagine that she'll focus on your episode with the whore Janie. It's my bet that she will not forgive that."

Hayes slid a piece of cardboard across the desk toward Michael.

"This is called a daguerreotype, Drieborg. Yes, that's you all right, on your back. On top of you is the whore, Janie. You remember her from the dinner. She sat on your lap then, much to your discomfort. This time both of you are naked, and you don't look at all uncomfortable. In fact, the two of you take a very good picture, don't you think? I'm told that someone gave the Congressman and his daughter a copy of this one. I don't think they should have any trouble recognizing you. You can keep that copy, Michael. Consider it part of your Washington City education."

"You bastard," Michael choked. "You and Bacon set this whole thing up, didn't you?"

"Whether I did or not, you must admit you are probably ruined with the Kellogg family, especially with pretty Miss Patricia. But do not fear. I will look after her now. Think of it, boy. Think of me instead of you in bed with her," Hayes taunted, smiling.

"No!" Michael shouted, grabbing Hayes by his shirt.

Just then, the side door of the office opened. Lt. Tom Smith, one of the aides Hayes used as an errand boy, stepped in.

As soon as Mike realized he had an audience, he released his hold on Captain Hayes, turned and left the room.

***

A week later, Michael was working on some documents in Congressman Kellogg's office.

"Mike, can I see you for a moment?" asked the Congressman.

Mike followed his boss into a private office. Once the door was closed after him, he was directed to a chair.

"Krupp tells me that you have worked hard and been very efficient in the months you have been with us, Mike," the Congressman commented. "From what I've seen, I would agree."

"Thank you, sir."

"I'm terribly sorry about this Hayes problem, Michael. To some extent, I feel responsible. I should have taken you with us last month when we went home for the spring recess. You could have been very helpful there, and all of this would never have happened."

"Not your fault at all, sir. Hayes was determined and would have found some way to discredit me."

"Possibly. Despite that daguerreotype of you in that whorehouse, I believe your story. It was most probably staged after you were drugged. I told Patricia as much. Nevertheless, she hasn't been able to get by this. Maybe she will in time."

"Thank you for your trust in me, sir. But I don't think Patricia ever will."

"The critical matter right now, Mike, is Captain Hayes," Kellogg interrupted. "He has informed me that he is seriously considering filing charges against you for assault. He claims to have a witness. Is he telling the truth?"

"Yes, sir, I'm afraid he is. I lost my temper after he told me what he intended to do with Patricia. I grabbed him by the shirt. That's as far as it went," Michael assured him.

"Well, he has agreed to drop the matter if you accept reassignment to a front-line cavalry unit outside of Washington. Do you agree to that, Michael?"

"Yes, sir, I will."

"With Lee on the loose, we need all the cavalrymen we can find. So, I will arrange for your transfer to your old Troop as a platoon leader. I have already talked with Captain Hyser. He assured me that he will be very pleased to have you back."

"Thank you, sir."

The two men stood and shook hands.

"God keep you safe my boy," Congressman Kellogg said as Michael left the office.

June 1863

Dear Family,

I am well, and I hope all of you are, too. Today I was reassigned to my old cavalry unit. There is a great deal of excitement and worry here in Washington. It seems that Gen. Lee has moved his army out of Virginia. No one actually knows where he went, but it is assumed that he is moving north. So, General Hooker is moving in that direction, too. The cavalry has the job of finding Lee. So, all available cavalrymen in Washington are being sent to units involved in the search.

I know you will all worry — especially you, Mamma. But working in Washington was not good for me. Here, men use their power over others for evil purposes. As a second lieutenant, it would be difficult for me to survive without compromising my values. Please try to understand and trust my judgment.

Love, Michael

Gettysburg

In May, just a month earlier, the Union Army of the Potomac, led by General Hooker, was dealt a serious defeat at Chancellorsville, Virginia. Now the Rebel army that had inflicted that defeat was on the move.

Led by General Robert E. Lee, the Army of Northern Virginia was 60,000 soldiers strong. Lee was determined to lure to a battleground of his choosing, the remnants of the same Union army he had defeated in May. This time he intended to destroy it and win the war for the Confederacy.

Toward that end, Lee divided his army into three parts. On June 3, General Longstreet's Corps was sent northwest toward Culpepper, Virginia, and thereafter through the Ashby Gap in the Blue Ridge Mountains. General Hill's corps would follow the same route a few days later. General Ewell's Corps would use the Chester Gap to move west into the Shenandoah Valley.

Stuart's Rebel cavalry was assigned to screen this infantry movement east of the Blue Ridge Mountains.

This sudden move caught General Hooker completely by surprise. Lee's army was on the loose, and no one actually knew where he was or where he was headed. Hooker sent General Pleasanton's 6,000 cavalrymen, toward Culpepper, Virginia, in hopes of finding the Rebel infantry and denying them access through the Blue Ridge Mountains to Pennsylvania.

Instead, Pleasanton ran into Stuart's screening force at Brandy Station. A fierce battle resulted there. Several skirmishes followed as Stuart's forces successfully screened Lee's movements from the Union cavalry, thus protecting the passage of Lee's infantry through the Blue Ridge Mountains and into Pennsylvania.

Hooker wanted to use his 100,000 men to attack the 30,000 men of Hill's Confederate Corps still east of the Blue Ridge Mountains. He proposed to engage them at Fredericksburg, Virginia. Once he destroyed Hill's force, he planned to turn and attack the undefended city of Richmond. President Lincoln and his military advisors refused Hooker permission.

They feared that before Hooker could destroy Hill's force, Lee would swing back south and have the Army of the Potomac trapped with Hill's corps on one side and Lee's forces on the other. This might leave Washington, D.C., exposed in the process. Therefore, they ordered him to keep the Army of the Potomac between Lee and Washington.

Hooker began to move his forces north and east of the Blue Ridge Mountains protecting the Capital. Meanwhile, his Union cavalry units continued their search for the elements of Lee's divided army.

***

Lieutenant Michael Drieborg caught up with I Troop of the 6th Michigan Cavalry Brigade in Pennsylvania. They were there searching for the Confederate cavalry of Jeb Stuart. It was near evening, and the men of his platoon were fixing coffee during a break in the search.

"Well, I'll be," exclaimed Stan Killeen. "Look what the cat dragged in, will ya? Our Washington dandy has returned. And may the Lord protect us, he's a lieutenant at that!"

"Now look, you guys," Mike retorted. "When the order went out for all officers holding nonessential positions to report for reassignment, it didn't surprise me that I was at the top of that list. But do I actually have the right unit? They told me I was being sent to a fighting cavalry troop. They must be right, though, since they also told me I was assigned to a platoon in great need of leadership." He smiled broadly. "I can't tell you how good it is to be out of that cesspool of a nation's capital. It's so full of bad characters, even you guys look good."

The men of his old squad gathered around, greeting him. They all shook his hand and clapped him on his back. They were clearly glad to have him back. Their celebration was short-lived, though. Before dawn the following day, I Troop was on the move again. This time they were ordered toward a Pennsylvanian town called Gettysburg.

After a day of continuous riding, Mike felt exhausted. He was grooming his horse along with the other men of his platoon who were doing the same.

"I didn't realize just how out of shape I had become," he told George Neal, now a corporal and in charge of Michael's old squad. "My back is killing me. I wish I could have had my old mount back. He and I were really comfortable with one another."

"So," George responded with a big grin, "now *you* are the one whining about his horse. I remember when I had trouble with my new horse. You turned me over to the tender care of Killeen here. Welcome to some of your own medicine, Lieutenant."

***

By the end of June, all three Confederate corps which made up the Army of Northern Virginia were west of the Blue Ridge Mountains, each moving independently on a northern route into Pennsylvania. Stuart's cavalry was still to the east, creating havoc while moving northwest of Washington and into Pennsylvania.

By June 30, General Kilpatrick's Union cavalry division, which included the Michigan Brigade and Michael's I Troop, was near Gettysburg, Pennsylvania. At the nearby town of Hanover, elements of the Michigan Brigade met the advance guard of Stuart's Brigade. Though suffering heavy casualties, the Wolverines from Michigan used the superior firepower of their new Spencer repeating rifles to stop the advance of the Rebel cavalry.

In the afternoon of July 3, Stuart ordered 3,000 veteran cavalrymen to charge the men from Michigan again. His aim was to break through and then attack, from the rear, the Union infantry forces facing Lee's army at Gettysburg.

New to battle, the men of Michigan were astounded by the roaring sound of several thousand galloping horses, of the cannon fire, and of the screams of wounded horses.

When the Michigan Brigade, led by their new brigade commander, General George Custer, charged into the oncoming Rebels, they were outnumbered more than two to one. Custer's men cut a swath through the center and were joined by a Michigan Regiment of dismounted cavalrymen attacking from each flank. Drieborg's I Troop was one of those attacking the rebel flank.

By five o'clock, the battle was over. Stuart withdrew from the field. He had not broken through the Michigan Brigade.

A truce had been agreed upon so that the wounded of both sides could be found and treated. But a heavy blanket of cordite smoke lay over the quiet battlefield, and its thickness made it difficult to find the wounded. Cries for help led the medical personnel of both sides as they roamed the field in search of their injured comrades.

Before a battle, men feared several things. First, they were fearful they would run from the enemy or act in some other cowardly manner. Then they feared being wounded and losing a limb. Finally, they feared being wounded and left undiscovered on the battlefield.

***

"What? What's happened?" Mike whispered.

"Easy now, Mike. You've been wounded. Not a stomach wound, so you can have some water." Henry Stewart from B Troop in the 6th Regiment lifted Mike's head and brought a canteen to his lips.

Henry was from Muskegon, Michigan, a good-sized village west of Grand Rapids. From time to time, he had joined his brother David's mess in Drieborg's platoon. He was assigned stretcher-bearer duty today because he was recovering from a severe case of diarrhea.

"Where's my horse?" Drieborg asked.

"Someone in your Troop probably has it. I'll ask my brother as soon as I see him. Let's get you to the aid station."

"Can you tell what happened to me? My left shoulder hurts like its on fire. I can't move my arm much at all, either."

"Let me look. Does it hurt too much to sit up? Easy," Henry cautioned. "That'a way. I'm going to tear your shirt some." Henry popped the buttons of Mike's tunic and exposed his chest.

"There it is, Mike. It looks like there's a puncture wound on your chest. There's a cut on your back, too. Probably a saber went right through. I don't see any bones sticking out. Don't seem like they'd take yer arm off for this."

"What? Take my arm? Christ! Don't be kidding a guy, Henry."

"Sorry Mike. I didn't mean to get ya upset," Henry apologized. "I don't know a thing about such things. I just seen a big stack of arms and legs by the operating table today. Guess it's on my mind a bit. I see some men worse off'n you. Can ya hold off a bit till I get them others to the aid station? It's just over that rise." Henry pointed to the east.

"It shouldn't take too long. I'll leave this canteen with ya. Yell out if ya get any worse."

With that, Henry left. Just sitting up made Mike's head swim. He was afraid of drifting off to sleep. He didn't want the stretcher bearers to forget him. On a darkened battlefield with all the dead lying about, it was a very real possibility.

Mike noticed that the quiet was broken occasionally by the scream of a wounded horse. Mike didn't even know if Stuart's attack had failed. Despite his best efforts to stay awake, he fell asleep.

"Mike." Henry shook him. "Wake up buddy. It's your turn now. The sleep ya just had probably did ya some good. This here is Tom. He's on stretcher duty today, too. Let's see if ya can walk. Come on, give it a try."

With that, they helped him stand.

"Whew! Head's swimming," Mike exclaimed. "Hold on to me Henry. Put my left hand inside my shirt, would you? Please take it slow." Mike put his other arm around Henry's shoulder as the two men tried to walk up the hill toward the aid station. "I don't know if I can walk much. I'm pretty dizzy."

Henry was much shorter than Mike and was having a good deal of trouble holding the bigger man up by himself.

"We better use the stretcher, Tom," Henry decided. "Give me a hand with him. Lay back, Mike. We'll have ya to the doc in no time. Here, take some of this stuff. It's called opium. It's supposed to dull the pain. We're not supposed to give the wounded any water, though."

"Why can't I have some water?" Mike asked, irritated. "I could drink a whole canteen of water right now."

"Don't know Mike," Henry told him. "They'll give ya some whiskey at the aid station, though; all ya want, actually."

***

"You have another one for me, Henry?" the doctor observed. "Get him on the table, and I'll have a look."

"Easy, Doc," Henry urged. "Mike's a close buddy. He's afraid ya'll chop off his arm. All it 'pears to be, is a hole in his back from a saber."

The doctor rinsed his hands in a bucket of water by the table. Then he wiped his wet hands on his bloody apron, ran his hands through his long black beard, and turned to Michael.

"A saber wound, eh?" the doctor wondered aloud. "Can you move the fingers of your left hand at all, Lieutenant? Painful, I bet. I'm going to move your arm some now. This motion will probably hurt. But I have to see if any bones are broken."

He began to slowly move Mike's arm as he probed for bone breaks. The left arm and shoulder were already badly swollen and feverish to the touch. Despite the stiffness, the doctor was determined to test the full range of motion. He ignored his patient's groans and completed his examination. He examined the collarbone as well.

"Nothing appears broken, Lieutenant," he concluded. "Seems you will keep your arm too. You should regain its full use, eventually. Your biggest enemy right now is infection, shock, and fever. We'll give you some more whiskey for shock and some more opium for the pain.

"We don't know much about preventing infection, Lieutenant. And, once you get infected, we're not very good at stopping it from killing you. Fever seems to be part of the shock and infection, too. We don't know much about shock, either. For now, just get as much rest as possible. My orderly, William, will come around and answer any other questions you may have. But more wounded are coming in, son, so, I need to move you along."

"What's going to happen to me now, doc?" Mike asked.

"We're sending you to the Regimental hospital, Lieutenant," the doctor explained. "It's a mile or so east of here. They will help you more there than we can here. William will tell you all about it."

"Back on the stretcher, Mike," Henry told him. "We're going to put ya on that horse-drawn ambulance over there. Sorry I can't go with ya, but I'm assigned to this aid station. Now ya need to get to the Regimental hospital. It shouldn't be more than a couple'a miles back."

"Swallow some more opium Mike. It will help ya with the pain. It might even put ya to sleep. The doc told me ta give it to ya. He told me it sort a' numbs things. Here, swallow some." He brought the vial of murky liquid to Mike's lips.

***

The ambulance was a horse-drawn cart that had no springs. There was no padding for the wounded men it carried, either. Besides Mike, three others were laid side by side for the short trip to the Regimental hospital.

The driver was in a hurry to deliver his load of wounded, so he kicked the horse into a trot, pulling the cart roughly over the rock-strewn ground of open fields.

Despite the opium, Mike felt every jolt of the journey.

"Hey! Slow down, driver," Mike shouted. "We want to arrive at that hospital alive. You're killing us back here."

The driver ignored his order. Pain shot through Mike every time the cart hit a bump or a wheel dropped into a hole. The other wounded

Troopers cursed the driver despite his assurance that he was trying to be careful.

This was worse than the doctor's probing of his wound. Even Mike began cussing the driver.

By the time they arrived at the Regimental field hospital two miles to the rear of the battlefield, the wounded passengers were exhausted. Mike's head throbbed, his shoulder ached terribly, and his body was hot and wet with sweat.

Mike and the four men were laid on hay in another barn which served as the Regimental hospital. *"It's such a great relief to be done with that ambulance ride,"* Mike thought. *"I don't care where they put me."*

An orderly took their names and made notes on the severity of their injuries. He pinned the note to the shirt of each man. Then he told them,

"After your examination here, you will be sent to a hospital in Washington by train. There will not be much individual care there for things like fever, infection, or diarrhea. Chances are you will all have some sort of infection and the fevers that come with it, too. There are no orderlies in the hospital during the night, either. So, you are pretty much on your own during that period of time.

"You'll be better off if you can get a person, like a family member or a friend, to nurse you. Your chances of recovery will be much better. In fact, if you can find one willing, you can be released to the care of a family located nearby.

"Oh, yes. If we get our hot rations today, you might have some soup and bread before you leave on the train," he added. "My advice, even if you don't feel like it, is to have the soup. Also, you'll need all the whiskey you can hold down to prevent shock. But you shouldn't drink any water."

Shortly thereafter, Michael was taken in for another examination. If he was to lose a limb, it would be decided in the field hospital. Medical protocol dealing with wounds to the appendages called for amputation as soon as possible. It had been determined that such action would lower the incidence of infection, gangrene, and death.

Two men carried Mike on a stretcher toward a long wooden table in another part of the barn. The man in a bloody apron was splashing water from a bucket over the table as two other men carried another soldier away.

"Right up here, Corporal. Help me get him on his right side," the doctor ordered. "That's good. Help me cut his blouse off so I can examine the area. Well, it seems the doctor at the aide station was right about a puncture wound, Lieutenant." The manipulation of the arm and shoulder was repeated. Pain shot through Mike.

Once the examination was completed, the doctor told him, "Don't appear to be any broken bones, either, not even the collarbone. Your arm's all right, too. Hard to tell, actually, when the whole area is so swollen and tender. Just to be sure, though, I need to do one more test."

He inserted a metal probe into the wound on Mike's back, searching for a projectile. Mike stiffened and moaned. Sweat suddenly poured down his face. He gripped the side of the table with his right hand during the doctor's probing.

"There you go," the doctor said. "I'm finished. I couldn't find a bullet, Lieutenant. The wound was probably from a saber. I'm going to clean the wound, bandage it, and strap your arm to your chest for the trip to a Washington hospital."

Using alcohol, the doctor swabbed the wound on both the back and chest." *Why is the man so rough?"* Michael wondered.

"*He ought to work for the Rebs the way he's treating me.*"

Michael was taken to another area of the barn to await transport to the railroad for his trip to Washington, City.

***

"I'm looking for a Lieutenant Drieborg," Captain Hyser inquired. "He was brought here late this afternoon. Can you tell me where I can find him?"

"Sir, I don't know but a few of the names," responded the orderly. "And that's not one of 'em I remember. Afraid you'll have to ask someone else. But I did see a lieutenant on the examining table a bit ago. Think he's over in that corner waiting to be taken to the railroad."

Wounded troopers were lying everywhere, it seemed. Captain Hyser had to step carefully as he moved to the back of the barn. That was where he found Michael.

"Mike?"

"Captain," Mike greeted him. "Am I glad to see another friendly face."

"Are you going to be all right, son?" Hyser asked.

"The doc said it was a saber wound, sir. Do you have any water I can have, Captain? They say water's not good for us. All they want to give us is whiskey. Craziest thing I ever heard."

"I'll get you my canteen as soon as we're done talking," he promised.

"Sir can you get a message to the Hecht family? I have their postal address in my pocket. They can find me at one of the hospitals in Washington. The way I'm burning up already, I think I'm going to need some tending to real soon."

"I sure will try, Mike. Don't know if I can get this out by telegraph today, but I sure will get a letter to both of them first chance I get," he promised. "You should try yourself as soon as you reach Washington. I also should contact Congressman Kellogg. He arranged for you rejoin the Michigan Brigade. You probably wouldn't have been assigned to us if not for him."

"Yes, sir," Mike responded weakly. "I should have thought of contacting him. Thank you. Did we stop Stuart, sir?"

"Yes, we did, and the boys in Gettysburg stopped Lee, too. Custer is hopping mad that we're not attacking Lee right now. Hold on, Mike, I've got to get back to the Troop. God bless you. We need you back with us soon, you hear?"

"It means a lot to hear that from you, Captain. Thank you, sir. I'll be back before you know it."

A few minutes after Captain Hyser left, an orderly brought Mike a canteen of water. "Don't tell anyone here I gave this to you, Lieutenant," whispered the orderly. "But that Captain who just seen you made me promise."

It was daylight before Mike was carried to an ambulance. He was burning up with fever and felt very weak. Despite the canteen of water, the captain gave him, he was still very thirsty.

***

The ambulance ride to the railroad bounced Mike and the three other wounded men in his vehicle around for the better part of an hour. Despite another dose of opium, pain shot through his body every time a wagon wheel hit a rock or a pothole. His wool clothing was soaked through with sweat.

Once the railhead was reached, Mike and the other wounded were placed on cots in a railroad boxcar. The cots were stacked from the floor to the ceiling of the car, thirty wounded men and one orderly to each boxcar.

The smooth motion of the train and the breeze flowing through openings in the sides of the moving boxcar were a blessed relief for Mike and the other wounded soldiers. But he was still refused water, so his dehydration worsened and his fever rose.

Michael was given more opium and whiskey. After sunset, the air cooled his body some and he fell asleep.

The hospital train stopped just inside the gun emplacements of Washington. The wounded men in each hospital car were examined there by orderlies. The most seriously wounded were moved first.

There were so many thousands of wounded from the battle at Gettysburg that the hospitals were full long before the trains were all unloaded. Consequently, only the most seriously wounded were taken there. The rest were assigned all manner of housing. Even the halls of Congress were used.

Mike Drieborg was one of those taken to the congressional office building and given a bag of hay to lay on in one of the hallways. His wound had become infected, and he was feverish and weak. For lack of water, his dehydration worsened. Despite this, he and the other wounded were considered ambulatory and were expected to fend for themselves.

So, even though his wound was not of itself life-threatening, his condition had become so. The infection, fever, and dehydration had to be addressed quickly if he was to survive.

The Kellogg Home

"Where did you see him, Sergeant?"

"Right over in that corner, I think, sir. He should be the only officer in this area."

Congressman Kellogg worked his way down the hall in search of Michael Drieborg. He found Mike half-conscious where he had been placed the day before, ignored by passersby.

"My Lord," he exclaimed. "Mike, is that you?" He knelt beside Drieborg, who was lying on his right side on a straw mattress, still in his boots and uniform. He was stunned by Mike's filthy appearance and awful smell.

"Sergeant," the Congressman ordered. "Get some men with a stretcher over here immediately."

He soon had Mike at his residence. There, Mike was bathed, shaved, and fed some hot chicken broth before being put into bed for his first real rest in days. Kellogg sent for a doctor he knew from one of the hospitals.

After the doctor examined Mike, he talked with Congressman Kellogg.

"The city is filled with young men suffering just like your lieutenant. Even with wounds not too serious, infection and other after-effects are killing thousands of them. Your young man is seriously ill, Congressman. The wound is infected, and I have nothing to solve that situation. The fever is caused by infection. Cold baths might help him some.

"But he is a strong young fellow who could very well survive this," the doctor continued. "Keep him clean and rested. Give him all the nourishment he can handle and make him take in a lot of liquid. Water is the best. I don't agree with giving these boys whiskey. Opium is used a lot, too. More than it should be, in my view. I suggest you keep it away from him. We have already seen cases of addiction turning up. If his fever doesn't abate in a week, send me a message, and I'll come by to look at him again."

"Thanks very much, Doctor. I consider your taking time for this a real favor. Call on me should you need my help anytime."

***

The next day, Michael felt a slight breeze on his face and saw it move the white window curtains near his bed. The sun lit the room brightly, as well.

"Good morning, Lieutenant." The greeting came from an unfamiliar male voice. "How are you feeling today?"

"Where am I?" Mike asked. He saw a man in uniform standing beside his bed with a cup of water in his hand and a towel hung over his arm.

"Today, you are in Congressman Kellogg's home," the man told Michael. "Yesterday, you were among the many wounded men who were brought here from the Gettysburg battlefield. You were placed in the hallway of the congressional office building. It seems that the hospitals here were full to overflowing with more seriously wounded. The Congressman received a message that you had been brought here. He searched the halls of his office building and found you under a staircase on the second floor, unconscious."

Michael was waking up some. "You have a soldier's uniform on," Mike observed. "Who are you; and what are you doing in the Congressman's house?"

"I'm Corporal Webster, Lieutenant," he told Michael. "I lost my left eye in a skirmish with Lee's boys down near Richmond. I've no place to go, so I've been helping out at the hospital as a nurse. The Congressman had me assigned to him to care for you while you are at his home."

"I'm so thirsty," Mike told him. "Can I please have some water? They wouldn't give us any at the Regimental field hospital. We could only have whiskey. It would help with the shock, they told us."

"That's what we have been told in the hospitals here, too. But the congressman's doctor told us to give you all the water you wanted. He said it would help lower your fever." Webster held Michael's head up while bringing the cup of water to his lips. "The doctor also told me to give you broth when you woke up."

Michael sipped some, but he was too hot and tired to finish the whole bowl. He allowed Webster to wipe off his body with cool towels. Then he fell asleep again. He was in and out of sleep for some time. Despite the water and the cool cloths, he was still feverish and sweaty.

Sometime later in the day, Congressman Kellogg came into his room. "Michael! Are you awake boy?" Kellogg asked. "Sorry to awaken you, but I need to talk with you for a minute or two. I've telegraphed my man in Grand Rapids and directed him to visit your parents and inform them of your situation."

"Thank you, sir," Mike responded weakly. "You have been most kind. If it hadn't been for you, I'd still be lying on that floor of your building. I'm grateful, but I don't want to be of any trouble to you."

"That's quite all right Michael," Kellogg assured him. "You fellows did quite a job at Gettysburg. You proved that Lee and Stuart are not so invincible. You know, your victory was the first over Lee since he took command of the Confederate Army of Northern Virginia. And we just received word today that we captured Vicksburg. We now control the entire Mississippi River. It has been quite a week."

"Does that mean the war is over?" Michael asked.

"Not likely. If General Meade had attacked Lee's retreating army, or at the very least cut off his escape south into Virginia, we would be negotiating a peace with the Rebs right now. But Meade did neither, and Lee escaped with his army. Now the war must continue.

"Anyway Michael, you are out of it for a while," Kellogg reminded him. "By the way, I sent Patricia back to Grand Rapids for the summer. I wanted her away from Washington's summer heat and infections.

"But I'm afraid Captain Hayes is still causing trouble for the aides," Kellogg related. "I fear that he might press charges against you after all, once he hears that you are here. So, I communicated with the Hecht family. They are most willing to take you to their farm for your recovery. It seems that Mrs. Hecht is a healer of sorts. They should be here sometime tomorrow. Is that all right with you?"

"Whatever you say, sir," Michael responded. "As soon as I am able, I'll write my parents."

"You get some rest now son," Kellogg told him. "I'll look in on you in the morning. Webster will be in the next bedroom. Just ring that bell on the bedside table, and he will come right in."

***

The Hechts arrived at the Kellogg home by ten o'clock the next morning. Their son Kenny was with them too.

Once in Michael's room, Mrs. Hecht removed the sheet covering his upper body. If she noticed his embarrassment, she didn't let on. She removed the bandage, washed his chest and scrubbed his torso with alcohol. Then she examined Michael's wound.

"The infection is causing the fever," she reported to those in the room. "On the farm, the men get cuts now and then. We clean the wound and cover it with clean bandages, but sometimes it still gets infected. Then we use a poultice to draw out the infection."

There was more she observed. "Michael, your wound looks as though it was not kept clean. Your bandage I removed is dirty, too. We must treat the infection if you are to recover."

"But we had the doctor here the other day, Mrs. Hecht," Congressman Kellogg told her, somewhat defensively. "He told us the fever was the problem. He did not say anything about infection."

"It is not your fault, sir," responded Ruben Hecht. "My wife knows about such tings. I don't know why your doctors don't. She vill take care of Michael."

"The poison has to be drawn out, Michael," Emma Hecht said. "To do that, I have to open the wound before the poultice can do any good. This will hurt some, but it is needed. Eh, Papa?"

"Ya, Mamma. I have vatched her do dis before, Michael," Ruben assured him. "She helps our neighbors who come to her mit infections and such. She even vorks on me and da children, too."

"If you can do something, Mrs. Hecht," Mike told her, "please, do it." She washed her hands in the bedside basin.

"Hand me that bottle of alcohol, Papa," she ordered.

She took a knife from her bag and cleaned it with the alcohol. She also soaked a clean cloth with the pungent liquid. Then, for a second time, she vigorously scrubbed Michael's chest around the wound with the cloth. Still under the effects of the last opium pill, Michael hardly winced at the sting of the alcohol or Emma's rough scrubbing.

She then placed her left hand on the swollen hot skin of his shoulder. And, with the knife in her right hand, she placed the point of the knife at the blackened center of the wound. With a quick movement, an inch of the blade disappeared into Michael's shoulder.

He felt that. "Oh! Damn, that hurts," he shouted.

Black liquid squirted out of the opened wound as Mrs. Hecht used her hands to put pressure on Michael's shoulder and continued to squeeze the black liquid out of the wound.

"This is good," she decided. "It can drain now."

Once she cleaned the area again, she applied a sticky yellow substance on his back before she bandaged the wound.

"This smells a bit, Michael, but it will draw out the poison. That should take care of the infection. Then the fever should go away."

***

It wasn't long before the Hechts' horse-drawn wagon was moving slowly through the Maryland countryside. Michael lay atop a straw-filled mattress. He was bare-chested but protected from the hot July sun by a blanket held above him on poles attached to the wagon's sides.

Mrs. Hecht sat next to him and cooled his head with water and wiped the sweat from his chest. All the while, she insisted he drink water.

"Imagine Papa," she angrily said. "They deny water to wounded men, and instead they give them whiskey. You'd think our doctors work for the enemy the way they treat our wounded. Even our sick farm animals would die from such treatment. They should put a woman in charge of the hospitals, Papa."

"Ya, Mamma. You are right."

Michael and Eleanor

The Hechts converted the barn's tack room into a bedroom for Michael. It was a bit crude, but Ruben had cut out a window for light and ventilation. Even with a dirt floor, the room was clean and airy. It was just right for the situation.

Mike lay on a hay-filled mattress which was supported by ropes tied across a wood frame. This had the advantage of being easily replaced and allowing air to circulate under his feverish body. To help cool his body, Mrs. Hecht had dressed Michael in a pair of her son's pants cut off at the knees and kept his torso bare as well.

"We want you to be as cool as possible, Michael." She had told him. Emma's daughter, Eleanor came into the small room.

"Holy smoke, I'm almost naked." Michael realized.

"Mrs. Hecht, can I have my shirt back?"

"No, Michael," she insisted. "Remember, what I told you; until we get your temperature down, we must keep you cool. No shirt for now, Michael."

"Laying here like this doesn't seem to bother Eleanor at all". He observed.

"How long will the fever last Mamma?"

Eleanor was the Hechts' eldest child. Very pretty, she was no longer a child. She had given birth to a son last year. At five foot eight, she had hardly shown her pregnancy, even at the end. Now, a year later, she had returned to her trim but full-breasted figure. In the intense heat of July, she was dressed in an airy dress of light fabric. She hardly noticed that she had been a little careless closing her blouse after breastfeeding her baby.

Michael noticed. *"I wonder if she knows that the top of her dress is not completely buttoned?"*

Emma was rubbing Michael's bare torso with a damp cloth.

"The fever should go away when the infection is gone, Eleanor. His body is fighting it right now. We can help him by wiping the sweat off his body, cleaning his wound when we change his dressing and getting him to swallow a lot of liquids.

"Watch me clean the wound Eleanor," she directed. "I just reopened the wound so now we need to put some more poultice on it. I mixed some fresh yesterday. It is in the cabinet over there.

"See how I spread it on?" She demonstrated for her daughter. "Now, Eleanor, you take this clean cloth and cover the dressing."

As Eleanor started dressing the wound, Emma continued, "Now, take the bandage and roll it twice around his chest. You must help her Michael. That's it, sit up some," she instructed.

"Oh! It hurts to move!" Mike told them.

"Sorry, Michael, but you have to help. Now Eleanor, move the bandage over his shoulder and back around his chest. "This will keep the dressing in place. I want you to do this in the morning and again before dark. In between changes, remember that you are to wipe the sweat off his body and give him water and hot broth."

"How much do I give him, Mamma?"

"Give him as much as he will take. You have to be tough mit him."

"Eleanor," she urged. "Make him drink these liquids. If you have trouble, call me."

"All right Mamma," Eleanor agreed. "But I need Robert out here with me. That way I can look after both babies."

"Come on, Eleanor," Mike protested. "I'm not a baby."

"Seems to me like you were doing a lot of complaining a minute ago, soldier.

"Who will look after Michael during the night, Mamma?"

"Kenny will sleep out here, Eleanor. If Michael has a problem during the night, Kenny will get one of us."

For several days, this plan seemed to work well.

Michael remained feverish, but each day he was a little bit less so. As he became more awake, he became more aware of his state of undress, he blushed with embarrassment.

Then, as he began to feel stronger, he experienced sexual arousal when Eleanor wiped the sweat from his body, or he felt her touch, or he saw her lush figure when she bent over him. He was especially affected when she lifted his torso and held him close to her in order to apply and secure fresh bandages.

After about ten days of care at the Hecht farm, Michael had managed, with Kenny's help, to visit the outhouse. Later, he was propped up in bed after Eleanor had changed his dressing and fed him some solid food.

She then began to breastfeed her young child Robert in a rocking chair not two feet from Michael's bed.

"Eleanor, do you think you ought to be feeding Robert in front of me?" he asked.

"For heaven's sake Michael," she snapped. "It is the most natural thing in the world. Have you forgotten that since you've been here, I've spent almost every minute of every day taking care of you? Where do you think I have been feeding Robert all that time? In this room, right by your bed, that's where. Sides, didn't you see you mother breast-feed your youngest sisters or your brother?"

"That was different."

"Oh, is that right? How, pray tell?"

"Come on El. First off, that was my mother and my sisters and brother. Second, you are a beautiful woman with her breast exposed right in front of a man, not her brother, parent or husband. Besides, in my weakened and almost naked condition, the sight of you is having an embarrassing effect on me."

"Well, you poor little boy," she teased. "Probably a good thing you are in a weakened condition, if you're having trouble controlling yourself. And say, what is this, you calling me El?"

"Just came out," responded Michael. "Besides, as close as we've been, it seemed right that I have a special name for you. You don't mind, do you?"

"I suppose not. Wait, I'm not so sure. I'll have to think about it. But then you can't mind if I have a special name for you, like Mikie or Michelle maybe. Would you now?"

"You wouldn't!" Michael exclaimed in mock alarm.

"Wouldn't I, really? Mikie!" She laughed.

"Lord, give me strength. Protect me from this woman."

***

Despite his continued protests, Eleanor followed her mother's directions cleaning Michael's wound twice a day. This was one of those times.

Eleanor stood alongside his bed with a pan of hot water in one hand and a clean cloth in the other.

"Michael Drieborg, If you think I am going to watch that wound get infected again, you have another think coming. Mamma says it has to be kept clean and that is what I intend to do. The least you could do is stop whining about it."

"I think it is fine, El. Can't you just leave it alone for a while? And, for your information, cavalry officers don't whine," Michael retorted.

"Well, it certainly seems to me that I am looking at one who does. Do you want to be the one who tells Mamma, Mister brave Lieutenant Drieborg?"

Michael avoided her stare and did not respond.

"I thought not. So, let's get that shirt off fella. This isn't the only thing I have to do today, thank you very much."

Michael sat on the chair by his bed as Eleanor approached.

She leaned over him and pulled off his shirt. Then, she unwound the bandage and began to scrub the wound vigorously with the cloth and hot soapy water.

"Hey! Take it easy, will you? My skin's still almost raw from the scrubbing you gave it this morning."

She ignored his pleas and continued scrubbing. "Want to play rough, eh, young lady?" he warned her.

She apparently paid no attention, for she kept scrubbing his chest. With that, he grabbed her right wrist in his and pulled her toward him. She was already leaning into him, so he didn't have to pull too hard. She tumbled onto his lap rather easily. His right arm encircled her waist and he pulled her close as he kissed her upturned lips.

After a moment, she brought her arm around his head and pulled him closer.

Finally, she leaned back some. "You like this kissing business, do you?"

"I've not done much of it, but I must admit it's pretty nice. How am I doing, El?"

"I haven't decided, but… hey." She sat up suddenly. "Do you mean to say that you think that I'm some kind of loose woman or something?"

"No," Michael haltingly responded. "I just thought that you having been a married woman and having a child and all… I just figured…"

"Oh, I get it," she snapped. "I'm the experienced, lonely widow seducing the innocent farm boy soldier far from home. Well, I never! You just better keep your mouth shut, soldier boy, while I finish putting this dressing and bandage on you."

Michael started to put his arm around her again.

"No, you don't," she ordered. "Don't touch me Michael Drieborg! You think about what you said just now."

"What did I say that was so horrible?" She stormed out of his room.

Letter Home, July 1863 Dear Family,

I hope this letter finds you all well.

Don't worry about me. I am doing fine. As you know, Mr. and Mrs. Hecht brought me to their farm to recover from the wound I received at Gettysburg. She told me that because I did not receive the proper care after the battle, the wound became infected. The infection caused my high temperature. She opened the wound so the infection could drain and put a smelly yellow paste, called a poultice, on it. Mrs. Hecht or her daughter Eleanor clean it two, sometimes three times a day and put more of that smelly stuff on it. My fever is gone now, so I guess that the poison is, too.

I've lost a good deal of weight. I'm almost as skinny as you, Little Jake. I'm still sort of weak too. Their son Kenny still has to help me to the outhouse.

I will write you again soon.

Love you all,

Michael

***

Ruben was sipping a second cup of coffee. Eleanor was feeding her baby, her sister had gone about her afternoon chores, Kenny was chopping wood and Michael was taking a nap.

"Mamma," Ruben asked, "how is Michael's wound coming along?"

"It is fine Papa. Now we keep it clean and begin to make him use his left arm. It is stiff right now and weak too."

"How about I get him to hoe in da garden tomorrow morning?" Ruben suggested. "He doesn't have to have much strength to move dat loose dirt around. Dat vill get his arm moving some."

"Goot idea, Papa," Emma responded. "Wake him up when you get up in the morning. It is time for that, too. He can eat mit us in the morning and begin before the sun is too hot. Work in the morning and rest in the afternoon."

"Goot," agreed Ruben. "Then it is decided Mamma. I will tell Michael at supper-time."

For most of the following week, Michael worked in the garden. By the end of the week, he was able to spend two or three hours in the morning, moving the soil around with a hoe. His left shoulder began to regain its full range of motion. The intense late July heat helped as well.

It was time for the second cutting of hay. Kenny guided a horse, pulling a cutting device. The farm equipment left neat rows of cut hay lying on the ground. The next day, Ruben guided a horse-drawn wagon between the rows while Michael and Kenny gathered the cut hay with wooden pitchforks and threw it up on the wagon.

It was hot work. The dust was flying, and everyone was covered with sweat and hay dust.

The girls brought lemonade out to the field. All three men welcomed the drink and the opportunity to wipe off their faces with wet cloths.

"Hey, soldier boy!" Eleanor shouted. "How you doing with this farm work?"

"Just fine, little girl," Michael responded. "Don't you remember? I worked these fields last spring when all this stuff was planted. Can I have more of that lemonade? It really tastes good."

"Your shoulder still feeling all right?" she asked.

"I'm still doing more work with my right arm than my left. The shoulder is still a little stiff. But with this heat, the muscles seem to be loosening up. The hay is light, but the pitchfork motion is helping. Muscle strength will come." He paused and then added, "You haven't cleaned my wound for a while. I thought you were determined it would not get infected again. Or don't you care anymore?" he teased.

"You know Robert has had bad stomach upsets the past couple of weeks. Probably from this heat," Eleanor reminded him. "Keeping him cool and comforted has taken all of my time. Besides, Mamma has kept an eye on it."

After supper that night, Michael begged off a checker game with Kenny and went for a walk toward the creek in the hollow behind the house. The sun was rapidly setting over the trees. A light breeze came up and the temperature was dropping. It was a nice change from the heat of the day.

Michael had taken one of Ruben's rifles with him, just in case. He was sitting against a very old and large tree trunk, enjoying the evening.

At the crack of a tree branch, he rolled over, rifle ready.

"Michael! Are you going to shoot me or invite me to sit with you?" Eleanor asked.

"Don't be testy, El. I was just being careful. Of course, I would like you to sit with me. Would you please?"

Eleanor joined him and snuggled close on Michael's right side. They were both silent, just enjoying the evening and one another. Lately, they had found it difficult to be close and not kiss. Tonight, was no exception. But this time, they kissed.

Eleanor rolled Michael on his back and lay astride his leg, controlling the kiss.

"To answer your question, Lieutenant Drieborg," she whispered hotly, "you are a pretty good kisser. I don't think there is much I could teach you. Are you going to take advantage of this lonely widow?"

"Lying on top of me like this, El, you must be aware of the effect you have on me," Michael warned her. "Yes, I want to make love to you. I love you, El. But it wouldn't be right. You parents trust me."

"Oh, Michael," she said, hugging him. "I want you to make love to me. I knew I loved you last winter when you and Swede would visit and work with Papa. Even at Christmastime, I think I knew. But I still felt so ugly for the longest time after my baby was born, I couldn't imagine you could ever love me. So, I was sort of cross with you all the time. I suppose I tried to frighten you away."

"It worked. You certainly convinced me back then. I figured you were still mourning your husband. But the care you have given me this summer and the affection you have shown toward me changed my mind. How could I not fall in love with you? I couldn't love you more than I do right now. Will you marry me, El?"

"Yes, Michael! I want to marry you," Eleanor responded, kissing him passionately. "But I am so afraid you won't come back to me; that this darned war will take you too."

On his side now, he drew Eleanor toward him. "Listen sweetheart. I'm not the least bit afraid. I know we have no idea what will happen. But to let our fear of what might happen in the future prevent us from loving one another as fully as possible in the present seems foolish."

"Thank you, Michael," Eleanor responded. "I need you to remind me of that. Yes, I will marry you."

They kissed again, tenderly.

Michael paused. "I think we should talk to your parents about this tonight. I intend to tell them that I want us to get married as soon we can. What do you think?"

"Yes, Michael," she agreed. "Let's tell them. But not right this minute." She rolled him over and lay atop him, once again pressing her leg against his manhood. This time the kiss was not only passionate, but long.

"Whoa there," Michael gasped, pulling away from her some. "Now I know why Adam took the forbidden fruit from Eve."

"And don't you forget it buster," Eleanor shot back, poking him in the ribs.

Michael helped her to her feet, and they walked to the house.

Kenny, Julia and their parents were still awake. Michael and Eleanor told them of their love for one another and Michael asked their permission to marry Eleanor.

"Wow!" Kenny shouted. "You're going to be in the family. Great!" Julia jumped up and hugged her sister.

Eleanor's parents were pleased, as well. They gave their permission. "Vhen we go to church tomorrow, ve'll talk to da pastor about da ceremony. Eh, Mamma?" Ruben asked.

"I agree, Papa," she responded. "If we see him before Mass starts, he could give the first announcement today."

"Goot idea, Mamma," Ruben agreed.

"Before da war Michael, vedding plans had to be announced three times at da church. But, during da war, it is only once. Time for bed, everyone," he decided. "Ve have much to do in da morning before church."

***

Later that night, as Emma and Ruben prepared for bed, they talked about Michael and Eleanor.

"Well, Papa," Emma said, "I'm not surprised. I've noticed how these two have looked at each other at meal time. They have been resisting their feelings for one another, I think. It is good they are talking with us about it. This Michael Drieborg will be good for Eleanor and baby Robert, too. What do you think, Papa?"

"You are right, Mamma. I had not noticed da looks. But he is a goot man for our Eleanor. Dey should marry vhile dey can. God vill decide vhat happens mit this var and if Michael survives."

"Yes, I approve, too. Isn't it exciting watching our daughter and Michael so much in love Papa?" Emma rolled toward Ruben in the dark and put her arm around him.

"Ya, Mamma. But dey are not da only ones in dis house in love, I tink."

Dear Family,

I am sorry if I worried you. It would seem that my wound was not serious, but the infection and fever were very serious. If it had not been for Mrs. Hecht, I don't know what would have happened. Nothing good, I am thinking.

Papa, I have been hoeing the garden most every day. Kenny Hecht, who is about Little Jake's age, and I loaded the newly cut hay on the Hechts' wagon yesterday. My left shoulder is loosening up quite well. I have very little strength, though, especially on the left side. I look for that to change as I become more active.

When I was brought here last July, Mrs. Hecht and her daughter Eleanor nursed me through my fever and infection. Of course, I got to know them on my visits to their farm last winter and spring. But, during my recovery here I realized that I loved Eleanor. She accepted my proposal of marriage and her parents approved.

I am sorry not to have involved you more in this decision or given you time to be present at the private ceremony at their Catholic Church. But this war has changed many things. It has taken away the luxury of time. Being wounded has made me realize that she and I must take advantage of the time we have together now. I hope you understand.

After we are married, Eleanor and I will travel to Lowell for a visit. I will still be on leave because of my wound. 'ill write as soon as I know how much time the Army doctors will allow me; and with our travel arrangements.

Love you,

Michael

Lowell Visit: October 1863

Two weeks later on a Sunday morning, Eleanor stood at the altar of her Maryland Catholic Church and married Michael Drieborg. Mrs. Hecht had repaired and cleaned his old uniform for the occasion; and Eleanor wore a dress she and her mother had made just for this marriage ceremony. Little Robert stood beside his mother and his aunt Julia while her bother Kenny served as Michael's best man.

After the ceremony, the church pews were pushed to the side and stacked. Then long boards were place atop sawhorses and covered with white tablecloths.

Most every family at the ceremony had someone fighting for one side or the other. Many had lost sons to graves or prisons. Still, such an occasion was welcomed by everyone as an opportunity not just to socialize, but to celebrate something joyous in the midst of a war zone.

Over forty adults with children from the area, as well as church members, were welcomed to the celebration. Every family brought food. After the meal, the tables were broken down and the center of the church cleared. Someone with a violin, another with a guitar and a third church member with a base fiddle joined their music to that of the small church organ for the dancing that followed.

No one wanted to leave. But traveling after dark was not wise. So, by five in the afternoon, the church was cleaned, the pews were restored, and all were on their way, including the newlyweds.

Eleanor snuggled close to Michael in their horse-drawn buggy. It had been decorated by the young kids with ribbons. They had even attached a sign to the back of the rig that told one and all that the couple in the buggy had just been married.

"Wasn't it all beautiful, Michael?" Eleanor gushed. "Everyone is so happy for us. I'm sorry your family could not come. But we are going to Lowell soon. I can hardly wait."

"I sure know what I can hardly wait for, Mrs. Drieborg!"

Eleanor giggled.

"And what could that be Lieutenant?"

With that, Michael pulled her closer to him with one arm and kissed her deeply.

Eleanor slid her free hand from behind Michael's head, down along his jaw.

"Oh!" exclaimed Michael. "You know that's driving me crazy, don't you El?"

She giggled again. "I can tell."

"I'm not sure how much more of that I can take."

"Find a grove of trees Michael," Eleanor urged. "I don't want to wait any longer, either. I want you, right now."

"It's not safe out here El."

"Safety be darned Michael Drieborg. Let's be reckless," she urged. "It's our wedding night, after all. You've made me wait long enough."

Eleanor continued to tease her husband. "You still want to wait Lieutenant Drieborg?" she taunted.

Very quickly, Michael found a stand of trees off the side of the road. It was well after dark before they reached the Hecht farmhouse.

The Hecht family had gone visiting relatives for a couple of days so the newlyweds could have the house to themselves. When the family returned, Julia would sleep in the loft, Kenny would take over Mike's room in the barn, and the newlyweds would use the girls' room in the house.

Until the Hechts returned, Michael and Eleanor hardly left the house.

***

War department personnel knew that Lt. Drieborg was recovering from his battle wound at the Hecht farm, so they forwarded his pay there. Responding to a written request sent him at the Hecht farm, he went to Washington, City, for a physical examination. The doctor pronounced him almost fit for duty. The War Department then told him that he could have another six weeks of recovery time. Then he would have to report for assignment.

After his return to the Hecht farm Michael and Eleanor prepared for their trip to Lowell, Michigan. First, he took Eleanor with him to Washington. He visited Congressman Kellogg's office, introduced his wife and made his loan payment.

"It is a pleasure to meet you, Eleanor. Both of you please accept my congratulations,"

"Thank you, sir," Eleanor responded. "I will always be grateful for what you did for Michael last summer. You saved his life."

"I did what I could. But I think your mother is the person you should thank the most. I suppose you already know that. Your wife is not only beautiful Michael, but well spoken too. Have a pleasant journey and enjoy your leave at home," the Congressman urged.

After they left Mike purchased a new uniform for himself and some travel clothing for Eleanor. Then they set off by train from Baltimore and headed for Lowell, Michigan.

Their first stop was Philadelphia, where they made room reservations in a hotel near the train station. After a nice supper, they took a leisurely walk. Many stores were still open along the lamp-lit downtown streets. Eleanor bought a tablecloth for Mike's mother.

They were both amazed at the sights. It was much cleaner than Washington Mike told her, and people seemed much friendlier and less in a hurry too.

As interesting and pleasant as it was, they were still newlyweds after all, and they had a private room with a big bed all to themselves. They soon ended their sightseeing and went to their room.

They had an early breakfast and boarded a train for the next leg of their journey.

The train stopped next in Pittsburg where they had time to stretch their legs and get some lunch. Mike and his Regiment had been entertained at that same train depot last December by hundreds of well-wishers and bands when they stopped on their way east to Washington City. It was much quieter now.

Supper in Cleveland and a walk along Lake Erie concluded the second day of their journey. They thoroughly enjoyed all the time alone together. They especially enjoyed the evenings.

Mike and Eleanor were up early the next day for the last leg of the journey. It took them to Detroit, Michigan by lunchtime where they changed trains. They now headed northwest to the state capital city, Lansing. By suppertime they reached the end of their train journey in Grand Rapids.

It was evening, and Michael's parents would not pick them up until the next morning, so they walked to the nearby Eagle Hotel. There were three well-known hotels in downtown Grand Rapids. Mike chose the Eagle because it catered to families. It had no bar and did not allow alcohol on their premises. He remembered that it also had an excellent restaurant.

After supper and their evening walk, Mike and Eleanor shopped downtown for gifts for his sisters and brother. Once it was dark, they returned to their room.

Mike was sitting on the bed watching his wife prepare for bed. "I so enjoy watching you, El."

"Will you ever tire of me Michael?" she asked.

"I could never get enough of you, sweetheart." He answered.

Eleanor turned from the wash basin, threw back her long golden hair, and handed a towel to her husband. "Dry me off, Michael."

Much later that night, covered with perspiration; Mike lay next to his wife's. On his elbow, he looked at her face. "You are so beautiful. I thought so the first time I saw you. Remember, El? It was December last year. Your father had brought the Swede and me into your house for the first time. You walked into the room and I knew right then that you were special. I don't think I had ever seen a woman more beautiful."

He kissed her lightly on the lips and cheeks. Surprised, he tasted her salty tears. "El, why are you crying? Did I hurt you or something?"

She reached up and pulled his head back to hers.

"No, sweetheart," she told him. "I'm just so happy. But I'm afraid, too."

"It's great that you're happy. But what are you afraid of?"

"I'm afraid that your family might not like me," she confessed.

"Such nonsense. They'll love you. Just be yourself."

"Michael, do you think we will be able to make love while we're at your parent's home?"

"I don't know El; probably not like we just did," Michael predicted. "But my parents will understand. They'll think of something to get us some privacy."

"Just in case, we should make the most of our time alone tonight, shouldn't we, big fella?"

Mike laughed. "And you say you're worried about me surviving the war. At the rate, you are driving me El, I may not live long enough to get back to the war."

"Poor little Mikie," she teased. "And they call us women the weaker sex."

"Whoever said that never met you, El."

There was not much sleep for the two lovers that night.

***

Michael's parents were expected to be at the hotel with their wagon around ten the next morning. Reluctant to get out of bed, the newlyweds had barely packed and had breakfast before Jacob and Rose Drieborg arrived to pick them up.

On the ride to Lowell and their farm, Jake asked Mike to sit with him on the front bench. They talked of the farm, their neighbors, and the town, and Michael told his father of his experiences of the past year.

As the miles dropped away, Eleanor realized that Mike's mother was much like her own. Her fears were replaced with warmth. She felt that she was home.

Once they had reached the Drieborg farm, they were all loudly welcomed by Mike's sisters and brother. They hugged Mike, and Eleanor, too.

"You didn't tell us Eleanor was so pretty, Michael," Susan chided.

"I was at a loss for words little sister," he responded as he hugged Eleanor to his side.

"We thought you would never get home," Ann added.

"We thought you were in a ditch or something, Papa," Little Jake chimed in.

"Come, Michael," commanded his father. "Change your clothes. We have chores to do, eh Little Jake? Or doesn't our son da cavalry officer clean stalls or milk cows anymore?"

"Some things never change, do they, Papa?" Mike laughed.

"Come Eleanor, you too. Everybody works," Mamma directed. "You can help Ann mit the peeling of the potatoes, no? Already, we are late."

By nightfall that first day, everyone was exhausted. Even the newlyweds were tired and ready for sleep. They had the girls' room in the house. Mike's sisters took the loft and Little Jake slept in Willi's old room in the barn.

Their days were full of farm work, talk and laughter. Neighbors dropped in or invited the Drieborgs to socials. Each Sunday, church turned into a day-long social event. Even big Jake seemed to enjoy the excitement and diversion.

"How are you doing with all this activity, Papa?" his wife asked.

"With the children here, Michael und Eleanor, maybe we are not paying much attention to the farm?"

"I am tired, ya. And I am even behind some on da farm work. But Mamma, believe me when I tell you, I wish dey would never leave us. He und Eleanor have brought laughter back to our home."

"They are so much in love, Papa. Eleanor is good for Michael too, I think."

"Dey remind me of us, years ago, Mamma," commented Jake as he extinguished the kerosene lamp and turned to hug his wife.

Mike and Eleanor stayed in Lowell until just after Thanksgiving. Shortly after their return to the Maryland farm of the Hechts, Mike had to report for duty. The wife he left behind was already pregnant.

Winter Encampment 1864

During the winter of 1863-64, the soldiers of the Rebel Army of Northern Virginia occupied the southern bank of the Rapidan River, a few miles north of Richmond, the capital of the Confederacy. The Union Army of the Potomac occupied the northern bank of the same river. Michigan's 6th Cavalry Regiment was part of that army.

There was little fighting during the winter. Pickets, standing guard on both sides of the river, did not look for opportunities to attack their enemy, either. But they did look for opportunities to engage in unauthorized conversation and trading. Tobacco and Richmond newspapers were prized by Union Troops, while coffee and boots were sought out by the Southerners.

Because of the long stay in one location, the men of both armies were able to erect more permanent and comfortable housing arrangements than would have been the case during the months of fighting. The men of Michigan's 6th Cavalry Regiment were able to erect rectangular log houses with peaked canvas roofs. A door and a fireplace with wooden chimney made each log dwelling dry and warm. This was most welcome, since this year's winter was unusually cold and windy for this part of Virginia.

To guard the Army's encampment, picket duty was required of each cavalry Troop every three days. Drilling new Troopers, training green-broken replacement horses, and learning new formations took a good deal of the intervening time. The hard winter required additional care for their horses too. But the men were still left with time on their hands.

As a result, the Troopers sought diversions. Reading was one such activity. Good readers were highly prized and could always attract an audience. The reading material was usually the Bible, since most men were quite religious and the book was carried in most haversacks. Other books, like *Uncle Tom's Cabin* and the works of Charles Dickens, were sought after as well. The Regimental band gave regular concerts. The sound of a violin, guitar, a Jew's harp or a fine tenor voice could be heard most evenings.

Soldiers were avid letter writers, too. Many a winter evening was spent catching up on letters home. Caring for personal clothing and other gear would likewise help pass a winter evening.

Card playing was widespread. But in some units, it was forbidden because it was considered corrupting and the root cause of gambling, drinking, violence, and insubordination.

Sometimes, after a good snowfall, a snowball fight would be organized. Up to hundreds of men, even entire Regiments, could be involved. Horse racing attracted large audiences and much wagering. The Michigan brigade commander, General George Custer, often put on a race by challenging an officer from another command. So, be it a snowball fight or a race, such rivalries were much encouraged by the commanding officers.

***

Michael had been reassigned his former cavalry Troop. Now, however, he was its commander, with the rank of Captain. Such wartime promotions were common. As the Army grew and casualties mounted, the need for officers grew as well. It was called a brevet promotion. This meant that he would hold that rank as long as the Army needed him to command a Troop.

Normally, officers did not fraternize with enlisted men. Actually, enlisted men preferred it that way. But the men who had trained with Mike back in the fall of 1862 felt differently toward their newly appointed Troop commander. They all had bonded with one another then and still felt that way toward one another, including Mike.

One evening, the members of Mike's old squad were relaxing in the warmth of their winter quarters. The Swede, Bill Anderson, Stan Killeen, George Neal and Dave Steward were sitting around the fire pit at the center of their hut. George was now the squad leader and Joe Hill was a recent replacement.

"Do you think Mike will be over to read again tonight?" Bill wondered. "Last time, he left off when Tom was sold south. I'm anxious for the rest of the story."

"My God, Bill! We've heard *Uncle Tom's Cabin* read by someone how many times? Five?" complained Stan Killeen. "You'd think you would get tired of hearing it. If you like it so much, why don't you read it quietly to yourself?"

"Yup, I suppose we have heard it read several times," George commented good-naturedly. "Sort of surprised myself how much I like it, Stan. The story still has a fascination for me I can't explain. I could read it for myself, but having someone else reading lets me sort of concentrate on the story better. Besides, Mike has a special way with his voice and all."

"I agree with you George," Bill concluded. "Remember that newspaper story Mike read to us? Old Abe himself, when he met Mrs. Stowe, the author of *Uncle Tom's Cabin*, said, 'So this is the lady whose book started this war.' It seems like you and I are not the only ones who like her story, George."

Stan changed the subject. "Since Mike got back from medical leave last month, he's spent more time with us than I would have expected. Most officers stay away from the men pretty much. He is different from the rest of them."

"I think so too, Stan," Dave observed. "He doesn't treat us much different now than when he was our squad leader and just a corporal. But as a Captain, he doesn't fun with us, or we with him much. Wouldn't seem proper, I suppose."

"He's turned hard some, too, though," added George. "Remember when he had to borrow money to save his folks' farm, leave us, and live in Washington? He almost got court-martialed there for trying to protect Kellogg's daughter. He got wounded at Gettysburg too. That will do something to a man."

"Being married myself and with little kids," said Dave, "I can see how he misses his new wife. And now she's pregnant. I know how that can affect a fella, believe me."

"I think we are sort of a support group for him," added Bill Anderson. "He can trust us and he's comfortable spending time with us. He asks me and Dave all kinds of questions about when our wives were pregnant, what our wives went through and all. Mike may have turned hard some, but I think it's because he wants to survive this war more than ever before. I know he swears some now, and he even drinks a little. But anyone who has been through what he has is bound to change some. He's still the best officer around here who I've seen. I'll follow him in battle any day."

"Me too," chimed in the others.

"We haven't had any dealings with the Rebs since Mike returned," warned Stan. "So, we don't know how he will be in a fight. We'll see. I don't trust officers much, though. We'll see if Mike isn't just another one protecting his hide at our expense."

"Hey George," said Stan, changing the subject, "who won the snowball fight this morning?"

"Actually, both sides claimed victory," George answered. "The snow was great packing. But once some of the troopers on the other side used stones in their snowballs, things got a little out of hand. When they did that, we just assaulted them with a little old-fashioned fist action. It took a few busted noses and such, but I think they got the message. They should play fair next time."

Bill Anderson asked of no one in particular, "Any of you hear more about that Richmond raid rumor? Sounds like it might be fun. It sure beats sitting here all the time."

"Come on Bill, you should know better," Dave chided him. "That's just a pipe dream; nothing more."

Richmond Raid: February 1864

Rumors were commonplace in every Army camp. Mike knew that, so he didn't pay much attention to them. In his experience these things quickly took on a life of their own. This was especially true during long periods of inactivity, like now. Most rumors never materialized. But that grim history never stopped soldiers from spreading them faster than a heartbeat. As a Troop commander, he would be told soon enough. In the meantime, why worry about such things?

He had heard the current rumor of a cavalry raid on Richmond the capital of the Confederacy that was supposed to involve the cavalry division of which the Michigan Brigade was a part. Variations of this rumor suggested that the target was the enlisted men's prison, Belle Island, located just outside of Richmond. Another insisted that the Libby Prison for Union officers in that city was the target. Still another target was said to be the Confederate President, Jefferson Davis.

Whichever it was, General Kilpatrick was said to have devised a plan and committed his cavalry division to carry it out.

By late January, another rumor spread that this plan had been approved with a date yet to be set.

At the end of the month Michael was briefed on such a mission. He realized that this time, the rumors he had heard were true after all. The plan was for elements of Kilpatrick's cavalry division to make up the attacking Union force. They were to ride to Richmond, Virginia, and free the prisoners held at both the Libby Prison for officers and the enlisted men's prison on Belle Island, located in the James River. The third objective was not to capture President Davis, but to capture and hold the city of Richmond itself.

Volunteers were sought from the division's various Regiments. The Michigan Brigade furnished Troops from all its Regiments, save the Michigan 1st. The troopers of that unit had just re-enlisted and were on veteran's furlough. But the Michigan 6th Regiment made up for their absence and furnished over three hundred troopers.

Captain Drieborg's Troop was part of that number.

"Can't believe we're doing this," exclaimed Stan. "You all know this is crazy, don't you? Remember, even Mike told us that when we heard the first rumor."

The squad gathered around with the other ninety men of Drieborg's Troop.

"Listen up!" snapped Sgt. Riley. "I'll not have any more a' yer yapping' about this. The decision has been made. Now's the time ta get ready. An' believe me, ya will be ready, all a' yas!

"At the briefing this morning, we were told that we should arrive at our target in three days. So, rations will be issued ta cover that period a' time. Cook yer meat and bake yer bread this afternoon. We won't be stopping ta sleep. Greatcoats, poncho, blanket, extra socks, and gloves will do. Pack a canteen full of water, cooked rations, coffee and a cup. Be sure to wrap the cup with yer socks and pack it in yer haversack. We don't want that cup rattling' making any noise. Leave all sabers here, too. Don't forget to draw three days feed for yer horse. That's it, me boys. Squad leaders will report to me after noon chow. A full inspection will follow the evening meal.

"Off with yas now," Riley concluded. "See to yer gear and check yer horses special today. Swede, better join me now to look over the mounts. If we don't, some a' these bozos would end up walking back."

***

After dark on Sunday, February 28, 1864, thirty-five hundred cavalrymen and a battery of artillery left their winter encampment. By midnight, the advanced guard of this force crossed the Rapidan River at Ely's Ford.

Another force of six hundred Troopers, commanded by Colonel Dahlgren, crossed the same river upstream to the northeast. This advanced force, of which Drieborg's Troop was a part, took the Confederate pickets by surprise without firing a shot. Since all the Rebel guards had been captured, no alarm was given. The raid had begun well.

The night was clear and very cold. Dahlgren had been ordered to proceed at a fast walk, without a pause. He did so throughout the first night. Captain Drieborg's Troop had been assigned to lead the way for this advanced unit of Dahlgren's. The remainder of the Michigan Brigade under Colonel Sawyer made up the rear guard, many miles back.

Keeping the space between units closed up at night was difficult. Large gaps in a long column of riders appeared periodically, especially when a column was strung out around a curve in the road. It often required men to spur their horses to a gallop to catch up. This march was no exception. Units were strung out for miles, and wide gaps appeared repeatedly in the darkness on these unfamiliar roads. Michael and the other officers of his Troop moved up and down the columns of riders keeping their men awake and moving at a quick pace.

"Close it up, trooper," Mike often said in the darkness. "Make it quick now!"

By daylight Monday morning, Michael's advanced party reached its objective, the Spotsylvania Courthouse. After a short rest, his unit turned west. Its next objective was to cross the James River twenty miles above Richmond, move down the south bank, and thus be in position to attack at ten o'clock Tuesday morning at the same time Kilpatrick's main body attacked from the north.

It was Monday night. Despite wearing their rain-repellent ponchos, cold rain had run down their necks and drenched most of the men.

"Captain," spoke Sgt. Riley, "we have two horses limping, sir. An' all the mounts need a rest, some feed, and ta be walked a while, if'n we expect them ta be worth a hoot for the attack. An' the men are drenched, sir. A short stop to change shirts would do wonders for morale."

"Sorry Sergeant," Mike told him. "We can't do much about the men. In this rain, we can't light a small fire for coffee or warmth, either; besides, it might alert the Rebs. But I'll suggest a pause for the horses." He spurred his horse and moved to the head of the column to talk with Col. Dahlgren.

Shortly, an order was quietly relayed to stop and feed the horses. Within a few minutes, another order had the men walk their horses.

"Couldn't get much of a stop, Sergeant," reported Drieborg. "Did you get those limping horses checked out?"

"Swede done it, sir," Riley responded. "Stones were wedged under the shoe for both a' them. 'Tis lucky that's all it was. Neither is lame, it would seem. Feed, water, and walking them for a while will do nicely. Do ya have any idea where we are, sir?"

"According to the Colonel, we are about half a mile east of the Goochland Bridge," said Captain Drieborg. "If we cross it within the next half-hour, we should be in position just west of Richmond to attack tomorrow morning as scheduled. So, don't count on any rest for the men, Sergeant. I'm told we will not stop until we are in position early tomorrow morning. Lord only knows how long that will take. We know virtually nothing about conditions south of the river. Bound to be touchy the closer we get to Richmond. Move fast and quietly is the order. But keep me informed about the horses, Sergeant."

"Right, sir."

South of the river, they moved at a trot on the main road toward Richmond. Every half-hour or so, the men walked their horses for a while. They stopped for a few minutes twice. The troopers gave their horses some feed and water, quickly remounting to resume their journey.

Shortly after seven the next morning, Dahlgren's troopers stopped in a sparsely wooded area three miles west of Richmond.

"Have the men disperse to the south of this road, Sergeant," Mike ordered. "In that stand of trees over there will do; no fires though. Have them feed and check over their mounts first, then eat something themselves. I expect this is the last opportunity for rest. But before they grab any sleep, have them check their gear for the attack. I've been called forward by the Colonel. I expect to be back shortly with more information."

"Yes, sir," Riley responded. Then, he spurred his horse to toward the rear of the column. "Squad Leaders, listen up! Form up on me. Come on, now; we don't have all day, after all."

He proceeded to give them their orders. "A'fore yas let the men get some sleep, make sure they've done what yas told 'em. Swede an' I'll inspect the mounts in fifteen minutes. Be quick about yas, now. We don't have all day, ya know. When the order comes, we leave with ya or without. Tell that ta yer men now."

A bit later, most of the troopers were asleep each man wrapped in his poncho and lying by his mount with the horse's bridle tied to his wrist. A light snow began to fall, driven by a brisk, cold wind.

"We're going to attack right down this road Sergeant," informed Captain Drieborg. "Seems that it goes right into Richmond. According to our map, it's the main road from the west too. It seems strange to me that there isn't more traffic on it. Makes me worry a bit about the reception we might be getting."

"A mite late to worry about that now, sir," observed Riley. "We knew this might be a wild ride. In another hour, we'll know fer sure. Get a bit a' sleep yaself, Captain. Ya need ta be fresh shortly. I'll listen for the order ta mount."

"Thanks, Sergeant," Drieborg said. "You've always looked after us, haven't you? All the men in the platoon, I mean."

"I've done me best, sir," Riley replied, somewhat surprised at Mike's complimentary observation.

Mike lay back on his poncho and placed his head on his saddle. He looked up at the predawn sky.

"Remember when all of us first reported to camp back in Grand Rapids a thousand years ago?" Mike said, aloud.

"When you singled me out to face the First Sergeant, I thought I would shit my pants. For a while there, I was thinking maybe I should have taken the thirty days in the Grand Rapids jail instead of joining the Regiment. As afraid as you two made me, I had a tough time not breaking that fellow Bacon in half. More than once, I was sorely tempted to do just that."

"Sorry ya didn't, boyo?"

"Not a bit," Mike responded quickly. "I'm glad I took your advice and held my temper. You know, though, I wouldn't be surprised if the jail they would have sent me to would have been more comfortable than this field." He laughed.

"But thinking about all the good and not so good things that have happened to me since I joined the Regiment, I have no regrets at all, Sergeant. Besides, where else could I be trying to sleep in an open field, middle of the winter, far from home, outnumbered, surrounded by people trying to kill me and planning to capture Richmond, the capital city of the Confederacy, with a few hundred men?"

"Put that way son, I don't think they ought a send ya on a trip north recruiting volunteers for the cavalry," remarked Riley with a chuckle.

"I must admit, Sergeant," Mike responded, "that would be a challenge. But if I could sell men on joining up, I'd know for sure I could make it in Washington City, after all."

***

At the very hour scheduled for General Kilpatrick's forces to begin their attack, retreat was sounded instead. The men were puzzled at the decision and disgusted with their leaders.

"I told you guys," taunted Stan. "Only one time have our Generals been decent in this whole damn war. That was at Gettysburg. Even then, we didn't follow up proper and finish Lee. Lincoln agreed with me and fired General Meade for that. Now we're within sight of Richmond, and we're retreating. Not a shot fired, even. No wonder this war has lasted so long. We've outnumbered the Rebs in every battle for the last year or so; we have better equipment and more ammunition, too. Damn.

"And with our Spencer rifles, each of us can get off seven shots in the time it takes a Reb to get off two. Tell me why the Michigan Brigade is the only unit to have the Spencer carbines? The Rebs are barefoot and half-starved, ta boot. It's enough to piss off a saint, I say."

"Being right this time, Stan, don't get us out of this fix we're in here," cautioned George, his squad leader.

"George," Riley ordered, "yer squad will be taking the point. We have to get ta that bridge we crossed yesterday an' hold it for the rest of the Colonel's force coming behind us."

"It's about twelve miles back," George remembered. "I believe we can get there well before dark, Sarge."

"That's good. Ya know what to do lad," Riley said. "Get going now. Be about fifty or so yards out. The captain will be with the second and third platoons. Swede an' I will bring up the rear. Get on with ya, now."

Drieborg's Troop was on the road moving at a trot. No walking the horses this time. They had to capture and hold the Goochland Bridge before any Rebs in the area knew of their intention.

Colonel Dahlgren's force of over five hundred men depended upon this bridge being captured and held. At a good trot, it should take the advanced guard no longer than two hours to reach the bridge, some twelve miles west.

The point squad of six riders was some fifty yards ahead of I Troop's main body. If trouble came, they would usually be the first to face it, giving ample warning to the rest of the Troop.

They were followed by two platoons of twenty-five troopers each, spread over another one hundred yards or so. These platoons had riders out on both flanks, as well.

Another fifty yards back of these two platoons followed the rear guard with Sgt. Riley.

Because of the winding nature of the turnpike, the three parts of this Troop would sometimes lose sight of one another when sharp turns were encountered. At these times, they were very vulnerable to attack from the flanks. So, they would close the gaps by spurring their mounts at a gallop. Their greatest ally was speed. So, despite the tired condition of their horses they rode at a trot, not walking their horses at all.

Captain Drieborg was with the two twenty-five-man platoons which made up the center of his Troop. He changed positions from the front to the rear, and back again to the front. Thus, he could keep track of both the point and the rear guard and thereby better direct their actions.

As Drieborg's point squad rode ahead around a curve, they moved out of his line of sight. Suddenly, rifle fire from the flanks was directed at his two platoons.

Several men fell in the first volley. A horse reared and screamed, blood streaming from its neck, while another horse leaped forward, throwing its rider. Gun smoke filled the air, reducing visibility. Drieborg fell from his horse into a ditch, unconscious. His Troop was momentarily leaderless.

At the same time, fire from the woods was directed at both the point squad and the squad acting as rear guard. The Union soldiers of these units dismounted and formed skirmish lines to attack their hidden foes.

Meanwhile, the Confederate attackers swept across the road and took the confused members of the second and third platoon's, prisoner.

Sgt. Riley took command of Drieborg's Troop. His men dismounted and silenced their attackers with their Spence repeating rifles… Then they ran forward into the woods to attack the Rebel main force from the rear.

The troopers laid down such intense fire that the Rebs withdrew with their prisoners to the other side of the road. By the time the Union point squad attacked from the other flank, the Rebel force had withdrawn from the fight entirely and taken their prisoners with them. Riley's

Troop commander, Captain Drieborg, was one of the prisoners.

Riley broke off the fight and did not pursue the retreating Rebs. He had his wounded to contend with. Besides, his Troop had been ordered to capture and hold the Goochland Bridge. Some five hundred mounted men retreating behind them depended upon it.

So, he reformed his men and headed west.

Taken Prisoner: March 1864

"Move, all of you!" a gray-clad soldier shouted. "Prod them prisoners an' get 'em moving, too."

Michael lay semiconscious on the ground. His collar markings showed that he was an officer. He vaguely heard voices above him.

"Can I have his boots, Pa?" asked a young boy standing directly over Mike.

"Leave him be son," an older voice replied. "You have a good pair. 'Sides, both of your feet could fit into one of his boots."

"But he's dead I think, Pa," the youngster insisted. "What use will he have for them?"

"Jus' look closer son," the older man said. "He ain't dead. He's got a nasty crease across his forehead, but he's breathing fine. He'll come to in a bit. We can't wait, anyway. Those Yankees firing at us out there are really pouring the lead at us. Here, help me tie him to his horse. We gotta get going, or you and I will be their prisoners instead. Your mother would sure give me what for, if anything happened to you."

"Well, how about my taking his long coat Pa?" the boy suggested. "You could sure use a nice warm coat like that."

"I'm just fine son. Rather be a bit cold than steal. Anyways, he'll be needin' this where he's a' going. Get up now fella," the older man told Mike. "We gotta be moving." He helped Mike get to his feet. "Put your arm around my shoulders. That a' way. My son and I are not regulars.

We're home-guard volunteers. We just help out now and then to protect our homes from you devils. I'm sorry about your wound, but you didn't give us much choice with you attacking our homes like you have. We'll help you till you get your wits about you. But don't take too long, 'cause we're gonna leave and get back to our farm shortly. They don't need us much now that your attack has been stopped."

Mike was silent for a time, but once he had his wits more about him, he asked, "Do you know where I'm being taken, sir?"

"If that don't beat all, Pa," the boy said to his father. "This officer called you, sir."

"Richmond, probably," was the response. "There's a prison they keep there for officers. It's called Libby Prison. No one has ever escaped from that place. It seems to me that your fighting days are over young feller. Till this war is finished, at least."

Michael had heard of the prisons maintained by the Confederates. If the stories he'd heard from exchanged prisoners were true, he wasn't looking forward to the experience.

He believed that southern prisons were places used to hold men until they were exchanged. During the wait, few efforts were made to make the prisoner's stay tolerable. There was no effort to protect the captured soldiers from the elements or to feed them properly. Food and clothing sent from the North for them were usually confiscated.

There was another rumor Mike had heard that dealt with the practice of prisoner exchanges. It was said that exchanges were not going to be made as frequently as they had been early in the war. Northern Generals had objected to the exchange system because they knew the men returned to the South would quickly rejoin their army. And, they argued, the pool of fighting men available to the Southern armies was very limited compared to that available to the Union army. So, they wanted every Rebel prisoner kept a prisoner in order to hurt the Southern armies.

Southern authorities objected to treating the captured Negroes of the Union Army the same as white prisoners. Instead, Negro prisoners were treated as runaway slave property. This practice caused the authorities in the North to threaten the stoppage of all exchanges. Thus, when the Union cavalrymen participating in the Richmond raid were captured, the chance of their return through the exchange system was slim; they just didn't know it. They thought the old system of prisoner exchanges was still in full operation.

Michael looked about him as he marched. He was clear-headed now, and his energy was returning. He was not thinking of being exchanged right now; he was thinking of escape. He realized that the men and boys who captured his unit in the predawn hours were little more than local militia. They were organized to defend their homes when word spread about invading Union cavalrymen. So they had been assigned to patrol along that road when Michael's Troop led Kilpatrick's retreat north.

He could see that they were only armed with squirrel guns and shotguns. Neither they nor the regulars with them were a match for the firepower of the Spencer carbines his Troop carried. But they had the advantage of superior numbers, they knew the countryside well, and they were angry. He could tell that by their attitude toward him and the other prisoners.

Now, they guarded him and the others with the rage of men defending their homes and womenfolk against intruders believed to have the worst of intentions. They swarmed around Michael and the several dozen other prisoners and herded them toward Richmond and an uncertain welcome.

Mike heard one of the regulars say that they were less than fifteen miles from Richmond. But for the first few hours, the walk through the countryside was slowed by wet snow and soft, muddy ground. It was difficult to keep one's footing, much less run. Even so, when walking through a thick stand of trees, he saw one of the prisoners try to escape. The man grabbed a shotgun from a boy sleepily walking beside him, hit him with the stock, and fled into the woods. Slowed by the poor footing and the dense underbrush, he had gotten but a few yards when he was cut down by musket fire from the regulars guarding them. Mike decided right then that he would have no chance, either. None of the other prisoners tried to escape either.

After an hour of walking cross-country, they reached a solid road.

***

It was just after noon when Michael and the other prisoners reached the outskirts of Richmond. They were marched in a long column of twos through the city, while local citizens gathered all along the streets to watch. They were mostly women and kids, but Mike could see some uniformed men in the crowds, too. They were all angry.

"Leave us alone, you Yankees!" was shouted time and again. "Your mamma would be ashamed of you!"

Some of the kids threw stones and balls of wet dirt at the prisoners. "Where are we going now?" Mike asked one of the guards.

"You officers are going to a real nice hotel just down the road a piece," he said, sounding very pleased at the prospect. "The enlisted men are going to that island out there. A real paradise, it is."

Libby Prison

As the prisoners neared the James River, the column was stopped. The enlisted men were marched over a bridge to Belle Island, a prison in the middle of the river. The officers were going to be housed in nearby Libby Prison.

The column of prisoners Mike was in had been joined by officers captured elsewhere. They were marched to the very four-story brick prison building Mike and his troops were supposed to capture.

"Formation, halt!" one of the guards shouted. Used to giving and receiving marching orders, the column of officers came to a halt and stood at attention.

Mike noticed an officer emerge from the building and approach his column of prisoners. "This is going ta be your home men. It's called Libby Prison. With your arrival it will house a few over one thousand Union officers as prisoners. This street you're standing' on is called Carey Street. Over to your left is the James River.

"Libby has the reputation of being escape-proof; and we intend to keep it that way. The guards and other Confederate military personnel are located on the first floor. All prisoners are housed on the upper three floors. Maybe a few of you are important enough to be exchanged, but most of you are not, since we haven't had an officer exchanged for some time. So, don't count on it. It seems your government has stopped such things."

He let that sink in for a minute or so. "So, once you enter those doors, the chance of you coming out before this war is over is slim to none. Get used to it."

***

The newest prisoners, those captured in Kilpatrick's Richmond raid, stood in single file in a first-floor office of the prison.

"Give me your full name, unit and home address," said a Confederate clerk sitting behind a desk.

"Michael Drieborg, I Troop, Sixth Cavalry Regiment, Michigan Brigade. Lowell, Michigan."

The clerk finished writing and looked up at Michael. "Before I was assigned this desk job, Captain, I was with Fitz Lee's cavalry Regiment. We an' the rest of General Stuart's cavalry met you boys a bit west of Gettysburg. Do you remember that sir?"

"I was there, Corporal," Mike responded wearily.

"Those repeating carbines of yours sure caused us some problems. You took us by surprise with those weapons, for sure. After that, we called you the Michigan Devils. Put me in this chair, too." The clerk showed Michael his crutch.

Mike remained silent.

"It gives me great pleasure keeping you out of this war, Captain." He grinned. "Jus you move to that stairway over there and wait, sir. Next."

Mike did as he was told.

Mike and the other new arrivals were housed for a time in the center room of the third floor. There, they were soon met by two Union officers.

"I'm Colonel Tom Rose and this is Major A.G. Hamilton. I was infantry and the Major was cavalry. We share responsibility for the internal organization and discipline of the Libby prisoners.

"Tomorrow, each of you will be interviewed by personnel of the prison Comman-dant's office. They will assign you to one of six rooms. We suggest that you respond to their questions with courtesy and dignity. We further suggest that you not reveal infor-mation about your unit strength, disposition, or movements. Using the basic infor-mation, you have already given they will notify our War Department of your internment here. Our government will tell your families of your situation."

"Just remember," Major Hamilton cut in. "They control our food and medical at-tention. They can also withhold our mail. They can deny us our packages, clothing, blankets or anything sent to us from the North." "You make it seem like we're supposed to just give up and act helpless," one of the newly arrived prisoners lamented.

"That's not what we're saying, Lieutenant," Colonel Rose corrected him. "But a bad attitude just challenges them to punish everyone. If you have a problem with the Rebs or another prisoner, your Room Committee is the first place you take it. The Committee will handle most problems. If the problem can't be solved at that level, the Major and I will take it to the Commandant's office."

At this point Major Hamilton took over. "Disrespect for fellow prisoners will not be tolerated. We must help one another if we are to survive prison. We must also exercise and keep as clean as possible.

"The Room Committees Colonel Rose referred to earlier are elected each month. The men on these committees are responsible for passing out food, mail, and any cloth-ing which might be sent here by our government. They assign latrine duty and General cleanup, supervise daily exercise and handle group problems. We rotate committee mem-bership monthly, so you can expect to be asked to serve before long. You will soon realize that the rooms are very crowded with prisoners. That makes it even more important for each of us to treat fellow prisoners with respect."

"Do you have any questions at this time?" Colonel Rose asked.

"Yeah, I've got one sir, with respect, of course. When do we eat?"

"Well Lieutenant, you just missed our main meal today: moldy hardtack with worms soaked in warm corn soup. How many kernels of corn did you find in your bowl today Major?"

"I saw at least three or four, sir. I was lucky. Yesterday, I didn't find any. Oh yes, there is a blanket here for each of you, compliments of the United States War Department."

"And listen," Colonel Rose warned. "As much as we preach about caring for one another and as severely as we punish stealing; this blanket, your greatcoat and your boots are important to survival here. They are more valuable here than money. Leave that kind of stuff lying around untended, I guarantee you, it will be gone faster than you can snap your fingers. As crowded as we are, you will never get it back."

Major Hamilton then assigned each new prisoner to a section on the second or third floor.

Mike headed up the stairs to the second floor. "Is there a Lieutenant Blanchard around here?" he asked.

"I'm over here soldier," Blanchard shouted. "You're one of the prisoners who arrived today, aren't you? One of Kilpatrick's Raiders, I guess."

"That's right. I was captured just a few days ago."

A prisoner seated against the wall by Blanchard said, "We've been expecting you boys for a couple of weeks."

"What? You knew we were coming?" Mike sputtered.

"Don't look so surprised Captain," said Blanchard. "It was in the Richmond newspapers two weeks ago. The Rebs were waiting for you. Don't get me wrong. I wish you had succeeded in freeing us and the boys out on Belle Isle, but you had no chance." He beckoned with his hand. "Over here. Let me introduce you to the men in your group. Then I'll tell you about your responsibilities."

"Hey Blanchard," Mike asked. "I need to write to my pregnant wife. Where can I get some supplies?

Dearest Eleanor,

By the time you receive this letter, the War Department may have notified you that I am missing and possibly captured. Well, I was captured and am now a prisoner. The building where the Rebs are keeping me is in Richmond of all places. There are hundreds of other

Union officers being kept here too. At least you don't have to worry about me being killed in battle.

More important to me, is how you and the baby are doing. Please take care of yourself. I love you so much. My thoughts are about you always. I don't know if my parents will be notified of my situation. Would you do that? I only have this small piece of paper another prisoner gave me. I don't know when I will be able to get writing supplies of my own. So, it may be some time before I can write again. In the meantime, remember that I love you.

Your loving husband,

Michael

***

During all twenty-one years of his young life, Michael had always been active. Sitting around with nothing to do was not something he enjoyed. But in captivity, at Libby Prison, there was nothing anyone could do, except endure.

However, Mike heard a rumor that someone was doing something. That someone was Colonel Rose.

Mike approached him. "Colonel Rose, my name is Michael Drieborg.

Can I speak to you privately?"

"You're one of those who just arrived, aren't you?" Rose responded. "Certainly, we can talk, Captain. Follow me."

Mike was led to an empty corner of the second floor. Mike assumed that this was the Colonel's private area, since a guard kept other prisoners away while he talked with Rose.

"This is Evan Schluckbier, my aide," Rose told Mike. "Evan, take a break while I talk with the Captain."

Once they were alone, Rose asked, "Now, what's on your mind?"

"Sir, I heard your Aide talking to one of the men in my unit here," Mike began. "He told the other man about a shift schedule. It seemed to me that they were talking about digging. Colonel, sitting around is going to kill me. I am healthy and strong and anxious to get out of here. Whatever it is you're digging, I can help. Will you let me?"

"Drieborg, let me be very clear right now about the conversation we are about to have. If I hear that you talked to anyone about our conversation, you will not survive to see another day. Do you understand?"

"Look, sir, I only want to get back to my Troop, and back to the war. If I can accomplish that by helping you dig, I have no problem keeping quiet about it. Besides, my wife is having our first child. I have no death wish."

Rose continued to question Mike. He asked about life on the farm, the circumstances of his enlistment, being wounded at Gettysburg, recovery, and his recent marriage. The conversation lasted over two hours. Mike's experiences in Washington, D.C., seemed of special interest to the Colonel.

"Tell you what, Mike," Rose told him. "Let me think about it. I'll get back to you with my decision. Remember what I told you. Talk about this to anyone, and you will never see your child."

"Yes, sir. I understand."

Within a few days, Mike had been accepted by the Colonel. Mike was excited to be involved in this prison escape effort. As the Colonel had explained it to him, the lowest floor of the building was on the river side of the prison. In that space, there was an unused basement room called the Rat Cellar. The prisoners knew about it because they were sometimes allowed to cook food on the stoves in that area. In one corner of the room was an unused fireplace. It had a chimney that ran through the ceiling of that room and through all three of the upper floors of the prison. Colonel Rose saw this chimney as an ideal hidden entrance to the Rat Cellar from the upper floors.

It was there, in the Rat Cellar, that Colonel Rose and his hand-picked men had begun digging an escape tunnel. The tunnel was headed toward a shed located a good thirty yards to the northeast of the prison building.

On his first night, Mike was given his assignment. "Follow me down this rope ladder Mike," the Colonel told him. Once in the Rat Cellar, Mike could see the tunnel opening on the north wall. He noticed that the opening was pretty small.

"Colonel," he said. "I don't think I can work in such a small space."

"Just give it a try, Mike."

Mike obeyed. But after pulling himself completely into the tunnel, he found the dark passage frightening. *I can't stand this. I have to get out of here.* He hurriedly pushed himself out and sat by the entrance, sweating and gasping for air.

"Mike. Don't worry about it," Col. Rose assured him. "We have other things that need to be done down here." So, Mike still had a four-hour work shift on one of the digging teams. He was assigned to pull out each bucket of dirt when a digger had filled it. Then he spread the dirt on the floor of the cellar. He spread it around and eventually covered it with straw. He also operated a billow fan to push air into the tunnel entrance.

The nightly effort was not without its dangers. Even though guards did not venture into the rat-infested cellar, one might stumble on their chimney entrance or a guard might notice fresh dirt on the knees of one of the conspirators. A fellow prisoner might even tell a guard in hopes of special privileges or food.

The dirt ceiling of the tunnel was a potential danger, too. On the first attempt, they had dug only ten yards, when the ceiling of the tunnel caved in. They feared guards might notice the depression in the ground.

When there was no interest shown by their captors, they began again after a few days. When the second tunnel had gone over twenty yards, they decided to poke through to the ground above. It was discovered that they had been digging on an angle and were still seven or eight yards from their shed objective. They had to start again. It took another week, but finally, one of the diggers poked his head through the ground inside the shed. The conspirators were ready.

***

One moonless March night, all the men involved in the digging successfully escaped through the tunnel and into the city.

Unfortunately, that same night, other prisoners discovered the chimney opening and followed Mike's group through the tunnel. By dawn, one hundred and nine men had managed to escape. That many men missing at the morning count would not be overlooked by the jailers. On the contrary, the Confederates immediately began an intensive search of the prison. Sure enough, after morning count, the guards found the chimney opening, which led them to the Rat Cellar and the tunnel.

This was the first escape of the war from Libby Prison. The Commandant was outraged, and he was determined to catch every single escaped Union officer. He alerted the Richmond authorities and the commander of the Confederate military. Cavalrymen, together with units of the infantry, began searching the city and, in ever widening circles, the local countryside.

Earlier, while the general prison population slept, Mike snuck through Richmond. It was around midnight. He and the other escapees figured that they probably had about six hours before their absence would be discovered.

He had traveled a good number of miles northeast of the city, following the tracks of the Richmond and York Railroad. It was almost dawn when he reached the Chickahominy River Bridge.

"Damn," he thought.

He figured that the bridge would be guarded, but he had hoped that he would find the guards still asleep. Instead, they were awake and cooking their morning meal. So, he moved back into the woods at the southern bridge approach, hid in some shrubbery and slept. He awoke at dusk and moved further east in hopes of finding a shallow place to cross the river. He eventually slipped crossing the river, thoroughly soaking his clothing and shoes. He was shivering from the bitter night cold, but continued to move through the Virginia countryside.

For a second time, he hid himself during the daylight hours. He moved only after dark. He was able to spot Confederate patrols during the night by their campfires. By the next dawn, he had reached the New Kent Courthouse some twenty miles from Richmond. According to the crude map each of the escapees had been given, Mike believed he was close to Union lines at Williamsburg.

He took a chance during the third day and crossed an open field in broad daylight. On a ridge, several hundred yards to the east, he believed he spotted Union cavalrymen riding south. They did not see him, so he began sprinting toward them.

Unexpectedly, a Confederate patrol on his right rode onto the field he was crossing.

"Pull up there, Yank," one of the riders shouted. "Or, you're dead in your tracks."

Mike stopped running. He could see the Union soldiers watching from the ridge, but the Confederates were closer. He was recaptured.

Andersonville Prison

Of the 109 prisoners to escape, forty-nine were recaptured. Michael Drieborg was one of those caught and returned to Libby Prison. The leader of the escape effort, Colonel Rose, was also recaptured. The Commandant of the prison was furious with him.

"Colonel," he fumed, "I gave you enormous authority in this prison. You betrayed the trust I placed in you."

"Yes, I did," Rose admitted. "But once I noticed a way to escape, the very leadership position you gave me obliged me to help my fellow prisoners escape."

"That may be Colonel, but it will not happen again, I assure you." Colonel Rose was placed in solitary confinement. The other recaptured officers were put in chains and imprisoned in the very room from which they had escaped, the Rat Cellar. Michael and the others were housed and fed in that room for over a month.

Early one morning, a guard removed Mike's chains. "Come on Captain," the guard ordered. "You're going for a little train ride."

Excited at the prospect, Mike asked, "Am I being exchanged soldier?"

"Afraid not Captain. There's a train just down the road ready to take you to Andersonville Prison in Georgia."

That stopped Mike cold. "I thought that the other officers' prison is in Milan, Georgia. Isn't Andersonville an enlisted man's prison?"

"That's true," the guard told him. "We've been shipping men there from the Belle Isle Prison, but the Commandant figgers that the officers we recaptured after the big escape are problem prisoners. So, off they'll all go on the first available train south, whatever its destination, officer or not."

"What of Colonel Rose? Is he being shipped south, too?"

"He was exchanged last week, I think. Anyways, he's gone north. Guess you're not a big enough fish for anyone to bother with Captain." The guard chuckled. "The good news for us is you're one Michigan Devil who won't bother us anymore."

Mike was shoved into a boxcar. There were so many men in his car, he couldn't sit or even fall down if he wanted to.

"Easy there, soldier," he said to a man who slumped against his side. "Hold on, we'll make it."

As the train traveled south, the weather cooled. That was a blessing during the several days of the trip south. Still, it was hot with body heat and the putrid smell caused many to throw up, even on empty stomachs. With no place to relieve themselves properly, the men in the car relieved themselves the only way they could. The train stopped occasionally for fuel, but the prisoners still suffered terribly. No food or water was provided. No opportunity to stretch their legs and properly relieve themselves was provided either. When the train jerked to another abrupt stop, the captives groaned, anticipating another long wait to bake in the hot sun.

Andersonville, Georgia. Officially known as Camp Sumter, nearly 33,000 POWs were held here during one period; 12,000 died and were buried here. COURTESY OF THE LIBRARY OF CONGRESS

Andersonville Prison

This time, when the doors were opened, the prisoners were ordered out of the cars. After days packed in these cars, most men could barely stand without support. Many just fell to the ground from the open doorway of their boxcar.

As each cattle car was emptied of its human cargo, the men who could stand were quickly herded from the train to just inside the wide-open gates of the prison. Once inside the guards withdrew and closed the large doors. The newly arrived prisoners were simply left standing there.

"Now, what do I do?" Mike wondered.

"Hey Drieborg!" he heard.

Still getting used to the bright sunlight, Michael squinted, shading the sun with his hand. He looked around and tried to find the familiar voice. Someone was pushing his way through the crowd toward him.

Suddenly he saw the man who had shouted at him. "Ransom, is that you?" exclaimed Michael.

The men hugged one another.

"I thought you were dead John," Michael said. John had gotten to know Mike some when he had visited his brother, who was in Mike's platoon.

"Not hardly," John Ransom told him. "I just feel that way some days though." He led Mike away from the crowd of newly arrived prisoners and onlookers. "I see you recovered from your Gettysburg wound all right. But you being an officer an all, what in heck are you doing here?"

Mike explained the circumstances.

"Well, I don't know anything about the conditions at Libby Prison," John said. "But if it was for officers, it had to be better than this place. Andersonville has only been up and running since April, but already the water is foul, fuel is in short supply and the food is terrible, when we get any. We don't see any of this changing for the better either."

The two men were still standing near the main entrance to Andersonville. Mike noticed that the entrance was on higher ground than the general camp. From where he stood, he could look across the entire prison to the far stockade wall. What he saw stunned him. From one stockade wall to another, he could see what had to be thousands and thousands of men in blue uniforms. And these were only the men who were not sheltered by tents and tarpaulins on poles.

"How many men are here?" Mike asked.

"Don't know actually. The Rebs just keep bringing in trains like yours most every day, full of men with just the clothes on their backs."

"Doesn't anyone get out of here?" Mike asked. "You know; exchanged?"

"No one has been exchanged since the prison opened this spring. As you can see, the place is very overcrowded. If that weren't bad enough, we're also in danger all the time from a large group of prisoners who prey on the weak. We call them the Raiders. Other than that, this is a paradise on earth."

Like Mike, John was from Michigan, too, and a cavalryman as well. He looked to Mike to be a lot thinner than when they had last talked. What was left of John's uniform was filthy and worn. His hair and beard were much longer than Mike remembered, and dirty, too. But he still had that ready smile, and Mike was happy to see his friendly face.

"Come over to my area," John suggested. "We're all cavalry guys. You probably will recognize Phil Lewis of the 5th Michigan Regiment. The others are all Michigan men too. You'll fit right in. But you have to abide by our rules if ya want to stay with us."

"What kind of rules John?"

"None that don't make sense Mike. We all exercise together every day. We take turns preparing and sharing our food together. We even pray twice a day. Even though you never win the war with the Graybacks, we pick 'em off one another all the time, anyway. We want each other to stay clean. We also take turns on guard through the day and night. Any problem with these rules?"

"No complaint from me," Mike responded quickly. "You're right, all those rules all make sense. But standing guard? We're all Union soldiers here in a Southern government prison. Is it that Raider bunch you were telling me about?"

"Afraid so. These guys roam throughout the camp; day and night. They take what they want. Most men in this prison are not organized like us. In fact, most prisoners are too sickly and weak put up much of a fight, so the Raiders rule the roost here. We figure the Reb guards get bought off to cooperate with the Raiders.

"Here we are. Hey guys, guess who just arrived on the latest train?" John announced. "You remember Mike Drieborg from the 6th Michigan? Mike, you remember Phil Lewis from the 5th Regiment? This is George Hendryx of the 9th. Sam Hutton there and Joe Sergeant are both of the 9th, too. Unless any of you have an objection, I asked Mike to join our mess here. Is that all right, or do you want him ta move on?"

Each of the men nodded toward John in approval.

"No one seems ta have a problem, Mike. So, welcome to our mess," John said, shaking his hand. "This little spot of heaven is now your home away from home."

"That's fine with me. I appreciate it guys. Anything I can do to help each of us come out of this alive, just tell me," Mike promised.

***

Before long, Mike had caught on to the routine and the demands of living in an open-air sewer. They boiled all water used for drinking or cooking. He took his turn getting his group's share of the food. He stood guard watching for the predator Raiders. He kept his clothing and his body as clean as he could, and he joined his mates in their losing battle with lice.

"What did you hear about food today Phil?" Mike asked.

"Word is, bean soup and cornbread again. We're supposed to get it this afternoon sometime. If it's anything like that last so-called soup we had, we'll be drinking barely warm water with a few worm-infested beans hidden at the bottom of a bucket of dirty water. So, complain to the cook." Phil chuckled. "Got a better idea?"

"Give me John's straight razor. I'll sharpen it on my belt and see if I can't get us some meat for our soup today."

"Oh, my Lord! Are you talking about rat meat? And you were the guy who would retch at the mere thought just a week ago."

"That's right Phil. But I've decided to survive this prison," Mike responded vigorously. "If eating rat meat will help me keep up my strength, I've got a better chance of surviving. So that's what I'll do. Now get me the damn razor. I'll trade a shave or two for a juicy rat."

Later that afternoon, the men of Mike's mess were eating their portion of the bean soup and cornbread given to them earlier that day.

"Not bad soup today, Phil," observed Sam Hutton. "The Rebs threw in some bits of meat this time."

"I had a bit of pepper stashed away that I used too," responded Phil. Joe Sergeant swallowed the last bit of his cornbread.

"John, if you stopped using your money for paper and pencils, you could buy salt and other edibles from the local farmers who sell stuff here. We would all be better off."

Sam Hutton interrupted. "Stuff it Sergeant! What John does with his money is his affair. Our mess eats better right now than any other around. We are healthier, cleaner and better dressed, too. You got any problems with that, I suggest you look for another group where you could do better."

"Knock it off you two," urged John. "Just tell us. Where did the meat come from?"

Phil Lewis had been in charge of this meal's preparation. "Want me to tell 'em Mike?"

No one spoke for a moment.

"No!" exclaimed John, sitting upright. "Not you, Mike?"

"It's like you said, John," Mike responded. "We can't survive for long on the stuff they give us here. We gotta have meat sometimes too. I gave three shaves for the two rats we used in our soup. Just don't any of you guys tell my mother or my wife that I did it, okay?"

"Joe won the pot on that bet," John told Mike. "Everyone else thought you would hold out longer. But he said you would eat rat meat, on purpose, in ten days ta two weeks of your arrival. So, he won an extra share of grub next time we get any."

Joe sat across from them grinning like a Cheshire cat. He was thin like everyone else Mike had seen since he arrived. But his hair was cut short and he had a bounce to his step. Mike thought that Joe's energy level and positive attitude were the result of the group's daily exercise and cleanliness routines. It sure couldn't be the result of the food around here.

"Don't take it personal Mike," Joe assured him. "I just made a lucky guess."

"If that don't beat all." Mike shook his head, chuckling. "You guys would bet on most anything. I know you bet on who can pick the most Graybacks; who can do the most sit-ups; even who relieves himself first after reveille. Is there any end to things you guys don't bet on?"

"You missed the most important event we're betting' on right now," Joe said. "Everyone in our group here but you, that is."

No one said anything. They just smiled and looked at Mike.

"You didn't," Mike exclaimed. "Not when my baby will be born?"

"You're close Mike," Sam cut in. "But that's not what we're betting' on this time. It's much more basic than that. Sex has something ta do with it though."

"Oh, I see," Mike realized. "Whether it's a boy or girl."

"You got it, my boy."

Mike laughed. "Is nothing sacred around here?"

"Nope," George Hendryx responded. "No harm was done, Mike. Besides, what else is there to do around here?"

"Staying alive." Mike asserted. "Doing whatever it takes to stay alive. That's what."

***

My Dear Eleanor,

I am well and hope you are too. When I was in Libby prison, I managed to escape along with a lot of other men. After several days, I was close to a Union cavalry patrol when I was recaptured and returned to Libby. The authorities there were very upset with me, so they sent me to a prison in Andersonville Georgia. I doubt if you can even find the town on a map. I miss you so. But, don't worry. I am just as safe here as I was at Libby. Remember sweetheart, I am still out of the fighting.

I suppose the War Department will forward your letters here now. Don't bother sending packages to me. No one here gets any. The guards brag about how much they enjoy things sent to us from our homes.

Please take care of yourself El. I love you.

Your loving husband,

Michael

The Raiders

In the Andersonville Prison, a group of Union prisoners had formed a group called the Raiders. This was a predatory outlaw group that robbed and killed their fellow prisoners for their own survival and ease.

They targeted newly arrived prisoners in particular. Depending on surprise, they plundered the newcomers of everything of value, usually leaving their victims naked and badly beaten. Long-time prisoners were not exempt from attack, either. The Raiders preyed upon the weakest, stealing blankets and clothing as well as any other item that struck their fancy. They viciously attacked at will.

The compliance of the Confederate guards, many barely teenagers, was easily bought.

Not ten yards from Drieborg's tent, a man was beaten in broad daylight. The event could not have been missed by the guards in the nearby watchtower. But as usual, they did nothing. The Raiders stripped the man of his clothing and boldly paraded back to their section of the camp.

The men in Mike Drieborg's mess were together for the only meal of the day. As they recounted the events of that day, Phil Lewis told of witnessing the beating near their tent.

"This fellow was poorly dressed," Lewis related. "I don't think he even had shoes. What he had couldn't have been the reason they attacked him."

"It wasn't for what he had," interrupted George Hendryx. "He was beaten and stripped to remind all of us that the Raiders could do this to anyone, even in broad daylight. They use fear as a weapon." George was from Battle Creek, Michigan. A cavalryman in the 5th Michigan, he had been captured at Gettysburg and was one of the first to be sent to Andersonville, Georgia.

"It's probably a good time to review our own defenses against such an attack," John Ransom suggested. "Two of us need to be in our tent area at all times during the daylight hours. Our goods should always be gathered in the center of this sleeping area with a man on either side. A shovel or piece of firewood should always be handy for each of us to use as a weapon."

John had been the brigade's quartermaster sergeant in the Michigan 9th Cavalry. He had been captured November 6, 1863, in eastern Tennessee. First, he was sent to Belle Island Prison outside of Richmond. Then, he was shipped to Andersonville when it was opened. He had been a slender man when he got here. Now he was actually skeleton-like. His clothing just hung on his frame. Because of his quartermaster background, the men of Mike's group had him manage their food and other possessions.

"Away from the mess," John continued, "we should always travel in pairs with a weapon in hand. We need to keep alert and not hesitate to defend ourselves. Should any of us be attacked, make a racket to get the attention of others and possibly their help. Have I covered everything?" "I think so John," said George Hendryx. George, like John, had come to Andersonville shortly after it opened. It showed in his face that he, too, had lost weight.

"As far as you went John, I thought it was fine, too," Mike added. "It's good to have a plan like that right now. There is some degree of safety in numbers. But what we are doing is not a real solution to our problem with the Raiders."

"Those of us who have been here the longest are doing the best we can," Sam Hutton retorted, taking offense to Mike's remark. Sam was another Michigander from the 9th Cavalry. Mike had noticed that he seemed to look at the negative side of everything. He seemed angry about his situation too. "We just have to survive one day at a time. That's our short-term goal. Our long-term goal of surviving this place is out of our hands. Our army has to win this war soon, or most of us will be dead before long."

"Look, Sam," Mike hastened to explain, "I'm not criticizing. And, I know I'm the new guy here. I sure hope all of you realize how greatly I appreciate your taking me into your mess. You guys probably saved my life. But I'm not blind. Every day that passes, I can tell that I lose weight and strength. As a result, I know I will become more prone to infection and disease. All of us face this same problem. I think we must solve this Raider problem while we still have our strength, or they will eventually deal with us as they did that poor fellow this afternoon."

John Ransom joined in. "Is there anyone here who would argue with Mike's description of our problem with the Raiders? Haven't all of us lost weight since we got here? Are any of us as strong as we were when we walked into this place? I think we also know that we will be easier pickings for the Raiders as time goes on. So I believe Mike is right. We need to come up with a plan to solve this problem now, not later. Do you have something in mind Mike?"

"Yes, I do. Do you guys want to hear it?"

"I'm not going anywhere special this evening Drieborg," Sam joked. "Besides, I need a good laugh."

"Give him a break Sam," admonished John. "Let's hear him out. Share it with us, Mike."

"All right," Mike began. "We have already admitted that we are all growing weaker. We also admit that the Raiders are not. They have all the food they want from the guards, probably packages sent to prisoners that the guards never delivered. The Raiders occupy the highest ground, with the cleanest water, tents, blankets and clothing galore. So, they grow stronger while we grow weaker. Nothing I see will change either situation unless we do something ourselves."

"Oh, yeah?" Sam retorted. "What's that, Captain?"

"We must destroy them. And we must do it very soon if we are to survive. There is no other option I can see."

"Just like that eh?" mocked Sam. "Going to march right up to their compound and do what, talk sense to 'em?"

"No, Sam," Mike responded. "Talk won't work and you know it. We have to kill them. It's as simple as that!"

"You and what army is going to do that?" Sam continued sarcastically. "Me Sam, and an army of prisoners who are fed up with living in fear; guys just like us who are slowly dying anyway; men like me who want a chance to survive this place and go back to their families; guys who refuse to die at the hands of these thugs.

"The beating the Raiders gave that poor soldier this afternoon only strengthened my belief that we have to do something while we are still physically strong enough to do it. But you're right about one thing, Sam. We six men are not nearly enough. It will take a platoon of men who are willing to kill other prisoners. No talk; just attack and kill them. I'm willing to take that risk. Are you?"

As he concluded, Mike's stomach was in a knot and his face flushed. He suddenly realized just how intense and angry he actually was. But he had presented his argument; it was now up to the five men who had welcomed him into their tent. So, he sat back and waited for some response.

"You know Mike, I've been in this prison since it first opened," John Ransom said. "There have been attempts to fight them before. Several were tried before you arrived. None ever succeeded in solving anything. In fact, those who tried force didn't live very long afterward."

Mike felt he had their attention, despite what John had said. He sensed that they wanted him to respond. He sat up with renewed energy.

"I've asked around and listened to some others too, John," Mike continued. "It seems that other attacks on the Raiders were just reactions to something the Raiders did. The other attacks were not well-organized efforts. On the contrary, the Raiders boasted of knowing about them in advance. So, the Raiders turned them into traps.

"On the Raiders' part, they attack well-scouted targets. They know in advance a good deal about their target and pick the place and time. They also have numbers and surprise on their side. In the past, by the time a group got organized to respond, the Raiders were ready and waiting.

"This time, we are going to pick the time and place. Nor will our attack be just a reaction to one of their raids. Instead, it will be a surprise of our own. Our intention will not be to loot, but to kill as many of them as we can, and retreat. Afterwards, we will set up a trap if they attempt a counterattack. If they do, we'll kill more of them."

"Let me get this straight Drieborg," asked Sam Hutton. "You propose to attack a group of fellow prisoners who are physically stronger, better armed and well organized. Is that about it?"

"Yup. That's it, exactly."

"Well, I swear," Joe Sergeant exclaimed. "I can see why we should destroy them, Mike. But how could we ever manage to do it?"

"I'll tell you how, Joe," Mike responded. "First, we have to maintain strict security while we recruit men to join us. You guys have been here long enough to know men you would trust. So, each of you will recruit and lead five men to make up a squad of six. I will help each of you to organize your squad, one man at a time. The members of your squad will know you and me, but not the others in his squad. In fact, each of you squad leaders will only know the members of your own squad. This will help us maintain secrecy. And only I will know the date and time of the attack."

"Seems like you've given this quite a bit of thought Mike," Phil Lewis observed. "How can you be sure all of us are willing to participate?"

Mike looked around. "If anyone is not up to it, just say so."

John Ransom jumped in. "Mike has answered my question about the failure of past efforts to stop the Raiders. Now he's answered Joe's question about how this attack can be pulled off. I, for one, think it can work. So, you can count on my help."

Mike waited for Sam, his severest critic, to comment. "All right Drieborg," Sam finally said. "I'm in, too." The other three men also agreed to recruit and lead a squad.

Over the next ten days six squads were recruited. Five men and a squad leader gave Mike a total of thirty-six men as his strike force. He spoke with each man about the killing purpose of the attack and the type of weapon each of them should find. He suggested a shovel or wooden stake two or three feet in length. Of course, a knife would be excellent too. He explained that surprise and darkness would be their major weapons. He didn't tell any of the recruits that each man would need a piece of white cloth tied around his head to identify him as a member of the attacking force. He kept this a secret. The squad leaders would supply this cloth moments before the attack began.

***

Mike wanted to implement his plan as soon as possible. When the last of the recruits were found, Mike met with the five squad leaders.

"How is your recruiting and training going?" he asked.

One at a time the squad leaders gave a report. They covered all the issues. Mike asked about weaponry, individual toughness and dependability. Mike seemed more interested in the character of the recruited men than any other attribute. He especially did not want men who could be bought off by the Raiders. He wanted angry men, like himself.

When John Ransom spoke of his squad, he brought up another matter. "I think you guys have noticed the last few days that I am having trouble walking. But one of my recruits is a Sioux Indian named Battist. He's a recent arrival and still healthy. He's quiet, but I sense that he is very tough and dependable. I've spoken to him and I think he is willing to take over my squad. I'd like to go get him now, unless any of you object."

"Well," asked Mike, "does anyone have anything else to say about this?" When there were no objections, he said, "Fine then. I think all of us have noticed your stiff leg John. Bring this guy over here right now. We'll talk with him and then decide."

Battist sat quietly in the circle of men. Many questions were asked of him. His answers were short and to the point. Finally, Mike asked him, "How do you feel about helping to lead this undertaking, Battist?"

"I feel as you men do," he answered. "We must kill these outlaw prisoners or lose our own lives. Your plan is my chance to survive and return to my people. I was a warrior of the Sioux nation. I was a leader of men in my infantry unit. I will go with you on this attack as a member of a squad or as a leader of a squad. Either way I am very good at killing. It is up to you to decide."

"Is there any objection to Battist taking John's place as a squad leader?" Mike asked.

There was no objection. "It's fine with me, too. So, you're in Battist," Mike told him. "We will not have time to speak to each man in your squad about this John. So, you will stay with Battist and your squad until we begin the actual attack."

"We can talk to each of them tomorrow," John suggested. "I'm afraid not," Mike responded. "We attack at dark tonight." "Holy shit," Sam muttered. "It's really gonna happen."

Mike nodded. "That's right. I'm satisfied that everyone is ready. And you all know that the longer we wait, the bigger the chance of discovery. So, with no moon tonight, it's got to be now. To get back to your question, John, Battist does not know any of the other men in your squad, so you will go with him as you round up your men. Explain the situation as you go to our attack site.

"You might as well get some rest now. Remember what we agreed upon weeks ago. Now that you know the attack is on for tonight, none of us leaves this mess area. Battist, you were told that before you joined us today."

Shortly before dark, the squad leaders rounded up the members of their squad. All men were accounted for as they gathered in preparation for their attack. Two squads were to lead and secure the entryway of the Raider area. Three squads were to follow on their heels into the heart of that area. The sixth squad, led by Mike, would head directly to the center of the Raider camp to locate and kill the leaders. All the attacking men tied a piece of white cloth around their heads for easier identification by other members of the attacking force.

There was no moon, so when the sun disappeared below the horizon, it quickly became very dark. *Perfect*, Mike thought. He sent off the first of his attacking force.

Without arousing the other prisoners, the twelve men of the first two squads quickly dispatched the Raider guards at the entrance of their compound. Then, these two squads moved to either side of the entrance and began using their clubs, shovels and knives to kill as many sleeping Raiders as they could. They remained near the entrance to secure the escape route for the other four squads.

With his heart pounding in his ears, Mike led the twenty-four men of the other four squads quickly into the Raider compound. He had his men move in pairs. Side by side, they used their weapons to attack the sleeping forms. A shouted alarm finally was sounded, but the Raider response in the moonless night was confused. They didn't know what was happening exactly or against whom to direct a response.

Mike had scouted the location thoroughly, and he knew where the leaders usually slept. He also knew how many paces from the entrance it was. He led his squad directly that many steps into the Raider area. His six men did not attack anyone they found on the way. Once at their destination, though, they began to use their weapons on anyone they found without a white headband. In the excitement and exertion of the moment, Mike shut out the scene around him. All he could hear was the groan of the men he hit with the sharp blade of his shovel. He brought it down on the sleeping forms again and again.

Suddenly, the shrill sound of a whistle interrupted his killing frenzy. That was the signal to break off the attack and withdraw to the entry that was being held by the two squads of men who had led the attack. The whistle sounded a second time. Mike hoped that the twelve pairs of men in his attack group remembered the signal too; and headed out of the compound.

At the rendezvous point Mike met with the five squad leaders for a few moments. "Are any of your men missing?" Mike asked them.

They each quickly reported that all were present.

"Then everyone is accounted for. That's great. Now, go back to your squads. Get them ready to receive a counterattack." *What a relief,* Mike thought. He wiped sweat from his face. His shirt was soaked with sweat as well. He crouched alongside the path they expected the Raiders to use and tightly clutched the shovel he had just used several times to kill sleeping soldiers.

The Raiders did not mount a counterattack. After an hour of waiting, the men of Mike's attack group discarded their headbands and returned silently to their own sleeping areas.

Trial and Punishment

The following day, a guard detail opened the large gates and entered the camp. They were looking for Mike Drieborg, and they seemed to know right where to find him.

"Are you Captain Drieborg?" the sergeant in charge of the guard detail asked.

"Yes, I am Sergeant," Mike responded. "What do you want of me?"

"I have orders from Commandant Wirz, to escort you to his office Captain."

"That's fine, Sergeant," Mike responded. *What the devil? How could he know my role in last night's raid so quickly? Whatever it is, I don't have much choice in the matter.*

Mike was escorted to the office of the Commandant.

He knew that the small wooden building twenty or so yards outside the gate was used by the Confederate soldiers. Thinking about it on his walk to the office of Captain Wirz, he decided that he wasn't all that surprised he had been identified so quickly. He was the only one of the attackers who had talked with all thirty-six men involved in last night's raid. One of them most likely traded information this morning for some extra food.

The guard closed the door behind him once Mike had entered the building. Mike stood at attention. He saw the Commandant sitting behind a desk located in the center of a sparsely furnished room.

"Please sit, Captain," Captain Wirz suggested and pointed to a straight-backed wooden chair in front of the desk. Mike sat stiffly, his stomach in a knot, awaiting a judgment of some sort.

"Guards reported to me this morning that a group of prisoners attacked another group during the night," he revealed. "I am also informed, Captain, that you planned and led that attack."

Mike had seen Captain Wirz many times at the daily morning count of prisoners. Much shorter than Mike, he usually rode his horse around the formations. He was always in proper uniform and sat well on his mount. He wasn't much over five foot six inches tall. He was mustached, but had his hair cut short.

Mike had seen him shout furiously when it became obvious that the prisoners had tried to increase the count of their particular group in an attempt to increase whatever ration would be given to them that day. It was a game to the men, a diversion, because they usually only succeeded in losing the miserable rations entirely.

"There it is," Mike thought." *He knows." Mike* felt his shoulders relax some as he sat back in the chair.

"Even if your information is correct Captain Wirz, what do you intend to do about it?"

"I have hoped for some time that you prisoners would successfully do what you and your men did last night."

"If we are to survive, it had to be done, sir. What will happen now, sir?"

"The renegade prisoners who call themselves Raiders have gone too far with their violence. So, I intend to lead a patrol into the camp today, identify and arrest their leaders. At least, I will arrest those who survived your attack."

"Why bother to tell me about it first, sir?" Mike asked.

"Because I want you to set up a court-martial to decide the fate of these men," Wirz told Michael. "Such a court will operate inside the prison and have the power to hear testimony and mete out punishment, even the death penalty. After you handle that, I need someone to organize the camp internally; draw up rules of conduct for the prisoners, and lead an enforcement team. Could you be that man Captain?"

"I would be willing to lead such an effort sir," Mike quickly responded. "But only if we can actually be in charge of our own internal security and only if you order your guards not to interfere with the enforcement of our rules. Nor can we tolerate guards trading with prisoners. They were in league with the Raiders you know, and gave that rotten bunch free reign inside the camp in exchange for food, clothing, cash, and other loot taken from other prisoners. If you want us to maintain order, it will be maintained. But keep the guards out of the camp. Also, will you allow us weapons of any kind?"

"Draw up rules of conduct Captain," Wirz instructed. "Lay out an administrative structure to enforce the rules and include an appointed court to punish prisoners who break them. Once I approve the rules and the administration you set up, I will order the guards to stay out of the internal affairs of the camp. I will also forbid them to trade with prisoners. There is paper and pencil in here for you to use.

"So, Captain," Wirz concluded, "we have a good start, eh? If you are willing let us put all of this in writing. I will personally arrest the Raider leaders. I would like to see their court-martial begin as soon as possible. I want only prisoners to serve on the judgment panel. Prisoners will also carry out the judgment of the court.

"As for weapons, I can allow you only wooden stakes, Captain. That should be sufficient. As I see it," Wirz told him with a wry smile, "it was sufficient last night, wasn't it?"

***

Mike and Commandant Wirz spent the remainder of the morning working out the structure for the internal administration of the camp.

"Of course, Captain," Wirz insisted, "I will want you to be in charge of the security force inside the camp."

"I'm afraid I cannot do that sir," Mike responded coolly.

"Why not, Captain Drieborg?"

"Because, sir, "Mike responded. "Anyone appointed by you would be suspected of being a turncoat. Actually, that man would most likely be killed the first day."

"Yes, I can see that," Wirz admitted. "Do you have any suggestions?"

"Yes, sir," Mike said quickly. "Let the men in each of the ten camp districts we have identified in this plan select their own leader. We could call them Marshalls; then, allow those ten men to select a chief Marshal. Each man selected will have to be approved by you. Of course, you can remove any of them if you feel it necessary."

After a good deal of such give and take, the structure was complete. "Now Captain Drieborg," Wirz said, "I want you to organize a military court for the trial of the Raiders. Can you do that by tomorrow?"

"Yes, sir."

***

Once he and Captain Wirz finished, Mike was escorted back inside the camp. This time, Captain Wirz and thirty armed guards stayed inside the camp and searched for the Raider leaders. Mike returned to his tent.

"We'd about given up on you Mike," commented Sam. "I thought for sure Wirz was gonna put you into the stocks for leading our raid."

"Yeah," John joined in. "I thought so, too. But you look fine. What happened?"

"It turned out that Wirz thought the Raiders had corrupted his guards and were seriously disrupting the camp," Mike explained. "In fact, he felt that he needed to do something soon or possibly lose control of the camp population. So, he was pleased we solved the Raider problem for him. I don't know if he knew about our raid before it happened, but he sure knew that I led it quickly enough."

"You were over there all morning Mike," Phil observed. "It didn't take you that long to find out what you just told us, did it?"

"I haven't gotten to the rest," Mike responded. "Wirz wants us to set up an internal security force for the camp. He wanted me to head it up. But I told him that whoever leads it should be elected by the prisoners, not appointed by him. I did work with him though on designing a security structure for inside the camp."

"Would we really be in charge of keeping order?" John asked. "And how would those who broke the rules be punished, if at all?"

Questions came fast and furious from the five men. Mike stayed calm and answered each question. He watched their reaction because he was worried they might think him a turncoat or somehow disloyal for having worked with Wirz on this plan.

"He also wants us to set up a court-martial panel of judges to hear testimonies and punish the leaders of the Raider group."

"Holy smoke," Sam exclaimed. "If that don't beat all. How do you plan on doing that, Mike?"

"John, I want you to be in charge of setting up the court. You can be the chief judge, or whatever you want to call it, too," Mike said. "Each of you squad leaders will pick one man from your squad to work with John on the trial. Pick another man to work with me on security for the trial. Sam, Phil, George, and Joe; I want you to find men who would be willing to testify against the Raiders at the trial. Wirz wants this set up today so the trial can begin tomorrow. He promises food right after the trial is finished. Any questions?"

There were none.

That same day, Captain Wirz and his men arrested over one hundred Raiders. He took them out of the camp and placed them in a compound under heavy guard. Over the course of a few days, he identified six men as the primary leaders. These six men were placed in chains some distance from the camp. All of this was happening very quickly.

The following day the trials began for the others. Each of the accused was allowed to pick someone from the prison population to speak to the court on his behalf. Witness after witness testified against the accused too. Despite their pleas for forgiveness and leniency, all the Raiders were found guilty of one crime or another. Punishments ranged from flogging to having one's head shaved. Once the punishment was administered, they were returned to the main prison. There, they found that many of their victims would deal with them more harshly than the court.

Then, the six Raider leaders were tried and sentenced to hang. Mike's security force constructed gallows on the morning of the hanging. When the convicted men were standing on the platform, they were each allowed to speak. A man named Delaney admitted that he had changed his name from Bierlein. He asked to be spared because he had been misled by evil men. He said that he had never seen his young son Robert either. He cried and begged to be spared.

Since five of the condemned Raiders were of the Catholic faith, Captain Wirz had asked Father Whelan, a priest, from the nearby town to be present. The priest asked the court to spare the life of the man who had also just begged for his life; the Bierlein man from Maryland.

Mike heard shouts from the thousands of prisoners watching the hangings.

"Turn him over to us. He'll soon wish you'd hung him." Loud cheers followed this suggestion. Those in charge of the hangings paid no attention to either.

Mike heard the man's pleas too. He was stunned to hear the condemned man's name. And, that his son's name was Robert. Mike was sure that this man was his own wife's first husband. Just the same, he watched in silence and without pity as a noose was placed over the man's head. The trap door opened under his feet and he dropped until the rope jerked his body to a stop. The fall did not break his neck, so he strangled to death, slowly.

"Could I ever tell Eleanor what actually happened to her first husband? Would her son Robert blame me for his father's death if he knew of my role in this matter?"

The Move to Savannah

"You hear the rumor, Mike?" John asked.

The two of them were in their small mess area. It was their turn to stand guard that morning.

"Are you referring to the one about today's meal?" Mike kidded him. "Or, maybe you're asking about the big prisoner exchange. Possibly you're talking about all those Union cavalrymen who came to visit last night?"

"Come on, Mike, stop kidding. Since we voted you the head marshal in charge of security inside the camp, you should know about such things. So, stop with the kidding around and just tell me what you know. Please."

"I don't know for sure," Mike responded seriously. "My guess is that something big is going to happen very soon. It's nothing Wirz or any of his Aides told me. But something about how the guards are acting leads me to suspect something unusual."

Late that afternoon, a locomotive arrived at the prison siding pulling twenty or so boxcars. Such an event in the past would mean that several hundred new prisoners would be added to the thirty thousand already in a camp built for ten thousand. This time, it arrived empty. Adding to the mystery, the locomotive just sat there all night belching steam.

The train did bring mail, though. It was passed out by prisoners who were called trustees. Mike was the only member of his group to receive a letter this time. Looking at the stamped envelope, he could tell it had been sent over six weeks ago. It was from Eleanor. Mike rushed back to his sleeping area to read it. He saw that it had been mailed July 10, 1864.

Dearest Michael,

Congratulations! You are the father of a beautiful baby girl. I guarantee that you will fall in love with her the instant you see her. I am fine. But your daughter is a big baby and I did have a hard time giving birth to her. I still have a little bleeding, but Mamma says it's normal and I should be fine soon. So, don't worry Mikie.

I do worry about you though. How awful if must be in that terrible place you wrote me about. I know you will not tell me how bad it really is, but I worry just the same. We all pray for your safe return. Papa needs this letter now because he is going into town. Remember how much I love you and miss you. Please take care of yourself.

With all my love,

Eleanor

***

"Hey you guys! I'm a father."

John was the first to pat him on the back. "Congratulations Mike." The others gathered around too.

"I don't suppose you have any cigars to pass out do you Drieborg?" Sam taunted. "Anyway, you know we got a pot hanging on this. Was it a girl or a boy?"

***

It was before the usual morning prisoner count. Michael and his deputy marshals were summoned to the Commandant's office building outside the prison walls.

They stood at attention in front of Commandant Wirz's desk.

"Captain Drieborg," Captain Wirz said, "you and your deputy marshals will organize prisoners who can walk unassisted into groups of five hundred. At ten o'clock this morning the first group of five hundred will be loaded on the train you have seen standing outside the walls. Other trains will be arriving every two hours until all the ambulatory prisoners are removed to other prisons. Some will head to Florida, others to camps in Alabama or Georgia. As you move each group of five hundred to the main gate, my guards will pull out any prisoner having trouble walking. Other guards will escort those able to walk to the boxcars. Do you have any questions, Captain?"

While still standing at attention, Mike responded, "Just two, sir."

"What are they?" Wirz asked.

"First, sir, what will happen to those who are left behind?"

"Our medical staff will care for them, as always."

"What of our belongings sir? Will we be allowed to take personal things like Bibles or journals, blankets, and shaving gear?"

Standing in front of the men now Wirz said, "There will be no room for any of that, Captain."

"Surely a Bible, a journal or at least a drinking cup will be allowed, sir," Mike insisted.

"No. Nothing is to be taken. That will be enough Captain Drieborg. If you do not wish to take on this responsibility, I will assign it to my guards. I believe you and your deputies are best suited to handle this large movement of men, but I could assign it to my teenaged guards.

"The choice is yours, Captain."

"We best handle it, sir."

"Good," Wirz said. "I too, believe this entire matter can be better handled by you and your deputies. Before you leave this building, Captain, you will devise a plan for the execution of my orders. Right now, I am going to speak to our medical personnel about this move. My Aide will inform me when you are ready to have your plan reviewed. It is now six-thirty Captain. The first train leaves at ten this morning. You have no time to waste."

With that, Wirz left the small room and the prisoners to their work. Mike turned to his ten deputy marshals.

"You heard the man gentlemen," Mike began. "Anyone have any idea how we should do this?"

John Ransom volunteered an opinion. "We'll have the morning prisoner count in a few minutes," he reminded everyone. "All the prisoners will be in formation. Seems to me, it will be an ideal time to organize the men. How about we get our first couple of groups right then and there?"

Sam, another one of the deputies, joined in. "Tell the guys that they only get fed if they cooperate. Then, we divide the camp into the groups we need. No cooperation, no food. You could even promise that the first group of five hundred will be the first to eat and get out of here."

"I think it's a great idea to use this morning's count formation to get us started," Mike commented. "Sam, you count off five hundred men, and I'll move them to the gate immediately. Food will be waiting for them there.

"Battist, while Sam and I are doing that, you count off a second five hundred and have them just sit on the ground where they stand.

"George, you and Phil will be responsible for getting the food to each group. We want to feed these men where they sit, before they are loaded up.

"While this is going on, the other six of you deputies will identify other groups during this morning's count. Just have them sit down and wait. Appoint one or two men from each group to help you keep order. Don't let them move. See that they wait for me and

Sam to join you. We need twelve groups organized today if we are to fill the train schedule on time."

"Can we tell them that they will be fed something as soon as they get organized?" asked Sam

"We all know that we need Wirz's approval before we make that promise," Mike reminded his deputies. "He'll review our plan in a few minutes. Hopefully he'll approve our suggestion about the promise of food too."

Wirz did approve the overall plan. He also saw that promising a meal for the prisoners if they cooperated would help with the control of the prison population.

Mike thought that all of the prisoners would be enthusiastic about leaving Andersonville. "With most of the men happy about leaving," Mike told Battist, "they will be more cooperative too."

Even the weather cooperated, with no rain. "*Our plan should work very well, too,*" Mike thought.

And it did. The initial groups of five hundred prisoners each left pretty much on schedule. Out of over thirty thousand prisoners, there were complaints, of course, especially from the disabled men who were to be left behind. But by and large, Mike thought the operation was working quite well.

By the end of the week, almost twenty-five thousand prisoners had been loaded on trains and moved from Andersonville. Mike Drieborg and his deputies would go with the last group.

Mike knew that John Ransom was worried. John hadn't been able to walk very well for several weeks. He moved around his cooking and sleeping area some, crawling mostly. He realized that the prison was being emptied and that sick men like him were supposed to be left behind.

"What about me, Mike?" he asked. "Are you going to leave me behind when you go tomorrow?"

"No, John," Mike quickly responded. "You're going with us. You personally saved my life when I came here. Don't worry, I'll see to it. But you will have to help me."

"I'll do whatever you tell me Mike."

The next afternoon, the last group of five hundred prisoners was formed and moving toward the gate.

Mike Drieborg and Sam Hutton were standing in the middle of the group. They held John Ransom between them.

"Keep your head up," Mike urged him. "Don't slouch or drag your feet. Hold him firmly Sam. We have to keep him moving."

"I got him Mike," Sam said. "John, use all your energy right now. Don't hold anything back. If you fall or look weak, the guards will spot us and pull you out of the line. Then, you stay and you're a dead man. The train is only fifty yards away."

"Keep your head up dammit! You've got to help."

The lines of men moved forward steadily. Everyone was anxious to get into a boxcar and as far from Andersonville as possible. Mike and Sam moved through the gate with John between them.

"Hey! You there!" a guard shouted, watching for such a ruse. "Are you holding that man up?"

However, the Confederate soldier couldn't stop the surging lines, and the threesome was through the gate before he could sort them out of the crowd.

Alongside an empty boxcar, Mike shouted, "Lift him into the car, Sam."

The two of them lifted their comrade and threw him through the open door of the car.

"Let's get over to the far side," Sam suggested. "We can get some air through the slats. I don't know where we're going, but it's got to better than the place we're leaving."

Despite the rush of air through the openings in the sides of the box-car, the heat and stench were sickening. Many of the men packed inside lost control of their bowels or vomited. Everyone had to urinate, which made the stench only worse.

Twice, the train had to pull over to a siding to allow a train carrying Confederate soldiers westward to pass. Waiting in the afternoon sun for the trains to pass created an oven effect, causing many to faint.

"Easy John," Mike urged. "It will be better as soon as we get moving. Are you alright Sam?"

"No, I'm not," Sam responded. "But I assure you that I will survive this."

"John and I will, too," Mike told him. "Right, John?"

John had fainted.

The next time the train stopped, it was early in the evening.

"What's all that commotion outside Mike?" Sam wondered aloud.

They heard a man giving a command outside of their car.

"Stand back, but have yer weapons at the ready." Someone shouted from outside the train.

Then, the door of the car was slid open with a bang.

"All right Yanks," an armed guard on the ground shouted.

"Outta there with ya now; no funny business, if ya please. Move into the field and towards the tree line. When ya find an empty spot, lay down. There's water for ya in the barrels ya see out there. Some food will be delivered soon."

The boxcar was a good three feet off the ground. The prisoners inside the car had been in a weakened condition before getting on the train. Now, after a day packed tightly in a hot boxcar, they were even weaker. All of them had difficulty getting out of the car to the ground. When Mike's turn at the doorway came, he jumped down safely and waited on the ground with outstretched arms for Sam to lower John. Once on the ground the three men moved to the shade of some nearby trees.

"Here, John," Mike said, lifting a ladle of water to his lips. "You must drink as much as you can."

Confederate medical personnel worked their way through the field.

"You there," one of them said. "The man you are holding, is he unconscious?"

"Yes, he is," Sam responded. "He has not been able to walk well for some time either. Today's ride has pretty much wiped him out. Who are you, mister?"

"I'm Doctor Martin. I run a nearby hospital. My staff and I are assigned to assist you men from Andersonville. Will you allow me to take your friend to my facility? We have set up a temporary field hospital just across the field."

"Yes, of course, doctor," Mike agreed. "Our friend's name is John. Can we go with him?"

"He will be fine soldier," the doctor told them. "You can walk to our medical tent later. It's located about a mile south of this field."

Mike and Sam put John on a nearby ambulance wagon. Then they returned to their spot and waited for their turn to eat. It was only some kind of mush, but the cornbread was fresh and free of worms. The water was clean too.

Then, they went to see John at the field hospital. He was awake when they arrived, washed up in clean clothing and resting on clean bedding.

He greeted them with a bright smile. "I had hot soup just before you came in. It had lots of meat and greens in it too. The fresh baked bread didn't have one weevil in it either. Can you believe it?"

"How do you rate such high-class treatment, John?" Sam asked. "We had cold mush of some kind."

The doctor had moved alongside John's bed. "He is pretty weak right now," he told them. "We'll give him all the vegetables, meat, bread and clean water he can manage. It will take a while for him to gain strength. I'm not sure about his ability to walk without crutches though. You men should leave him to us for now. He needs rest."

"Thanks, Doc," Sam said. "We'll see you tomorrow John unless they move us again, that is. Save your meal scraps for us, will you?"

"You two saved my life you know," John managed. "But don't count on any meal scraps for a while."

"That's thanks for you," Mike said with a laugh as he and Sam left. They returned to the field where they had been dropped off earlier in the evening. As soon as they found an open spot, they sat down. Even with the August heat, the clean air was refreshing. Sleep came quickly.

The next day, the rising sun awoke Mike and Sam. A Confederate officer shouted for the men's attention.

"We've dug latrines south of the tracks," he directed them. "If we catch any of you relieving yourselves north of these tracks, instead of this designated area, you'll get no ration today. We will not have this area become an open latrine, like the one you just left. It will be a couple of days until we move you to a permanent prison facility.

"A medical team will be here soon to examine those of you who are sick. Food and more fresh water will be here shortly too. As long as you act responsibly and don't cause problems, you will be fed good food and given good medical attention. Become unruly or try to escape and my guards will shoot you. Carry on."

Later that afternoon Mike and Sam were relaxing in the shade of a tree.

"Sam," Mike mused, "I woke up during the night and took a piss back in the orchard over there. I noticed that with no moon out, I could hardly see my hand in front of my face. So, once it gets dark tonight, I intend to escape west along the railroad tracks. I bet I'll find one of our units in that direction. Want to go with me?"

"I don't know if I'm strong enough," Sam responded. "I want to escape too, but I don't want to hold you up, especially the first night."

"Thanks for your concern," Mike said. "You're right about covering a lot of ground the first night. Come on Sam, you're strong enough aren't you? I'd hate to leave you behind. I got sort of fond of you for some reason."

"Thanks Mike. But the train ride took a lot out of me. You probably didn't notice, but I got up three or four times last night. I got the runs something fierce. So, I'm feeling pretty weak in the knees today. You've seen back at Andersonville what that can do to a man. With a few days of rest, food and clean water, I should be stronger. Right now, though, I don't think I have enough energy to get more than a few miles west.

"I would slow you down for sure. It would be easy for the Rebs to catch us Mike, if we're together. Besides, I don't know that I won't need the kind of attention John is getting right now. So, thanks for the offer, but I don't think I should chance it. Ask one of the other guys from our group or one of the deputies like Battist. He's strong as an ox and could probably outwalk or outrun even you."

"All right Sam," Mike conceded. "I'd wait a few days for you to get your legs under you, but I'm afraid the Rebs might move us again or do something to block this opportunity. So, I'll check it out with the other guys and Battist. I hate to leave you though. Tell you what. You can have my share of John's meal scraps."

"Enough Drieborg," Sam retorted. "Just leave. Get back to that wife and baby of yours."

Mike reached out and gave Sam a hug. "Never thought I would do that, did you? I know that you as much as anyone else helped me survive Andersonville. I'll never be able to thank you enough."

"I never thought I would meet an officer in this damn army I could admire and trust, until you. God bless you Mike."

Within an hour, Mike had talked with the others. They felt the same as Sam did. They needed time to regain their strength. But they all encouraged Mike to take advantage of this opportunity to escape. Only Battist, the Sioux Indian, was anxious to go.

Escape to Union Lines

Michael and Battist waited for nightfall to begin their journey west. The bald Indian and Mike had become close friends since they had teamed up to attack the Raiders back in Andersonville Prison. He was a bit shorter than Mike and arrived at the camp as a strong muscular fellow. Like Mike, he had lost some weight, but not his determination to survive.

After the trial and hangings of the Raider leaders, Battist had become one of Mike's most dependable deputy marshals inside the prison. He and his assistants were tough. Some prisoners even thought them vicious. But everyone knew no one broke the new rules in their section of the prison without swift and severe punishment. Most of the prisoners appreciated that. They felt safer. Battist was a quiet fellow, and he knew how to preserve his strength. So, when he made a suggestion, Mike listened.

"Mike," he said. "We have just a few hours till dark. Let us rest in the shade by the tree line to the west over there." So, that's what they did.

"Take off your shoes," he directed. "We must rest our feet, too, now." Mike thought the suggestion was a bit strange. But Battist had been an infantryman. They marched a lot. What did cavalryman know about foot care?

Mike trusted that Battist knew what he was talking about. Besides, he just seemed to expect Mike to follow his direction in this matter. So, Mike took off his shoes while they waited. He lay back on the grass and looked up at the darkening sky.

I wonder what Eleanor and the baby are doing at this very minute. O my Lord! The thought of her breast-feeding has gotten me aroused. I haven't had that experience in awhile. Had Eleanor named our little girl already? I think she said we would do that together when I returned. Or had she? I'll read her last letter again tomorrow morning when Battist and I stop to rest. For now, I should pray.

"At Andersonville, my group had prayed together each day. But, I have not thought to pray on my own in quite some time.

"Thank you Lord for delivering me from Andersonville, he began. And, I ask for Your blessing, Lord on our escape attempt tonight. And, please Lord, take care of Eleanor and my baby daughter."

Mike watched as the sun set. As he had noticed last evening, when the sun went down here this time of year, it became dark quickly, really dark. Still, he and Battist did not make their move immediately. Instead, they continued to lay by the tree line at the western side of the field. Battist suggested that even though it was dark, they should wait a while for the thousands of prisoners to settle down and the guards to relax some. Mike agreed.

When they did move, they slipped into the shoulder-high shrubbery they had noticed growing a few feet from the railroad tracks. Just a few yards away from the edge of the camp, they paused and crouched low behind the shrubbery. No rifle shots or shouts followed them. They seem to have succeeded thus far.

"We can move now," Battist said. "I'll go first. In my experience, you white men make more noise than a herd of buffalo. After I get five yards or so ahead of you, I'll signal for you to follow me. Do it slowly and step softly until we get further away from the camp."

For the next hour Battist led Mike at a very slow pace through shrubbery and small trees. Then he paused and waited for Mike to move forward.

"We are far enough away to begin walking more quickly," he told Mike. "For a white man, you walked pretty quiet, Mike. You only sounded like one buffalo instead of a herd."

"Funny," Mike said irritably. "Can we move now?"

Without another word Battist moved ahead. Mike followed, feeling guilty for every sound he made with his boots.

The two walked briskly for another hour. With no stars to guide them, they continued to move along the railroad tracks. However, they knew it wasn't safe to stay that close to the tracks for long, because that's where their pursuers would search first. At their next break, Battist suggested they move several hundred yards to the north, away from the tracks.

After walking all night, they stopped by a shallow stream just after daybreak. They had their fill of clean water and then slept in a thicket of pine trees, taking turns standing guard. Shortly after sundown at the end of a day of rest, they headed west again. At one point, Battist smelled chimney smoke before they even saw the farmhouse where it came from. Battist changed their route further north to avoid the expected farm dog barking and giving them away. They picked up their pace.

On the fourth day, Battist was sleeping while Mike was standing guard. The only noise he had heard in the past hour was the growling of his empty stomach. Suddenly, to the south of him in the direction of the railroad tracks, he heard men talking. He shook Battist, motioning him to be quiet. They lay low and waited for the voices to fade. The voices stopped.

Instead, they heard the sound of horses crashing through underbrush. That noise became louder as it got closer. Before Mike or Battist could react, two men on horseback were upon them with pistols drawn.

"Hands up you two," one of the riders ordered. "And don't move a muscle, or you are dead men."

Threats like this were not new to Mike or Battist, for they had heard such orders given by guards at Andersonville many times. They stood up as directed and remained very still, hands on their head.

"Are those rags you're wearing Union uniforms?" the other horseman asked.

"Yes, what's left of them, trooper," Mike answered. Battist was silent and did not move.

"You steal 'em?" the Union trooper suggested.

"No, they were issued to us some time ago," Mike explained, "before we were taken prisoner and sent to Andersonville."

The two horsemen looked at each other at the mention of that prison.

"That may be mister," said the trooper with corporal's stripes. "But before we put these pistols down, tell us what unit you're supposed to be from, and how you got here."

Mike and Battist identified themselves and told their stories to the two men in Union uniforms.

"Well I'll be," one of the men exclaimed. "You walked all the way from Savannah? I suspect that's quite a hike."

"You two can put your hands down now," the other trooper told them. "We can't be too careful down here in Reb country, ya know. My name is Tommy Wheelright, and that's Bill First. We both hail from South Bend, Indiana. That's a small farm town just over the border from Niles, Michigan. We're with General Kilpatrick's cavalry division. For the last few weeks, our job has been to tear up railroad track and generally cause all the disruption we can. Our division is headed for the Georgia state capital next, I think. Word is, we might just burn that city to the ground."

"After the treatment the Rebs gave us at Andersonville," Mike told him, "that wouldn't trouble me at all."

"You have anything we could eat?" Battist inquired.

"I've got a little hardtack in my pocket," Corporal Wheelright answered. "How about you, Bill? You got anything for them to eat?"

"Just half a biscuit and some water in my canteen is all."

"Sounds good to me," Mike told them. "We haven't had anything to eat in four days. Anything you have would be a feast right now."

"We are on picket duty Captain," Wheelright informed him. "We were just about ready to make our last swing around when we ran into you."

He turned toward his fellow trooper, Bill. "Now that we know who these guys are, let's get them back to camp. The Captain can get them some proper food."

On the ride back to their encampment, the troopers shared their mounts with Mike and Battist. It was a good hour before they arrived. Once there, the former prisoners were fed as soon as their situation was explained to the Troop commander. There were no spare uniforms to give them, but they were each provided with a horse. The following morning, the Troop was relieved, and Mike and Battist rode to the Regimental headquarters with their rescuers.

The Regimental commander, Colonel Williamson, welcomed Mike to his noon meal. "Don't worry about your companion Corporal Battist," he told Mike. "He asked my aide if he could eat with the enlisted men of the Troop you rode in with this morning. I suspect that he did not feel comfortable with all the officers here at Regimental headquarters."

"Thank you for taking care of him Colonel," Mike said. "If it hadn't been for enlisted men like Battist, I would not have survived Andersonville, I assure you."

"That may be son," the Colonel responded. "But to hear him tell it, you're the one primarily responsible for saving a lot of lives in that hell-hole of a prison. Anyway, join me and my staff for something to eat this evening. I would like to hear more about Andersonville and your escape. That is, if you don't mind. Are you hungry?"

"Believe me," Mike assured him, "after Andersonville, I could eat a horse."

"But for now, Captain," the Colonel added, "if you don't mind my saying so, you not only look pretty ragged in that clothing, but you need to wash up. I understand why you are this way, but I'm sure you will feel better cleaned up. I know the rest of us at supper tonight will enjoy your company much better if you don't smell quite so bad as you do now. Besides, we can't have you going to see General Kilpatrick tomorrow, like you are."

"No, sir," Mike responded, "I don't mind. You're absolutely right. I'll feel much better after a scrubbing. This will be the first time since last February that I've been able to clean up properly. But there is not much I can do about my clothing."

"My quartermaster has a clean uniform and shoes for you. The officers' shower tent is over that way. My aide will show you the way."

"Thank you, Colonel. But sir, what will happen to my companion Corporal Battist?"

"I'm going to have him accompany you to General Kilpatrick's headquarters tomorrow Captain. For now, we'll call him your escort. His staff will know where the two of you are going from there. How does that sound to you?"

"Fine, sir."

That evening, Mike joined the Colonel, his staff and a few other officers for supper.

"So, Captain," one of the Colonel's aides asked, "you were a congressman's military aide before you fought at Gettysburg?"

"That's true Major," Mike confirmed. "I'm afraid I didn't last long as a fighting man though. During our scrap with Stuart east of Gettysburg, one of his boys stuck me with his saber. The wound and the infection that followed took me out of the fight until last January."

"How in heaven's name did you get yourself sent to the enlisted men's prison at Andersonville?" another officer at the table asked.

The questions kept coming, so Mike gave up trying to eat and put down his knife and fork. He told them of his reassignment to the Michigan Brigade last January, volunteering for Kilpatrick's raid on Richmond, his capture and imprisonment at Libby Prison. They were fascinated with his tale of the big escape from Libby and his subsequent recapture. Then he told them that because the Rebs thought him a potential troublemaker, they sent him to Andersonville as punishment.

The Colonel rose and lifted his glass of wine. "I salute you Captain Drieborg, and wish you a speedy return to good health."

The other officers at the table rose in agreement. "Hear, hear!"

Mike didn't quite know what to say. So, he too rose, raised his glass and said, "Thank you, gentlemen. And here's to President Lincoln and the United States of America."

***

After the best night of sleep, he'd had in months, Mike prepared to leave Colonel Williamson's encampment.

"I can't thank you enough sir." With that, Mike came to attention, saluted, and walked away.

Within an hour, both he and Battist were riding fresh horses westward. They were cleaned up, freshly uniformed and on their way to the corps headquarters of General Kilpatrick.

"How are you feeling, Mike?" asked Battist.

"The food was most welcome. I can't describe how good it feels to be clean after all this time."

"The people of the Sioux nation wash their body every day of the year. So, it has been very hard for me to endure the filth of prison. I agree that the food today was good, but cleaning my body and putting on clean clothing restored my pride."

They rode well into the evening. As they were making camp, Mike said, "I want to be returned to a combat unit. How about you?"

"In the infantry division, I joined when the war started, there was an entire company of my people. I want to rejoin them. Last I knew, they were fighting up in Maryland someplace."

The two men camped out for two nights with the trooper escort Colonel Williamson had provided them. Still deep in Georgia, they moved carefully, not even lighting a campfire to brew coffee or cook some food at night. In daylight, however, a small fire would not likely give them away. So, in the morning, after sunup, they enjoyed a cup of real coffee and some biscuits.

By the afternoon of the third day, they reached division headquarters.

***

"Welcome Captain Drieborg, Corporal," said an officer with Colonel's insignia on his shoulders. "I'm Colonel Donald Best, General Kilpatrick's Aide. The General is tied up in a meeting right now, but he asked me to make you comfortable. Is there anything I can get you while you are waiting?"

"We would sure appreciate some hot coffee sir," Mike responded. "And maybe we could shave and clean up some while we wait."

"Sergeant," Colonel Best ordered, "take these men over to the officers' wash tent. They need shaving gear, towels and some clean underwear and socks. When you and the corporal return, we'll have that hot coffee."

"Thank you, Colonel," Mike said, saluting their host.

When they returned, the Colonel greeted them with the promised coffee. He directed them to two canvas chairs while they sipped the hot brew and waited for the General.

"I must tell you," Colonel Best commented, "you certainly needed to shave and clean up."

"You should have seen us back at Colonel Williamson's Regimental headquarters," Mike said with a chuckle. "We were wearing rags and smelled to high heaven. Even Corporal Battist, an Indian had stubble."

"While you were cleaning up, I read the dispatch Colonel Williamson sent outlining the experiences you've had since last February, Captain. Your involvement was described some too, Corporal. What unit were you with at the time of your capture?"

"I am a Sioux Indian, sir," Battist answered. This was the first time he had spoken since he and Mike had entered the division camp. "I was a squad leader, First Platoon of G Company of the 24th Wisconsin Infantry. My company was made up of Sioux Indians, except for the officers, who were white men."

"How did you like serving under white officers Corporal?" the Colonel inquired.

"Once we trained them sir, they were good fighters."

"At Andersonville," Mike interrupted, "we had some bad apples. They were ruthless men who preyed on the weak. Battist and I led a group of prisoners and eliminated those bandits. Afterwards, Battist was one of my security deputies. He and his squad enforced the rules in a section of the prison. I don't recall that there were any repeat offenders in his section. He is the one who helped me escape from Savannah last week."

"Would you like to rejoin your unit, Corporal?" asked Colonel Best. "Or would you prefer a leave to go home first?"

"If it is my choice Colonel, I want to go right back to my unit."

"Colonel," Mike cut in, "if I may suggest, sir. This man not only helped me escape, but saved many lives at Andersonville by protecting those who were too sick and weak to fight for themselves. Can I recommend him for promotion to sergeant before he goes back to his unit?"

"You certainly can Captain," the Colonel responded. "Unit commanders like you were before you were captured, promote in the field all the time. I'll get my clerk to write up your recommendation for your signature. I'll approve it and give a copy to our new sergeant here to take with him. The other two copies will be needed so the promotion will be official and he will be paid properly. I'm sure we can find some sergeant stripes around here to put on his blouse."

"Thank you, sir," Mike said. "He's earned it."

All of this was taken care of by the time General Kilpatrick concluded his meeting.

"General," Colonel Best informed him, "this is Captain Michael Drieborg, recently escaped from Andersonville by way of Savannah."

"Welcome Captain," Kilpatrick said, extending his hand. "Would you give me a minute? I need to visit the latrine. I never had a minute to sneak out since that danged meeting began."

"Certainly sir," Mike responded, smiling.

The General wasn't long and motioned to Colonel Best and Mike to follow him to his quarters.

Once settled, he addressed Mike directly. "I'm told that you were with Dahlgren last winter on the Richmond raid. Sorry mess, as it turned out. But I'm glad you survived it, and imprisonment. Would you mind telling me as much as you can remember of your unit's part in the Richmond attack, your capture, imprisonment and recent escape?"

"Of course, sir," Mike assured him.

"Dan," Kilpatrick directed his Aide, "would you get a clerk in here to take notes of Mike's story?"

Mike spent the next hour recounting what had happened since last February.

At one point, the General interrupted and asked, "In Colonel Williamson's report, he said something about you being an Aide to Congressman Kellogg. That must have been prior to all of this."

"Yes, sir, it was."

As was the case with most of the high-ranking officers in the Union Army, General Kilpatrick was very politically aware. He was the one who had gone over the head of his commander, General Meade, to sell the idea of the raid on Richmond to General Halleck, the Army chief of staff.

Since the failure of that raid, he had been out of favor in Washington. If it hadn't been for his mentor, General Sherman, he would probably be chasing Indians out in Arizona. Still, he had political ambitions. But tearing up railroad track and burning barns in Georgia would not get him any headlines back home. He needed an opportunity to redeem himself. Maybe Michael Drieborg would provide that opportunity.

Michael told the General of his 1862 enlistment, saving Congressman Kellogg's daughter, and the subsequent assignment as his Aide.

Kilpatrick knew Kellogg was a powerful member of the House Committee on the Conduct of the War and close to President Lincoln.

"Dan," Kilpatrick again addressed his aide, "please telegraph Congressman Kellogg in Washington. Tell him that his former aide has escaped from Andersonville Prison and is safely in my camp as my guest. Ask him if he has any instructions."

He then turned to Mike. "Please continue."

"Sir, if you don't mind, could I say something else?" Mike asked.

"Of course. What is it?"

"What of the other prisoners, sir?"

"The ones you left behind in Savannah?"

"No, sir, the Union soldiers the Rebs refused to relocate from Andersonville. Thousands who were too weak to walk were left behind there, sir. Before we were moved, those of us who were still healthy took care of them. We brought food and boiled water for them. Now, no able-bodied men are left in the camp to do that. When we left that stinking hole, over three hundred men were dying every day. Unless something is done quickly, the death rate will climb dramatically."

"What do you suggest?"

"Andersonville is lightly guarded sir," Mike related. "And the guards there are boys and old men. If you would send a Regiment of cavalry, the place could be captured easily. That's what I suggest, General."

"I would like nothing better than to order that right now Mike," Kilpatrick told him. "But my orders, as they now stand, prevent me from doing what you suggest. What I can do is wire General Sherman with the information you have given me and propose that he allow me to move against Andersonville as soon as possible.

"For now, though," he said, rising from his chair, "I have another staff meeting. Dan will see to it that you are fed and get you set up with a place to sleep. This evening I would like you to supper with me and my entire staff. I am sure they will enjoy hearing some of the things you have told us here. We will have a few newspaper reporters attending, too. I know they will be interested."

"Of course, sir." Mike stood, saluted and walked toward the headquarters tent to report to Colonel Best.

Later that afternoon, Kilpatrick was talking with his aide Colonel Best.

"Dan," he mused, "remember a few months ago when the Rebs allowed some reporters to see Andersonville Prison? Stories, drawings and photos about the prison were published in papers and magazines all over the North. It caused a firestorm of outrage. Can you imagine the publicity up North if my Troops freed the thousands of sick and dying prisoners at Andersonville? I would be back in favor. I'll bet that I could be elected Governor of Rhode Island. Let's take a look at Drieborg's suggestion."

That evening, several news reporters were at General Kilpatrick's supper table. They were quite impressed with the guest of honor, Captain Michael Drieborg. Mike told of his capture, imprisonment, and escape. They peppered him with questions. They also took photographs of Mike with the General and with his staff members until the evening light no longer permitted it.

"That will do it for tonight gentlemen," Kilpatrick's aide announced. "You can continue your interviews with the Captain tomorrow."

After everyone had left, the General talked briefly with Mike. "You did a good job with those fellows, Mike. Dan brought me a telegram just before our meal. I've been ordered to send you to Washington tomorrow morning. You are to report directly to Congressman Kellogg. I expect you know where his office is. They told me that the President is interested in your story and doing something about Andersonville, too."

"Why am I of so much interest sir?" Mike asked.

"I don't think it's about you personally. It could be that it's more about the focus you can help them bring to the Andersonville prisoner issue. You would like to help in that cause, wouldn't you?"

"Absolutely sir," Mike responded without hesitation.

At sunup the following morning, Mike and an escort headed north to the nearest railhead for his trip to Washington City.

Sent to Washington City, September 1864

A week later, on September 15, Michael arrived in Washington City. He walked directly from the train station to the congressional office building located just a few blocks away.

He signed in with the guards at the main entrance. After they checked with Congressman Kellogg's office staff, he was escorted to the second-floor office of the Congressman.

"This sure looks familiar," Mike thought. *"It's still dark-looking, with all that dark wood covering the walls."* Before he could say hello to George Krupp, the Congressman's chief Aide, the Congressman himself burst into the room and greeted him.

"Michael, welcome," he gushed.

The two men shook hands. Then the Congressman gave Mike a welcoming hug.

"Thank you, sir. It is an understatement for me to say that I am happy to be here," Mike responded. "Excuse my appearance though. This uniform was all General Kilpatrick's quartermaster had available. I must look like a scarecrow in it."

"I will admit you look a lot thinner than when I last saw you. Some good food will take care of that, I'm sure. We'll also arrange for you to be properly outfitted later today."

Before they moved to the Congressman's private office, George Krupp, still the office Manager, stepped up. "Mike, welcome back," he said as they shook hands. "How are you feeling?"

"Considering the time, I spent at Andersonville, I'm feeling pretty good. I should regain my weight as well, given decent food and clean drinking water."

"It's great to see you," George said. "I'll talk to you later, Mike."

Once Mike and the Congressman were alone and the door closed in Kellogg's personal office, the two men seated themselves in leather chairs near a window. Michael spoke first.

"I can't tell you how happy I am, overjoyed actually, to be out of that place, sir. But could I first speak to you on behalf of the thousands of prisoners still there who are not fine?"

"Of course, Mike."

"I spent the last five months living in the worst conditions you could possibly imagine. Five other prisoners took me into their group when I first arrived and made it possible for me to survive. Together we fought hunger, water polluted with human waste, exposure to the elements and attacks by marauding fellow prisoners. We looked after each other Congressman. And, with God's help, we all survived. I doubt I would have survived without them.

"There were many other groups of men like ours, of course. When one of the men in their group came down sick, his comrades fed him and saw to his needs. But now sir, there are thousands and thousands of Union soldiers still imprisoned in Andersonville who have no comrades to care for them. The sick were left behind when the able-bodied prisoners were all moved to other prisons. They will surely die. When I left there two weeks ago, prisoners were dying at the rate of three hundred a day. That figure should be much higher now that the able-bodied prisoners have been taken to Savannah. With General Kilpatrick's forces so close to Andersonville, thousands could be saved. If it can be done, sir, don't you think it should be done?"

"Absolutely," Kellogg agreed. "We had a fierce debate last April over the issue of prisoner exchange. Some of us wanted to continue the exchange practice. Unfortunately, the Confederates did not honor the terms of the previous exchanges. Instead of returning to their homes as agreed, their exchanged prisoners returned to their army and fought us again. So, others here in Washington made a powerful case for depriving the Confederate Army of thousands of seasoned fighters.

"Also, we wanted our imprisoned Negro soldiers exchanged, too. However, the Confederates considered these Negro prisoners as escaped slaves, not legitimate combatants. So, they refused. As a result, we stopped the mass exchanges of all prisoners."

"Sir," Mike interrupted, "we kept hearing rumors of exchanges. We thought, maybe our turn would come next month, or at the latest the following month. It never did, of course. You can't imagine the depressing effect that had on those of us in prison. We felt abandoned. It seemed to us that our government didn't care about us anymore. At the morning count the Rebs even teased us about it.

"They would say things like, 'Looks like your government got all it needed from another prison.' Or, 'You Andersonville guys got passed up again.' They gave us the impression that exchanges were an ongoing activity, but not for us at Andersonville. They insisted that the officers at Milan Prison were being exchanged, but not the enlisted men at our place. But now our army is in a position to do something about the men at Andersonville, sir."

"You're right about that Mike," Kellogg responded. "With your help, I think we will do something."

"With my help? Sir, I'm only a lowly Captain who has hardly even fought in this war," Mike wondered aloud. "What could I possibly do that would have much influence?"

"Quite a bit actually," Kellogg assured him. "First off, it would help a great deal if you would be willing to take the time and visit with the House Committee on the Conduct of the War. They are very interested in learning about Andersonville and your thoughts of liberating the prisoners there. It might take a few days of your time. Can you delay your trip home for a few days?"

"Certainly sir," Mike quickly responded. "You said 'first off.' Does that mean there's more I'll be doing?"

"Yes, it does," Kellogg explained. "But I have to wait till later to tell you about it. Trust me on that?"

"Of course, I will sir. While all of this is going on, sir, would you send word to my wife in Maryland and my family in Lowell that I am safe and here in Washington?"

"Oh, my heavens!" Kellogg exclaimed, sitting up straight in his chair. "You don't know do you?"

"What, sir?"

"Your wife's family contacted me last month in the hope that I could get a message to you. I'm sorry there's no easier way to say this, Mike, but a week or so after she gave birth to your daughter, your wife Eleanor, died."

Mike just sat for a bit, head bowed. "My Lord," he said finally. "Eleanor's letter telling me of our daughter's birth did reach me, but she said she was fine. And all this time she's been dead, I've been thinking of myself. What of our daughter? What of her sir?"

"The Hechts also told me that they are caring for her and that she is apparently very healthy. I can arrange for you to leave right away for the Hecht farm if you wish. I certainly would understand if you left right now."

With that, Mike stood and moved to the window. Through misty eyes, he saw the street below filled with marching soldiers, wagons, and horse-drawn cannons. He knew the war would continue and men would continue to die in battles and at prisons like Andersonville.

He turned to the Congressman. "No, sir. I want to go there right now, of course. But if by staying here in Washington I can help save the lives of even some of the prisoners still at Andersonville, I will stay. This may seem callous to you, sir. Maybe it is. My grief is small compared to the anger I still feel toward the Rebs for what they allowed at Andersonville. I can't seem to let that go, however much I grieve for Eleanor.

"No, sir. I will stay here as long as you think necessary before I take time to grieve for my wife and go to my daughter. I'll send a telegram to the Hechts and tell them of my situation and that I will be out to see them as soon as I can get away."

"Thank you, Mike," Kellogg concluded. "My office will make arrangements for you to do that when we are done with our conversation. I had hoped you would agree to help me on this matter. I've arranged for you to meet tomorrow with the entire House Committee on the Conduct of the War."

Just then, the regulator clock on the wall reminded them that it was three o'clock. "We're late young man," Kellogg stated, heading for the hat rack and the door to the hallway.

"For what, sir?" asked Mike, standing and somewhat surprised. "Your appointment with my tailor is in fifteen minutes. Can't have you traipsing around the nation's capital looking the way you do now, can we? Afterwards, the cook is expecting you at home for a special meal."

"Thank you, sir," Mike said. "But I don't think I would be fit company tonight."

"I understand. But Patricia is in Grand Rapids right now. You and I will have the house to ourselves. Besides, Michael, cook expects us for supper. And you know how testy she can get when her plans are disrupted. You wouldn't want me to get in trouble with her, would you?"

"Of course not, sir," Mike responded, smiling for the first time since he had been told of Eleanor's death.

"Then, you and I will get to bed early. Tomorrow will be a busy day for both of us. Is that all right with you Mike?"

"Yes, sir."

That evening at the Kellogg home, Michael enjoyed his first real meal since leaving the Hecht home and his wife last January. The thought of her caused him to tear up some and eat quietly. He hoped the congressman didn't think his quiet manner impolite.

Over coffee later, Michael felt better and asked, "Is Captain Hayes still in charge of the committee aides, sir?"

"I meant to tell you eventually Mike. But no, he is not. Remember the fellow who was Congressman Tower's aide? I've forgotten his name. But he was the one who verified the assault charges Hayes made against you."

"How could I forget him?"

"Anyway," Kellogg went on, "he got into some personal troubles. Beat up some woman down on Hooker Street. She went to the military police and filed charges against him. She also claimed that her assailant and Hayes paid her to help them frame some people and entrap others. You were identified as one of the men she had been paid to frame.

"The military police checked out her charges through their Hooker Street inform-ants. They used the evidence they accumulated and her testimony to threaten this fellow with prison unless he cooperated. So, he agreed to cooperate. Subsequently, Captain Hayes was arrested and brought before a military court. This aide and the woman testi-fied against Hayes at his trial. Several men he had been blackmailing for money also testified against him. There wasn't much he could offer in rebuttal. He was then found guilty of all charges. Hayes was given a dishonorable discharge and sentenced to a year in the military prison in Detroit, Michigan."

"I suspect I know why I was his target," Mike said. "I was just a newly appointed lieutenant who had never even met him. But he started riding me my first day on the job as your Aide. It was a mystery to me until you left town during the Easter recess last year. That's when he ordered me to have dinner with him and the other aides at Molly's. You remember that brothel on Hooker Avenue?"

"Yes, I remember," Kellogg responded. "The aide who testified against Hayes told the court that your old enemy Carl Bacon had paid Hayes to harass you and set you up on the occasion of that dinner at Molly's brothel."

"When Carl showed up at that place," Mike remembered, "I suspected he was behind it all. But everything happened so quickly afterward, I was back with my troop chasing Rebs at Gettysburg before I gave it much thought. It didn't matter much to me by then. But how did Bacon even know Hayes?"

"You might recall that the Grand Rapids Eagle newspaper reported that you saved my daughter from that runaway wagon. It also followed up with another article about your promotion to my staff. Hayes told the court that Bacon contacted him shortly thereafter and offered him money to harass you. When that didn't satisfy his need for revenge, Bacon paid Hayes to entrap you at Molly's brothel. Of course, you know the rest."

"Does Patricia know I was set up?" Mike asked.

"Yes, she does, Michael. There is something else I wanted to tell you, too. The reason General Kilpatrick did not immediately dispatch cavalry units to free the prisoners at

Andersonville was because his orders did not permit it. Such a move on his part would have slowed his drive toward Savannah considerably. It would have isolated his force deep in enemy territory and thus put his entire command at risk. In addition, your presence in his camp posed a problem for him and the President."

"How in heaven's name was I a problem sir?" Michael asked, shocked.

Kellogg explained. "Every large element in our army has newspaper reporters hanging around. They send dispatches daily to their papers in the North. It just so happens that Kilpatrick thrives on such publicity. He's had very little good press since the fiasco of his failed raid on Richmond last winter. He could have used your presence for the advancement of his own personal agenda. So, you can see how your experiences could soon have been reported throughout the North.

"We do not need newspaper reporters writing stories about how the Lincoln administration has been ignoring the plight of prisoners you have described. Imagine what damage that could do in the North to him and our war effort in an election year. The President does not need that when we are on the verge of winning this terrible war.

So, I had General Kilpatrick ordered to send you here to me. Here, you can help me accomplish what General Kilpatrick was not allowed to attempt. Do you understand what I have told you Michael?"

"I do now sir. Thank you for the explanation."

"Besides," Kellogg continued, "after the capture of Atlanta, General Sherman sent an entire cavalry Regiment under General Stoneman to capture the Confederate prison for officers located in Macon, Georgia, and then capture the enlisted men's prison in Andersonville. The prison at Macon was supposed to be lightly guarded.

"Instead, the entire attacking Union force was captured. No one is especially anxious to have a repeat of that fiasco.

"You needed to know about these things before your appearance in front of the House Committee on the Conduct of the War tomorrow. There are a few border state Democrats just looking for an issue to use against President Lincoln in this fall's election. They would love to use news about the plight of the prisoners at Andersonville to turn the people against the President.

"Now that I have told you why General Kilpatrick's hands were tied on the issue of the capture of Andersonville, the hidden agenda of the Democrats on the House Committee on the Conduct of the War and how you might have inadvertently hurt the President and the war effort by remarks to newspaper reporters, I think you are better prepared now to testify tomorrow."

"Thank you, Sir. I think you are right. Still, I will answer truthfully any question they pose. I'll not even reveal my anger about our government's refusal to exchange prisoners with the Rebs. I only hope that I can help you affect the liberation of the boys at Andersonville."

"That's fine Mike. Now, it's getting late. You have a full day tomorrow."

Once upstairs in his bedroom, Mike sat down and wrote one letter to his parents and another to the Hechts.

Dear Family,

Please believe me when I tell you that I am fine. I lost a lot of weight in prison, but with all the good food around here, I can assure you that I will regain it quickly.

I am writing this letter to you from Congressman Kellogg's home in Washington. He has asked me to stay here for a while to help develop a plan to free Union prisoners held by the Confederacy. If you could see the terrible condition of prisoners held by the South, you would understand why I am willing to delay coming home for a visit in order to help them.

I did not know until the Congressman told me today that Eleanor died. I still find it hard to believe. I will try to visit the Hecht family as soon as possible. I will write you again soon. Right now, I am very tired. It has been a long day, and tomorrow promises to be another very busy one, too. But before I sleep tonight, I must write the Hechts a note.

I love you all,

Michael

He paused in his writing to wash up and prepare for sleep. This would be his first night in a real bed since last December at the Hecht home. Eleanor had been beside him then. Just remembering her caused his eyes to tear. He sat back on his chair at the writing desk and cried. He could not remember ever having cried before. The thought of never seeing Eleanor again caused him to lose control and start sobbing.

After a while, he washed his face, blew out the light, and lay on the bed. He would write the Hechts tomorrow.

President Lincoln

The next morning, Captain Michael Drieborg was dressed in a new uniform appropriate for a Captain of cavalry. After yesterday's appointment, the Congressman had asked his tailor to have one ready by this morning in time for Mike's appearance before the committee. By ordering a rush job, Michael was at least presentable for his testimony.

The Congressman and Michael arrived in time for the opening of the Congressional Committee on the Conduct of the War. A larger room was used so other interested members of Congress, the Administration and the War Department could attend.

"Gentlemen, allow me to introduce Captain Michael Drieborg of the 6th Michigan Cavalry and the Michigan Brigade. Since you saw him last as my aide, he has fought at Gettysburg, where he earned a Purple Heart. Upon recovery from his wound, he was given a troop to command and participated in General Kilpatrick's Richmond raid last winter. Within sight of Richmond, he was captured after being shot. He spent time in Libby Prison located at Richmond.

"While there, he was part of Colonel Rose's escape team. This was the first, and so far, the last, prisoner escape from there. Like Colonel Rose, Michael was recaptured and returned to Libby Prison. You might remember that Colonel Rose was one of the last officers exchanged.

"But the Rebs felt that Michael and the other recaptured officers were troublemakers, so they sent them to other prisons. Michael was sent to the enlisted men's prison in Andersonville, Georgia. While being transferred by the Rebs to Savannah a few weeks ago, he escaped and found his way to Kilpatrick's force west of that city. At my request, he was sent here to give us an update on the conditions in Andersonville."

"Captain," the chairman of the House Committee asked, "would you like to start the discussion with some comments?"

"Yes, sir, I would," Mike responded.

"Before you begin, you are not under oath here, so you may speak freely."

"Thank you, sir."

Over the next two hours, Mike discussed his experience at Andersonville Prison. He concluded his statement with this observation: "Please keep in mind, gentlemen, General Kilpatrick's forces are within striking distance of the lightly guarded Andersonville Prison."

"Thank you, Captain. Are there any questions, gentlemen?"

"Yes Mr. Chairman. I would like to ask the Captain something," the Congressman from Ohio said. "Captain Drieborg, about this Raider bunch you told us about. Was this an Andersonville phenomenon, or is it common in all Reb prisons?"

"It did not exist at Libby Prison Congressman," Mike responded. "I was warned not to leave my gear unguarded, but there was no organized band of men preying on the weak. Libby Prison houses Union officers and was tightly organized and disciplined by the officers themselves. I was not housed at the enlisted men's prison on Belle Island on the James River at Richmond, but rumor had it that such an outlaw group operated there, too. Beyond that, sir, I have no information for you on this subject."

The committee chairman recognized the Congressman from Tennessee to speak. Congressman Webster was one of those committee members Kellogg had warned Mike about. A fat man, he lounged back in his tall leather chair and began to question Mike.

"Do you expect us to believe, Captain, that the killing of these so-called Raiders, who were your fellow Union prisoners at Andersonville, was justified?"

Michael straightened in his chair. His heart began to race and he felt his face flush.

"Sir, Confederate guards conspired with these outlaw prisoners in exchange for loot. They used these thugs to steal our food, clothing, shoes, blankets, packages from home, and the supplies sent by the Union government for our use. Often, the Raiders took the very lives of their fellow prisoners. The Confederate guards protected them.

"We prisoners had a choice Congressman. One was to suffer it in silence, weaken and die. The other choice was to fight back. Those of us who still had the strength to do so decided to fight back. We successfully stopped the vicious activity of this outlaw group by the only means at our disposal, sir, brute force.

"By doing so, we also forced the Rebs to allow us to establish order in that prison where none had existed before. The outlaw leaders we captured were given a proper trial, convicted and hung. We thus created an atmosphere in the prison that gave thousands a better chance to survive. Yes, sir, the killing of these outlaws was justified."

Webster leaned forward, arms on the table. "Do you realize Captain, that you could be brought up on charges of murder for what you have just admitted doing in that prison?"

As he spoke, Mike could see his jowls shake with the emotion of his threat.

The room was silent. Michael sat quietly regaining his composure. His hands were still folded on the table in front of him. He took a deep breath, slowly leaned forward, and looked the politician from Tennessee in the eye.

"If that is your intention, Congressman, it might help you to know this, too. I personally organized and led the attack on the outlaw prisoners I just spoke about. In addition, it might please you to know that during the attack, I personally killed several of the Raiders."

Webster jumped to his feet. "How dare you speak to me that way captain!"

Mike's initial reaction was to laugh at the fat, sputtering little man. He looked so comical. Instead, Mike just smiled and settled back into his chair.

"In fact, sir, I will be happy to engage you in a public debate on what I and some of my fellow prisoners did in our own defense at Andersonville anytime you please. A press conference would be fine, too. I would especially invite the reporters from the papers in Tennessee to attend. Their readers would be interested to know that you were one of those decision-makers here in Washington who decided to end Union prisoner exchanges because the Confederates refused to treat their black prisoners of war the same as their white prisoners," Michael continued heatedly. "How would that go over in Tennessee, Congressman?

"Most Union soldiers didn't like the President's Emancipation Proclamation when it was issued. He was called all sorts of nasty things by our soldiers. Imagine what the white voters back in Tennessee would call you when they find out that you decided to leave white Union prisoners to rot in Southern prisons because of your concern for black Union prisoners of war?"

Kellogg cut in. "Don't mind my Democrat colleague from Tennessee captain. If it were up to him, we would turn the other cheek and end this war on the South's terms. He is a McClellan supporter in this fall's Presidential election, don't you know." Kellogg chuckled.

"He seems to forget that a decision was made in the spring to end prisoner exchange, and that he, as a member of this very House Committee, and his current Presidential candidate, General McClellan, were both part of that decision, too.

"You don't have to worry about Captain Drieborg Webster. The captain is just one lone veteran soon to be decorated by the President himself. But you do have me to worry about. I'm the hard case here. I have been polite with you too long as it is. So, if you start a fight, I'll give you a war. And, my Copperhead colleague, I will crush you."

The committee chairman broke in. "That's quite enough, I think, gentlemen." He gaveled the heated exchange to end. "Thank you for joining us today, Captain. Several of us have asked Congressman Kellogg to schedule private sessions with you over the next few days. Will you be available?"

"Of course, I will sir."

"Right now, I understand you have an appointment with President Lincoln, Captain. So, you are excused."

As they left the congressional office building, Michael commented, "Whew. I sort of blew it in there, sir. Sorry."

"You didn't, actually. That guy has been espousing near traitorous opinions for some time, and we have allowed him to get away with it because we didn't want to run the risk of losing Tennessee to the Confederacy. Believe you me, Mike, I'll crush him one of these days."

***

"So, I have a personal appointment with the President. Do you have any more surprises for me, sir?"

"You'll see, Michael. You'll see."

The President's waiting room was crowded with men.

"Some of these men have appointments Michael," Kellogg told him. "But most of them do not. They are just hoping for an opening. All of them want something from the President."

Congressman Kellogg went directly to the President's appointment secretary and informed him of Michael's arrival.

"Yes, Congressman, it will be just a few minutes. Please stand by that doorway. The President is expecting you and the Major. In fact, you will be next to see the President."

"What is this 'Major' business about?" asked Michael of his Congressman.

"Patience Michael, patience," Kellogg told him. "You'll soon find out."

As predicted, the two were shown into President's Lincoln's office without having to wait more than a few minutes. It wasn't a very large room, Michael observed. A rather plain desk was positioned in front of two very high windows to take advantage of the light. At the other end of the room, Mike heard wood crackle in a fireplace. He saw several high-backed chairs surrounding a low table in front of the fire. He and the Congressman walked toward the desk.

"Mr. President," Congressman Kellogg said, "allow me to introduce Major Michael Drieborg of the 6th Michigan Cavalry, lately a prisoner at Andersonville Prison in Georgia."

President Lincoln stood and walked around the desk, hand outstretched toward Michael. "Major Drieborg, welcome. It is not often that I get to meet with an escaped prisoner."

The President was as tall as Michael, but more tired looking than Mike had imagined. Mr. Lincoln's black suit and vest were commonplace in Washington, but his clothing was wrinkled and hung loosely on his slender frame. His shoes, Mike noticed, were not well polished, either." *He would never have passed one of Sgt. Riley's inspections,*" Michael thought.

"It is a great pleasure sir," Michael responded. "As the son of immigrant Dutch farmers, this is an unexpected honor for the Drieborg family."

"Thank you, Major. The honor is mine, as well. Please sit down, gentlemen." He directed them to the chairs by the fireplace. "Warm yourselves by the fire. You might need a bit of warmth after that chilly reception given to you by Congressman Webster of the House Committee on the Conduct of the War. Our friend from Tennessee gave you a nasty time, I hear."

"I was sort of wondering whose side he was on, sir," Mike responded.

"There are times I wonder, too. Eh, Kellogg? Your Congressman here can control him, I expect."

The two visitors sat in straight-backed chairs facing the President. Kellogg was relaxed, one leg crossed over the other. Michael sat rigidly, both feet on the floor with his hands joined in his lap.

"Michael did very well by himself, as I am sure you will soon hear, sir," Kellogg informed the President. "He needed no help from me."

"Sir, may I ask why you are calling me Major?" said Michael. "The last I heard I was a Captain in Michigan's Sixth Cavalry Regiment."

"Haven't told him yet Kellogg?" the President responded. "Let us have our little fun, Major. You'll find out soon enough."

"Yes, sir," Mike responded, still puzzled.

"I asked to see you, because I wanted to thank you personally for bringing the plight of the soldiers held prisoner by the Confederacy to our attention. I regret that my attention and energy has been devoted to our 250,000 men fighting the Rebel armies. Your reminder is timely and welcomed. I have asked the War Department to immediately focus attention on liberating our troops held prisoner at Andersonville Prison. We can't do much about Libby Prison and Belle Island Prison in Richmond, Virginia, just yet. But I think we can do something about Andersonville, and I assure you, we will," the President concluded.

"Can I be of any help sir?" Michael asked.

"Yes, you can. I'm going to award you that new medal Congress recently authorized. It is called the Congressional Medal of Honor. It seems to me you've earned it."

"Thank you, sir," Michael responded. "But how will that help liberate the prisoners at Andersonville?"

"Excellent question young man," the President said. "Be careful of this fellow after the war Kellogg. He might just get a notion to run against you for Congress."

"He would be a tough opponent Mr. President," Kellogg responded.

"You will be given the medal by me at an awards ceremony, Major.

"On that occasion, we will have people from the newspapers present. The ceremony will give me the opportunity to tell them of your conduct at the prison, of your escape and of the news you brought us about the terrible conditions at Andersonville. And, of course, the ceremony will be an excellent opportunity to announce our intention to liberate that prison as soon as possible. I think they will write stories for newspapers throughout the Union in support of the liberation effort. This should gain the public's support for the project.

"These same reporters will most likely interview you for additional stories which will also be printed throughout the North. The general public seems to understand an issue much better when they have a person like themselves to identify with. The publicity we obtain for the issue should gain additional public support for the plight of the Union prisoners still at Andersonville Prison.

"It might mean you will be stuck in Washington for a few more days, though," the President warned. "I've been told of the unfortunate death of you wife Major. Please accept my condolences and those of Mrs. Lincoln. Can you assist me on the liberation project for a bit longer?"

"I've already told Congressman Kellogg that I will stay here as long as necessary."

"Excellent, Major." The President nodded. "Then you and I have an understanding?"

"Yes, sir," Mike responded quickly. "We do."

President Lincoln turned to the Congressman. "Kellogg, check with my appointment secretary on your way out. He will set everything up."

Returning his attention to Michael, he said, "I would like to visit with you more, Major, and hear firsthand about that terrible prison. But you see, I am a prisoner of sorts, too. All you have to do is look at that waiting room out there. Everyone out there wants something from me. I can't even get away for lunch."

"I understand sir," Michael told him. "I will do everything I can to help you free those prisoners."

Washington Celebrity

Later that day, the Congressman and Mike were having a late lunch at the Willard Hotel. Michael asked, "Just what is this medal business all about, sir? I don't think I did anything so great that I earned any special honor. Lots of men I know did much more."

"That, my boy, is part of your charm," Kellogg told him, smiling. "You accomplish the heroic and consider it normal behavior. By the way, Michael, you are puzzled when people call you 'Major.' Obviously, you don't realize it, but the Congressional Medal of Honor carries with it a promotion of one grade in rank. So, when the President of the United States awards you the highest decoration this country can give a soldier, he will address you by your new rank, which is Major Drieborg."

"My Lord, sir," Michael sighed. "I wish Eleanor and my parents could be here to share this honor with me."

"Well, one thing is for sure, Michael. We can't have you in that makeshift uniform my tailor threw together for you today. You still look like some skinny Michigan bumpkin. My tailor should have your uniforms ready tomorrow. A dress uniform is being made as well. You are going to look the part when the President awards you that medal," Kellogg promised.

"How can I afford your tailor, sir? I'm penniless," Mike protested.

"No, you're not. All your back pay since you were captured last winter is waiting for you at my office. You will be paid, by the way, as a Major for that entire period. So, you can easily afford new uniforms, dress, blues as well, complete with boots, hat, sword and overcoat, all the things to properly outfit a Major in the United States cavalry. Don't let me rush your meal, Michael, but that tailor expects us in another thirty minutes for a second fitting. He'll get real cranky if we are late."

"Dress blues, too?" Mike asked surprised. "Seems like an awful waste for just one ceremony."

"Under normal circumstances I suppose it would be son," Kellogg agreed. "But once you receive the Congressional Medal of Honor from the President himself, you will be a celebrity in Washington. As such, you will be invited to all sorts of events here. Remember your deal with the President? He expects you to publicize his plan to free the prisoners at Andersonville. The newspapers will help, but your presence at functions here in Washington can help with influential people whose support the President needs."

During the following week, George Krupp, Congressman Kellogg's office manager, arranged a daily schedule for Mike, now Major Drieborg. Every day, Kellogg took Mike to visit with groups of congressmen. He hosted interviews with newspaper reporters in his office for the new Major. Michael also called on members of Congress about the Andersonville prisoners from their districts.

The evenings provided an opportunity for Kellogg to take the now properly outfitted Major to social gatherings, sometimes more than one.

"Seems to me that I am taking up all your time Congressman," Mike said. "It makes me feel a bit guilty."

"I have spent most of my time with you, that's true," Kellogg responded. "But understand something. Once word got out that President Lincoln invited you to his office for a private meeting, and that you would receive the Congressional Medal of Honor, my office has been deluged with inquiries and invitations. Everyone around this town wants to meet you and hear of your experiences.

"As a result, Michael, you have raised the awareness at all levels of government and society here in Washington of the plight of our soldiers at Andersonville. That awareness is vital to the liberation project. Now, thanks to you, I think everyone in this city supports the President's plan to liberate those prisoners. Taking you around and introducing you to politically and socially powerful people has not been a bad thing for me either Michael. It has given me the opportunity to meet more of them, possibly gain favor with them and thus gain access to them in the future."

"If that is the case, sir, I am yours to use. Who do we see next?"

***

After a late afternoon meeting with several powerful United States Senators, the two men were walking toward the Congressman's home.

"Michael, did I forget to tell you that there is a surprise waiting for you at my home?" Kellogg asked.

"You know sir, I'm beginning to suspect you forget such things on purpose," Michael responded good-naturedly. "No, you didn't tell me."

The entryway of the Kellogg home was called a vestibule. It was in that small room, just inside the front door, where an employee of the Congressman would take visitors' coats and the guests would clean their shoes before entering the house's main carpeted hallway. Once in that hallway, rooms behind double doors were located both to the right and to the left. The Congressman moved toward the room on the right and swung open the doors before stepping aside.

Michael stood looking into the room. He could hardly believe what he saw. There stood the entire Drieborg family from Michigan, and all the Hechts from their Maryland farm.

"Michael!" the young people shouted.

His brother Little Jake, his sisters Susan and Ann, and Julia and Kenny Hecht all rushed up to him excitedly, hugging and kissing him.

As they pulled back, he looked down at a toddler pulling on his pant leg for attention.

"Robert?" Michael said as he bent over and picked up the two-year-old boy.

They hugged for a moment. Then Michael's stepson said, "Mamma's gone to heaven, Michael."

"Yes, she has, Robert. She wanted to stay with us, but God wanted her in heaven." Michael moved toward his father, still holding the little boy. The three hugged.

"This is your Grandpa Jacob, Robert."

"We have already met, haven't we Robert?" Jacob announced. "We are friends already now."

Michael's mother carried an infant toward him. "This is your daughter Michael."

"Robert," Michael asked, "who is this?"

"That's my new sister," the little boy responded.

Mike hugged his mother, the two children pressed between them. "Thank God you are well, Michael," she said.

He approached Ruben and Emma Hecht. Both embraced him as well.

"I did not know about Eleanor until just a few days ago. I still haven't accepted the fact that she's gone," he told them.

"Yes, Michael. All da time we expect to see her walk into the room, too."

"What do you think of your new daughter, Michael?" asked Emma Hecht.

"She is beautiful Emma. She has such dark blue eyes," Michael observed. "But she's so tiny."

"Her mother named her, Eleanor," Ruben told him.

"Oh, my goodness!" Michael exclaimed as he sat down, still holding Robert. The wind seemed to go out of him. He paused for a moment, turned to his stepson and said,

"Robert, what do you say we hold your sister Eleanor? Will you help me do that?"

For a while the three of them sat quietly, Robert on Michael's left arm and Eleanor on his right.

Soon, though, the young people could stand it no longer.

"Tell us what happened to you at Gettysburg."

"What was prison like? How did you escape?"

"Did you really go to the White House and see the President?"

So, he told them. The Hechts already knew of his wound and his recovery at their farm. But he spared everyone the details of the prison camps.

Finally, he turned to Congressman Kellogg, who was seated quietly by the doorway listening to Michael's narrative. "I know this was your doing," Michael said. "How can I ever thank you enough sir?"

"It is my pleasure, Michael," he responded.

"What is going to happen to you now, Michael?" his father asked.

"Well Papa, I promised the President that I would help with the liberation of Andersonville Prison. But, right now I don't actually know how I will be involved with that. I do know, though, that as long as the war is still being fought, I am a soldier.

"So, I don't know what my immediate future holds. And, here I am, with a baby daughter and a toddler who thinks I'm his real father.

"Their mother was the bond that held all of us together. Now she is gone. I didn't even know that much until a few days ago. So, I need all of you in this room to help me handle this situation."

After Robert and baby Eleanor were put down for a nap, everyone met once again in the Congressman's living room.

Michael addressed both families. "I need all of you to participate in this discussion. You, too, Congressman, if you wouldn't mind," he suggested. "Everyone has a stake in this. So, it seems to me that everyone should be involved. Keep in mind that I promised the President to help with the liberation of Andersonville Prison. After my obligation, here in Washington City is taken care of, I will probably be assigned to a cavalry unit until this war ends. So, what do you think, Mamma?"

"You put a baby in the arms of a mamma or a grandmother Michael, and you do not get a practical answer to that question," she responded.

"Your mamma is right Michael," Emma Hecht agreed. "Well Papa, Ruben, what do you think?"

"Give me und Ruben a few minutes alone together, eh?" his father told him. "Congressman, is der another room we could use?"

"Of course. Just follow me please."

"Would you please join us, Congressman?" "Certainly Mr. Drieborg."

The three men were gone for nearly an hour. When they returned, Jacob Drieborg said,

"The three of us discussed the situation. Until dis war ends, Michael can't care for da little ones. Besides, Congressman Kellogg tells us that Michael must stay here in Washington to finish the plans to free dose poor prisoners at Andersonville. Eh, Ruben?"

"Ya, Jacob," Ruben responded. "We tink little Robert should stay mit us, vhere he is used to all of us."

"And Eleanor vill be with da Drieborg family in Michigan," Ruben finished.

"So, what do the rest of you think of dis?" Jacob asked.

"How can we be without Eleanor?" Julia Hecht complained.

"You know we would take good care of her," Susan interjected.

"Oh, I know that, Susan. But we lost my sister, and now little Eleanor, too? It's so hard to face."

"I know that this is not easy for you, Julia," Emma Hecht said. "But Papa and Mr. Drieborg are right. this is something we must do, I think."

"We would love to have you come home with us and help care for little Eleanor," added Rose Drieborg.

"Oh! Could I, Mamma? I would love that so," Julia gushed. "What an adventure. And I could be with Eleanor."

"Papa, what do you think?"

"Vell, Mamma, it vould be hard for us," Ruben responded. "But it vill be good for little Eleanor and Julia, too. I tink ve should say yes."

Emma nodded her assent.

"Oh, thank you, Papa," Julia exclaimed, hugging her father and then her mother.

"Well, Michael," Jake asked, "What do you think of our ideas here?"

"I think you, Ruben and the others have come up with a plan that makes sense to me."

***

Later that evening, Mike had a moment alone with Congressman Kellogg.

"Excuse me sir," Mike began. "I arrive in Washington, and the next day you have arranged for me to appear before the Committee on the Conduct of the War and meet with the President of the United States. It has also been decided to award me the highest medal the government can give and promote me to the rank of Major. If that isn't mysterious enough, my family shows up all the way from Michigan, and I've just picked up new tailored uniforms."

"Young man," Kellogg responded with a laugh. "Mysterious? There is nothing mysterious about it at all, Michael. Haven't you realized by now that I can accomplish miraculous things?"

"I do now, sir," Mike responded, shaking his head. "I sure do now."

***

Two days later, the President and Mrs. Lincoln welcomed the two families to the White House for a noon meal. Afterwards, Mrs. Lincoln took them on a tour of the newly renovated building.

"I want you to know that you are the first visitors to see the completed work we had done here on the White House," she told them. "I am very proud of what Abraham and I have done to this place. It was so dark and dismal when we arrived. I wanted to brighten it up."

"I think you did that," Rose Drieborg commented. "It is truly beautiful."

"Thank you for saying so," Mrs. Lincoln responded. "I have taken much criticism for bothering to do this with the war and all. But it was all paid for by donations from citizens. No tax money was used. Many of the paintings and much of the furniture was just lent to us. That didn't cost anything either."

Later in the afternoon, everyone gathered in one of the large banquet rooms.

Members of both the House and Senate were joined by representatives of the Army, Washington society and newspaper reporters. When President Lincoln entered the room, everyone stood.

"Thank you all for joining us today," the President began. "Once Mrs. Lincoln heard that both Mrs. Drieborg and Mrs. Hecht were to be here with their children and grandbabies, she told me she couldn't leave them alone with all us men. I suspect she thinks they need her protection.

"So, she decided to join us today as we honor them and their son. Let me tell you, it is a real treat to have her here with me. Because, just like on the Illinois farm of my youth, my day here starts early in the morning and seldom ends until after dark. Jacob, you and Ruben understand that kind of work day, don't you?

"I can't resist another observation," President Lincoln announced. "There are two people in this room, I know for sure, who will ask nothing of me. Allow me to introduce Master Robert Bierlein and Miss Eleanor Drieborg."

Julia moved forward with the infant Eleanor. The President took the baby in his arms.

Kenny Hecht escorted his nephew up to stand by the President, who knelt down and shook the little boy's hand.

Robert looked up at the tall man and asked, "Are you really Mr. Lincoln?"

"Yes, I am, young fella. Do you think your sister will ask me a question, too?"

"She doesn't talk yet," responded Robert. "She just cries."

The President shrugged. "Well, there is at least one in the room who will not ask me for something."

The children were returned to their families, and the President turned to the crowd.

"Today we meet to honor your son, Jacob and Mrs. Drieborg, and your son-in-law, Ruben and Mrs. Hecht. You all have a right to be proud of him. He has proven himself to be a man of great character and the kind of young man we can depend upon to rebuild this country after the end of the war."

The President continued, recounting the reason the Congressional Medal of Honor was awarded to Michael Drieborg.

"I am pleased to confer on Major Michael Drieborg the highest award a grateful nation can give one of its soldiers. This medal was authorized by the Congress earlier in the war. So, with me today is the Speaker of the House of Representatives and the Leader of the United States Senate."

Once all three men congratulated Michael, the President pinned the medal to Mike's jacket. He then turned to the audience and announced, "Ladies and gentlemen, may I present to you Major Michael Drieborg!"

To applause, photographs were taken of Michael and the President. Other dignitaries posed with him as well. Even more photographs were taken of the families and the Lincolns. Michael was interviewed, as well. Mrs. Lincoln escorted the Drieborgs and Hechts to a reception held in an adjacent room and stayed with the ladies and children for some time.

The President took Jacob and Ruben around the room, introducing them to dignitaries. But he wanted some time with the two farmers, alone. So, he led them away from the crowd into another room. They sat and talked for some time.

"You can't know, gentlemen, what a treat it is for me to visit with you like this. I haven't spent this kind of time with men still in farming since before I was first elected President."

Ruben and Jacob were peppered with questions from the President about their farms. How had the shortage of farm workers impacted them? Were they clearing and planting more acres because of the inflated prices? How was their debt structured? What impact would the end of the war have on prices and debt repayment? How was public sentiment about the war in western Michigan and with Ruben's neighbors in Maryland?

Then, the three men walked through all the floors of the White House. But it was clear that the visitors were most impressed by Lincoln himself.

"Gentlemen," the President told them, "you have spent the last two hours answering my questions. Thank you for putting up with me. I am so isolated here and bombarded with requests from people who have special agendas. You have provided me with a breath of fresh air. Is there anything special you would like to ask me?"

Jacob and Ruben looked at each other for a moment.

"Yes, sir, "Ruben admitted to the President. "Ve too, are isolated and know little of da var,"

"Mr. President," joined in Jacob, "how soon will dis war end?"

"I don't know gentlemen. I wish I did." He hung his head sadly.

It was late in the afternoon before the White House reception was concluded. The President found his wife and her guests going from room to room, having a good old time.

"Mr. Lincoln," she said somewhat testily, "you may be done with Ruben and Jacob, but we ladies are not finished. If you must rush back to your office, do so. Leave the men with me. They might find the rest of our tour enjoyable. Would like to join us gentlemen?" she asked. It really wasn't a question.

The three men knew there was little choice, so Jacob said, "Ruben, shall we join da ladies?"

"Ya, I think so, Jacob."

The group went on, leaving the President of the United States standing alone in the second-floor hallway.

Later that afternoon, the families returned to Congressman Kellogg's home for an evening reception.

For the next few days, Ruben and Emma Hecht and Jacob and Rose Drieborg were the hit of the Washington social scene. Each evening, their son and Congressman Kellogg took them to a social function at a fashionable Washington home. Each afternoon, the ladies were guests at an afternoon tea in those same fashionable homes. Of course, Major Drieborg was expected to escort them.

Meanwhile, the Congressman took Jacob and Ruben on tours of the city. His guests could not believe their eyes when they saw the open pens with tens of thousands of cattle and horses awaiting shipment to the armies in the field. They were also stunned when they saw thousands of cannons standing wheel to wheel.

Then Kellogg took them to warehouses full of food, weapons, and clothing. He showed them the nearby rail center, teeming with boxcars and flatcars attached to hundreds of engines belching steam and headed south or west.

"How come our government has not ended dis war already, Congressman?" asked Jacob. "So many supplies and weapons must mean we have thousands and thousands of men fighting for da Union."

"Ya," joined in Ruben, "how come?"

"Until now, gentlemen," Kellogg explained, "we haven't had good leadership, and the Confederacy has. With poor leadership, we have squandered our chances time and again to inferior numbers of poorly equipped rebel soldiers who were better led."

"But mit all dose cannon and horses..." Jacob muttered.

"Sad, isn't it?" Kellogg commented. "Tell me. If I offered you a rifle which could be fired seven times a minute without reloading against an advancing enemy, or a muzzle loader which might allow you to get off three shots a minute, which of these rifles would you chose to fire in battle?"

Ruben responded first. "I vould choose da rifle I could fire seven times mit no reloading, of course."

"So, would I," Jacob chimed in.

"Me too, gentlemen," the Congressman agreed. "Can you imagine the firepower of a hundred-man infantry company equipped with this kind of rifle? At three hundred yards, those men could fire seven hundred bullets a minute at an advancing enemy without taking the rifles from their shoulders. Multiply that times the one thousand men of a Regiment, or the five thousand men of a division, all concentrating their fire on the enemy advancing across an open field.

"Some of us believe that the war would have ended a long time ago. However, two years ago it was decided by our military leaders that such a weapon was too wasteful of ammunition. As it stands right now, only the cavalrymen of the Michigan Brigade have been furnished these rifles."

The two farmers just shook their heads.

"I don't understand dis Congressman," Ruben commented sadly. "Is dis what you call politics?" Jacob asked.

"I'm afraid so, gentlemen," Kellogg admitted. "I'm afraid so."

Reporting for Duty: September 1864

Once his family and the Hechts had left Washington, City, Michael reported to the War Office for assignment.

Michael stood at attention in the office of the chief of staff, General Hallack. "Major Michael Drieborg reporting for duty sir."

"At ease Major," General Hallack directed. "Have a chair. You've been assigned to a committee whose members are to plan the liberation of Andersonville Prison. The House Committee on the Conduct of the War has recommended we free the prisoners there immediately. The President has concurred. He also wants you involved, so you will be. Think you can be of help?"

"I certainly hope so, sir. I will do whatever I can."

"In fact, Major, you are to keep both me and the House War Committee informed on the entire project. Were you aware of that part of your assignment?"

"No, sir. I wasn't. I can understand the need to keep the War Committee informed. I worked for Congressman Kellogg as an aide to that committee at one time. But I don't know just how I will keep you informed, sir."

"My aide will brief you on that Major."

"Besides, sir, as I see this liberation project, it must be done quickly and rather surgically. All this sharing of information you want could put the entire effort at risk, in my opinion, sir."

"I share your opinion concerning speed Major. But I am curious. What do you mean 'at risk'?"

"Well sir, northern newspapers are already full of stories about Andersonville Prison and talk of liberating the prisoners there," Michael explained.

"Confederate forces in that area surely will now be on the alert for such an attempt. Speed is critical, it seems to me. An involved planning process could put our liberation forces there at risk. You might remember, sir, the plan to liberate Libby and Belle Island prisons with a raid on Richmond last March? It turns out that it was reported in the Richmond press a week before we attempted it.

"So, I fear that the sharing of the project's plans you spoke of will not only slow everything down, but increase the chances that the Rebs will hear of the details before we even get there. That is what I mean by 'at risk,' sir."

"Let's just concentrate on the necessity for speed, eh Major? The topic of information leaks could be seen in a bad light by those in Congress, as well as by those around the President. It would not do for a recipient of the Congressional Medal of Honor to be accused of defeatism."

"I certainly didn't mean it that way, sir," Mike protested. "I believe that I still have a lot to learn about Washington!"

The General laughed heartily. "The trick Major, is to survive long enough to accomplish your mission. The President's sworn duty is to keep this country together by winning this war. He has assigned the War Department and our armies in the field the mission of accomplishing that task.

"As a part of that overall responsibility, he has added the freeing of the prisoners at Andersonville as a current priority. You were used to increase awareness and thus gain public and congressional support for it. You and the President achieved that part. Now, you have been charged to help with the on the ground accomplishment of that project.

"So, keep in mind what the objective is before you speak. Will what you say help or hinder the successful accomplishment of the project? It doesn't hurt, by the way, to also ask yourself how everything you say will help or hinder your career, either."

"Thank you for the lesson in Washington survival, sir. I'll not forget it."

"One more thing Major," the General cautioned. "This is an election year for the President and all the members of the House of Representatives. One third of the United States Senate is up for reappointment by state legislatures too. What you say and do reflects on the President because he told the public and the people of this town that he trusts you and that you are his guy. He told me that too. So, now I must trust you."

"I won't embarrass the President sir, or you," Michael promised. But he wondered if he should have taken the opportunity a few days ago to leave Washington and visit the Hechts and his own family in Michigan. He knew he could have. Too late now though.

***

"Good. Now, let us get on with this project. I have put together a small group to plan this thing. You are going to meet with them right now."

In an adjoining room, General Hallack introduced Mike to a group of several military men of field rank, one lady, and a gentleman in the military dress of a surgeon.

"This is Colonel Rose, Major. I think you already know one another," the General prompted.

"Yes, sir. We do," responded the Colonel as he shook Mike's hand. "He was a member of my tunneling team when we escaped from Libby Prison last April. Good to see you Mike."

"Thank you, Colonel," Mike responded.

"By lunchtime today I want a complete plan for the liberation, removal, and care of the prisoners at Andersonville Prison," the General directed. "In your plan, you must identify all the resources you will need for the successful accomplishment of that project. You will present your recommendations to me after you share a lunch here in this room.

"While you and the President were out gaining public support for the project, Major Drieborg, the specialists in this room were at work too.

Each in his or her specialty has brought to this table today what they think will be needed.

"Allow me to add another piece of vital information Colonel Rose, before I leave you to your work. Field recon information I received this morning from General Kilpatrick's men suggests that the prison is still lightly defended and that there is no large Rebel force in the area.

"And finally, I would remind you of a stipulation you have already accepted. Later today you all will be transported south to join our forces there. Under no circumstances will you be allowed contact with anyone until the liberation is completed. Are there any questions at this time?"

There were none.

"Fine. I will leave you to your work." With that, the General left the conference room.

The committee went to work immediately. Colonel Rose solicited ideas and data from each member. Coffee and a light lunch were served, but the discussion was not interrupted.

Early in the afternoon, General Hallack was notified that the committee was ready to present him with a plan.

"Sir," Col. Rose began, "the committee has asked me to present the overall plan. Major Jenson, an experienced quartermaster, will touch on supply and transportation needs. Major Howard, a medical doctor, and Mrs. Barton, a nurse, will deal with healthcare issues."

"Fine Colonel," General Hallack commented. "Please proceed."

"Sir, if you will look at page one before you," requested Rose. "We have settled on the recommendations you have before you as those best suited to accomplish the liberation, treatment and transportation of the prisoners at Andersonville.

"First, we suggest that a Regiment of cavalry be detached from one of General Kilpatrick's divisions to capture the prison with all possible speed and that you order that attack today. Second, we suggest that the rest of that cavalry division be ordered to move to the relief of the prison, tomorrow. The primary role of this large force would be to deny to the Rebs all likely routes of counterattack, implement procedures for medical care of the critically ill and organize the removal of prisoners to treatment centers.

"The attached documents, sir, clearly call for supplies and transport far in excess of what a cavalry division would normally carry in its inventory. So, General Kilpatrick's quartermaster people will have to strip his entire Corps to come up with the supplies and transport that will be sufficient for the removal phase of the operation.

"We want to emphasize sir," Colonel Rose continued, "that we do not believe it necessary to slow down the schedule we have recommended while the General's people are identifying and organizing the supplies and transport at the Corps level. We think the prison needs to be taken and secured while they are doing that sir.

"Additionally, we have left the logistics and timing of prisoner removal to General Kilpatrick and his commanders. We believe they are best positioned to manage that stage. Does anyone wish to add anything at this point?"

"Yes, sir, I do," Michael offered. "I suggest that the lead attacking Regiment be directed to capture and imprison the Andersonville Commandant, Captain Wirz. He has much to answer for, sir, and should not be allowed to slip away. Nor should he be allowed to destroy the prison records."

"Why should we make a special effort in the case of this one man, Major?" asked Gen. Halleck.

"Because sir, in my opinion he was responsible for the unnecessary deaths of thousands of our soldiers," Michael responded.

"They died because of the lack of basic sanitation and the foul water we were forced to use. It was within Captain Wirz's power and means to have prevented such conditions. Also, his guards conspired with other prisoners to steal our supplies. He and his guards stood by and allowed these prisoners, we called them the Raiders, to beat and kill prisoners at will."

"Our committee agrees General," Col. Rose said in support. "We also wish the General to advise the commander of the attacking force to seize all available records which Captain Wirz might have."

"I see. His capture and the seizure of all available records will be included in the orders. I appreciate the work you and the committee have done, Colonel Rose. I will consult with those in command of our forces in Georgia, and those in Tennessee. It may be necessary to leave Kilpatrick's force in place as a buffer between the Confederate Army and the prison. Instead, we may bring the forces needed to accomplish this project from southern Tennessee or Atlanta, Georgia. This decision will be made today.

"And," the General warned, "the suggestion you have made for Troop movement to begin today may prove to be faster than we can manage. But rest assured the attack on Andersonville will be under way as soon as possible."

The meeting broke up at that point and within the hour the members of the Liberation Committee were aboard a train headed for Chattanooga, Tennessee.

***

"I was just given a cable sent from General Hallack's office," Colonel Rose reported to his committee members. "While we've been on this train headed south, a cavalry Regiment has been dispatched to Andersonville from Chattanooga, Tennessee, not one of Kilpatrick's near Savanah, Georgia. We are told that this Regiment should reach their objective in two or three days. Follow-up cavalry units with extensive supplies should join them at Andersonville shortly after its capture. We should be close behind."

Mike remembered his first train ride.

"My cavalry Regiment was moved by train from Grand Rapids, Michigan to Washington City. We were greeted in towns along the way by crowds of cheering and flag waving well-wishers, bands and a lot of food. This trip is certainly different."

This was Rebel country; and his train had traveled without a friendly stop since it left Washington.

Even with only fuel and water stops, it took his committee members almost a week by rail and wagon to reach Andersonville. The final leg of their journey was on horseback. Mrs. Barton rode alongside Mike. She was a nurse representing the Sanitation Committee which assigned nurses to all the Federal military hospitals.

"My heavens, what is that smell?" Mrs. Barton complained. "Does anyone know?"

"Yes, mum, I do," Major Drieborg answered. "That's the prison you smell. I believe we are still more than two miles or so away, but the light breeze you feel carries the smell. You see, the camp is one big cesspool. It doesn't help either, that the smoke from thousands of cooking fires gets trapped inside the high walls. You'll soon see mum."

"Then," Mrs. Barton firmly stated, "we'll just have to tear down those high walls."

"Yes mum, that's a great idea."

"How could you stand that smell, Major?" she asked, handkerchief over her nose and mouth.

Mike chuckled. "It was not by choice. I never got used to it actually. But I did adjust," he assured her.

Within the hour, they saw the vast prison camp. Smoke from hundreds of small cooking fires hung low over the camp and the valley in which it was located. A slight breeze blew smoke toward them, along with the smells Mrs. Barton had complained about.

They paused to let their horses drink from a stream of cool clear water rushing down the slope and disappearing into the northern end of the camp.

"This is the only source of water for drinking, cooking or washing," Michael pointed out. "Before it gets into the camp, it's not only badly muddied, but is polluted with the human waste of the Confederate guards who bunk up there. If that wasn't bad enough, once the stream is inside the camp, all the human waste from the prisoners pollutes it further."

"Then we'll just have to move clean water to the men before it enters the camp!"

"I certainly like the way you solve problems mum," Mike said. "You act quickly and directly."

Mike noticed two things right away. The large double gates of the prison stood open, and the guard towers were now manned by Union Troops. They used the high structures to watch for approaching Rebel soldiers, not to keep prisoners in the prison compound. There were probably Union patrols on picket duty in the countryside as well.

***

Upon his arrival, Mike directed his attention to Captain Wirz.

"Captain Wirz I am Major Drieborg. I'm here to place you under arrest."

"The name Drieborg rings a bell. I've met you before, haven't I Major?"

"Yes, Captain, you have. I was recently a prisoner here at Andersonville."

"Oh, yes. I recall now. It was the matter of the outlaw prisoners. The Raiders, wasn't it? You led a group called the Regulators. Your group killed a few of them and arrested some. I insisted upon a trial for them, as I recall. You convicted and hung them. Did I remember all that correctly?"

"Yes, you did."

"So, it's my turn now, is it Major?"

"Yes, it is sir. I am to escort you to Washington City with all possible speed. You will stand trial there."

"You will not have a difficult time with me Major. But why am I getting all this attention? Do you have so many soldiers that you can provide an armed escort all the way to your capital for a mere Captain who was just following orders?"

"That is what I was ordered to do Captain," Michael responded. "I'm just following orders, too. You can help make this easier if you will direct me to the records you maintained. Those files will go with us."

"Certainly," he agreed, quite agitated. "But what will become of my family? Are they prisoners, too?"

"No, they are not. They are free to leave this camp."

"What is to become of them? I am their sole support. I have no other family in the Confederate States to care for them."

"I am sorry sir. I have no authority to address your family problem. But you can stay with them here until we leave, if I can have your word that you will not attempt to escape."

"You have my word, Major."

"Now sir, please show me your records."

Captain Wirz and his staff had maintained very detailed records. Prisoner arrivals, deaths, and even recent transfers had been carefully recorded by date. In addition, the amount of food, medicine, and supplies with the dates received were also recorded. It took Drieborg and his staff of three men a week to sort and secure the files for travel.

Journalists from the North had been allowed to travel with the Liberation Committee from Washington City, to Andersonville. At Andersonville they took hundreds of pictures of the dead and the emaciated, near-dead prisoners. These pictures and the stories had been sent to newspapers and journals throughout the North.

By the time Mike was ready to take Wirz and his prison records north to Washington, the photographs and stories published in northern newspapers had caused a surge of anger toward the entire South in general and Captain Wirz in particular.

A squad of six Troopers escorted Wirz north by train. Mike was surprised that their route and exact schedule seemed to be public information. They were met at each stop by angry crowds. On one occasion, they were attacked by a mob when they were changing trains. Wirz was seriously beaten before Michael and his squad could fight their way out of danger. At another stop, the train was almost derailed by a mob. The conductor had to plow through the crowd in order to escape.

Once in Washington City, Mike turned over his prisoner to the military authorities. Reading the newspapers, Mike could tell that Wirz had become a lightning rod for the pent-up anger felt by Northerners over the cruel treatment Union captives had received in Southern prisons.

Under these circumstances, Secretary of War William Stanton ordered Captain Wirz to stand trial by a military court with the charge of the capital crime of murder.

Michael and Patricia Renew Their Friendship

Shortly after his return to Washington with his prisoner Mike paid a morning visit to the Kellogg home. Since his parents and the Hecht family had left Washington, he had not had an opportunity to thank the Kellogg staff for the hospitality they had shown them. The door was opened to his knock, and Adam welcomed him inside the house.

"Good to see you Major," Adam said in greeting. "How are your father and Mr. Ruben getting on?"

"Good morning to you too Adam," Mike replied. "They are both fine as far as I know. I just stopped in here this morning for a moment. I wanted to thank you and Mable for being so kind to my family. I would have stopped in sooner, but I've just returned from Georgia."

"I read about our boys at Andersonville Prison being liberated," Adam noted. "A fine piece of work you did there, Major, freeing all those starving men. God be praised, sir."

"Yes, praise God indeed," Mike agreed. "Would you mind if I went to the kitchen and talked with Mable and the rest of the staff?"

"Come right ahead, sir. Mable should be the only one here right now, but she will be most happy to see you again."

They proceeded through the house and into the kitchen area. The room was still warm from breakfast, and Michael could smell fresh bread in the oven.

"Well, I'll be," Mable said. "Look who the cat dragged into my kitchen." She moved toward Michael and wrapped him in her strong arms. She was almost as tall as Mike, but much heavier. She and Adam were married. They had both been with the Kellogg family since Patricia was a toddler.

"How is that family of yours Major?"

"As far as I know, they're in good health Mable. I stopped in today to thank you for all you did for them last month. They had a wonderful time here."

"It was my pleasure. Except, you know, I had an awful time keeping them two ladies out of my kitchen. They always wanted to help. I guess they never been waited on a'fore."

"That part is true, they never had," Mike responded. "You spoiled them so much that my father feared he would have to hire a cook once my mother returned home."

Suddenly Mike heard a familiar voice behind him. "Well, what do we have here?"

He turned around and saw Patricia standing in the doorway to the dining room. She was smiling at him, one hand on her slim waist and the other on the door frame. Her blond hair was pulled up on top of her head and her snug yellow dress showed off her figure. She was a beautiful sight to Michael.

"Doesn't the mistress of this house rate a hug, too?" She held out her arms toward Mike and he stepped joyfully into them. Adam and his wife moved back a bit. Adam left the room and Mable returned to her cooking.

Patricia put her arm through Mike's and led him out of the kitchen to the front parlor. "What is all this hoopla I hear about you from my Washington friends?" she asked in feigned surprise. "Are you that hero they're all talking about?"

"If they're telling you about that handsome Major who has practically won the war singlehandedly, I'm not," Mike joked. "But if they're talking about a farm boy from Michigan who is still mystified about all the fuss being made about him, I'm your man."

"Nice to see you're still so humble Michael," Patricia quipped.

"You know Miss Kellogg," Mike said, not letting go of her arm, "before I actually saw you standing behind me in the kitchen, I knew you were there, because I have never forgotten your perfume. But I had quite forgotten just how beautiful you are."

"My, my," she gushed, hugging his arm closer to her side. "You are certainly not that shy farm boy from Michigan I remember. Where did you learn that kind of smooth talk Major?"

"You'll be surprised how much I have learned since we last saw one another."

They faced each other on the room's loveseat. Patricia continued to hold Mike's hand. "Everyone in Washington seems to know all about you and your adventures except me," Patricia pouted. "I can't stand it. Please tell me everything."

"Not everything," Michael protested.

"If you value your life," Patricia threatened, "leave nothing out."

For the next hour, Michael told her nearly everything that had happened to him since she had ordered him out of this very house after the Hayes affair a year ago. But he did not mention everything.

"I was so sorry to hear of your wife's death Michael," she told him. "You were in prison when she died, Father told me. He also told me that you have a daughter now. How is she?"

"Thank you for asking, Pat. Little Eleanor is with my parents in Michigan right now. I'm told she is fine."

"Later this week, Friday in fact, we are having a dinner party here," Patricia said. "Will you be my escort that evening? It seems that you have been the guest of honor at everyone's house in Washington but mine. Do say you will, Michael."

"How can I refuse such an invitation?" he quickly responded. "Besides, I suspect that there would be one less hero around Washington if I refused."

"You're right about that Major Drieborg," Patricia exclaimed. Then she slid closer, lifted her hand to the side of his face, pulled his head to her and kissed him. Michael was surprised but did not resist. Instead, he pulled her to him and returned her kiss with passion.

Between kisses, Patricia rested her head on his shoulder.

"Will you forgive me for not believing you about that awful Hayes business and those terrible photographs?" she asked.

"I will, but only on one condition."

She sat up and gave Michael a surprised look. "What condition?" she asked cautiously.

"That the next time you are angry with me, you will not throw me out of the house until you cool down."

"That's a pretty tough condition Major," Patricia teased. "But I'll promise not to ask you to leave when I'm still angry, if you will make a promise to me."

"What?" It was Michael's turn to stiffen and look a bit surprised.

"That we will do things together only because you want to, not because my father wants you to. Agreed?"

"No problem. I can agree to that."

"One more thing." Patricia moved close to him.

"You want another promise?" Michael was wary this time.

"Absolutely! No more photographs of you in bed with a prostitute."

"Fine, as long as you don't throw me out of the house again," he promised.

Before she could say another word, Michael pulled her close and kissed her again. That took care of any conversation for a while.

Mike stayed for lunch that day, too. Over the next few weeks, the two spent as much time together as his duties would allow. Walks were their favorite. Each day they either had lunch downtown or supper at the Kellogg home. Mike escorted Patricia to private dinners and some Washington social events, and, as often as possible, they had private time together in her parlor. This time, Mike never refused her anything she asked of him.

Planning the Wirz Trial, Fall 1864

The Northern press hounded Secretary of War Stanton's office for information about his infamous prisoner, Captain Wirz. At first, Stanton turned them away, considering their pleas for information a bother. However, one of his Aides suggested that his cooperation with the press could actually encourage public support for the Union cause if he used Captain Wirz's notoriety. With a Presidential election in November, it could help re-elect President Lincoln, too.

So, he relented and called a press conference. Stanton promised the press that Captain Wirz would be made available for questions on that occasion.

The press conference was held in a federal courtroom. Secretary Stanton took the elevated seat behind the bench usually occupied by a judge. The prisoner, Wirz, was seated in front of the bench. All of the reporters who had proper credentials were seated behind the railing in the public seating area. This courtroom had a gallery that would accommodate important Washingtonians who had special passes for this occasion. Everyone was searched at the entryway and armed guards sat between the prisoner and the audience.

"Welcome, ladies and gentlemen," announced Secretary Stanton. "Today you will have an opportunity to question the Commandant of Andersonville Prison. It was there that thirty thousand of our brave Troops were housed as prisoners. It was also there that as many as three hundred of them died each day. We believe the evidence will show that the leaders of the rebellion are responsible for these deaths. We also believe that Captain Wirz could have helped prevent the appalling conditions and thus could have saved the lives of many of our boys.

"I have also asked Major Drieborg to join us today," Stanton continued. "You will be allowed to question him later. You might recall that he was a prisoner at Andersonville and he escorted Captain Wirz from Georgia to this city just last week.

"Now, let us proceed. You of the press have drawn numbers. Whoever has number one, please come forward and show your card to the sergeant stationed at the railing."

There was a bit of shuffling until the first reporter began the questioning

"Captain Wirz," the man began. "We have all seen the terrible photographs of the prisoners at Andersonville. Do you accept responsibility for the conditions there?"

Wirz was chained to his chair, so he answered the question seated.

"No, I do not accept responsibility," he asserted. "The records will show that I did the best I could with what I was given. The prison was designed to house ten thousand men, but my superiors sent many more than that. As you were told today, it recently housed as many as thirty thousand men. I did the best I could."

The second question addressed the issue of who was responsible. "If you did the best you could with what you were given, who should we blame, Captain?" the next reporter asked.

"I am just a soldier following orders, sir," he responded. "It was not my fault that the prison was so overcrowded or that I did not have sufficient food to give out each day."

The following questions attempted to get the captain to implicate Jefferson Davis, President of the Confederate States, or some other well-known, high-ranking Confederate official.

Captain Wirz continued to assert that he did the best he could given the circumstances. He did not accuse anyone in particular for inadequate supplies or overcrowding. And, so it went between the reporters and the prisoner.

Finally, a reporter asked a question of Major Drieborg. "I'm Burt Green of the *Grand Rapids Eagle* newspaper. I have a question for Major Drieborg who, by the way, is from a town in my area of Michigan. Major, what do you have to say about Captain Wirz's insistence that he is not responsible for the conditions at Andersonville?"

"He was responsible for much that contributed to the horrible conditions there. At his trial, I believe we will prove that," Mike asserted.

"The only point I would concede is that he was not responsible for the number of prisoners sent to Andersonville. Aside from that, I know from my time there, and the meetings I had with him when I was his prisoner, that there were many things he could have done to save lives. He refused to do them. He is definitely responsible for that."

Mike's comments were greeted by shouting from people in the audience demanding that Wirz be hung for his role.

"Get Jefferson Davis, too!" someone called out.

Secretary Stanton banged his gavel for quiet. "Mr. Green's question will bring this press conference to an end. The trial of Captain Wirz will begin next Monday in this very room. We will award passes using the same process as for today's press conference. We thank you for coming and now, ask everyone to clear the room. Those with the appropriate pass will be allowed to remain to take photographs."

As Mike was leaving the courtroom, Mr. Green called out to him. "Major, can I speak to you privately for a few minutes?"

Mike walked to the railing and briefly talked with Mr. Green.

"I'm afraid I can't tell you much more than you heard in the press conference, Mr. Green," Michael explained. "I've been told not to talk about Wirz's role for fear of compromising the prosecution."

"Nothing like that, Major," Green responded. "I just wanted to visit with you some. You are quite a celebrity around Grand Rapids. I don't know how many copies of the *Eagle* your family buys, but we seem to sell a lot more when something about you is featured."

"Follow me, Mr. Green. We can talk some in that adjoining conference room." Once there, Mike asked, "How can I help you?"

"Is there anything you can tell me about the upcoming trial that wasn't revealed today?"

Mike shook his head. "I don't have much to add today that will not be revealed during the trial."

"Did you know that President Lincoln was much criticized for not moving sooner on the liberation of Andersonville?"

"All I know about that," Mike responded quickly, "is that as soon as I arrived in Washington after my escape, the President called me to his office to discuss the question of liberating the prisoners at Andersonville. With the fall of Atlanta, he was most interested in liberating Andersonville. It certainly impressed me that he was determined to free our troops there as quickly as possible. Will you tell your readers that, Mr. Green?"

"Certainly; will you meet with me again? I would like to keep our readers up to date on the trial. Coming from you, it would mean a great deal to me and to our readers."

"I can't imagine my opinion being of any interest to your readers. But I would be glad to help you if I can."

"Thanks, Major," Green said in parting. "I'll be in touch."

***

The prosecution team was headed by Colonel Norton Chapman. Major Drieborg was assigned to his staff.

Michael was directed to interview former prisoners so that witnesses could be found who would best support the charges against Captain Wirz. Drieborg also searched the prison documents that he had brought north. He was looking for additional evidence which would help support the charges against Wirz.

The military court was made up of General officers. General Lew Wallace directed a panel of six Generals and three Colonels. Secretary Stanton knew that several of these men had political ambitions. So, he believed that they would deliver a verdict the public would approve.

"Major Drieborg," Col. Chapman asked, "Have you finished with your report on Captain Wirz?"

"Yes, sir." He handed the Colonel a written list.

He took a few moments to review the document Michael had given him. "I see you have not chosen to list the specific act of cold-blooded murder."

"That's right sir. I never saw him kill anyone, nor have I interviewed any prisoner who witnessed such an act. But I believe a good number of his actions caused the death of prisoners."

"Please proceed then Major."

"In all sorts of weather — rain, shine, hot or cold — he made all the prisoners stand outside for the daily morning count. If his count was disrupted for any reason, he would order it to begin again. With as many as thirty thousand men standing in ranks, it was sure to be disrupted at some point. Many times, actually. So, the counting process would often take hours.

"Also, prisoners would move around so that they would be counted again and again. By this method, the prisoners thought their food ration could be increased."

"What would Wirz do when he discovered such tactics?" asked the Colonel.

"Sometimes he would withhold all rations for a day or more. On occasion, he became so enraged that he would charge into the ranks and strike prisoners with his heavy sidearm. He would become especially angry when prisoners would laugh at his use of English. It only made things worse, of course, but it was the prisoners' only means of fighting back. These morning counts caused many to become ill. In the heat, hundreds of men passed out. Barefoot men suffered greatly in the cold. The rain soaked our clothing. We had to wear the wet clothing until the heat of the day dried it on our backs.

"Those who chose to report for sick call were usually taken outside the prison to a medical facility. Few who went to the prison hospital were ever seen again. So, those of us who were not too ill or too weak, cared for our own sick. Wirz was a medical doctor. He could have corrected these things.

"He never did anything to correct the water situation, either. There was a small stream that entered the camp at one end and exited at the other. Before the water even got inside the stockade, it was polluted by waste from the guards' latrine. Once inside the camp, that water became more polluted with human waste. We had no choice; we had to use that polluted water for drinking and cooking. As a doctor, he knew the effects this practice would have on our health.

"The diagrams and commentary I have attached to the documents, sir, clearly show the water problem. Also attached, is a description of a solution which could have been put in place by Wirz to avoid this problem.

"He allowed guards to shoot prisoners who walked close to the stockade. It was called the 'Dead Line.' He even gave them furlough as a reward for such shootings."

"Was this line marked?" asked the Colonel.

"No, sir," Mike responded. "It was whatever the trigger-happy guards thought it was. In addition to this neglect, he allowed a group of prisoners we called the Raiders to operate openly in collusion with the guards. They beat, bullied, and killed prisoners at will, stealing anything of value. That's as far as I've gotten sir."

"Fine," the Colonel told Michael. "That is a good start. We can work with this list. Now, your job is to find more witnesses who will testify to these acts. We have enough to start with. But, I want more, many more. We don't have a lot of time for this, so be aggressive. Should anyone be reluctant, subpoena them. Arrest them if necessary and drag them back here if you have to. You understand Major?"

"Yes, sir. But in a combat zone, I can't see myself ordering superiors officers to give me much of their time. Nor can I picture them turning healthy soldiers or troopers over to me."

"You're probably right," the Colonel agreed. "I'll get you written authorization from Secretary of War Stanton. He wants this trial to start next week and he wants Wirz found guilty. He'll give us the cooperation we need."

"Don't you think my job would be better handled by a military lawyer, sir?"

"No, I don't. You'll be fine. Actually, I believe you are better suited than any lawyer around this office. You are a combat veteran who was wounded at Gettysburg, held as a prisoner at Andersonville and a recipient of the Congressional Medal of Honor. It would be hard to beat those credentials with soldiers in the field.

"I am also going to assign two troopers, both sergeants to this detail. That should help you with any reluctant witness. By the way," the Colonel warned, "keep good expense records. Pencil pushers around here are very touchy about such things."

"One last thing, sir, if you don't mind," Mike asked.

"No, I don't mind. Go right ahead."

"Sir, even if this disqualifies me from this assignment, I must tell you that what I experienced and saw at Andersonville has left me with a deep hatred for Wirz. I want to see him convicted and hung in the worst way."

"Far from disqualifying you, Mike. It makes you the man for this job," Drieborg's superior told him. "I want my staff to have such a fire in the belly, a hate like you described. I suspect that you will not let anything or anyone stand in your way. That's the kind of attitude that will get us the conviction and sentence we want."

"I'll do my best, sir."

"See my aide on the way out for the money and travel vouchers I've ordered to be set aside for you."

Mike figured he would be gone at least a week on this assignment. So, before he left the city by rail for Chattanooga, he said his goodbyes to Patricia.

***

Over the last several weeks, except when he was out of Washington on assignment, Mike had been Patricia's constant companion. He met her for lunch, escorted her to the theatre and dinner parties, and helped her father entertain his evening guests at their home.

He had become very comfortable with Patricia and more than attracted to her. In fact, it was becoming very difficult for him to resist her clear invitations for greater intimacy. It would be easier if only she weren't so beautiful. What a smile she had!

The way she sat and walked close to him, holding his arm against her breast, left Mike in a constant state of arousal. When she walked into a room, paused in the doorway, and smiled, he could often feel his face flush.

He wondered if she could tell.

"How is it, Major, that a war hero like you gets red in the face when a girl just walks into a room?" she teased.

She could tell.

One evening, he was at a dinner party in the Kellogg residence. On such occasions one of the guests would usually ask him about prison life at Andersonville. He would respond with a sanitized version of how it was there.

But tonight, the talk at the dinner table was all about the President appointing General Grant overall commander of all the Union forces.

"What do you think about the President's decision Major?" one of the ladies at the table asked.

"Mum," Michael responded, "I am in no position to evaluate the decisions of the President. But I have confidence in him. Besides, from what I read, General Grant has demonstrated that he wins battles. I'm certainly for that."

"I would agree with that," said a Congressman from Indiana. "I know that there was a dark spot in Grant's past. Liquor, I think. But Major Drieborg is right. Grant wins battles. If he can finally finish Bobby Lee, I don't care if he drinks a barrel a day."

"The best reports from my War Committee indicate that his old liquor problem is just that — past tense. I believe his wife accompanies him everywhere, except the battlefield. That would keep any man sober." Kellogg chuckled.

"Is that a derogatory remark aimed at all women?" Patricia cut in rather sharply. "Or, is it just your experience Father?"

"Michael, be forewarned," her father said. "You may be in trouble. As you can see, my daughter is no shrinking violet."

"Don't drag me into this one, sir," Mike quickly responded. "Besides, you're the one in trouble here, not me."

"Wise choice Michael," responded the Congressman. "But to answer your question, Patricia; it is a compliment to womankind; and praise to the General's good sense."

After everyone had left, Patricia and Mike were alone in the living room.

They sat on the couch close to one another. Michael had his arm around Patricia's shoulder.

"Did you agree with my father, Michael?"

"If you mean, do I agree with him about you being no shrinking violet?" Michael asked. "Anyone who knows you would agree that you have views of your own and that you are outspoken about them. Do I think it is a bad thing? No. Actually, it's part of your charm, Patricia."

"I'm happy that you think I'm charming." She leaned forward and brought his arm lower around her back and under her arm. Then, she looked up at him, inviting a kiss.

Michael obliged her.

She slipped onto his lap, put her arms around his head and returned his kiss with passion. Her kiss took his breath away.

"Love me, Michael," she urged.

"Surely you know how I feel about you Patricia." He wrapped her in his arms.

"I didn't mean that Michael. I want you to make love to me."

"Your father is right upstairs."

"I don't care where he is. Make love to me. Right here! Right now!"

"Patricia, please," he pleaded, pulling back from her a little. "I would like nothing more than to make love to you right now. You must be able to feel how aroused I am. But I can't betray the trust your father has placed in me."

She pulled out of Mike's arms and stood in front of him, hands on her hips. "My father should have nothing to do with it Michael Drieborg." Angrily, she threw her head back and taunted him.

"Maybe I'm not desirable enough for you. Maybe that prison did something to you. Maybe you're still mourning for Eleanor. Whatever it is, you must not want me like I want you."

"You're mistaken about all of that."

"Maybe we aren't meant to be together," Patricia continued angrily.

"The last time you became angry with me, Pat, you threw me out of the house. And, I recall, just a few weeks ago you promised not to do that the next time you became angry with me."

Still standing in front of him, she folded her arms. Her face became flushed, and she hissed, "Stop it Michael! This is not a joking matter. Maybe you had better leave before I say something I'll regret!"

"Come on Patricia. Let's talk this out."

"Just go home Michael," she stormed. "I'm too angry to deal with this right now."

Mike was getting angry too. So, without further argument he left as she had asked.

As he walked to his quarters the cool evening air felt good on his face.

"What a woman," he thought. *"I don't know what to make of her sometimes. She is passionate one minute, and instantly angry the next. But there is one thing about her that's never changed — she always wants everything her way. I know we share a pretty intense physical love for one another. There was more than that between Eleanor and me. Whatever that bond was, it is not present with Patricia."*

Early the next morning, he boarded a train and headed south to interview several former Andersonville prisoners who had been found in a field hospital in Atlanta, Georgia. He did not expect to return for at least a week.

He traveled southeast to catch up with Sherman's army in hopes that he might find a few former prisoners already reassigned to that army. Staying away from Washington and Patricia for a while might be a good idea, too.

When Mike returned to Washington City, he called on Patricia. He was welcomed at the door by the butler, Adam.

"Good morning, Major, please come inside," he said. "It's a mite cold out there today."

"Thank you, Adam," Mike said. "Will you ask Patricia if she could see me?"

"I'm sorry Major. She and the Congressman went back to Michigan for a week or so. She didn't want to go without seeing you, she said, but she did leave a note for you sir. Just a moment, I'll get it for you."

Adam gave Mike the envelope Patricia had left for him.

Mike walked to the nearby park that he and Patricia had frequently used for their evening walks. In fact, he sat on the secluded bench where they shared many kisses. He took her letter out of his overcoat pocket and opened it.

Dear Michael,

It seems like I am always saying that I'm sorry. But I am sorry that I am not in your arms right now. As you have discovered, I can be pretty angry when something I want is denied me. Thinking about it, I have come to understand your reluctance to make love to me the other night.

Keeping the promise you made my father is a matter of honor for you. At times, you are too honorable. But It is probably one of things that I love about you So, it is silly of me to have let my pride get in the way of accepting your decision that night.

Please forgive me. I know I broke my proise to you when I lost my temper and asked you to leave. But don't you break the promise you made to me and run off to a brothel. My father has promised that we will be back before the end of the month. I can't wait to hug and kiss you.

Till then, Patricia

Visit to the Hecht Farm

It was going to be a beautiful October day. Michael could feel a pleasant chill in the mid-morning air. The sun was getting high in a clear blue sky. It would be a great day for a ride or a battle. He decided to take a ride.

He packed his haversack for a two or three-day stay and rode to the Hecht farm. He had not seen the family since the medal ceremony last month, so this visit was unannounced. He knew a visit was long overdue. He arrived in the evening, just in time for late afternoon chores and a good meal with the Hecht family.

Mid-morning of the following day, he was in the Hecht barn rubbing down his horse. Eleanor's son Robert came runninto the building.

Almost three years old now, Robert was a stocky boy, growing like a weed and full of energy.

"Here you are!" Robert shouted.

"He is getting tall, like his father". Mike thought as he remembered Robert's father when he stood on the gallows at Andersonville Prison, begging for his life.

"I had done nothing to save the man." Mike recalled. *"The little fellow has his father's curly blond hair too."*

"Sure," Mike responded. "Where did you think I would be, Robert?"

"I don't know. I was afraid you had left without saying goodbye."

"I wouldn't do that to you," Mike promised. "You're my buddy. Here." Mike handed him a brush. "Want to give me a hand with my horse?"

"Sure. I've helped Kenny with our horse, Blue lots of times."

"I'll bet you're pretty good at it, too."

"Grandpa says so."

"Take this brush to his front legs. Not too hard. He likes a gentle touch."

"Oh, yeah! I can tell he likes that." The young boy hesitated. "Mike?"

"Yes, Robert?"

He had stopped brushing and faced Mike, frowning and looking very serious with hands on his hips. "Mike, are you my real father?"

"Your real father was killed in the war, Robert." "Does that mean I don't have a father?"

"Not exactly Robert," Mike told him. "Your mamma wanted me to be your father."

"But I don't call you Papa. Should I call you Papa?"

"Would you like to, Robert?"

"Yes."

"Then you can," Mike said. "I would like it a lot if you did."

"What is little Eleanor's name Mike, I mean, Papa?"

"Why, it's Eleanor Drieborg, of course."

"And your name is Michael Drieborg?"

"That's right, Robert."

"*Where is all of this going?*" Mike wondered. "Then how can you be my poppa when I don't have the same last name as you and little Eleanor?"

"Robert, I hear Grandma calling us for dinner," Mike told him. "Let's you and I talk about this after we eat and you take your nap."

As they walked out of the barn, Robert balked at the idea of a nap. "I don't wanna take a nap," he protested. "I want to talk. Can't we talk?"

"Sure. We can talk all you want, Robert, after your nap, though. Now, let's get our hands washed for dinner."

They approached the sink by the pump. Hand soap was on the counter, and a towel hung there for their use.

Robert continued to complain. "But my hands aren't dirty. I don't see any dirt on them. Why do I have to wash them?"

"Because that's what is expected of men," Mike explained. "We wash our hands before we sit down at the table to eat. You might just as well learn that now, young man."

"Are you going to wash your hands, Mike?"

"Of course, I am. Even though I can't see the dirt there, I've been working on my horse. So, I know I must wash them before I sit down at your grandma's dinner table."

"I worked on the horse with you," he surmised. "Then I should wash my hands, too."

After a hearty noon meal, Robert was droopy-eyed. Although still protesting some, he allowed Mike to tuck him into bed. He agreed to the nap only after Mike had promised him a story. In just a few minutes, he was fast asleep.

Michael retreated to the kitchen, where everyone relaxed over pie and coffee.

"Is Robert full of questions all the time?"

"Ya," responded Ruben. "He is interested in most everything."

"He certainly is. I'm not used to being around a little tyke. Does he pester you with questions, too?"

"Come to think of it," commented Emma, "he started about the time we returned from visiting you in Washington. Seeing you, the President, and your family seemed to release questions like in a flood breaking loose. So much is on his little mind. Where had his mother gone? Why had God taken her from him? Why didn't little Eleanor come home with us? Where were you? Our answers never seem to satisfy him. Did he pursue anything special with you, Michael?"

"I could not believe it. He nailed me good with a series of questions just before dinner," Michael explained.

"He started with questions about who was his father. Then he got into why his last name is different from mine and Eleanor's. You called us to dinner and saved me from having to answer that last one."

"How are you going to answer that one?" Kenny asked.

"I don't really know," Mike admitted. "Eleanor and I talked about that, of course. But he is Eleanor Hecht Bierlein's son, raised by you, the Hecht family. Makes more sense if he took your name," Mike thought aloud.

"That might make sense to us adults," Emma interjected.

"But I see Robert looking to you as his fathe," she continued. "If you refuse him your name what would that tell him, Michael? Would it tell him that you don't want him? That you don't love him? That you don't want to be his father?

"Just' because I am a mamma, I don't know what goes on in the mind of an almost three-year-old boy who woke up one day last summer to find his mother gone and you a prisoner somewhere. I do know Michael that you are very important to him. I also know that this little boy, God bless his pure heart, has asked you the big question. He wants to know how important he is to you. He wants to know if he is important enough for you to truly become his father. Or, is he only worth a weekend visit now and then when you have nothing better to do? I think you know the answer Eleanor would expect of you Michael. But she is gone and now Robert wants to know what he can expect of you. We do too.

"I do not think he will let up on you about this. He is just a little boy reaching out to the man he was told would be his father. It is not too complicated, I think, Michael."

"I do want to be his father, Emma!" Michael responded a little too loudly. "But until this war is over, how can I assure him I will survive it? In the meantime, would he be better off in Washington with a housekeeper most of the time, rather than here with you?"

"No! Of course not," Emma sharply retorted. "These are problems, I know. But I think you use them to help you avoid answering the real question Robert is asking. Many other men these days have the same problems. They face them. Can you?

"I may be a simple farmer's wife with no education or position. But remember Michael, I was in the room when the President of the United States told everyone that you are a brave man who has the best of character. I was there too, when he gave you the highest medal our government can award. And now you can't face a little boy and tell him how he fits into your life?"

Michael did not respond. Kenny sat leaning forward, elbows on the table, his pie fork still in his hand. He had never heard his mother talk in this way, especially not to Michael. Ruben, as was his habit, listened quietly, smoking his after-dinner pipe, as his wife Emma spoke.

Then, she looked directly at Michael across the table, with tears in her eyes.

"You haven't even asked where Eleanor is buried."

Emma rose from the table, carrying her dishes to the sink.

"Michael," she said quietly, "I think you had better leave our house, now. You may return only if you decide to be a father to Robert. But do not wait long to decide. I will not have Robert wondering if you will ever return his love for you."

"Mamma!" said Kenny, shouting. "How can you tell Michael he has to leave? He is family too, isn't he?"

"He can be Kenny, but it is for Michael to decide if he wants to be part of our family. Robert has lost one father to this war," she declared. "You must tell us before the end of the year Michael. After the New Year comes, we will tell him the war has taken you, too."

"But Mamma, this is Michael," Kenny started to protest again.

"Dat is enough talk Kenny," Ruben admonished quietly. "Mamma knows about dese tings. It is best for Robert, too I tink. Da sooner Robert knows da better for him; und for us too. Mamma is right. You must decide Michael. Da sooner, da better."

With that, Ruben put his pipe into his mouth, moved to the doorway, and put on his work coat. "Come, Kenny. You have vork to do. Michael vill tell us vhat he decides. Da sooner da better, eh, Michael?"

***

As he rode away from the farm, Emma Hecht's words rang in Mike's ears.

"She sure took me by surprise. Obviously, she had thought about this before my unexpected visit. She is one tough lady. I found that out after I was wounded at Gettysburg. She snatched me up from the Kellogg home and brought me back here. I was feverish from infection and dehydration. I was told that I was darned near dead.

"I thought her treatment of my wound was pretty rough. But, she didn't pay any attention to my complaints. Each time I tried to avoid one of her treatments Eleanor would threaten to tell on me. That always did it. I'd rather endure the treatment than face her mother's rath.

"That was child's play compared to how she treated me today. I think I would rather face the Rebs again than take another scolding from her.

"I could have come out here since they visited me in Washington earlier this fall. I have been busy and out of town some. But, I could have made it out here sooner. Instead I have been having fun as the Washington celebrity with the beautiful girl on my arm. I haven't even taken time to mourn for Eleanor or to think of Robert. Emma knows. Her comment about what Eleanor would expect of me sure hit home too.

"Actually, I had not thought this problem through before coming here yesterday. But I will now. If nothing else Emma Hecht has touched a nerve. She made me ashamed of myself. I will give the Hecht family and Robert an answer.

"Oh, my God. I have never even mentioned Robert to Patricia. Good thing that she is out of town for a while. I don't look forward to talking to another strong-willed woman about this just yet."

Michael's Problems

It was noon in Washington City. The dining room at the Willard Hotel was crowded with men who held power and those who wished to influence its use.

Congressman Kellogg often invited Michael to join him at the midday meal. He knew Michael had no designs on power or wished to influence its use. He had learned to trust Michael and never worried that he would disclose their conversations with others. Thus, he was able to relax, enjoy his lunch and Michael's company, and watch the hectic scene at the Willard Hotel.

"Have I ever told you much about this place Michael?" asked Kellogg.

"Bits and pieces sir," Michael responded. "From what I've seen each time you've brought me here, the men who run this place would make pretty good field Generals in our Army."

Kellogg chuckled. "Hadn't thought of it that way. I'll mention it to the President next time I see him. He'll get a good laugh out of your observation. He probably will agree with you, Michael.

"Let me see," he considered. "I might as well start at the beginning. The hotel was first opened in 1847 by the Willard brothers. They bought six buildings along Pennsylvania Avenue and opened this place in February that year just a few hundred feet from the Capitol building.

"By the time this war began in April of 1861, they had expanded. Now they are the largest eating place and hotel in the city. They lodge guests in hundreds of second-floor rooms spread along three hallways.

"Each hall is served by a large bathtub, indoor plumbing and even a toilet. Only place in the city with those things.

"The ground floor, where we are seated, is the scene of frantic activity all the time. The large dining room, bars and smaller meeting rooms are served by a kitchen ninety-some feet long with several open fire pits. I'm told that cooks prepare over twenty-five hundred meals each day. Watch the fleet-footed waiters Michael. They almost run through the kitchen's swinging doors to deliver the meals and I bet they do serve that many meals here.

"Aside from what you see, there is much more you cannot see. This building is the scene, right now probably, of more government-related decisions than anywhere in this city outside the President's office. Men are here today trying to obtain an Army commission. Others are trying to obtain manufacturing contracts for all manner of things needed for our war effort. Bribes are likely being offered and even accepted by government officials right now, in this very room. I wouldn't be surprised in the least if a Congressman or a Senator wasn't involved in that kind of transaction too.

"In fact, several Confederate spies are probably here today, hoping to pick up some bits of information useful to their cause. And tonight, right at that long bar behind you, all of the activities I mentioned will continue to take place. Change how you look at this place and the people around us?"

"Definitely," Michael responded, laughing. "Now, I find myself seeing shady types who might be spies and evil-looking lobbyists handing out bribes. Right now, I'm listening for a high-ranking Army officer talking too loudly about our army's future activities. I don't think I will ever be in here again without looking and listening for those types of things."

"Sort of fun isn't it, Michael?" concluded the Congressman. "It is absolutely fascinating sir. Absolutely fascinating."

"Oh, here is our food. It's not as well prepared as either of us would get at home, but it will do. Besides, I come here for the fun of the watching, not the eating."

After the plates were cleared, both men were served coffee.

"I know you don't smoke Michael," commented Kellogg as he lit a cigar. "But I do enjoy a good cigar after a meal. Have you and Patricia patched things up?"

"Not really, sir. I was out of the city for a week after she kicked me out of your house, and you two were back in Michigan until this week. I've been working long hours with the prosecuting team preparing the final arguments in the Wirz trial. So, I haven't had more than a few hours here and there to myself. But I think I have put off seeing her because I'm also struggling with another personal matter."

"What would that be Michael?"

"I've simply avoided thinking about the issue of my responsibilities as a father. Since my return to Washington last summer, I've not thought much about my obligations as a father to either Eleanor or Robert. My visit to the Hecht farm convinced me that I cannot put that off any longer."

"Did anything in particular happen when you were at the Hecht farm?" Kellogg asked.

"Yes, sir. Mrs. Hecht happened. Patricia isn't the only lady I've had trouble with lately. Emma Hecht threw me out of her house too."

The Congressman laughed heartily. He laughed so hard, that he began to choke on the smoke he had just inhaled from his cigar.

"I'm sorry Michael. I don't mean to be insensitive.

"Patricia told me about her spat with you. I told her how much I respect and appreciate your response to her invitation. I can't imagine it was easy for you to turn her down."

"No, sir, it wasn't. Patricia simply has to walk into the room, and I can feel my blood pressure mount, among other things."

"Well put, Michael," Kellogg interjected. "She is a beautiful woman who knows how to get a man's attention. Surely Mrs. Hecht had a different reason than Patricia's to throw you out," he continued with a chuckle. "Again, I'm sorry. I couldn't resist making that last remark."

"No apology needed, sir. The comparison you made is funny. I can use the humor." Despite himself, Mike laughed too.

"More seriously, Mike, do you want to tell me about the situation with the Hechts, and the boy?"

"Thank you, sir. I would appreciate a friendly ear. I could especially use some advice from you. A shortened version of what happened is that I was out in the barn grooming my horse when the little guy joined me. He pestered me with questions about my being a father to him. I avoided giving him an honest answer. After the noon meal he was put to bed for a nap and I joined the Hechts at their kitchen table for pie, coffee and some conversation. The pie was great; the conversation was not.

"I told them of Robert's questions. I couldn't believe a child not yet three years old could trap a guy with such a series of questions. We could use him on the Wirz prosecutor team, believe me. Anyway, he got me to volunteer to be his papa. Emma called us in for dinner, so I didn't have to answer him about the last name issue he questioned me about, right then. After we ate, he was put down for a nap, and I told his grandparents of our conversation and that I had avoided answering his last question.

"That's when Mrs. Hecht came right after me. She believed that Robert is in a highly emotional state right now. She thinks it was caused by his mother's sudden death and my lack of involvement since they visited me in Washington. She told me I was a coward, the decorated war hero who would not even answer a little boy's questions. As she explained the pain I was causing this three-year-old child, she became quite angry. She asked me to leave their home and not return unless I was willing to be a father to Robert as I had promised his mother."

Kellogg remarked. "I remember her when she and Ruben picked you up at my home last summer after you were wounded. She certainly impressed me then, as a very strong-minded woman. She was here for the award ceremony with your family too. Once again, I was quite impressed by her. She is quite a lady."

"No question about that, sir. And, she nailed me accurately. As she said, I have used the war and my current assignment as an excuse not to think about either child, or my obligation to them."

"What are you going to do about it?" asked Kellogg

"I want to be a true father to both children. But now that my assignment with the Wirz trial has concluded, I don't have a clue what my next assignment will be or where. Even if I knew these things, how could I care for one child, much less two, alone?"

"Not easy I can tell you,"interjected Kellogg. "Raising Patricia, even with the help of her aunts and nannies, has not been easy. But maybe I can help to clear up at least one of the problems you identified. I would like to get you assigned to my Congressional War Committee staff, effective after you return from the home furlough you have been given. That should be after Christmas, as I recall."

"Yes, sir, that's correct," Mike responded. "You seem to step in and rescue me all the time. But with thousands of men still dying, in a war far from won, how can such an assignment be justified?"

"Michael, our war effort does not need another dead hero. But alive, you can be valuable to the War Committee and to me personally."

"I have learned to trust your judgment Congressman. Whatever you have in mind, I will do it happily."

"Good, I'll arrange it. As for the other problem, you must manage that without any help from me."

"I think you are referring to my finding help to raise these children, or a wife perhaps?" Michael surmised.

"Perhaps. How soon will you be able to talk with Patricia?"

"I have some time tomorrow morning sir. I had hoped to call on her then, at your home."

"Like Ruben said Michael," the Congressman said with a smirk, "da sooner da better."

"Ouch!" Michael replied in mock hurt. "I didn't realize this side of you sir."

"There is still a lot about me you do not know young man. Over time, you will learn more. But for now, I must return to my office. That's where I meet with people who want something of me, not here at the Willard. Good luck on the helpmate issue."

"Thank you, sir. I expect I'll need a lot of that."

Mike hadn't expected that his upcoming employment problem would be solved with such ease. He should have known; tell your congressman about it and it would be taken care of.

Next, he intended to talk with the other Kellogg, Patricia. He hoped she would be willing to help him solve his other problem. He needed help raising two children.

Conversation with Patricia

Mike was approaching the Kellogg home.

"Pat is an early riser. So, ten in the morning doesn't seem too early an hour to be calling.

"I need to talk with her before she and *her father leave for Michigan in a few days. I might as well face her today, if she's home. Maybe she is out and about already. If the strong attraction I feel for her is to develop into something more we must talk over some serious issues; my daughter Eleanor; my deceased wife's first child, Robert; what I will do for a living after the war and where we will live."*

"Good morning, Major," greeted Adam. "It is nice to see you again, sir. Please come in," he invited. "Is it cold out there this morning, sir?"

"Thank you, Adam." Michael stepped into the vestibule. "It's warming up a bit. But there is still a chill in the air."

"Here now, let me have your hat and coat sir. The Congressman had an early breakfast and has gone to the office. Miss Patricia had her breakfast too and is in the sitting room. Would you like me to tell her that you are here?"

"Yes, Adam. I would appreciate that."

Adam walked down the hallway. He went into the sitting room and closed the door behind him.

He returned shortly to the hallway where Michael was waiting.

"Major," Adam informed him, "Miss Patricia will see you now." Mike entered the sitting room. Patricia stood in the sunlight by her desk. As soon as the door was shut, she glided across the room toward him. Arms outstretched, she walked into his arms and held him tightly. Her familiar perfume filled Mike's senses. He returned her embrace and kissed her.

Mike wondered how he could have refused this woman's invitation to make love.

She pulled away slightly, still holding his arms, and looked into his eyes. "I've missed you so, Michael," she whispered. "I was foolish. Forgive me? Again?"

"Of course, Patricia," he responded, hugging her once again. "Since that evening, you have never left my thoughts or my heart. The time apart helped me realize how much you mean to me," he happily revealed.

"Oh, yes, Michael!" she assured him. "I was afraid I had lost you for good. Hold me, Michael. Hold me close."

"I don't ever want to let you go Patricia."

They moved to a nearby couch. Facing one another, they held hands. "Patricia, your beauty takes my breath away."

"Oh, Michael," She put her hand on his cheek. "I'll never tire of you telling me that. But I need more than just those words. I need you to tell me that you love me. I need you to tell me that you want me at your side always. Can you say those things too?"

"I can Patricia," Michael said, pulling her into his arms again. "And I want you to be my wife."

She pulled back and looked at him through tear-filled eyes. "Yes, Michael! That's what I want too. With all my heart, I want to be your wife."

Michael bent forward and kissed her. She moved her arms up his chest, put her hands on the back of his head and returned his kiss.

Patricia broke the kiss, brought Michael's hand to her lips and leaned back against the arm of the sofa. "Have you talked to Father about this?"

"No. I wanted to talk with you first," he assured her. "I'm pretty sure your father knows how I feel about you. I don't want to ruin this moment Pat. But before we go any further with this, I must bring up the question of the children."

"If you are referring to Eleanor…" Patricia interrupted. She raised her hand and caressed his cheek. "You needn't have any fear about that; I want to be a mother to her. I know I will love her. And because she is so young right now, I believe she will come to consider me her real mother and love me too."

"That's wonderful," exclaimed Michael, genuine relief showing on his smiling face. "I'm sure you will be a great mother for Eleanor. But what of Robert? Have you thought of him as part of our family too?"

"He is Eleanor's son by her first husband, isn't he?" "Yes."

"My goodness Michael," Patricia said, pulling away from him just a bit more. "I haven't given that possibility any thought. Believe me, I will be most comfortable with Eleanor as my daughter. Actually, I look forard to becoming her mother." She stiffened, inching further away from him.

"But mothering a little boy, not even your son? Heavens! I had hoped that you and I could have our own son. I truly love you, Michael, but you need to give me time to think about this."

Michael thought he might as well drop the other shoe now rather than later.

"There is something else Patricia." "What? Not more children, I hope!"

"Oh, my no, Pat, "But it's something important enough for us to talk about now rather than later. It's the matter of what kind of work I will do after this war ends."

"Won't you keep working here in Washington, Michael?"

"I suppose I could," Mike admitted. "I am sure your father would help with that. But how would you feel about being a farmer's wife back in Michigan?"

"Really Michael!" she responded sharply.

Michael saw her sit up straight and slide a bit away from him. He knew from past experience with her that this posture might mean trouble.

"Think about it. Can you picture me baking bread, milking a cow, or killing a chicken, or whatever else farm wives usually do? Look at me. Haven't you always seen me dressed the way I am today? Would this be practical attire for daily life on a farm? Can you see me milking a cow, gathering eggs or baking bread dressed like this with my hair all done up? I doubt it."

Mike could tell that she was working herself up.

"Your mother and Mrs. Hecht, your sisters, Eleanor's sister, they all were raised on farms. They know farm life and are probably very skilled at carrying out the responsibilities of a farm wife. I would not be, Michael. I have been pampered by servants as long as I can remember. I have never even fixed a meal in my entire life."

Michael covered Patricia's hand with his. "Please, Patricia," he urged, "I am not demanding anything of you at this point. But we do need to talk about these things before we go any further. These are not decisions we should leave until after we're married."

She suddenly stood and walked to the other side of the room. When she turned around and looked at him, Mike could see that her face was flushed. *Is it passion or anger?* he wondered.

"Yes. I can see that. We do have to discuss these things first. Please understand Michael. I love you very much and I want to be your wife. And, I want be a mother to Eleanor. But I might as well tell you right now, I cannot be a farmer's wife."

"Are you kicking me out again?" Michael teased.

"Oh, stop that, Michael" she snapped. "This is not a teasing matter. If you want a definite answer right now, I would have to tell you that I am not only totally unprepared to be a farmer's wife, but I do not want to be a mother to Robert either."

She began to walk briskly from one side of the room to the other in front of Michael. Her face was still flushed. She hugged herself for support.

Michael rose too. "Come here, Patricia." He watched her quickly move into his outstretched arms. She wrapped her arms around him, put her head against his chest and began to cry softly.

"Is that it, Michael?" she whispered. "Is there no hope for us?"

He hugged her more tightly. "Of course, there is," he assured her. "I believe we can work through this."

"I want to believe that, too," Patricia responded.

Mike stood back a step, still holding her arms in his hands.

"Congress will soon be adjourned for Christmas. Your father told me that the two of you were returning to Grand Rapids until the first of the year. With the end of the Wirz trial, I've been given extended leave.

"So, I intend to return to Michigan as well. I haven't been home in two years. Can I call on you at your home in Grand Rapids?"

"Only if you understand that I cannot be a farm wife or a mother to Robert," she asserted more strongly than she had intended.

Tears forgotten now, she reached out to him. He pulled her into an embrace once again. They stood in the center of the room kissing. Patricia's body movement and her kisses were getting Mike aroused again. It didn't take much.

However, he had to leave.

"I have to report for a meeting. We're finishing up the Wirz case. I don't want to leave right now, but I must."

"I understand Michael," she said, giving him a quick kiss. She put her arm through his and walked him to the front door.

"I will see you in Grand Rapids Patricia," he said as he put on his overcoat and left the house.

"Whew! I certainly did not want to leave her this morning. She was so passionate I'm sure we would have ended up making love had I stayed much longer. I would not have refused another invitation from her.

"I know, I love her physically. I long for her touch. I love to hold her in my arms. The touch of her lips on mine is exciting and arousing. I can't get enough of it. But there doesn't seem to be anything more than this physical attraction between us.

"Our attempts at discussion have never ended very well. At least, they haven't for me. So far, it must be Patricia's way and no other. That can't be a good foundation for a marriage.

"And, she just made it very clear to me that I must abandon any thought of farming. Instead, she expects me to work in Washington for the rest of our life together. And then, I know that I would always be dependent upon the Congressman or some other politician for a job. Would I end up hating Pat for that? I probably would.

"And, Patricia would be responsible for my decision to abandon Eleanor's son Robert. Would I eventually blame Pat for that too? I probably would. Is she worth all that?"

Wirz Verdict: November 1864

The trial of Captain Wirz had been in session Monday through Friday, since early October. He was charged with several counts of murder. If convicted, the military court-martial could sentence him to death by hanging.

The prosecution team had pursued an interesting line of attack. First, they had hoped to link the President of the Confederacy, Jefferson Davis, with responsibility for the deaths at Andersonville Prison.

Second, they wanted to convince the court that Wirz, as Commandant, was directly responsible for conditions in the prison and the deaths that resulted.

And, third, they argued that Wirz could have alleviated the conditions at the prison with the resources at his disposal and that he failed even to attempt to positively change those conditions.

The prosecution utterly failed to prove the first charge against Jefferson Davis. Even for a very biased court, there was simply no evidence to support such a charge.

The second charge did not survive very well, either. Wirz was appointed Comman-dant well after Andersonville was constructed and the prosecution could not blame him for the overcrowding. Neither could they support a claim that he stole food or other supplies sent for the prisoners. The evidence was clear that he and his staff of aides and guards ate little better than the prisoners.

It turned out that the third charge was easily proven. Major Drieborg had identified dozens of eyewitnesses to the cruelty of prison life. He also recruited engineers who showed, quite graphically, how the water supply the prisoners had to use could have been made cleaner and how human waste did not have to be the infectious problem it actually had been. Most damning was their testimony that it was within Wirz's authority to change both of these major problems. They contended that his records proved he had the supplies and labor force to change these two things for the better.

The members of the military tribunal gave the legal staff defending Captain Wirz little sympathy or cooperation. His lawyers were very limited as to what evidence they could submit. Conditions in Union prisons similar to those at Andersonville were ruled inadmissible too. In the last analysis, their defense rested on what Captain Wirz himself had said. In a very overcrowded facility he had done what he could with the resources he was given.

It wasn't enough.

The verdict of the court was swiftly decided: guilty as charged. The punishment was harsh. It would be death by hanging.

As soon as the sentence was carried out, Michael headed for his home in Lowell, Michigan.

Trip Home: November 1864

Travel in wartime was a challenge. The fastest method was by train, so everyone wanted to travel that way and everyone wanted a ticket as soon as possible. Soldiers going home on leave had limited time and so they were in a hurry, of course. Businessmen and lobbyists pursuing contracts and influence were in a hurry too.

Michael had taken his new bride Eleanor to Michigan just about this time last year. This time however, he discovered that travel by train was more difficult to arrange.

"Good thing I made my arrangements weeks ago." Even though he hadn't known when his role in the actual trial and sentencing of Captain Wirz would be concluded, he bought his tickets in advance, anyway. He could always sell them if he needed to, most likely at a profit.

Trains headed to the Midwest had to first go to Philadelphia or Pittsburg. From one of these railroad centers, another train would take its passengers and cargo first to Cleveland and then Detroit. Michiganders would transfer there to other trains bound for the interior of the state. Michael would catch another train there for his home.

Most travelers bought the most available and inexpensive seat they could find. Such tickets entitled them to travel on straight-backed wooden seats. Rows of these would require three passengers to sit side by side and back-to-back. Thus, some passengers would see the oncoming landscape, while others would see where they had been. Their gear would be stored on racks above their heads and in the space under their seats.

For the more affluent and influential travelers, each train included first-class accommodations. They could purchase tickets for this less crowded, more comfortable — even opulent — seating. Railroad personnel would assist such passengers with their luggage and provide them with food and refreshment throughout their trip. Congressman Kellogg and his daughter Patricia traveled in such a car. Major Michael Drieborg did not.

He chose to travel on a railroad car reserved for army officers. Less lavish than the first-class cars, it was still much less crowded and more comfortable than the less expensive coach cars.

He shared a padded leather-covered seat with a fellow Union Army officer. Major Robert Lilley was from Michigan too. He lived seventy miles northwest of Detroit in a farming community called, Lapeer. Though a bit larger, it was much like Michael's hometown of Lowell.

Both men were raised on a farm, so they had much in common. A good six foot four inches tall, blond-haired and blue-eyed, Bob Lilley had a friendly smile and a keen wit. Michael and Lilley hit it off from the start.

Both were the eldest sons of European immigrant farmers. They shared stories of growing up on a small farm, and, of course, they swapped stories of the war.

They quickly discovered that they had both served in the Army of the Potomac. Both had fought at Gettysburg as well. Bob had not been wounded though.

"Where did you fight at Gettysburg?" Bob asked.

"My cavalry Troop was part of the Michigan Brigade," Mike related. "Jeb Stuart tried to attack the rear of your infantry units at Gettysburg with three or four thousand mounted men. Three miles north of your position, my brigade of a thousand or so troopers stopped him from doing that."

"My goodness! I've heard his cavalry was pretty good. How in heaven's name were you able to stop that many Rebs with so few of you?"

Mike chuckled. "I suppose we just didn't know any better. But actually, the Spencer rifles we had, sure helped."

"I've been told that a soldier can get off seven shots a minute with that weapon," Bob said. "Is that true?"

"Actually, after you get into the rhythm of handling the weapon, you can get off twelve to fourteen shots a minute. So, we were able to lay down some devastating fire that day."

They continued to talk of war most of the trip to Philadelphia and during dinner their evening in Pittsburg, as well. They walked around downtown for a while after they had had supper.

"Bob," Mike said, stopping on the sidewalk, "did you think we've been followed during our walk tonight?"

"Actually, no. I have been so captivated by the tales of your cavalry exploits I haven't noticed anything like that. Could it be that you are nervous around crowds of people after spending so much time with horses?"

"Do all infantrymen make sarcastic comments like that about cavalrymen?"

"We were always too busy fighting Rebs to pay much attention to you guys," Bob said, chuckling. "Besides, we were told that the cavalry was out scouting, not fighting. That's why I was so interested in your story about that small cavalry battle you fought at

Gettysburg. It was the first fight I had heard about that you cavalrymen had; with the rebs that is."

"Enough Lilley, that's enough," Mike said in exasperation. "Right now, I want a quiet room and a good night's sleep."

The next morning, they boarded a train headed west toward Cleveland. Both of them would travel together further west to Detroit. Their conversation continued. Major Lilley had heard much of Andersonville Prison, but had never talked with anyone who had been imprisoned there. He was fascinated with Mike's tales of life at the prison.

By the time their train pulled into Detroit that evening, they were fast friends. After they finished supper, they went for a walk along Woodward Avenue before turning in for the night. Woodward was Detroit's main business street. Its sidewalks were illuminated by gas lamps. Despite the hour, the two men noticed many people on the sidewalks and saw a good deal of horse and wagon traffic on the broad avenue.

They repeatedly interrupted their walk to look into the windows of the shops lining the avenue. Bob was surprised that so many stores were still open at that time of day. This was not at all like the rural town he had known. Michael was used to such evening activity because of his experiences in Washington City.

They entered several retail shops to take a closer look. In an Irish linen shop, both men bought a handmade tablecloth for their mothers. Further up the boardwalk, the glass window of a shop they were passing shattered. The sound of a fired gun followed.

Mike felt pieces of glass on his face as a nearby gas street lamp shattered from a second shot. He dropped to the ground alongside Bob Lilley. Both men pulled out their service revolvers. From the darkness ahead, they caught sight of the muzzle flash of a third shot and they returned fire. After they had fired several times, they heard a scream. There were no more shots from that direction.

Mike heard the report of a gun from behind them. He turned over and saw a man some ten or fifteen yards behind him pointing a pistol in his direction. He fired two quick shots at the man and saw him disappear behind a building to Mike's right. He couldn't tell if the man had been wounded and fell in that direction or moved on his own. It was suddenly very quiet. There were no more shots fired at him and Lilley from either direction.

Leaving their packages on the sidewalk, they rose. Guns still drawn, Mike ran back to check out the man who had fired at them from behind. Bob Lilley ran forward toward the source of the first shots. Ten or so yards ahead, in the darkness between two buildings, a man rolled on the ground in pain.

Lilley saw the wounded man's gun on the ground. He kicked it away. Mike quickly joined him and put the muzzle of his pistol to the man's neck. "You make a move mister, and I'll blow your head off," Mike promised.

A pair of policemen, alerted by the gunfire, spotted them in the darkness and rushed over.

"Hold it right there you two," one of them warned the two soldiers. Both policemen had pistols drawn.

"Put your weapons on the ground and place your hands on your heads."

Both Drieborg and Lilley complied.

"One of you tell me what this is all about."

Lilley identified himself and Michael. He told the Detroit policemen of the attack on them as they had left the linen shop down the street. One of the policemen went down the street to check out the story Lilley had told.

He quickly returned. "The shop owner supported his story. Their packages are still on the sidewalk. I think he's telling the truth. The wounded guy on the ground is the attacker, seems to me. Either of you know this guy?"

"I was just about to roll him over when you told me to put my hands on top of my head, officer," Mike told him. "Can I do that now?"

"Go ahead."

Mike rolled the man over on his back. "My Lord!" he exclaimed. "It's Hayes."

"Why did he attack you two?" one of the officers asked.

Mike told the officers a quick version of the Hayes episode in Washington. "I didn't think he was out of military prison yet."

"Our station house is just down the street," one of the two policemen said. "We best go there and sort this all out."

"Officer," Mike interrupted. "We were also shot at from behind. I returned fire, but the guy got away. I saw some blood on the corner of the building. Could you check out the back of the building here? He could still be around."

"Sure, soldier," the policeman agreed. "Good idea. Come with me."

The other officer told Lilley, "This fella doesn't look as though he's going to die on us. We can drag his sorry butt to our Police Station in no time."

The other officer and Bob Lilley picked up Hayes and dragged him across the street. Once there, Hayes was interrogated. It was made clear to him that if he cooperated and made a statement, he would get medical attention.

Because Hayes thought he was seriously wounded, he thought he was going to die without immediate treatment. So, he was most cooperative and signed a written statement, confessing to the shooting.

"Since I got out of prison, I've had no money or prospects," he explained. "Carl Bacon paid me to follow Drieborg from Washington. We were supposed to kill him when he got to Detroit. I would attack from the front and Bacon was supposed to fire from behind. I should have known he would let me take all the blame whether I was successful or not."

"We're going to turn this fella over to the Army Provost Marshal," an officer said. "He attacked two serving U.S. Army officers. That's a federal crime. They'll get this Bacon fella eventually. But until they do, you watch yourself, Drieborg."

After the Detroit police had taken statements from both Lilley and Drieborg, they were given their packages and weapons and sent on their way.

"Thanks for helping me back there, Bob," Mike said. "I might've been killed or in jail possibly, if not for you."

"You're welcome. But remember, that Hayes and the other guy, your old friend Bacon, were shooting at me, too. After all the battles I've been in without getting so much as a scratch, I would have been furious with you if I was killed in Detroit, Michigan, just seventy miles from my home. You're sort of a dangerous fellow to be around Mike," Bob joked. "You've told me of your adventures, but I never thought you'd make me part of one."

"Come on, Bob," Mike moaned. "Give me a break."

"Is there anything more I should know? Maybe I should walk a few yards behind you, or the other side of the street possibly. I think you at least owe me breakfast."

The next morning, they met in the dining room.

"I think we should take that table over there," Lilley suggested. "There's no light over there," Mike observed. "There's no window or ceiling light either. It's downright dark."

"Exactly," Bob responded with a wide grin. "And I get the seat against the wall."

Mike paid for the meal, too.

Bob Lilley's train would take him north to Lapeer. Mike took the train headed northwest to Lansing. From there, another train would take him west to Grand Rapids where his father would be waiting for him at the railroad station.

Before the train was very far down the tracks, Mike got his Spencer carbine out of his bag, loaded it and set it beside him. His action attracted many stares from fellow passengers. But with Bacon on the loose, he felt safer. He also sat against the back wall of his railroad car. Lilley had a good idea there.

Julia and Michael

As the train pulled into the Grand Rapids railroad station, Michael looked through the railroad car window for his father. Of course, he was there. Standing beside him on the train platform was his brother Little Jake. When the train finally stopped, Mike jumped down onto the platform and walked quickly toward them.

"Wow, little brother," Michael exclaimed. "Are you ever going to stop growing?"

"You squeeze me any tighter Mike," he gasped, "an' I'll stop for sure." His father opened his arms to him. They hugged and slapped one another on the back.

Holding Mike at arm's length Jake said, "It is good to see you son. You look well."

"Thank you, Papa." Mike responded.

"It is good to have you home son," Jake said, hugging his son one more time. "Who knows, maybe God will answer our prayers and dis war will end before you have to get back to it."

"Wouldn't that be a great Christmas present for all the families of our country? Eh, Papa?"

"Hey you two," interrupted Little Jake. "It's almost dark already, and Mamma's holding supper for us. I'm hungry. Let's go. I've loaded your stuff in the wagon, Mike. You two can talk on the way, can't you?"

"You're right, little brother," Mike agreed. "Thanks for loading my stuff."

They had traveled less than a mile when Jake stopped the wagon at the foot of the Fulton Street hill. "You two boys will have to walk alongside da wagon till we get atop dis hill. It's too steep for our old plow horse to manage with all of us in da wagon."

"What did I tell you little brother?" kidded Mike. "You've gotten so fat, not even the horse can pull you up this nothing hill."

"Me?" he retorted. "Last time I saw you, you were skin and bones, with your uniform just hanging off you. Now look at you. You're almost busting your buttons."

"I must admit, I have put on some pounds since you were in Washington last September. Now I need to turn this weight into muscle."

"Great idea," his brother agreed. "Cold weather's here. You're just in time to help me chop the wood we'll need for the winter. That ought to take care of all that flab you're carrying around your middle."

"That's not all, son," interrupted Jake. "Remember when you and Swede were here? There are still families with da man away at da war. We still need to chop wood for dem too. Soon, before da winter hits, we'll repair deir houses and barns; even do some butchering for dem. Not everyone fights in da Army Michael, but we men at home and our sons like Little Jake help out where we can. While you are here you will help us with dat again, ya?"

"Yes, Papa," Michael responded. "Of course, I will."

When the wagon reached the crest of the steep hill, Michael opened his duffle bag and took out his Spencer carbine. He held it across his lap when he sat on the wagon seat next to his father.

"Why do you have your rifle out of your bag Michael?" his father asked.

"I had some difficulty during my stop in Detroit." He told of Bacon's attack on him. "Unfortunately, he got away."

"Sounds to me dat he went too far dis time Michael. He attacked another officer too. Now he has da Army after him. Even his father can't blame dis on you."

"I think you're right Papa. It was fortunate that Bob Lilley was with me that night. Old Harvey Bacon won't be able to dismiss Major Lilley's sworn statement so easily."

"Just the same son," warned Jake. "Don't mention dis at home. I'll tell your mamma about dis. There is no need to upset da girls."

"That's right, Papa."

"You hear me Little Jake?" asked his papa. "Not a word now." "I understand Papa."

"When we go into town Saturday you stop to see da Justice of da Peace. I want to make sure he gets all dis information from da Detroit Police Department. You carry your pistol, Michael. I'll put da rifle in the wagon too. We can't be too careful until dis crazy Bacon person is captured. How is Congressman Kellogg son?"

"He is fine Papa. Congress is in recess right now. He is a man of fine character. He sure looks after me too."

"And the fighting; how is that going?"

"Both armies are dug in for the winter. So, things are much calmer in Washington right now."

"What of his daughter Patricia?" Jake inquired. "Have you become close to her again?"

"Yes, I have. She is a very exciting woman."

"But is she good for you and your children, Michael?"

"I need to talk with you about that" Michael admitted.

"So, talk already," Jake urged.

"She and I have talked about marriage," Michael revealed. "But she told me flat out that she was not suited to be a farmer's wife."

"What do you think of dat, Michael?"

"She is right. She was raised as a city girl, a big city girl actually. She is best suited to be a high-society woman. And while she told me that she would gladly mother Eleanor, she would not accept little Robert in her house."

"It is good dat she knows herself dat well. And it is good dat you realize it, too."

"What happens when you get back to Washington City after this time at home?"

"The Congressman has assured me that he would find me employment in Washington City. when I return in January. But I don't think I would want to live in a place like that permanently. I miss the farm too much."

"We can talk of dis again Michael," promised his father. "I don't think you should bring dis up in front of the whole family yet though. We should think about it some before you decide." Jake turned to his younger son.

"Did you hear me, Little Jake? What you hear we talk about just now, say nothing to anyone."

"Yes, Papa," he promised.

***

It was fully dark as they pulled into the Drieborg's yard.

Jacob stopped the wagon between the house and the barn. He turned to Michael.

"Son," he directed, "you go right away into da house. Mamma and da girls are excited to see you. All day long dey talk of nothing else. Come Little Jake. You help me get da horse into da barn. We'll take Michael's baggage into da house when we're done rubbing da horse down and feeding him."

"Yes, Papa."

"Michael's here!" his sister Susan shouted.

Rose turned from the stove and rushed toward him, wiping her hands on her apron as she approached.

Michael hugged her and twirled her around.

"Enough! Enough, Michael!" she shouted. "You make me dizzy."

His sisters, Susan and Ann, were joined by Julia Hecht in the excited welcome. Hugging him and crying for joy they led him toward the dining room table.

"We saved everything from our supper Michael; ham, sweet potatoes, apple sauce and rolls, too." Susan told him.

"Mamma's rolls!" he exclaimed. "I've really missed your cooking, Mamma."

"Not tonight, Michael," his mamma informed him. "It is Julia who cooks the supper. They are her biscuits and apple pie, too."

Julia had moved to the stove and was stirring a pot of applesauce. Michael took his first good look at her. She had changed a good deal since he had seen her last. He noticed that she was taller than her sister Eleanor had been, and had brown hair instead of blond.

But he did not remember that Julia had such a full figure. There was no doubt about it: she was not the skinny girl of just a few months ago.

"*No*, he thought, *she is now a beautiful woman.*"

She turned her head a bit in his direction and smiled coquettishly.

"*Is she flirting with me?*" Mike wondered.

They continued to look into each other's eyes, as though no one else was in the room.

Their reverie was broken when Little Jake burst into the room from outside. "Where's the food Mamma?" he shouted. "I'm starved."

"You're always starved runt," his sister Ann retorted. "Have you washed your dirty hands? Besides, Mamma is not in charge of the meal tonight. Julia fixed it. So, ask her."

"It's coming, Little Jake," promised Julia, speaking for the first time since Mike had arrived.

"Before you eat anything," Rose said to her son Jake, "we will say the prayer of thanks. Ya?"

"Yes, Mamma," Little Jake agreed.

"Living with all these women is not easy Michael. You've been away, but you'll soon find out how hard it is." His brother told him.

"Sit down, Jacob," his wife suggested softly. "Julia has everything warmed up. Susan and Ann will pour da milk and coffee. But first Papa, will you say da prayer?"

"Thank you, Lord, for bringing our son Michael home safely to us. Continue to bless da Drieborg and Hecht families, deir labor and da food on our table tonight. And Lord, bring peace to our country, soon. Amen."

The girls and Mrs. Drieborg had eaten earlier that evening, so they just watched happily as the three hungry men ate. They intended to join the men for apple pie though.

Excited to have Michael home, everyone broke the usual mealtime silence with questions, conversation and laughter. Even Jake joined in.

Finally, the supper dishes were cleared and everyone had a piece of Julia's apple pie. Michael and his brother had two slices each.

"Good meal Julia," complimented Mike. "This is the best meal I've had since I was in your mother's kitchen a few weeks ago."

"Oh, tell me Michael!" she exclaimed. "How is everyone at home?" The conversation continued well beyond the usual Drieborg bedtime.

Finally, Jake announced, "Dat is enough for tonight children. It is time for bed. We have work to do in da morning; you too, Michael. No easy government job here. You are a farmer again."

"All right, Papa," chuckled Michael. "I'll do my part. Please wake me in time to help with the milking."

"If Eleanor doesn't wake you up sooner son," his mother warned him. "She often is hungry in the middle of the night."

"That would be fine with me Mamma. I'm looking forward to seeing my daughter again."

With that, he stood and hugged his mother and his sisters. He turned and opened his arms to Julia as well. She stepped forward and pressed her body to his, rather suggestively, he thought.

"It's good to see you again Michael," she said. Then, after giving him another squeeze, she stepped away and joined his sisters in the bedroom they shared.

Mike watched her as she moved away from him.

"Good night, Julia," he whispered.

***

Jacob and his wife Rose were preparing for bed. They could hear freezing rain being blown against their bedroom window. Rose pulled a heavy drape across the glass.

"It is so good to have Michael home, Papa." Rose said as she pulled on her winter sleeping clothes. "He is looking well too."

"Ya, Mamma," Jake agreed. "He is. But he will have to get used to farm work after all dat big city living I think."

"The children were excited to see him," Rose continued. "Julia was especially happy."

"Why Julia so much, Mamma?"

"She is in love with him, Papa," Rose told him.

Jake stopped his preparation for bed. "How can you know dat? Michael just arrived tonight."

"Women can see such things," Rose revealed. "Before Michael got home, even, I noticed the way she talked about him. Since she has been here, she talks like a woman in love. Didn't you see how she looked at him tonight? She did not hug him like a sister. No, Papa, she is in love with him."

"All da girls gave Michael a hug tonight," Jake objected. "Why was her hug so different?"

"Men don't notice things like that . Michael too, noticed how much Julia has grown up since he saw her last."

"Are you trying to tell me dat Michael is in love with her too?"

"No, Papa. Not yet, anyway. We will see what happens though." They were under the covers holding one another.

"If you know so much, Mamma, tell me how much snow we are going to get tonight."

"Enough, already." She poked him with her elbow. "It's late; sleep papa."

***

Before many days had passed, Mike had once again adjusted to the farm routine. It was just after dawn one morning. He and his father were in the barn. Michael was into the rhythm of milking the farm's cows and goats. For the first few minutes that morning, all he could hear was the hiss of the warm milk hitting the inside of the milk pail. The fresh warm milk gave off steam in the cold November air.

"Tell me Michael," asked Jake sitting on a milking stool in the other cow stall. "Do da people you have met in Washington know anything about life on a farm?"

"Soldiers do. Most of them were raised on farms. But the civilians in Washington — at least the ones who have the power, and their wives — know little or nothing about farm life. That's with the exception of President Lincoln, of course."

"After da war could you live and work in a town like dat?" Jake asked.

"I could, Papa," Mike answered.

"Could you be happy der?"

"Let me answer your question this way. I have hardly been home for a week, but I've not felt so relaxed and content since I left home and joined the cavalry two years ago. This is where I belong. But I could survive in Washington if I had to."

"What about your children?" his father persisted. "Would it be best for dem to be raised on a farm like dis or in a big city like Washington?"

Mike did not respond immediately. He stopped milking and finally responded. "Papa, I've come to know, trust and admire men who were raised in cities. I believe them to be men of good character because they were raised by good parents. So, if it was Eleanor and I raising our daughter and Robert, we could do a good job no matter where we lived. The children would be fine?"

"But Michael," his papa reminded him, "Eleanor is gone. You are talking nonsense. What if your wife was the Congressman's daughter Patricia? Would da children be fine den?"

"No, Papa." Michael admitted. "They would not."

"Why not, Michael?"

"First of all, she has refused to be a mother to Robert. And, I don't believe she is willing to mother any child of Eleanor's or her own. At least, not as I understand mothering. She would turn over that responsibility to others, I'm sure."

Mike's father continued to pursue the point. "So, son, will you marry her anyway?"

"What I would like to do and what I should do are two very different things," Mike responded without hesitation.

"She is a beautiful, intelligent and a very exciting woman. Despite those qualities, I am beginning to understand that they are not enough. Besides Papa, aside from the issue of the two children, I just don't fit into her high-society world. So, I don't see how I can marry her. It's on a farm where I am most content. It's on a farm where I want to live my life and raise my children."

"Farm life is not very exciting, son," Jake responded. "It is not at all like your life in Washington City, I think. We live and work alone, from dawn to dusk, most every day. Our daily routine never changes, either. And the good Lord decides if we get good crops or bad. Take awhile before you tell Mamma or da children of your decision. We talk some more about dis later."

"I have decided another thing, too," Mike told him.

"Ya," his father answered patiently. "What is dat son?"

"I've realized that I want to be a father to Eleanor's son Robert." Michael's father resumed his milking.

"It is time to finish here, son. Mamma will have da breakfast ready soon."

"Good, Papa. All this talking has made me hungry."

Michael felt relief telling his father about wanting to be a father to Robert. With that decision, he knew he had also decided against marriage to Patricia. He realized that his father was probably right about keeping this to himself, for now. But the Hechts had told him a month ago that they wanted a decision soon. He had better write them.

Later that day, Michael wrote the Hechts of his decision about Robert.

Dear Ruben and Mrs. Hecht,

I was not able to get back to your farm before I left for my parent's home in Michigan. I hope this letter finds all of you in good health. Everyone here in Lowell is fine. It seems that Julia is in good health and is looking forward to returning home.

In January, I must report to my superiors in Washington for a new assignment. I think that I will continue to work in the city, probably for Congressman Kellogg. But I have no definite word on that. I could still possibly be assigned to a combat unit. Whatever it turns out to be, I will return by train to the city in late December. If you wish, I will bring Julia with me then.

I can assure you that I want to be a father to Robert. I haven't figured out how I can accomplish that until this war is over. But I love the little guy, and I can't imagine a life without him.

I will write again soon.

God bless you all.

Michael

Meetings in Grand Rapids

In early December, Mike dressed in his officer's uniform and traveled by horse to Grand Rapids. He had written Congressman Kellogg and had received confirmation of a meeting with the Congressman at his office in that city. He had also written a note to Patricia asking her to see him. She agreed as well.

"How is your leave going son?" asked Kellogg. "It's been two years since you did farm work. How are you holding up?"

"Fine sir," Mike told him without hesitation. "In fact, I am sure now, more than ever actually, that farming is what I want to do when the war is over. And sir, that's what I want to talk to you about. When we last met, you told me that you had an assignment for me in Washington, doing something for the Joint Committee on the Conduct of the War. Before you go to a lot of trouble for me, I wanted you to know my decision about farming after the war."

"Thank you for your concern, Michael," Kellogg responded. "But you might remember that I also told you that you would be of service to me too in this new assignment. That is still true whatever you decide to do after this war. So, rest assured, my arrangement for your next job does not extend beyond the war. Does that make you more comfortable about accepting?"

"Definitely, sir," Mike responded. "I just did not want to mislead you or take advantage of you."

"You know it has been my experience that men who go home on leave find it so comfortable that they can't imagine any other environment as satisfying. It sounds that you're having that kind of feeling now too."

"Funny you should bring that up, sir. My father and I were out in the barn doing the first milking of the day when I told him how I felt. He reminded me that farming was work from dawn to dusk. He stressed that it was more up to God than the farmer how good the harvest would be. He told me to think about it some more and we would talk later."

"He gave you good advice. I will respect your decision when the war ends, whatever it turns out to be. What of the other problem you shared with me before we left Washington? Have you solved the problem of raising the two youngsters without a wife?"

"No, sir," Mike admitted. "That's the other issue I wanted to share with you now. The morning after you and I talked, I did have an opportunity to discuss this matter with Patricia. I asked her to marry me sir, and she accepted."

"Well young man, she could not have made a better decision in my opinion," Kellogg said with a big smile on his face. "So, why is there a problem?"

Mike looked at the floor and responded carefully. "Patricia said she wanted to marry me. But when we began to talk of where we would live and what I would do after the war, she was adamant that she was not suited for farm life and therefore would not even entertain the idea of being a farmer's wife.

"That wasn't all. She said that she would love to be a mother to my child, Eleanor, but she would not be one to Robert, my late wife's son by her first husband. I suggested we think about these obstacles and talk later. I hope to talk with her about these things later this morning."

"If you were a betting man Michael," Kellogg asked, "what would you give for the chances that you and Pat could work this out?"

"Well sir, thinking over the reasons Patricia gave me for her rejection of the notion that she might become a farmer's wife, I have to agree with her. I can even understand her refusal to join me in raising a child who is not even mine. But every time I even think of Pat, I think of how beautiful she is and the physical reaction I feel when I'm just in the same room with her.

"I felt that with my late wife, Eleanor too. But she and I had a closeness, a union of sorts that I have never experienced with Pat. And, what's more important, I have come to believe that Pat and I would never develop that kind of love.

"So, I would not put any money on our working these things out."

Kellogg rose from his chair and extended his hand to Michael. "I sincerely hope that you two can work this out. But I fear that if either of you gave in on any of the issues you two have, it would tear your marriage apart, later. I don't wish that kind of heartache for either of you. Certainly, I do not want that for my daughter, who I love dearly. But not for you, either, Michael. For you see, if you haven't noticed yet, I love you too, like you were my son."

"Thank you, sir," Mike responded, somewhat shaken by his mentor's declaration. "Patricia and I may be unhappy for a time if we cannot work out these differences. But it is far better for us to endure that, than to create a marriage harboring resentment."

"Thank you for your concern for Patricia, Michael," Kellogg concluded.

*****

Michael rode east from the Congressman's Grand Rapids office on Monroe Street to where it met with Fulton Avenue. He rode his horse up that steep hill to Prospect Street on which Mr. Kellogg maintained his Grand Rapids home.

Suddenly, Mike realized. *"I rode up this same street two years ago when Papa took me to the cavalry training camp."*

After he tied his horse's reins to the hitching pole, he walked up to the door of the three-story home and pulled the bell chain.

Mike was surprised to see Adam welcome him to the Kellogg's home.

"Well, my goodness, if it isn't Major Drieborg," Adam greeted him. 'Give me your hat and coat sir."

"Adam, I thought you and your wife Mable took care of the Washington home when the Congressman and Pat were out of town," Mike inquired, a bit surprised at seeing Adam.

"We usually do sir," he replied, hanging Mike's coat and hat in the vestibule closet by the front door. "But for Christmas, we all come here to Grand Rapids. It's a family custom. Believe me, with all the white snow and the Christmas celebrations in this house, it is a real pleasure. Mable and I really look forward to it.

"By the way Major, how is that family of yours; you know, your papa Jake, your mamma and that little new baby of yours. How are they, sir?"

"They are all fine Adam. Thank you for asking about them. Could you ask Patricia if she has time to see me for a few minutes?"

"Yes, sir. I think she is in the front sitting room. She is helping her father prepare for his annual Christmas party for all the important people of this city. She is preparing the invitation list and such. Let me ask her, sir."

Adam returned to the entryway rather quickly. "Right this way, sir. Miss Patty is anxious to see you."

Michael moved into the room. Patricia was already standing in front of her writing table looking directly at Mike, a smile on her beautiful face. Once they were alone, she hurried into Mike's arms. Before they had even spoken Mike kissed her. She almost knocked him over with the sudden impact of her body against his.

While Mike held, and kissed her, the thought occurred to him that if the kiss stopped, they would have to talk. And, if they talked, they would have to discuss their differences.

That led him to realize that,

"If we stop this kiss, we will probably never hold and kiss each other again." he thought.

Neither of them seemed willing to step back and say the first word. Finally, they did break that first kiss and move back a step, but they still held each other's arms.

"Since you left the house Michael, I have missed you so," Patricia whispered, catching her breath.

"I have thought a lot of you too, Patricia."

They walked each other to a nearby sofa and sat close to one another. Mike put his right arm around her, kissed the side of her head, moved down to her neck, and kissed her again. Her skin felt hot to his touch. It seemed even hotter when she tilted her head back and met his lips with hers again. She brought her right arm up and put her hand on the back of his head, moving her body close to his.

They continued to hold and kiss one another. Then, Patricia sat back and broke the silence.

"Michael, remember when you were lying on top of me in the middle of that muddy Washington street? Did I arouse you then, like I can feel I do now?"

"No Patricia," Mike responded, his face reddened, clearly feeling and responding to what she was doing with her hand.

"Being close to you like this cannot be compared to that situation in a million years."

"Do you want to talk now, or enjoy the touch of my hands, my lips and my body against yours?" Patricia asked mischievously.

Mike loved what she was saying, but it wasn't getting them to the discussion he knew the two of them had to have.

"Patricia, please," Mike almost gasped. "You are driving me crazy."

"Do you want me to stop Michael?" she teased.

"No, Pat... no... yes," he stammered. "We have to talk. And, I can barely think clearly about anything while you're doing these things to me."

"Very well," she agreed. "More character showing up I suppose. But I can save you the trouble. There is nothing to discuss. I am not cut out to be a farmer's wife. Surely, since we last talked, you have thought about what I said. Can't you admit it, Michael? It would be absolutely ridiculous for me to even try to be a farm wife. Picture me milking a cow in this outfit. Feel my smooth hands. Do they feel rough to you? How long do you think these fingernails would last carrying wood or hoeing a garden?

"If it is a farm life you want you must marry someone who is from that background. You certainly should not marry a woman who has been pampered and spoiled all her life, like I have.

"You may love a woman like that, Michael, but you should never marry one. The decision is in your hands though. I love you and will help raise little Eleanor as her mother. But I cannot be a farmer's wife and will not be a mother to a child who is not of your issue."

Mike waited a few moments before responding. "You are right. If it is a farmer's life for me after this war, then I should look for a woman who is accustomed to farm life. I have come to realize that too Pat. You've made that very plain and I appreciate your openness and honesty. On top of that, you are most comfortable in the social atmosphere of Washington City and of Grand Rapids. I am not.

"The physical love I feel for you is very strong, as you know. But I have also come to realize that it is not enough on which to base a marriage. It is not enough for me to abandon little Robert. Nor is it enough for me to abandon the possibility of being a simple farmer."

Mike stood and faced Patricia, still seated on the sofa.

"Believe me Patricia, any love we might have for each other would eventually be destroyed by the resentment we would feel over whatever either of us had to give up to hold on to one another, now.

"You have called the sense of obligation I feel toward Robert a duty. Whatever you call it, my life will include both him and little Eleanor."

"Then, this is goodbye, isn't it?" Patricia whispered. "What a lousy Christmas present, Michael."

"Be angry with me if you must. But simply put Pat, we could never work out our differences."

With that comment, Mike stood and left Pat sitting alone in the room. He retrieved his coat and hat and left her home.

His horse was still tied to the hitching post, patiently waiting. Mike wiped the newly fallen snow from the saddle, mounted and headed east on Fulton Street toward his father's farm.

"What a physically exciting woman! Shouldn't I feel sad that it is over between us? Shouldn't I feel regret that I will not hold her in my arms and kiss her ever again?

"But I don't. Instead, I feel like a burden has been taken from my shoulders. I feel relief.

"Why am I thinking of Julia right now?"

Last Days at Home

Christmas at the Drieborg farm in Lowell was a bittersweet celebration. Michael could see that his parents and siblings were happy to have him home. In his mother's eyes, he also saw the sadness she felt over his approaching departure and return to the war.

Working with his father had been different during his leave. Before his enlistment in the Union Army, he had worked side by side with his father. Back then, Mike remembered him to be very preoccupied with the task at hand and not into conversation with his eighteen-year-old son.

"Stop da talk now Michael," Jake would say. "We have work ta do."

Now, the two of them talked all the time while they worked. Jacob did not just respond to his son's questions, but actually asked questions himself. Most surprising to Mike, his father even sought his opinion now and then.

"What do you tink of dis General Grant, Michael?" Jacob asked one time. "What are da important people in Washington City saying about him?"

Mike decided that all the experiences he'd had while in the Army, being awarded the Medal of Honor by the President of the United States and promoted to the rank of Major, had an impact on his father's attitude toward him.

Early one morning in late December, the two men were in the barn milking the farm's two cows.

"Michael," his father began, "Tell me again what da Justice of da Peace, Mr. Deeb, told you about Carl Bacon."

"When we were in town last Saturday, I went to his office and inquired about Bacon. I wanted to know if he had been arrested for attacking me and Lilley in Detroit. I thought I already told you this Papa."

"Ya you did Michael. But I want to hear it again."

"All right. Mr. Deeb told me that Carl had been found in a Lansing hospital and arrested. Because he broke his parole agreement when he attacked me, he was returned to the federal prison in Detroit. He also will stand trial for assaulting Union soldiers and attempted murder. That should take care of him for a while."

"Dat is probably true. But do not trust da Bacons ever, Michael," Jacob warned. "Even if he is in jail a long time, he or his father will try to get even mit us Drieborgs."

Mike knew that he would always treasure these quiet times they had together during the early morning milking of their cows and goats. Alone in the barn, Mike's father would ask him questions about Army life and about the men he had come to know in the cavalry and in the prison.

In turn, Mike sought his father's advice about how he could best take care of Eleanor and Robert. Of course, they talked about the problems their farm neighbors were having with animals, crops, and running their farms with the papa in the army.

However, the time passed all too quickly. The Christmas holiday came and went.

Michael had received an answer from Ruben and Emma. The Hecht family was very happy that he had decided to be a father to Robert and they were anxious to help him raise the boy until the war ended. They also told him that they missed their Julia very much and would appreciate it if he brought her back to them when he returned after Christmas.

She would join him occasionally when he was alone working in the barn, and they would talk. Their mutual interest in Eleanor and Robert was a frequent topic of conversation. They also shared their thoughts about farm life, raising children, crops, animals and such.

One afternoon, when Eleanor was taking her nap, Julia joined Michael in the barn. There was a fierce snowstorm outside and everyone else was enjoying the warmth of the house. So, the two of them knew they would be alone for a time.

She asked Mike, "What will the trip to Maryland be like Michael?"

"What do you mean, Julia?" Mike responded, somewhat confused about what she wanted him to tell her. "You rode on a train when you came here with my family. The train ride will not have changed much since then. Of course, we will be traveling east and south this time, instead of north and west the way you came."

"You are so funny Michael. I know that part," she said good-naturedly. "I want to know about staying in a hotel on the way back. You've told me that we will spend two nights in hotels during our trip, right?" she asked quite specifically.

"That's right," Mike answered, not knowing where this line of questioning was taking him. "And?"

"Where will I sleep? On the way here all the girls, including your mother and Eleanor had one room; your father with Little Jake had another. What about us? Will we have separate rooms?"

"My goodness Julia," Mike said without trying to hide his exasperation. "Of course, we will. Do you think for a minute that I would not treat you properly on our trip together?"

"What has made you think that I wouldn't want to share a room with you?" Julia shot back heatedly. She said this to Mike without any sign of embarrassment. He did not even see her blush.

"Am I too ugly for you Michael? Or, do you think that because you were married to my sister, I can't have feelings for you? Is it somehow wrong for me to love you?"

"Slow down young lady," Mike said, surprised. "In the first place, you're not ugly. Far from it. You are a very beautiful and desirable young woman."

Julia cut in, "But not beautiful enough to love? And not desirable enough to share a room and a bed with? Is that what you are trying to say to me, Michael?"

"Give me a chance to get a word in edgewise Julia. Will you please let me speak for a whole minute or two?"

Julia sat back on her straw seat. "Oh, all right, you can talk."

Mike noticed that she was smiling at him. Or was that a smirk of self-satisfaction on her face? He was still standing across from Julia in one of the stalls where he had been repairing some of the leather horse tack when she had joined him a half an hour or so ago. He moved around the stall boards that separated them and took a seat on another bale of straw a couple feet in front of her. He leaned forward with his hands on his knees.

"First of all, I want us to leave your sister Eleanor out of this conversation. Your feelings for me or mine for you should have nothing to do with her. Will you agree to that?"

"Yes," Julia whispered in response.

Is she mocking me? Mike asked himself. Actually, he was getting a little irritated with her attitude. *How did she get me into this situation anyway?"*

"All right now, where was I?" he thought aloud.

"Oh, yes. Whether you are desirable or not has nothing to do with staying together in the same hotel room. That is not something I would allow until we were married."

"Are you asking me to marry you, Michael?" Julia asked mischievously. She sat up, put her hands on her knees and leaned toward him.

"She is mocking me," he decided.

"Oh, my Lord," he laughed, throwing he head back. "You tricked me, didn't you Julia?"

"I'm sure that I don't know what you're talking about Michael," she said still mocking him.

"You are the one who brought up the topic of marriage not me. What kind of a man talks about marriage with a well-brought-up young girl and then pretends he never said anything of the sort?"

Michael was speechless. He looked at Julia in utter amazement.

"How has she maneuvered me into this? Wirz would never have been found guilty, much less hung, if she had been his defense attorney. But, I can see that the fat is in the fire now. I can play her game." Mike reasoned.

"Julia, do you love me?"

"That's not the question Michael," she snapped.

"It is the only question, the most important one actually. Do you love me?" he insisted.

"Oh, all right Michael. Yes, I will marry you."

"That's not what I asked you Julia. I'm not going to marry anyone who does not love me. Do you love me?"

"She did it again." He realized.

Right when he thought that he had her trapped on his terms, she changed the rules of the game. Where had that shy little girl he used to know disappeared?

Julia reached out and took both of Mike's hands in her own.

"Yes, I do love you." Then she stood and pulled him up with her. She brought a hand to each side of his face and drew his lips to hers. Their lips touched, but ever so lightly. Even when Mike put his arms around her they stood some apart, hardly touching.

Suddenly, Julia pulled back from Mike's embrace.

"Wait just a minute Michael Drieborg," she said hotly. "If you think that I go around kissing a man who hasn't even told me that he loves me you've got another think coming. Until you learn some manners around me you can just go and kiss that pig over there."

Then she stormed out of the barn.

Watching her disappear into the swirling snow toward the house, Mike couldn't help it. He stood there, slapped his hand on his leg and laughed out loud.

"What a woman!" For a moment, he remembered how her sister Eleanor had teased him in much the same way before he had married her. *"It must run in the family."*

***

That evening, Mike was helping wash little Eleanor before her bedtime diapering. Julia was washing the baby and he was waiting with a towel to dry the infant. He leaned close to her and whispered, "I love you."

Without even looking at him, she said, "Is it so much a secret that you have to whisper? We are leaving here in two days. How can we leave without telling your family that we love each other and intend to marry? Don't you think we should tell your family now?"

"This girl has me figured out for sure." Michael realized.

He decided right then and there that he might as well admit it and go for the whole brass ring.

"After you put Eleanor down for the night," he promised, "everyone will be around the table. Let's tell them then. Is it all right with you that we wait that long?"

That brought a smile to her face.

After the announcement, bedtime that night came a little later than usual for the Drieborgs.

"Oh, Julia, we are so excited for you," Susan gushed. Ann hugged her. "We are so surprised. When did you two decide all of this?" She asked.

Without batting an eye and with a perfectly straight face, Julia told Ann, "This afternoon. We were just sitting on straw bales out in the barn talking about nothing in particular and out of the blue he up and asked me to marry him."

"She's right Ann," Mike said. "I sure surprised Julia this afternoon."

***

Jacob and Rose were in bed. Their kerosene lamp had been turned off. The two of them were listening to the wind howl outside.

"It seems dat you were right, Mamma," Jake commented.

"So, you do remember that I told you Julia loved Michael da night he came home on his leave?" Rose gloated.

"Ya," Jacob admitted. "You were right about dat. But you have not told me yet when da snow will stop falling."

Afterword

It was a bitterly cold afternoon when Major Michael Drieborg and his traveling companion Julia Hecht arrived in Detroit. Heavy snow delayed their journey from the western Michigan town of Grand Rapids. So, they were late some, getting to their connecting train to Cleveland, Ohio. They struggled with their luggage against a strong wind as they hurried to catch that train.

Once on board they were relieved to be out of the wind, but they quickly discovered their new passenger car was hardly warmer than the outside temperature. In 1864, trains used by the average traveler were not very well insulated against the outside cold and were poorly heated, if at all. This railroad car had a potbellied stove at one end of the main aisle. Someone was feeding wood into it. So, it didn't give off much heat yet.

The passengers could still see their breath turn to vapor.

"Here Julia, move closer," Michael urged her. He put his arm around her and pulled a blanket over their torso and lap. As the train pulled away from the station, they could see that the cloud cover had blown off and the sun had brightened the countryside.

"We can't see much outside Michael," Julia observed. "The frost on the glass of our window is too thick."

"Give that stove a chance," Michael urged her. "We'll feel the warmth soon. It will heat up this car before you know it and that frost will melt. We should see a lot of countryside before we arrive in Cleveland."

"Actually, I don't mind the chill Michael," Julia smiled. "It feels nice and cozy being held by you under this blanket."

"It is nice, isn't it?" Mike agreed.

"But the stove is at the far end of the car Michael. It would be much warmer if we moved closer."

"It would, but you'll soon be surprised how hot it will be down there. Besides, it is safer with our backs against the wall at this end of the car. The only way anyone can enter this car is through the door at that far end."

"Are you still worried about Carl Bacon; the fellow who attacked you in Detroit? I thought he was in jail for that."

"I'm told that he is in federal jail. But with his money, he has a long reach. So, it's better to be safe than sorry."

"I suspected that's why you've had your pistol on the seat beside you the entire trip."

They were both quiet for a while. In the silence, Michael leaned his head back against the seat and closed his eyes. He began to think of this same train ride a year ago.

Julia's sister Eleanor sat at my side on that trip. She was my wife. We had been married that October at her church in Maryland. I had to report for duty in Washington City then, too. So, we were returning to her parent's farm in the East after a visit to my family's farm here in Michigan.

"Could it only have been a year ago? It's hard to believe; so much has happened since last December."

His thoughts were interrupted by a soft voice.

"Michael, are you asleep?" Julia whispered.

"Hmmm?" He responded. "I don't know sweetheart. I guess I was sort of dozing a bit. Are you alright?"

"I'm fine Michael." She answered. "But I've wanted to ask you something ever since you returned home on leave last month."

"Sure. What is it you would like to know?"

She sat up and turned on the seat some and looked directly at Mike. "When is this terrible war going to end?"

"You don't beat around the bush do you Julia?" Michael chuckled in response. "But to be equally blunt, I don't know."

"Come on Michael," she prodded. "If I am going to be your wife, I need a better answer than that. Remember, I was in the room at your parent's house when your father and you talked about the war. You told him how you thought it was going. Can't you tell me too?"

"Yes, I can Julia," Michael admitted. "I did tell my father what I knew about the war situation. And since you want to know, I should tell you too. Just remember, I've been away from Washington for almost two months. Most anything could have changed during that time.

"Wait a minute," he decided, "You know what might help? I had a map of the United States and the Confederacy I used when my father and I talked about this. I still have it in my bag I think. Let me look." Mike rummaged around in his duffel bag. "Here it is Julia. It even has all the major cities marked too. Are you ready to start?"

**Civil War
United States**

"Yes, I am Michael. But first tell me, what is that line from Lake Michigan all the way down the page?"

"That's the Mississippi River, Julia. Since last July 4th, the Union controls that entire river from New Orleans on the Gulf of Mexico all the way to the Canadian border in Minnesota. This map shows the river ending in Chicago, Illinois. That city is right here on the shore of Lake Michigan." Mike pointed out.

"Farther south though," Mike drew her attention to the state of Georgia on his map. "General Sherman captured the city of Atlanta this past fall. And I just read in the Grand Rapids Eagle newspaper that his army captured the port city of Savannah recently." He pointed to another dot on his crude map.

"It seems that Sherman has almost 70,000 men in his army and he is now moving toward Charleston, South Carolina." He moved his finger to a dot north along the Atlantic Ocean. "There he is opposed by a Confederate army less than half that size."

"Isn't Charleston the city where this war actually started?" Julia asked.

"Yes, it is. South Carolina militia used cannon located on the shoreline of that city to bombard the Union's Fort Sumter which controlled the Charleston harbor. That attack started the war."

"North of that, in Virginia," Michael directed Julia's attention further north on his map. "General Grant has surrounded the Confederate capital city of Richmond and its sister city to the south, Petersburg. His army of 150,000 men is opposed by General Lee's reb army of about 50,000 soldiers."

"Do you see that, Julia?" Mike asked before going any further.

"Yes, I can see where you are pointing and I heard what you said. But I don't understand how our two very large armies can be stopped by two very small Confederate armies. And, unless I'm mistaken, I heard you tell your father that our bigger armies have more supplies and better weapons, too."

"You are not mistaken. I did tell my father exactly that."

"So, why isn't the war over?"

"Well, actually for all practical purposes, it is over."

"Come on Michael," Julia snapped. "Don't toy with me here. You said the war is still being fought. Soldiers are still dying. How can it be over too?"

"The war continues right now because armies don't fight much during the winter. And in the early spring months of March and April it's too muddy to do much either. So, while there is very little chance anymore for the Union to lose this war, we probably have to wait until late April to win it. Does that clear up the confusion some sweetheart?"

"Sort of Michael," Julia answered tentatively. "But let me think about what you said for a while. We can talk about it again, later, can't we?"

"Sure, we can." Michael assured her. He held out his arms to her. "Get back over here young lady. I still need some warming up."

"One more question first."

"What's that?"

"If this war is over, just what will you do when you report for duty?"

"Congressman Kellogg told me that I would be working with his Joint Committee on the Conduct of the War. He expects that our men who have been held in Confederate prisons will need a lot of help recovering their health and getting back home. As I understand it, my job will be to make sure that happens."

"It doesn't sound like you'll be in any battles then." Julia surmised.

"Not according to the Congressman, anyway." Michael told her.

"Alright mister," Julia warned. "Just you make sure you aren't. Now, where are those arms you want to hold me with?"

***

"I don't know what the future has in store for us." Michael thought. *"The only thing I know for sure is that Julia and I will be sleeping in separate rooms tonight."*

About the Author

Michael J. Deeb was born and raised in Grand Rapids, Michigan. His undergraduate and graduate education centered on American studies. His doctorate was in management.

He was an educator for nineteen years, most of which saw him teaching American history and doing historical research.

His personal life found him as a preteen spending time regularly at the public library, reading non-fiction works of history. This passion has continued to this day. Teaching at the college, university and high school levels only increased his interest in such reading and research.

Since 2005, he and his wife have lived in Sun City Center, FL. In the fall of 2007, he finished the historical novel *Duty and Honor*. The sequel, *Duty Accomplished*, was completed in 2008. *Honor Restored*. Following this, Dr. Deeb published, *The Lincoln Assassination, 1860* and *The Way West* to conclude the *Drieborg Chronicles*. They are all available in print or eBook form at HistriaBooks.com and all major book retailers. Signed copies are available at www.civilwarnovels.com.

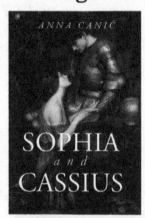
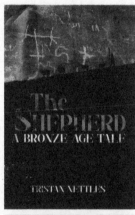

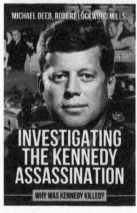